Rise From the Embers

The Embers

LIGHTNESS SAGA

BOOK 4

STACEY MARIE BROWN

ALSO BY STACEY MARIE BROWN

Contemporary Romance

Buried Alive

Blinded Love Series
Shattered Love (#1)
Pezzi di me (Shattered Love)—Italian
Broken Love (#2)
Twisted Love (#3)

The Unlucky Ones
(Má Sorte—Portuguese)

Royal Watch Series
Royal Watch (#1)
Royal Command (#2)

Smug Bastard

Paranormal Romance

Darkness Series
Darkness of Light (#1)
(L'oscurita Della Luce—Italian)
Fire in the Darkness (#2)
IL Fuoco Nell Oscurita—Italian
Beast in the Darkness (An Elighan Dragen Novelette)
Dwellers of Darkness (#3)
Blood Beyond Darkness (#4)
West (A Darkness Series Novel)

Dedicated To:

Ember, Zoey, Kennedy, and Fionna
For being such strong women who inspire me to be a better person.

Eli, Ryker, Lorcan, and Lars
For being the reason I'm single.
Damn you all for being such sexy beasts!
Why can't you be real??

ONE
Fionna

Sirens wailed through the air, and I bolted up from packing the suitcase laid out on the bed, fear shooting through my veins, a folded blouse in my hands. Evening descended into the room, casting shadows over the unmade bed. The sheets were still tangled from when Lars and I had explored each other all night.

We had only shared the bed once before everything went wrong. Before he was taken from me.

My heart pounded in rhythm with the loud hammering sirens. We were under attacked.

Lars was no longer himself, but his blood was, so the shield would have let him back in without warning. This was someone else…

I knew in my gut who that someone else was.

Stavros.

The new King had come to take what he felt was rightfully his: his throne, this house, and whomever was in it.

"Shite!" I thought we'd have more time. It had been only a few hours since the stone had seized Lars. I hadn't even had time to call my sister.

Terror thumped through every nerve, and fear curled in my throat as I ran down the hall, my feet smacking against the wood floor. "Piper!" I screamed. My only thought was getting to my daughter.

"Mummy?" she cried as I burst through the door to her room. She sat on her bed next to an already packed suitcase, covering her ears. "I saw a mean man, Mummy." She rubbed her head. "He looked sort of like Darz. Where is Mr. Darz?"

"Piper." I ran to her, cradling her to me. "You know that trip we talked about earlier?"

1

She nodded, cuddling me. Giving her up for adoption was the hardest thing I ever did, but now she was back in my arms, I was never going to let her go. "We have to go now."

"But Mr. Darz… We can't go. What if he can't find us?"

My lids squeezed together at the sound of shouting inside and out, cutting through the protective shield alarms. We had to leave. Now. Stavros would not be kind to me. At best, I could hope for torture and a cruel death. If he felt how much power Piper already had, he would make her one of his slaves.

"He will come back to us. Lars will find us again." I tried to comfort her, but it felt more like I was saying the words to myself. It hadn't even been two days since we returned, but she'd already forged a strong attachment to Lars, as though she'd known him before she ever met him. Perhaps, in a way, she had. Similar to my mother, who was a strong seer, Piper already had visions at the young age of five, though Druids didn't usually come into their own until much later.

"Ms. Fionna! *¡Niña!*" Marguerite yelled from down the hall, her footsteps already leading her to this room. Her short plump figure filled the doorway, her face screwed up with worry and distress. "Ms. Fionna… *He* is here, isn't he?" I had filled them all in on what had happened abroad and what we had to do. What Lars made me promise.

I nodded, helping Piper off the bed. "Hurry, put on your backpack." I kissed her head.

Bang!

Gunfire boomed outside, and Piper ducked. She didn't cry or scream, but her eyes were wide with fear, triple the size of mine.

"We have to go, Marguerite. Now." Time might already be against us getting out of the compound safely.

She nodded, her face turning stern. "I ready, Ms. Fionna."

The pounding of feet snapped my head to the doorway. Nic, the sexy Spanish incubus, stood there in a T-shirt and jeans, his forehead lined with furrows. "Are you guys all right?"

"Uncle Nic!" Piper ran to him, her rucksack bouncing on her back.

He picked her up, set her on his hip, and kissed her temple. His face was impassive, but I knew he was just trying to act calm. "Hey, squirt."

While Lars and I were abroad finding the lost Cauldron of Dagda, one of the four treasures of Tuatha Dé Danann, Piper had become especially close to Nic and Marguerite. I felt both grateful and envious of my daughter's attachment to them. Over the weeks, she had come to rely on them, trust them. Love them. She and I were still strangers. Her trust would grow over time. Hopefully along with my forgiveness of myself.

The shrill of the alarms stopped, halting us in place. Our gazes found each other. What did that mean?

"Nic! Marguerite! Get the Druid out of here now," a man bellowed up the stairs. I recognized the voice as Travil, one of Lars's right-hand men. "Stavros has broken through the shield."

My tongue stuck to the roof of my mouth with dread. Stavros was King now. The shield bent to its new ruler.

"Shite," I whispered.

"Come on, Ms. Fionna. Follow me." Marguerite motioned out the door, starting to jog down the hallway.

Good thing I had prepared earlier to leave.

"Go, take Piper." I nodded to Nic, running for Lars's bedroom. "I need to grab my bag." It was not a change of clothes I was desperate to retrieve. No, my bag held four extremely important items: The Spear of Lug, the Sword of Nuada, the Cauldron of Dagda, and one more. I thought Lars had taken the Stone of Fáil, but Travil had found it laying near the front door. Either the stone had discarded it when it entered Lars's body, or it had fallen from Lars's pocket when he attacked Nic on his way out.

It was merely a rock now. Useless. Empty.

All the treasures were uninhabited and void of their powers because the Stone of Fáil had drained the remaining gems of energy after it worked its power on Lars, claiming his body. I still wouldn't take the chance of letting the items fall into Stavros's hands. He could probably find a way of reviving them or using them to take over the world. Besides protecting Piper, Lars had made me promise to take them and run to Eastern Europe, where the King did not rule.

I planned to head to Budapest in the morning, settling in Piper with Marguerite and Nic before I came back and fought to get Lars back. No little rock would take the man I loved from me.

Shoving my feet into my boots, I grabbed the bag and strapped the sword to my back, masking it with a spell. People would not be able to focus on it; their eyes would look away.

Clangs of metal and gunfire assaulted the house, slicing at my chest. The noises moved closer, sounding right outside the door.

"Ms. Fionna!" Marguerite yelled my name from below with desperation. My feet skimmed the stairs, jumping down the last four. I rounded the corner to see her waving me to another set of stairs. I knew how far Lars's underground kingdom went, built with rooms to hold enemies both inside and out. But if Stavros was taking over the house, locking ourselves in a room would be stupid.

"No." I shook my head. "We need to get away from this house." I peered around. "Where's Piper?"

"With Mr. Nic." She nodded to the stairs and grabbed my hand. "Trust, Ms. Fionna. I get us out."

Crash.

The front door splintered, and the piercing cry of strighoul broke through. My heart plummeted. Directing Marguerite down the stairs, I zipped after her, shutting and locking the door with a spell. It would only hold for a while.

Being a powerful Druid trained in black magic was useful, but it came with faults, especially against a High Demon King. I had to pull my Druid magic through the earth, asking for its permission, which took a lot out of me. Black magic used even more. It wasn't natural and went against the laws of Druidism, which were grounded in nature. My body paid the price, and I'd almost died on a few occasions.

We knew Stavros would take over the house; we just hadn't thought it would be so soon. I wouldn't waste my fight on this. If I was alone, I might take the chance. But now I had Piper to think of and to get Marguerite to safety.

Lars was the one I'd tear apart my soul for. And soon I'd be going after him to do whatever needed to save him.

Our feet echoed down the passage, Marguerite leading the way into the section deep in the earth. She reached a wall and pushed at some hidden button. I gasped as the wall swung open, leading into an underground passage. Torches lit the dark passage.

"Mr. Lars always has a way out." Marguerite pointed for me to follow.

I stepped into the room after she closed the door behind us. Silence dripped in my ears, vacant of any struggle or fight happening above. I could hear only my breath and heartbeat pulsing in my ears. Softly Marguerite pattered ahead. For a woman of her age, she was fast and nimble, like a ninja.

The tunnel was made of old stone, similar to the one I had gone into in Prague and Scotland, with curved ceilings and torches lighting the way. I wasn't surprised Lars had built tunnels here. Most leaders of the world had ways to escape if anything grave ever happened.

Shadows lingered heavily through the passage, my head jerking at every slight noise. Finally, we reached a staircase that led up to ground level. A door leading out was slightly ajar.

"Nic and Piper." Marguerite tipped her head, telling me they had already gone through this way. The need to see my daughter waiting for me on the other side kicked my legs into overdrive. I leaped up the last few steps and shoved my shoulder into the heavy metal exit.

It moved easier than I thought, and I stumbled into a forest, my boots crunching on pinecones and leaves. "Nic?" I called out softly. I had no idea how far we were away from the house. The door was embedded in a boulder so seamlessly that walking by it you would never know it existed. "Piper?"

Anxiety caught in my throat, clumping in my stomach. My skin itched, the telltale sign of magic brewing, informing me something was wrong. I took a few more steps, my head jerking in every direction, Marguerite right on my tail. I skimmed my bottom lip with my tongue, my mouth watering with a spell.

"You utter one word and I will gut this adorable little version of you as I squeeze her babysitter's brain into mush." Amusement colored a deep familiar voice, and my throat tapered to a sliver.

No. Please. No. But my tiny strand of hope died when Stavros stepped from the trees with a group of strighoul. One held Nic at knifepoint, another had Piper.

My whole world tipped over, spinning me until I thought I would vomit. My hand twitched to grab the sword, to strike him. But Piper's life was too important. I would take no chances.

Strighoul moved around me, knives bumping against my skin. My muscles locked down, fear pumping through me. The one thing that could kill the Unseelie King was at the bottom of my bag, empty of its power. Worthless. The Spear of Lug. One of many secrets royals liked to deny was that the sword ended a queen, and once upon a time the spear had killed the High Demon King, Balfor. It could do the same to Stavros.

"My attack on the front was a distraction. Sent the vermin running out the back." Stavros shook his head. He looked stronger, younger, and healthier than when I had seen him last in Scotland. Now Lars's magic coursed through his veins, giving him vibrancy. Stavros's yellow-green eyes glowed with hunger and power. His long jet-black hair was tied back, and he wore slacks and a button-down shirt, which was half open like some cheesy billionaire on a yacht. It still appeared sloppy and ill fitting, as if he were dressed for a role. He was thinner and less muscular than Lars, but you couldn't deny the striking resemblance.

Except he was nothing like the man I loved.

"Let her go," I pleaded. "She's merely a little girl. Innocent in this. Take me."

"Oh, Fionna. You greatly disappoint me. That was so cliché and expected." Stavros's mouth quirked up with amused malice. "Makes me have to retort with something just as formulaic. And I *hate* that." He sighed heavily. "But here it goes; hopefully my delivery will be less trite than yours." He cleared his throat, preparing for his delivery like an actor. "You know I won't do that. This little one?" Stavros reached over, running his finger over Piper's face. She flinched but didn't cry; instead she glared back at him. Nic, Marguerite, and I all jerked for her, but the knife on her throat dipped in until she whimpered. A drop of blood slipped from her neck. Stavros leaned over, catching it on his fingers, taking his hand to his lips he licked it off. His eyes darted to me, growing serious. "My. My. You've been holding out on me, Druid. I thought having you as my prisoner would be… *stimulating*… but she is going to be even better."

A guttural cry throbbed in my throat, coming out as a grunt. What could I do? If I tried a spell, Stavros would kill Piper and Nic before I could even summon the energy.

"Just think about when I find my great-niece. That dae. What fun I will have." He rubbed his hands together smugly. "Ember is my next reward. Soon I'll have a whole collection of the most powerful fae. And yes, that includes you and your sister too." He winked. "I don't want you to feel left out. Now, where is my nephew? I thought he'd be cowering with you."

"He's not here." I pressed against the hands holding me, smirking at him. "You're too late Stavros. Lars is out of your reach now."

His lids lowered and he searched my face as though to assess a lie. I could see the slight confusion in his eyes, and my mouth twisted with satisfaction.

"Something claimed him first. *Much* more powerful than you," I spat through my teeth, enjoying stabbing each word into his gut. "You may take the throne, but it won't be for long. He will come for you."

"What are you talking about?" Stavros stepped close, looming over me. "He has no power to fight me anymore. I will kill him when the coward is ready to face his fate like a demon. It's only a matter of time."

A smug grin curled my mouth.

His nose flared with frustration, sensing I knew something he did not. He reached out, grabbed my throat, and squeezed down, cutting my oxygen. I had a funny way of inciting the demons I had encountered to physically touch me instead of using their powers. Wonder what that said about me?

"Whatever you think you have over me—" His nails dug into my skin, his lips brushing my ear. "You don't. I have been planning this for decades.

Trapped in that hole. I had nothing else but to plot my nephew's demise. There isn't anything I haven't prepared for. I will always be five steps ahead of you."

"Of course," I replied complacently.

He snarled loudly.

In the world of fae, information was power, both revealing or hiding it. But I was going to keep this secret to myself. Stavros didn't need to be forewarned on what was heading for him.

The Stone of Fáil would make its presence known.

"You can't rattle me with your false self-assuredness, Druid." He took one step back from me. "I have seen and lived through it all. I am the most powerful fae alive."

"Oh, it's not false." I cocked an eyebrow. "You might be the most powerful fae *alive*." The stone was not technically alive or fae. It was Druid made.

Irritation lined Stavros's forehead. "I've had enough of your mouth," he snapped. "I can think of better uses for it." He nodded to a strighoul. Out of the corner of my eye, I saw one pull out a gag.

Fuck. No.

Straining against my captors, a dark spell worked its way up my throat.

"No. Mummy. Don't." Piper's voice rang out, but it was too late, the hex gushing over my tongue like a river. With a crack, power emitted from me, crashing into everything in its path like a trolley, slicing huge wounds and tossing people as it barreled forward. Every figure in a hundred-yard radius, collapsed back down to the ground with a chilling crunch, not discriminating between good and bad.

"Piper!" I screamed. My gaze snapped to where she had been standing. Bodies scattered over the forest floor, the smell of blood tickling my nose. *Oh my gods. What did I do?*

Her frame stood exactly where it had been, untouched by my magic. My hand went to my chest, a relieved cry breaking from my lips. It took me a moment to realize a ripple of energy surrounded her, protecting her.

My mouth dropped open.

Holy shite. Was she doing that? She was five. How did she know spells? Or was her magic that ingrained in her genes? It would protect her even when she wasn't aware of how to do it?

"Piper…" I took a few steps toward her. I knew Marguerite and Nic were hurt from my spell, but getting to my daughter was my first goal, selfish or not.

7

"It's supposed to happen this way." She hugged a small toy doggy clipped onto her backpack zipper in her hands, as if it gave her comfort. "I've seen it, Mummy."

"What are you talking about?" We didn't have time for this. Stavros and his men were starting to get up, limiting my window of possibilities to get out of here.

"You will see."

Her statement baffled me for a moment, but my instinct to protect her overrode whatever she was trying to tell me. My legs carried me to where she stood, my hands reaching for her.

Bam!

A body rammed into mine, taking me to the ground. Stavros growled, pinning my arms with one hand, covering my mouth with the other.

Did he think that would stop me? We had clashed before. I fought him both times as close to death as I was capable. "You are making this so much easier." He snarled as blood squirted from the wounds in his chest, dripping down on me. "You are my property now, Druid. I will enjoy torturing you very much. But I need you to do a job for me first."

I snorted into his hand; my glare narrowed in on him.

"Not only will you do this for me, but you will do so quickly." He leaned in closer to my face. "Betraying one you love for another. I simply get giddy at the idea of Lars's expression when he realizes it's you who has deceived him." His grip strangling my wrists, he inched even closer, whispering. "You will bring Lars and Ember to me. And you will do it without a fight because your daughter's life is balancing on what you do next."

A guffaw went through his fingers. I shook my head.

This time Stavros lifted his eyebrow, his mouth curving with condemnation.

"Take the baby Druid away." Stavros didn't take his eyes off me as he spoke to his men. "She will be a great asset."

"No!" The word tore up my throat as I kicked and struggled against him.

"Stop, Fionna," he ordered. "I will kill her right now. Or maybe I should just kill you instead?" *You will be no use to her dead. Keep it together.* "Do as I say and she lives. Take your pick."

A tiny whimper gurgled in my throat. When it came to my daughter, there was no choice.

"Procure the whore. I know he is one of Lars's pets. He will also come in useful as a spy," Stavros motioned to Nic, who was being lifted up by strighoul. The wounds, my uncontrolled magic that had slashed across his body, still gushed from his stomach. I lay in horror, watching a handful of the vile creatures move Piper and Nic farther away from me. Stavros grabbed my jacket and roughly tugged me onto my feet.

Panic thumped in my ears, curling around my throat. I couldn't let this happen. I growled, my eyes still on Piper, her head turned back to me. Her eyes were calm, and I saw her mouth move. *It's okay, Mummy.*

It was far from okay. I had given her up so this kind of thing wouldn't happen, but the moment I took her back, promised to keep her safe, my worst fears came true.

"You will bring your lover to me here, along with my *niece*." Stavros's mouth curved in a cruel smile and straightened my jacket, brushing me off, as though I were his doll. His superiority mocked me at every breath. He had me this time. The spell Piper had thrown around herself clearly didn't protect her from people or weapons, only magic. I also didn't want to trust it wouldn't happen again. Her safety was my main priority.

"If you hurt her—"

"You'll what, Fionna. Spank me?" He gripped my jacket lapels, tugging me in closer. "More time for that later. Just bring my gifts to me within two weeks and I assure she will go unharmed."

At his last words, I felt energy enter my head, filling it until I cried out in pain. I dug my fingers into my scalp. An invisible hand punched into my throat and stomach, snapping me forward, gasping for painful bits of air. The pressure intensified and I clawed at my throat, my vision blurring. My knees hit the ground, more agony climbing my spine.

Stavros stood over me laughing, but I barely noticed him, my darkening gaze on the little form being taken away from me.

Nooooo. I cried in my head. *Piper.*

I had let her down. Again.

She remained turned toward me until she disappeared behind a tree with Nic. My body slumped forward, my face hitting the leaf-covered ground, the sharp smell of damp dirt ramming into my nose.

Marguerite might be dead. Nic and Piper were now prisoners. And I had to convince the Stone of Fáil, which had claimed Lars as its own, to give itself over to a tyrant. And that wasn't even covering the fight to get Lars back from the stone. If that was possible.

As unconscious grappled for me, pulling me down into its web, my mind didn't go to Piper or Lars.

It went to my sister.

A force built inside me before I was lost in nothing.

"KENNEDY!" I cried into the last bits of light. "Kennedy! Help me!"

With a snap, the wormhole closed, and I floated away into oblivion.

9

TWO
Kennedy

"KENNEDY! Kennedy! Help me!"

A scream tore from my throat, and my torso jackknifed up from my slumber. Pictures and scenes ran through my mind so quickly it was hard to grasp the threads as they slid from my head. My heart battered against my ribs, as if it desperately wanted to be freed. Sweat trailed down my temple, my lungs frantic for air.

"What?" A figure jumped beside me, sitting up. "What happened?"

My hand went to my chest, confusion and terror choking my breath. The voice echoed in my soul, shredding every nerve up my spine, leaving me raw and at the edge of tears.

"Hey. You're okay. You're home, li'l bird." The man moved closer to me, his hand rubbing my back. "This is real."

My head snapped to the silhouette beside me. Moonlight filled the room. My body instinctively knew and responded to him. It felt like a lifetime ago that Lorcan had come back from his afternoon hunt, not just a few hours ago. The moment he returned, he pulled me out of a meeting, made love to me on our balcony and then on the bed, before I passed out from exhaustion. Okay, making love sounded too nice for what we did. Though he was still mostly beast, I was the one shrieking like an animal.

He ran his hand through my hair, touching my ear. "What do you smell?"

That one question brought me instantly back to the present.

Lorcan.

Our bedroom.

Castle.

Vision.

"Ken, what do you feel? Hear?"

For once I didn't want to answer his questions, my gut twisting in my stomach. This vision was different. I didn't want to escape it. I wanted to remember every detail, crawl back into it, as if someone were calling for me. Needing me desperately.

"Ken?" Lorcan brushed a strand of hair over my ear.

"Something's wrong." My hand still knotted between my bare breasts, as if the secret were locked under my ribs.

"Must be Tuesday." Lorcan rubbed his face, waking himself up.

"No." My brow furrowed. I shook my head and tears sprang into my eyes. Emotions I couldn't seem to fight stirred in my gut. "This feels different."

"Different how?"

"As if someone is calling for me. They need me." I shoved the covers off, standing up, needing to move. Bits of the dream zipped through me, like one of those flip books, but they were going too fast for me to understand the whole story. All my visions were important, but this one jabbed at my gut like a woodpecker in a tree. I reached for a T-shirt and leggings.

"Where are you going?"

"I don't know… but I need to move." I started to pace the room, my hands rubbing fiercely at my skull, trying to remember my vision.

A man who looked similar to Lars flashed into my head, a cruel smile curling his mouth.

"Ken." Lorcan got up, his naked and unbelievable physique strutting over to me. "You need to breathe. Relax."

"I can't." I scrubbed harder at my head.

Lorcan grabbed my hand, stopping me from drawing blood. "The more you try, the more the images are going to slide away from you. You need to meditate. Or have sex. It helped last time."

I glared at him. Normally I would be all for that, but not this time. I hurt inside. Not physical pain, but as though I had lost something dear to me.

I cared about a lot of people, but there were very few I would destroy everything for. One was the man standing in front of me. My best friends, Ember and Ryan, came next. And my sister, who had returned home the day before.

My sister and I were so newly acquainted we were still strangers really, but a bond existed I couldn't deny. A connection.

A gasp clotted in my throat, almost choking me.

"Oh my god." Adrenaline punctured my heart, speeding it up with terror rushing through me. The voice came in solid this time. *Kennedy, help me!* "Fionna!" I yelled, my legs already aiming my body for my door.

Visions.

A man who looked like Lars but wasn't.

The compound taken over by strighoul.

A little girl and Nic at knifepoint.

Marguerite bleeding on the forest floor.

Fionna calling for me.

I hear you, sister. I'm coming, I shouted back in my head. I doubted she would hear or feel it, but it made me feel better.

"Torin!" I bellowed to the soldier standing guard outside my door. I felt Lorcan come up behind me, and I knew he was still naked. He didn't care about being "appropriate." Being naked was as normal as breathing to a dark dweller. But here in my wobbly kingdom, he was already a source of gossip and ridicule. Normally, I'd have him throw on some pants, but my mind was solely on my sister.

"Majesty?" Torin jerked to his full stature, bowing his head to me.

Things were still extremely awkward between us. Torin had expressed his love for me not so long ago, but there was no way I was getting rid of him. He was one of the only people I trusted in this castle. I hoped we could eventually get back to being friends. Torin's eyes slid to the figure behind me, his lips thinning with disgust. *Yeah. Probably not.*

"I need you to get a troop to Lars's. I think it's being attacked. My sister..."

He nodded again, not hesitating before he barked into his walkie-talkie. He had grown used to my visions and responded immediately to them, no questions asked, another thing I adored about him. He really had my back. I hoped someday he would find the happiness he so desperately sought and deserved.

More of my guards ran into my outer chamber. The only one missing was Castien. He was on wall watch tonight, making sure the spells and security were set for the night. Castien was the only guard with permission to live off grounds. He and Ryan lived with Lily and Mark in a large cabin next to the dwellers' ranch.

Dwellers.

I opened my mouth, turning my head to Lorcan.

"Already on it." Lorcan tapped at his temple. "Already have Dax and Dom heading there now."

Damn, I loved this man.

The dwellers communicated through a mind link. To be closer to their leader without being associated with me, Lorcan's group lived in a house deep in the forest, just bordering my lands, close enough for their links to still work.

"Gonna head out there with them." He moved closer to me.

Be careful, I said to him through our mating bond, which grew stronger every day. His notorious bad-boy grin hooked the side of his face up.

"Now, what's the fun in that?" He leaned over, his hand clasping the back of my head fiercely, his lips finding mine. The kiss was quick but stuffed full of promises for later. Heat pricked down my body, flushing my stomach with fire. I didn't seem to be getting any less immune to the power he stirred in me, even with a simple kiss. Lorcan didn't do anything half-assed or without passion. Killed. Loved. Hated.

He nipped my bottom lip before he whirled back to the bedroom, rushing out the glass doors. A few moments after he disappeared, a howl tore through the night, heating my flesh. My body had become conditioned to the sound of the beast, which turned me on. I knew what he was like when he came back from a hunt.

"My lady?" At the sound of Torin's voice, I whipped back to him. His eyes still lingered on the door from where Lorcan had left, his face strained with anger. This had to be hard on him. Torin and the Dragen brothers went far back, their hatred for each other steeped in history. Torin's enemy had taken away the woman he thought was meant for him. His mate. Not once, but twice. First Ember and then me. Ember was even once his betrothed. That had to sting. And every day he had to see and hear Lorcan and me together. My heart went out to him.

"What else would you want me to do?" Torin's gaze finally came back to me.

I took a deep breath and began to move without responding.

"My lady?" He trailed after me, switching the direction of the other guards heading for us. The activity roused people from their activities. They poked their faces out of doors and down hallways with curiosity. At least this time I was dressed in more than my underwear.

They followed me to the communications room. Against all the hope I felt, I wanted to try contacting Lars's compound. I clicked on the line that went directly there. It buzzed with its version of a ring. We were supposed to be getting an updated mobile prototype soon, putting the walkie-talkies out to pasture. Something told me it was now on hold for the unforeseeable future.

13

Nerves flickered at the base of my neck, and with each ring my heart skipped a beat, waiting for someone to pick up. The longer it rang, the more fear sank in my stomach like a rock. No matter the time, someone was always on duty at Lars's. Business, threats, and situations didn't stick to nine to five. I still hoped my visions wouldn't come true, but with every moment that passed, the truth set in.

"Majesty. I don't think anyone is go—" Sturt, the ginger-bearded guard, stopped talking when we heard a click.

"Oh good, is my order for a hot little queen on her way? I hope you got my requests. She needs to get on her knees and call me King." A deep, unfamiliar voice came over the device, sounding delighted with himself. "I prefer them feisty, but you should know when to bend over and take it. You must understand who is master."

My mouth parted, my feet automatically stepping back from the gadget, as if he could see me. He laughed in my silence.

"You're a delicate thing, aren't you? I apologize for my crude words. I thought it best for me to be up front about my wants… before our relationship progresses any deeper."

"Who-who are you?" I stepped back up, rolling my shoulders. "Where is Lars?"

"Did your sister forget to tell you about me? I'm hurt. Let me introduce myself. I'm Stavros, the true Demon King. Lars is no longer here, but you can leave a message after the beep."

What? What does that mean Lars is no longer there?

"So your sister really didn't mention me?" he said, then sighed. "Thought I made more of impression on her. Not to mention me at all is simply inconsiderate. Well, I'm pretty sure I made an impression this time. She might be a little brain damaged now. Dammit, I'm always too rough with my toys."

Bile burned up the back of my throat.

"What did you do to her? If you hurt her—"

"What is it with you Druids? Always threatening. All talk and little substance behind it. You should know when you are overpowered and outplayed, dear Queen. I will not be as lenient as Lars. Do you know how many will cheer when I take over? No longer will they have to suffer an incompetent Druid for a leader. The fae will throw fucking parades in my honor. It was logical to have Seelie and Unseelie leaders when the fae were in the Otherworld. But that no longer applies. One world, one ruler."

"And you think that will be you?" I countered.

"I don't think," he stated. "I know."

His confidence grated at my nerves. Who the hell was this guy and where was Lars? What was going on? I hated not knowing. It gave him the upper hand.

Think, Ken. What do you know?

1. He is powerful. Even over the airways, I could feel it.

2. Lars is gone. The why and where was a mystery.

3. My sister's alive. Maybe barely.

4. This man has taken over the compound.

5. He calls himself Stavros.

I needed to find out about him. Get him talking.

"You are clearly powerful if you took over Lars's compound…" I let the last syllables drift a bit, leading him to continue.

"My nephew was weak from the start. He was never the true King. I was. He played house, but I will make sure it is brought back to glory days."

Nephew? Lars had an uncle? I knew next to nothing about Lars's personal life. He was the type of man so serious and intense you forgot he'd ever been a child or had a mother and father. He was simply a king. He had told us about his antics with his twin brother, Devlin. They were very mischievous kids, and the reason a cave in Greece collapsed and started a dragon legend.

"Lars is no longer the King, sweet Druid. You will have to deal with me."

Nerf-herder! Was Lars dead? I knew that was the only way power transferred from one King to another.

"And when I say *deal*, you or your people will take the brunt of your disloyalty. So, if you are planning to send your troops here, you might rethink that move."

My heart froze, my entire body going still. I could barely swallow past the thick terror in my throat.

"I was kind enough to let your sister live, but she knows the deal. She obeys me and does what I asked of her." His playful smugness twisted my stomach. "There is only one ruler. I'm sorry, but you've been demoted. This is no longer an equal partnership. You both work for me. I look forward to meeting you in person, Kennedy. If you obey me, I will try to make this transition as easy as possible. But take one step I don't like, and you will be severely punished," he taunted. "I will be in contact again soon."

He hung up, leaving the room in utter silence.

"Lock down the castle. Get Castien. He should be doing his walk around the border," Torin ordered my guards, Georgia, Sturt, and Rowlands. They dashed from the room in response.

"Contact the dark dwellers, along with Lily, Mark, and Ryan." I turned to my other guard, Vander. "Until we know what is going on, I want them here."

Vander bowed, heading for another walkie-talkie on the wall. The dark dwellers might refuse. They didn't like coming here, even though Queen Aneira, who had tortured them, was dead and the castle was no longer on the Light side. After the barrier between the Otherworld and Earth fell, our worlds meshed together. The dwellers still danced around this place as if a bomb were about to go off. Lorcan lived here only because of me but would happily live somewhere else if I ever wanted to quit my job, as he'd said many times.

I stood there, still staring at the walkie-talkie. A million questions banged against each other. Where was Lars? What happened over there? And, most of all, who was Stavros?

I didn't trust him, but my Druid senses told me he was telling the truth.

Whoever he was, Stavros was the new Unseelie King.

👑 👑 👑

"We can't get anywhere near the property," Cyren, a captain of one of my groups stationed closest to Lars, said through the device. It had only been twenty minutes since Stavros's call and my castle was on full lockdown. "He's already changed the spell with his own."

Torin dropped his head forward, his hands splayed on the table. So far all the teams stationed close to Lars's compound were struggling to get anywhere near it.

"Dammit." Georgia paced the room. Castien had rolled out a map on the table, outlining the territory our team walked. It was a larger space than Lars's original property border. Stavros was quick to "change the locks," making our access difficult.

Lars had granted my top soldiers entry into his compound for emergencies, as I did for his men. It looked as if our admittance had just been rejected.

"Have you seen my sister? Marguerite or Nic?" I asked into the device, running my hand through my hair.

"No, my lady," the captain responded. "We've seen no one from the house. But we will keep searching the perimeter."

16

"There might be strighoul hiding out. Watch your backs." Torin's voice was tight. The way his shoulders rode up his neck like a jockey near the finish line, I could tell he wanted to be there. Since our return from Ireland, he had been even more obsessed with his job and protecting me. Fae usually didn't need a lot of sleep, but he appeared ragged and stressed. He was horrified that I could have been killed on his watch by someone right under our noses, by someone he trusted.

Thara. His best friend and my second-in-command betrayed us, giving our whereabouts to Luuk, who opposed my rise to the throne. Luuk had been one of Aneira's favorites and managed half of the European Seelie and hated Druids.

Sadly, Thara did this out of a broken heart, not her dislike for a Druid leading the fae. I had spoken with her since, while she was being kept in the dungeons. She still held her head high, but her shame soiled her like a dark stain. She lost respect for herself, knowing she shamed the position she held and the person she loved. Or used to.

Even if I couldn't let her out of jail, I had forgiven her. Torin, on the other hand, wouldn't even go down there. He stood at the door to the dungeon but had yet to make it below. His anger was palpable, but I also sensed his sadness, his loss. I don't think he knew how to function without her by his side. She had been there since they were young and went through training together. He had taken her for granted. Now that she was not with him, he was withdrawn, over-focused, and short-tempered.

We all missed her. She knew Torin so well; she would understand before he did, without a word, what his next move was. My top tier had experienced a few stumbles lately, allowing us all to see how much Thara had done.

My feet moved over the stone, pulling me back to the present. My stomach twisted in knots. *Fionna.* That was my only thought. I had recently found my sister. I couldn't lose her.

"Keep searching for her." I stormed up to the table, staring at the walkie-talkie as though she would pop out of it. I didn't even want to think about Marguerite or the rest of the people in the house. What would Stavros do to them? Killing them would be too easy. He sounded as if he enjoyed torture, breaking those who opposed him.

"Kennedy!" My name roared through the castle, ice spreading down my spine. I whirled around, feeling my mate's presence, and my heart sank in my chest. His voice was taut. Frantic.

Shit times a thousand.

17

The sound of my feet slapped against the floor, my ears pounding with blood. I let my body follow the link to him, his energy rushing over my skin.

My guards tried to run past me to intercept him, but I pushed through them and into my room, my toes sliding over the rug and coming to a halt.

"Oh. Gods. No." My hand went to my mouth, my heart stopping for a beat.

Lying in Lorcan's arms was my sister's limp body, blood dried around her head and nose, bruises and cuts layering her face and hands.

"Fionna!" I screamed, my knees crashing down next to her body.

"She's alive." Lorcan tried to reassure me, but my hands still moved frantically over her face and body, trying to feel the life pumping through her body.

"Fionna?" I gripped her face, her skin cold and damp, but her heart was strong.

"She wasn't the only one we found." Lorcan's features crunched with anger, nodding back to Dax and Dom, who carried in Marguerite. Both of them were naked like Lorcan from having shifted from beast to human again. "We smelled their blood. They were almost a mile away from the compound."

A tortured cry gurgled from my lips as they laid Marguerite next to Fionna, her body covered in blood and cuts as well.

"Anyone else? Nic? Goran? What happened to Lars?" I spouted.

Lorcan frowned. "I smelled Nic had been there… but no sign of him."

I chewed on my lip, pushing away all theories and stared at Fionna.

"Goddammit!" Torin squatted next to me, his fury rising to the group standing around us staring in shock. "Someone get the healer. Fucking do something. I shouldn't have to tell you this," he snapped.

Sturt was the first to move and ran out of the room, talking on his device.

I looked at my sister, still cupping her face in my hands. "You're going to be okay. You are safe now," I whispered to her, more for me than her. A small groan rumbled in her throat. "Fionna?" I called her name a couple more times, her lids flickering, as though she were trying so hard for consciousness.

"Pip-er…"

"What?" I leaned in closer to her.

"Piper…" She moaned again.

"Who's Piper, Fi?"

18

"My daughter," she mumbled. The statement was an arrow to my chest.

"Daughter?" My mouth dropped. "Fi?" I tapped her face. "What are you talking about?" Daughter? How did I not know I had a niece? Why hadn't Fionna tell me? Where was she now?

"Fionna!" I shook her harder. A hand clamped on my wrist, causing me to jump. I peered down at my sister's face, her eyes wide open.

"Get. Ember. *Now*," she choked out before her eyes closed, unconsciousness stealing her from us again.

THREE
Ember

Bones crunched, my back rolling over the gravel, grating my skin like cheese. The momentum thrust me up on my knees, and my blade sliced out for my attacker's legs. A guttural scream peeled at layers of the night air, blood spraying from the troll. The ugly bastard went down screeching like a banshee, singing for death.

Wiping at my brow, the sticky jungle felt the same as another layer of clothing, sweat sliding along my back.

"*Brycin,*" a deep voice screamed into my head, the dark dweller link bursting to life. I knew that tone as if it were my own, and what it meant. My sword swung along with my body, the tip carving into the gray lumpy form leaping for my back.

Bright eyes met mine, a mix of green and red. Eli's jet-black beast growled before his scythe-like claws tore through another group of pointy-eared, large-nosed creatures. Greenish goo poured from each body, turning the ground tacky and disgusting.

This was supposed to be a simple mission. A sighting of these normally reclusive creatures had been called in from Rio de Janeiro, South America, which seemed to be the hot zone lately. But on a night of observing, we spotted a whole band of them coming together. More and more showed up each night, increasing our anxiety. Similar to wolves, they resided in small, tight family units, and usually did not get along with other groups of their own kind. They were extremely territorial. Coming together like some war party went against their nature and meant it was time to worry. We hadn't been planning to kill anyone until we found out what was going on. But shit happens.

Trolls don't have great eyesight, but they have excellent noses. And in my defense, they attacked first.

"To the left, girly." Cal zoomed by my head, and I whipped around, parrying as a troll the size of a boulder came stomping for me. Trolls could range from a small bear in size to a minivan.

Its roar echoed off the trees and rocks, its gray eyes set on me.

"Come on, pretty boy." I winked at it. Trolls took great offense at being called "pretty." It was comparable to calling a human ugly. They took great pride in being hideous, smelly asses.

"Shut up." It growled at me, its beefy arm swinging out for me, forcing me to jump back. "You're smaller than what I ate for dinner. You're a little prepackaged appetizer."

His other arm pivoted faster than I was expecting and slammed into my body. My feet tore from the ground, pain vibrating through every bone. I crashed into the dirt, spine first, sliding over rocks, twigs, and bushes until I skidded to a stop.

"Owwww." I looked up at the canvas of night, the stars winking at me as though they were enjoying the show. Out of the corner of my eye I saw Eli's beast slashing at the horde circling him. He was lethal, but more than two dozen of them hurled their massive weight at him. A handful could crush his bones. Simmons and Cal were trying to help fight from the sky, but stabbing out the trolls' eyes only seemed to piss them off more.

Crap on ash bark.

The skies were clear, no sign of a storm, nor were we close to any electricity. I knew what I had to do, but I had to admit summoning that other part of me always made me nervous. I liked it. Too much. One of these days it wouldn't want to be put away.

The troll's feet pounded the ground, jogging for me, his arms in the air, ready to smash down on me.

Taking a deep breath, I closed my eyes briefly, letting the demon feel the threat, understand the peril my mate was in.

My lids shot open, my vision shifting, sharpening. I knew my eyes had turned black. The sensation of power flooded through each vein, blocking anything other than the impression of control. No fear. No pain. No emotions.

I rolled as the troll's fist hit the earth and jumped up. My arms opened, my focus solely on the monster. As if an invisible hand picked it up, the huge troll flew into the air, ramming back into the wall of stone with a crack, his body pinned. Every step I took sang his death, my sword vibrating with excitement in my hand.

"Sorry." My voice sounded robotic. "This packaged snack will give you heartburn." I drove my blade deep into his heart and twisted. His

21

screams only pumped me with more excitement. His form twitched and bucked against the rock. With a single cry, death claimed the leader.

I smiled.

"Brycin?" A voice called in my head. The sounds of a struggle felt distant, but I could feel the pull of the mating bond. My demon side had become even more protective over Eli. You hurt him, you dealt with the black-eyed monster.

Whipping around, I waved my arms in front of me and a handful of the trolls circling him went flying, sucking more energy from me. The demon was powerful, but it did have limits. Everything had limits and balances, in nature and certainly in magic.

Nature gave me another burst of energy as I sliced into one troll after another, the dark dweller in me snapping and growling with vengeance. Fairy. Demon. Dark Dweller. Most of me enjoyed the kill way too much.

Slice. Stab. Cut.

"Stop, woman. They're all dead."

Slice. Stab. Cut. Repeat.

"Brycin. Stop!" A hand clutched my elbow, slightly shaking me. My head snapped up, breaking me out of my trance. Green eyes stared down into mine, bringing me back to earth. My anchor. My heart.

My narrow sight eased, adjusting back to normal. Dozens and dozens of bodies were slumped over the ground, a few still gasping their last breaths, but otherwise it was quiet. Still. All were dead or soon would be.

A heavy sigh escaped my lungs, my shoulders dropping. When the demon took over it was identical to a drug. I could conquer the world. When I came out of it, it probably wasn't much different from a junkie coming down from a high. I felt sick, twitchy, exhausted, depleted, and restless in my skin.

Hands moved to my face, cupping, tilting it up. Eli's naked body pressed against mine. "Fuck. That never gets any less hot." Eyes twinkling, he thumbed away blood and goo off my face.

"I think there is something seriously wrong with you."

"I *know* something's wrong with me," he smirked. "I fell in love with you, didn't I?"

"That in itself should be enough to get you locked up." I leaned into him, my muscles soft as Play-Doh. His thick-corded body was like heaven. Most days, I wanted to stay naked against him all day.

"I'm not the only one who's a danger to society." He leaned in closer, his lips only a breath away from mine, his dick pushing heavily into my hip, throbbing and hot.

A shiver ran down my back, my mouth curving into a mischievous grin. "Maybe we should shackle ourselves away from society for a while."

Eli rumbled, his mouth brushing mine. "That sounds like an excellent plan."

Our mouths crashed together, our tongues quickly finding each other, turning our kiss hungry and desperate. Another kink between us—we both got extremely turned on after a fight. The more blood and carnage, the closer it got to death, the hotter the sex.

His hands started tugging at my clothing, wanting no barrier between us, our lips frantic with need.

"Oh. No. I am not going to be subjected to this again." Cal whizzed by my head. Crap, I totally forgot about them. "Yeah, did you and dickbag dweller forget we were here *again*?"

"Cal, maybe we should leave my lady and Sir Eli alone."

"I agree with the motorized Barbie," Eli grumbled against my mouth, loud enough for the pixies to hear.

"*Barbie?*" Simmons gasped. The sound of his mechanical wings hit my ears. He lost his real wings in the war when Aneira stomped on them with her heel, shredding them. "I'll have you know, sir, I am a world-renowned flyer. Not someone to be disrespected."

"Every. Damn. Time." I pulled back from Eli, shaking my head. Eli's grin only widened. He lived to get under the pixies' skin. Usually it was Simmons who fell for it. Not that the pixies didn't get Eli back. Their relationship basically thrived on pranks and insults. But I knew they all cared for each other, though none would ever admit it.

"Oh, don't listen to the overgrown kitten." Cal landed on my shoulder, folding his arms over his Woody the Woodpecker T-shirt, leaning against my neck. "He's still sensitive over his little curlies being waxed with honey." Cal snorted in my ear.

Eli's lids narrowed. "Huh, I wonder where the juniper juice that went missing earlier could possibly be? Oh, wait." Eli rubbed his hand over his ripped torso. "Right here. Soooo good."

Cal straightened and stomped his foot into my muscle, fury rolling off the dark-haired little man. "That is *too* far, dweller. You will pay—"

"Okay, let's stop right here before we say things we regret." I held up my hands, interrupting Cal. Sometimes I felt more like a mom refereeing three small boys. "Why don't you and Simmons do a flyover and see if there are any more trolls in the vicinity?"

Cal grumbled, still making a knife-slicing motion across his neck to Eli.

"Simmons?" I looked over my other shoulder for help.

"Come on, Cal." Simmons motioned to his friend. The blond six-inch pixie, dressed in a 1960s Ken doll pilot outfit, his swizzle stick sword attached to his belt, flew into the air.

Cal huffed, pointed two fingers at his eyes, then pointed them at Eli before taking off.

"I really am a babysitter."

"You can sit for me anytime you want." Eli stepped closer, his arms circling me. "But how about you just sit *on* me instead." His nose skated up my neck, sending heated chills through my system. I saw him naked more than I saw him clothed, but it never ceased to get my blood boiling. We'd been together for a while now and our lust had only increased, the need consuming us, and the sex even better. Every time felt as if we hadn't seen each other in months.

Bodies of trolls spread over the ground at our feet like land mines as Eli picked me up, my legs curling around his waist. My fingers trailed over his tattoos, following the path to his hip before my fingers took a detour, my hand grasping his length.

"Fuck." He hissed between his teeth, ramming me back into the wall next to where I killed the leader of the troll group. Yeah, we were demented and loved it that way. His hands frantically tugged at my jeans, heat flowering through my nerves, my clothes rubbing almost painfully against my skin. Eli wrapped his hand around my ponytail, yanking my head back, his tongue sliding up my throat, tasting the blood slightly oozing from a wound on my neck. His fingers worked down my jeans and pushed my underwear to the side, sliding inside me. Light flickered behind my eyes, air rushed into my lungs, and my legs squeezed him closer. He gripped my hair, his fingers curling, moving in and out of me faster and faster.

A tingling started at the base of my spine, his thumb rubbing me. "Oh gods." I gnawed on my lip, tasting the metallic tang of blood, mine and others'. Humans might find that gross, but my dark dweller part loved the taste of blood. I rocked my hips rougher against Eli's hand.

Eli pulled out, dropping my feet to the ground, and rammed me back before lowering himself on his knees, tugging my jeans and panties down. His hands opened my legs, his lips brushing over me. Teasing. Enticing.

"Eli," I growled. He peered up, his eyes melting me with their heat. He paused a moment before his mouth consumed me.

My hands in his soft brown hair, I tossed my head back, my moan piercing the air. He was a genius at this and knew exactly what made me lose my mind. My head grew fuzzy, his tongue moving in deeper, faster.

His fingers joined in, racing me to my orgasm. It would only be the first of multiple, before we would leave and head back to the hotel, where we'd finish. It was like that most nights for us.

Buzzzzz.

My backpack rattled from across the space, a ring humming through the sky. *No. Not right now.*

Eli growled, and instead of letting up, it only spurred him on more, sucking and nipping fiercely. My body bucked wildly, as though I had no control over myself.

Swear words hissed from my mouth, my nails digging into his head, tugging at his hair. Pain was another thing we enjoyed. Not extreme or anything, but just enough to ignite more fire between us.

"Ember? Eli? Are you there? Pick up!" A woman's voice came over the walkie-talkie. Damn Lars for adding that feature. I liked when you could pretend to ignore the buzz of the device. Now it fuckin' talked to you without even picking up.

Eli still ignored it, determined to finish what he started. His sharp teeth bit down and lights exploded across my vision, a cry tearing across the sky. For a moment I was there with the stars, losing all sense of gravity.

"Ember, please, if you are there, pick up. This is an emergency!" Kennedy's voice shot me back to earth with a thud. Eli held me up, keeping me from collapsing to the ground. Air heaved in and out of my lungs, my muscles even more like gelatin. My body still convulsed with aftershocks. Damn, he was good.

Eli got up, showing all signs he was ready for his turn, and walked over to the bag, retrieving the device.

"Hey, Kennedy. What's going on?" Eli spoke, his taut ass facing me.

"Eli, oh thank the gods." The tone of Kennedy's voice pulled me off the wall. I tugged up my pants. I knew my friend well; something was wrong. "I need you guys to return immediately."

"Why? What's going on?" Eli turned, his eyes finding mine. I took unsteady steps to him. Between using the demon magic and Eli's magic tongue, I was surprised I could function at all.

"I don't want to say over this thing. I need you both to come to the castle *immediately*. Everyone is here and waiting for your return."

"Everyone?" I repeated, my hand clasping Eli's bicep. "Ken, tell me what's happening."

"Ember, there is no time. Please. Get here as soon as you possibly can." The line went dead.

My gaze darted to Eli's, panic brushing at my insides. We had gone through a lot of "emergencies" with Kennedy and fighting for the kingdom. Our work as bounty hunters was always dangerous and sometimes exceedingly ugly. But never once had I heard fear in her voice like that. She was always centered. In control. Even when she found her adopted family had perished in the war, she had held her head high and focused on all those suffering from the effects of the war. She had become a force, even more so with Lorcan by her side, which had taken me awhile to admit.

Lorcan was far from my favorite person. Used and threatened by the old Queen to kill my biological mother, he also kidnapped my friends, one of whom had been murdered. Yet Kennedy had busted apart some of my perceptions of Lorcan. I'd come to see he had a good heart. But he would always be the one who killed my mother.

I was trying to accept him. To my shock, I no longer hated Lorcan. I could see his positive attributes, especially when I saw him with Kennedy. Shit, you could not deny those two were mates.

He and Eli were also trying hard to build back trust and a relationship, along with Cole. Lorcan was in my life no matter whether I wanted him there.

Eli pulled out the extra jeans and T-shirt in the bag and got dressed while I yelled for Cal and Simmons. Alarm rang through me at the distress in Kennedy's voice, which replayed in my mind. I had no idea what was happening, but deep in my gut I knew it was bad.

I just had no idea how huge the bad would become.

We headed for the closest fae door in the forest. Since the wall between worlds had fallen, they weren't really called "Otherworld" doors anymore. There were a lot more of them, and they tended to move and morph, often unpredictable. But for some reason, I could maneuver easily between them, getting to where I needed, whereas most others got lost in them, sometimes for years. The only other person who could use the doors with ease was Lorcan. Scary to think our minds worked similar enough we both understood them. I probably should talk to a therapist about that.

But the poor humans. With magic heavy in the air now, the doors became completely invisible to the eye, even to some fae. Fae could feel the magic, but humans couldn't decipher between what was merely air and what was a door. So many had gone missing or landed in another country. Not sure why they were complaining. It was an instant vacation.

Our boots pounded into the dirt as Eli and I ran toward the castle. Simmons and Cal flew ahead of us. It had only been about twenty minutes since Kennedy contacted us, but it felt like hours, desperation to reach her gnawing on my bones.

I couldn't see them, but I could sense fae guards lining the walk above the bridge.

"Halt! State your business." A woman stepped out from the entrance gates, holding up her hand.

"Get out of our way, fairy," Eli growled.

"You take another step and I will shoot you where you stand."

"Are you new? Do you not know who we are?"

Wow, that sounded pompous, but it was true.

"I know exactly who you are, but many can take on your face, your form. I will not simply let you in."

"Brielle, let them enter."

A familiar male voice came from behind her, his slim muscular body striding to the gate, dressed in his elite guard attire, signaling his top status among the soldiers. He wore the symbol of three rays, of Awen, the symbol used by the Druids on his chest.

"But, sir. What if they're impostors? We heard he can do that…"

"Believe me, no one could duplicate these two." The dark-haired, violet-eyed guy winked at me. "I can feel their stubborn bullheaded auras from here. No one can be as much of a pain in ass as these two."

"Castien!" I ran to him, and he embraced me.

"Hey, Em. Good to see you." He squeezed me then stepped back. "Eli."

Eli nodded, coming around to my side.

"Cal and Simmons already preceded you." He nodded behind him.

"What's going on?" Eli asked.

All humor dropped from the beautiful fae's face. "Follow me. They are all waiting for you."

"Who is *all*?" My feet worked double time to keep up with his pace as we entered the castle. My skin still crawled when I came through here, reminding me of so many things I'd rather forget: the blood that once painted the walls, the horrors Aneira put all my loved ones and me through. I had to keep reminding myself this was Kennedy's home now.

I was eternally grateful not to have to be Queen. Seriously, I couldn't think of a worse job for me. Traveling the world, hunting with Eli and my pixies, was where I belonged.

Kennedy was a perfect Queen. Kind, fair, strong. I wished the non-fae

27

haters would give her a chance to be the amazing ruler she was. They hated her merely because she was a Druid and not fae.

Ignorance at its finest.

Castien stayed quiet, his legs moving at a brutal pace through the hallways, leading us to a section I had never investigated, making me feel guilty about how little I had visited Kennedy here.

Castien clutched the double doors, swinging them open. Heads whipped around, taking in the new arrivals. Cal and Simmons darted into the room before us, settling on a bookshelf.

"Ember!" My mother's voice sprang from the throng, her tiny figure shoving the huge men to the side as she ran for me.

"Mom." I ate up the last of the distance between us, wrapping my arms around her. Lily may have been my adopted mother, but she was the only mom I had ever known, and therefore my true mother. A fox-shifter with gorgeous auburn hair and brown-and-orange eyes I always envied, I spent most of my youth thinking she was dead. I had found her body, what had remained of it, but it was all a ruse. Lily knew Aneira was getting too close, so she faked her own death and went into hiding to protect me. She got caught and spent years locked away in a dungeon.

"Please tell me that is not your blood?" Mark was quick to join her, gathering us up and hugging us both.

"Mostly not." I grinned at Mark. My stepdad was the best man in the world. The lack of blood connecting us meant nothing. He was my dad. After my mom's fake death, he raised me and stayed by my side when I accidentally burned down schools, went into a mental facility, and endured doctors shoving mind-numbing drugs down my throat.

Little did either of us know I wasn't crazy… I was fae.

I basked in the love of my parents for a moment before I stepped away, taking in the room full of all the people I cared about. It was almost overwhelming.

"Hey, my spicy one."

"Ryan." I flew from my parents' arms to his. Ryan and Kennedy were so embedded into my soul they were a part of me. Their friendships had gotten me through the darkest times in my life.

I stepped back from him to see Cole, Cooper, West, Rez, Lorcan, Dax, and Dom. Giving the first four a hug, I nodded at the other three. We weren't at hugging level yet.

West gave me an extra squeeze. "Hey, darlin'." He kissed my temple, grinning at Eli. "I missed you. Not that bastard so much, but definitely you."

I teared at the sound of his Southern accent, the love in his words. We had almost lost him a while ago, which was why Eli and I moved back to the ranch. After their nephew Jared's death, we needed to be far away from the memories, but the close call with West brought us home. These people were our family. Our world.

West and I would always have a close bond. From the night in the bar when he protected me to the moment I found him in Aneira's dungeon, we were linked. He once told me I saved his life that day, gave him strength to fight the demons and darkness instead of giving into them.

"Missed you too." I nuzzled into his chest. My dweller loved being back with the pack.

I couldn't imagine what it felt like for him to return to the castle. I didn't care for this place, but this had to be a living nightmare for West. His time here had been horrendous. I knew it went darker, deeper than he ever let on. Being back here had to rekindle those nightmares.

Eli greeted his brothers with pounding back hugs, but the reunion was a lot more subdued than usual. The one thing dark dwellers showed emotion for was family. Every time Eli and I returned to the ranch, whether gone a week or a month, the guys wrestled and beat up on each other like wolf pups, giddy to play with their siblings and reclaim the dominance order.

But tonight the room was drenched in apprehension, keeping everyone tense and reserved.

"Where's Gabs?" Eli peered around the room.

"She and Alki were on a mission. They are heading here now," Cooper answered for his twin sister's absence.

"I'm so glad you are all here." A voice came from the doorway, pulling us away from our family reunion. Kennedy stood there in jeans and a T-shirt and boots, but still looking every bit the regal Queen. Her expression was strained, but she reached for me. I took her hand and squeezed it. She gave me a pained smile, dropping it as she descended farther into the large room. It was the first time I really took notice. We were in the library. A beautiful two-story room with large windows on one side overlooking the blue lake below. Tables and comfy sofas were placed around to enjoy the books and the view.

"You wouldn't tell us anything." Cole spoke, stepping in front of his clan, rubbing at his thick reddish-brown beard.

Kennedy rotated around, her back facing the windows, her petite form standing strong. How much she had changed since the shy girl I knew in school. Kennedy had cut her waist-long hair to her shoulder blades, and it was a little darker than her natural color. I also knew under the shirt she had a nipple ring and a raven tattoo. When she returned from her "trip" abroad, we had a catch-up night. A few glasses of wine and she told Ryan and me about these changes. That was also the night she told us the truth about Lorcan. Ryan didn't take it so well. But slowly it was getting better between them. It broke my heart to see the two best friends not talking. They were the true soul mates.

"I thought it better to do this all at once. My sister still doesn't have the energy to explain it over and over."

I knew of Kennedy's sister, Fionna. We had learned about her on the night of our slumber party, but I had never met her. As far as I knew, she was still supposed to be locked in my uncle's prison after she attacked him.

Speaking of... Where was Lars? This seemed important for him to be at. Unless...

"Oh. No. Ken, you didn't." I stepped closer to her. "Please don't tell me you kidnapped her from Lars." Oh gods, that would be awkward. My best friend against the only blood relation I had left. And the frickin' High Demon King.

Not smart.

A strange expression ghosted Kennedy's face. "No, I wouldn't say that."

"Then what? Where is Lars anyway? If this is such an emergency, shouldn't he be here?"

"He should." An Irish lilt sounded from the doorway, spinning my head around. My mouth parted.

A gorgeous woman walked in slowly with Torin, his hand on her elbow, her skin still showing signs of healing cuts and bruises. She had the same long silky brown hair and eyes as Kennedy. She was a few inches taller, but they shared the same petite frame and freckles sprinkled over fair skin. The resemblance left no doubt they were related, but right away, I could sense that was where the similarities ended. Fionna held herself tensely, as though she were ready to attack, to fight. No naivete or sweetness shown in her eyes. She stared at all of us as if she were daring us to lunge for her. Kennedy told me she was a powerful Druid, one strong enough to toss Lars on his ass, which impressed me. And to be honest, it made me like her right off. She had something extra about her, something which demanded your attention.

She moved past Torin, pulling away from his hold on her arm, her chin high. It was a move to show she held no weakness in a room full of fae. She ignored Kennedy's assistance and faced us like a warrior ready for battle.

Then she spoke words I never expected to hear, ones that ripped the ground out from under me.

"The King has fallen."

FOUR
Fionna

Silence rebounded after my statement, eyes boring into me. I didn't remember every name in the room, but I had learned enough through my own investigations and Kennedy to figure out who each of them was. I wanted to know exactly what I was walking into. Who was in charge. What to expect. Torin, Lorcan, Castien, West, and Rez were the only faces I recognized.

"Lars is no longer King." Emotion flicked quickly through me, my heart splintering, but I shoved it back before it made it to the surface. It was taking a lot for me to even stand. Whatever Stavros had done to me had destabilized me. I stood here for my daughter. For Lars. I would never stop fighting until I got them back.

Kennedy knew everything. About Piper, about me and Lars. Stavros. The stone. All of it. She was the only one who would get certain details. She might trust these dark dwellers, but I didn't.

"I'm sorry, but *what*?" Ember was the first to break the tense silence. Even with blood and some greenish goo all over her, the girl was unnerving to behold, and not entirely because of her two different color eyes and hair. She was unearthly beautiful. So striking that it was unsettling. I could see how people were drawn to her. And feared her. Her mate was even more intimidating. Gorgeous. I wasn't blind. Tall. Broad. His brown hair hung to his shoulders, scruff lining his strong jaw and face, and his green eyes popped even in the brightly lit room. Ember and Eli together were overwhelmingly beautiful.

But looking around, each man and woman in this room was unbelievably sexy. I already could sense who Cole was, the leader of half

31

the dark dwellers. Power and confidence leaked from him. He was more reserved than I had imagined, someone who watched, noticed every detail, but no doubt as ruthless as the rest. And of course, with his reddish-brown beard and hair, intense hazel eyes, he was sexy as hell. That was fae for you. But Eli and Lorcan had a bonus "danger" chromosome or something. Part of me wanted to run and the other part fancied throwing myself at them.

My feet yearned to shuffle nervously, but I glued them to the floor, not letting one ounce of anxiety show. I had lived too long preparing to fight and kill fae. Just because I was on their side now didn't make that feeling disappear completely.

Kennedy didn't touch me, but her eyes gave me the strength and comfort I needed to go on. It was still peculiar to have a sister, one I only knew as an infant and thought dead until a few months ago.

"Lars is no longer himself. Stavros, his uncle, is now King and contains all the power. He is holding my daughter and Nic as collateral until I bring Lars and Ember to him. Marguerite and I barely made it out. Stavros has taken over the compound and Lars's men."

More silence followed my statement. Blinking eyes.

Kennedy stepped closer to me. "It's true. That's why I had you all come here. We are on lockdown. I spoke with this Stavros earlier. Lars is gone."

The same as a wave coming into shore, the room flooded with the chaos of yells and questions being thrown at me.

"What?"

"Gone?"

"Excuse me?

"What are you talking about?"

"What do you mean *gone*?" Ember pushed to the front. "Where is he?"

"Guys!" Kennedy held up her hand. "Be quiet. Let her answer."

Ember's gaze landed on me like a cement brick, fear crimping her pretty face. "Where is Lars? Where's my uncle? He would never leave. That's not like him."

"I know." My gaze met hers head-on. "He thought he was doing the right thing. For you, them…" I motioned to the group, holding in my emotions. "For my daughter. *For me.*"

Ember's head jerked, taking me in, her eyes widening.

"Crap on ash bark," she whispered, realization opening her mouth. "Are you guys… together?"

"Yes." The knot in my throat bobbed as I swallowed. "That's not important right now. What is… is the Stone of Fáil is now controlling Lars.

I tried to stop him, but he couldn't fight it. And he knew he didn't have enough power to kill Stavros. He made a decision for his people. But it was the wrong one. His body may be Lars, but his mind is not in control anymore. And Stavros is here, claiming his right to the throne, and he is the furthest thing from a democratic leader."

"You mean we have another Aneira." Eli folded his arms. "Another ruler who wants Ember for a play toy? Are you fucking kidding me?"

"I wish."

"Okay, start from the beginning." Cole moved forward, rubbing frantically at his beard. "Where did this Stavros come from? Where has he been?"

Not one to overshare, I did understand they needed to hear the whole story. I began to divulge my story, though I left out how Lars and I had bonded. No one except Lars and I needed to know about that, or the sex. The *incredible* sex. *Shite, I missed him.*

I described how we went to Prague and Scotland to get the cauldron. How his uncle showed up in different forms, taunting Lars. How Lars broke the cauldron saving my life, but now the stone had nothing to counterbalance it.

"Wait." Ember held up her hand. Terror and liquid lit up her one blue and one green eye like fireworks. "Not only do I have some asshole great-uncle I didn't know about, but he can shift into different people? And he is now the true King? And the only things that could have taken him down, the actual stone and the cauldron objects, are now useless pieces of metal? And Lars is being held captive by the energy of this stone, the Stone of Fáil, inside his own body?"

"Unfortunately, yes." I nodded.

Ember let out a small growl, turned her face for the window, and walked to it, her hands shaking at her sides.

I understood her fear, her sorrow, more than anyone. It took everything in me to keep calm. I wanted to lash out and storm back to the compound and get my daughter, to fall on the floor and cry.

"It's supposed to happen this way. I've seen it, Mummy. You will see."

I moved to the tight circle, my mind trying not to think of my daughter scared and possibly hurt. The line between me losing it or not was growing thinner with every passing second.

"Lars's father never killed his uncle but locked him away and spelled the chamber enough that the power of the King transferred to him, then down to his sons. But now Stavros is back, and when he challenged Lars, the energy willingly returned to him. He has all the power, but he still wants Lars dead, so there is no question he is the leader. Some fae will follow him, but I think most will still stand by Lars. Stavros wants no uncertainty. What he has planned will make Aneira's actions look like a child's temper tantrum. And with his gift of shifting into different people, we have to be even more careful."

"Guys, we have a lot to discuss and to plan on how to deal with this." Kennedy brushed back her loose hair. "But first, I want you to get what you need from your homes and come back here. I want you protected and safe within the castle walls."

"And you think it's safe here?" West's head was already shaking. "No fuckin' way I am stayin' here."

"West, I know this must be—"

"No." He gritted his teeth while Rez took his hand in hers. I saw him take a staggered breath at her touch, calming himself. "You have no idea."

"Stavros will come after you anywhere." I planted my feet strong on the floor, looking straight at West. "He has been studying Lars for years. Knows all the players. This is not something he planned on an impulse. He's been hiding out in South America, gathering his troops. Preparing. Learning all about his enemies."

"South America?" Ember's head jerked away from the glass.

"Yeah. Why?"

"That's been a hotbed for fae activity lately. Large groups of strighoul." She licked her lips, glancing at Eli. "We just left a group of trolls congregating together. Every night more and more came, as if they were gathering for a war party. And you all know that goes against their nature."

"Shite." I dropped my head, rubbing it. It had to be connected to Stavros. I didn't believe in coincidences. He had brought the strighoul with him to Scotland. It would be like him to have a massive army ready to fight us. "He is preparing for war."

"He's going to fuckin' get one." Lorcan leaned against the far wall, his expression emotionless, but I could feel the anger radiating off him. He knew Kennedy was also on the new King's hit list. Stavros would probably love to collect almost everyone in this room.

"This is the only place guarded well enough to protect you." Kennedy's gaze danced to everyone in the room. "We have been through so much together. Shared so much loss. I will not allow any more of you to be hurt if I can help it. For some, I understand this place brings back horrendous memories. But please… try. We need each other more than ever now." She gulped, blinking the unshed tears gathering in her eyes. "The thought of losing anyone of you… Nic and my niece are already too high of price. We will rescue them. And *we will* get Lars back as well."

"Are you ordering us?" West shifted on his feet, holding Rez's hand tighter.

Kennedy watched him for a bit.

"No." Her voice was quiet.

West pinched his mouth together, looking at the floor.

"Fine." He bobbed his head. "I'll do it for my family."

"Thank you, West." Kennedy clasped her hands together. There were a few beats of silence before she spoke again. "I'd like us to gather again in a few hours. I know we are all tired and it's the middle of the night, but I don't want to waste a minute. He is already way ahead of us."

Cole bowed his head at Kennedy and made for the door.

"Dax, Dom, and I will do another perimeter run." Lorcan slid up next to Kennedy, kissed her forehead.

"I'll go with you." Eli moved to his brother's side. Lorcan stared at him before giving him a nod, looking a little surprised.

"I'm going to stay here." Ember joined the circle, glancing over at me, like she was not done probing me yet.

"Hey, Coop." Eli yelled at the blond surfer-like dweller walking to the door. "Can you grab some extra stuff from the house for us?"

"Sure, man." He nodded before he left the room, followed by most of the party.

Eli leaned over and gave Ember a kiss before he and Lorcan left the room as well, only leaving Kennedy, Ember, and me.

The moment the door swung close, Ember's gaze snapped to me. "Please tell me he's still there. That there's—" *still hope.* I could sense her unsaid thoughts.

"I think so." My hand went to my stomach. "The arsehole better be."

Ember barked a sharp laugh.

"I think Lars met his match."

"Yeah." My finger went to my mouth, trying to hide the soft smile. "And I certainly found mine."

"I'm sorry about your daughter. We will get her back. And no one touches my sexy incubus and gets away with it." Ember mouth flattened. "How's Marguerite?"

"She's in the healing unit. She'll be fine. That woman is tougher than all of us." Kennedy leaned back on the desk, exhaustion dragging down her usually smooth face.

Ember sighed with relief, running her hands over the dried blood on her brow. "Tell me everything about this stone. I skimmed over the other treasures, the sword being my only concern at the time."

This was going to be a long night.

"The Stone of Fáil and the Cauldron of Dagda are similar to yin and yang—the brains of the treasures, so to speak. The sword and spear are merely their weapons, neither good nor bad; they take on the holder's intention.

"The stone and cauldron have agendas. The stone especially. The more power it can take and absorb, the better. It will promise all your wishes to come true while sucking life from you until you're dust and then it moves on. The cauldron was designed to counter its power. Control it."

"But they were kept separate."

"Druids realized their mistake quickly when fae could not resist using the gifts for their own personal gain. Wars, famine, diseases. They destroyed everything so the Druids hid them away, separating them in hopes no one would ever find them all again."

"Leave it to Lars." Ember folded her arms, pacing around the table. "Why did he do it? I knew giving him the sword would bite me in the ass someday. But he's too smart not to realize what would happen. I didn't think even his lust for power would lead to this."

"That's not the whole story." I sat on top the table, putting my feet on the chair. "He felt he had to. To protect his kingdom."

"From who?"

"Himself."

"What?" Ember swung back to me. A small groan came from Kennedy.

"He said you foresaw it, Kennedy."

"What I saw was Lars destroying everything in his path." She rubbed her temples. "But it wasn't Lars. I could feel it… The man I knew was gone." A strangled cry vibrated in her throat. "It's coming true…"

"But why? Why was he protecting us from himself?"

"He was afraid he was going insane." I linked my fingers together. "Like his uncle… like your father."

Ember hissed in a breath.

"It runs in his family. He thought it was slowly happening to him. With the treasures together, he believed they would help him." I opened my hands. "Or throw him over the edge."

"Shit. Shit. Shit." Ember stomped her boots, her fists clenched. "Ah! Damn you, Lars. Why didn't you talk to me? Maybe I could have helped."

I could feel her frustration. Sympathize with it. "That's not Lars."

"I know, but dammit, he's really fucked us. We're fighting both a crazy great-uncle and the stone for him." She took a deep breath. "Okay, what else do we know about the stone? Any weaknesses?"

"Besides the broken cauldron?" I shrugged. "I don't know."

"Wait." Kennedy jumped up. "I have a few books where I made notes in the margin."

"Of course you did." Ember shook her head, smiling.

I couldn't help a stab of jealousy because Ember knew her so well. They had years together, while I had only known my own sister for a few months. Many of which I'd spent in a dungeon.

Kennedy strode to a shelf and grabbed two books with sticky notes peeking out the tops. My sister was definitely the organized one. She walked back to the desk, stroking the leather covers as if they were beloved pets.

"I haven't had time to read them over, just tagged where they talked about the stone."

She opened the first book and Ember took the other, quickly scanning the marked pages. I peered over Kennedy's shoulder at the book. We were quiet, scanning over the information that seemed to be simply explaining the history.

"What's this?" Ember spoke, turning her book to face us, where a design occupied the bottom part of the page.

"It's the Druid symbol for the stone. Basically, it means 'mark' or 'signature,'" I said, the years Owlyn had me study everything on Druid history coming back to me.

"Holy..." Kennedy gasped, grabbing the book from Ember, her eyes growing round. "Nerf-herder..."

"What?" My heart thumped, feeling the shock whisking off her. Her finger traced the symbols, one that looked similar to the mathematical symbol *pi* but with vertical lines curved out at the end. The second was similar to a lowercase cursive R.

"I know these symbols," she whispered.

"You should. They're Druid."

"No." Her eyes shot to mine. "You don't understand. I've seen them in person."

"In person?" Ember frowned with confusion

"On a person." Kennedy swallowed, standing up straight. "They were scarred into her skin like a brand." She turned away walked the few steps to the window. "I *can't* believe I forgot. I saw her in the vision as well... *Shit!*"

Ember and I looked at each other, both sets of our eyes wide. I didn't know Kennedy well, but I bet she rarely swore.

Fear instantly ran down my spine, and I stood straighter.

"Who, Kennedy?" Ember began breathing rapidly, her anxiety evident to all of us. "Who did you see?"

FIVE
Zoey

Zoey...

My name was like a rope, pulling me forward. Even though I felt frozen with dread, my body moved without my permission.

You can't fight me. The robotic voice pounded my heart. All I could see was darkness, but its presence whispered in my ear, my muscles jerking. *The time has come.*

"No." Panic pounded in my throat, barely letting me speak.

A strange laugh rippled up my throat.

The more you fight, the more I will enjoy your fall. You know it's true. You dream of me all the time. I am in every thought and fiber of you.

My heart pounded, feeling the truth like a dagger to my soul.

Come to me.

My mind screamed no, but my body moved down the tunnel, a glinting light at the end, beckoning me to grasp for it. I needed it. Wanted it. I could not resist the call; it sang in my blood the same as a craving. My arm lifted, the marks on my hand glowing as I reached out for the power.

Cries of pain, shrill and shattering, rocked through me.

Suddenly I was on the other side of the light, in a street filled with crumbled buildings, burning cars, dead bodies, and blood pouring into the gutters. *Oh gods, no.* Familiar faces lay at my feet, their dead eyes burning into my soul. People I loved. I peered at my hand, dripping with blood. I had killed them.

Labored breaths hacked at my lungs, spinning my head. *No-no-no-no.*

"Zoey." A voice rang through my head. Only one other being stood in front of me, his back to me. Tall, dark, and familiar.

"Lars?"

Lars's head jerked to me. His eyes were black, a creepy smile stretched across his face, which was covered in blood. The power radiating from him pulsated against my chest. My muscles locked up against a terrible feeling of doom.

"This is only the beginning. You are mine, Zoey. Forever."

🐉 🐉 🐉

I bolted up with a cry, sweat drenching my chest and trickling down the back of my neck. Throbbing singed my palm, the stone's marks flaring with life. I rolled it tighter, squeezing it until my nails dug into my skin, blending the pain together. My head pounded with the remnants of the dream as I gazed into the dark room, confused as to where I was. The fan dusted my skin with cool air, goosebumps dimpling my flesh. It was humid and hot, but the dream stamped an icy path along my spine.

Framed pictures covered the dresser. A painting Ryker got for me at the street market hung across from me. My bed. My pillows. My room.

The loneliness of having spent years in foster care, tossed from home to home, still reared its ugly head, making me forget I had a permanent home and people who loved me. A family.

My eyes dropped to the empty place next to me. "Ryker?" I called softly. I knew he had come to bed with me last night. The memory of him thrusting deep inside me wiped the last bits of the dream away, my naked body flaring at the memory. I shoved off the sheets, my toes touching the wooden floor. I pulled on one of his T-shirts I loved to sleep in.

Peru was heading into its winter months, but summer wasn't ready to fully let go, drenching the earth with rain and humidity.

I padded from the room on bare feet, the house quiet, everyone asleep. I headed downstairs, listening for any sound of Ryker. Sometimes when he couldn't sleep, he would jump somewhere or work on the car he bought me. This didn't happen as frequently as it used to though. Our time and energy had been taken up completely by something else.

The low murmur of the TV drew me toward the family room. I turned the corner and stopped, my heart lurching in my chest.

Sprawled out on the sofa on his back, one arm by his head, the other curled over the bundles on his chest. It shocked me how much love I could feel without exploding.

Curled up on his stomach contently, our son's tiny form looked even smaller beneath Ryker's large paw. Sprig was sound asleep, almost in the same position, facing the other way. Matty, our border collie, rolled up on the floor in front to the sofa. My boys.

Hell. My heart couldn't be any fuller. I was so lucky. I never believed this would be my future. That fate would lead me to a fae who would be the love of my life. Every day I fell more in love with him.

My gaze slowly traced Ryker's face. His gorgeous blond hair was now shaved on either side of his head, but he still kept the middle long, letting it flop to either side. His beard was starting to grow out from his summer trim, only highlighting his strong jaw. His broad shoulders and long ripped torso barely fitting on the couch, he twisted his head, a deep sigh heaving from him, his hand rubbing our son's sleeping back unconsciously.

Our son, Wyatt, or *Buachaillín*, as Sprig called him, which meant boy, had been born a few months ago. Our little warrior. Not that he had much of a choice coming from two fighters. He made a strong entrance. The little guy decided he was ready after only seven months, which didn't surprise Ryker. Fae usually arrived earlier than human babies.

Sleep was not something we got much of anymore, though I was lucky to have so much help between my sister, Lexie, Annabeth, and even Croygen, a pirate and Ryker's longtime cohort. Annabeth was busy trying to run both Honey Houses with Lexie, who had suspended college for another semester to help me out. Honestly, I think her pausing school had more to do with being near Croygen than anything, which disturbed me on so many levels. Nothing had happened, that I was sure. But I could see how smitten she was around him. It reminded me of my crush on Daniel.

A figure moved near me, leaning against the opposite doorframe. When Croygen did go out, it was usually all night. He was still a pirate, and I knew he needed to let off steam with girls and booze. I never wanted him to feel trapped living here. I was surprised he was home before the sun rose.

I turned toward Croygen. With dark hair and eyes that glinted in the light of the TV, he was so striking he was almost pretty. He came from Spanish and Asian descent—tall, lean, but corded with muscle. His almond-shaped eyes, tan skin, and smoldering stare could bring anyone to their knees. I was not above admitting it had almost been me a couple of times. But my heart always belonged to Ryker, even before I realized it. Croygen was my best friend, another person crucial to have in my world. Yet, a few times I got the feeling he thought he didn't belong here. But there was *nowhere* else he belonged. He was as much as my family as the rest. Every person here made this place a home.

My gaze ran over him, a teasing grin on my mouth. "I'd take a shower before Lexie wakes up. You smell like flowery perfume." Croygen's eyes skated to mine without moving his head.

"Zoe..." he growled.

"What?" I shrugged. "I'm simply saying."

"You know it's not like that."

Yet.

I bunched my mouth together, fighting back my quip, staring at my sleeping boys. Both of us were silent for a moment.

"He used to be the guy who'd drink me under the table and still be going after I woke and drink me under again." He shook his head at Ryker. "And I'm the fuckin' pirate."

"Well, take a shower for me. From the way you smell, I'm thinking you drank enough for the both of you." I rubbed my foot over the other.

"I have to pull his weight too." Croygen sighed dramatically. "I am always making up for his shortcomings."

"If you keep doing it, he'll never learn," I tsked.

"And that is my failing... I have such a soft heart for those lesser than I."

"And a soft dick," a deep voice mumbled from the sofa as Ryker shifted.

I clapped a hand to my mouth, fighting a laugh. Not wanting to wake the baby, I had woke another instead. I might have preferred the baby.

"Huh? What?" Sprig's head lifted. "Honey? Did you say honey? It's breakfast, right? I mean, it must be close. I feel as if I've been asleep forever. I am starving. I mean really, really starving. Do we have pancakes? Oh, let's go get some churros. I can have those mango thingys to tide me over. Oh, what about—"

"Fuuuuucckkk." Ryker groaned softly, his lids blasting open, glaring at Croygen. "You woke him, you deal with him."

"Do I look like a fucking zookeeper?" Croygen shot back.

"No. More like a monkey's uncle." I winked at the pirate. His beautiful eyes squinted at me.

"Thought you were on my side."

"When it comes to feeding him..." I held up my arms, motioning my head at Sprig. "Each man for himself."

"Fine. Next time I'm throwing your ass under the bus," Croygen sneered. He and Sprig resembled two five-year-old brothers, constantly picking on each other and fighting. But when no one was looking, I would see Croygen sharing his food with him or Sprig climbing up on his shoulder. "I'll take this little guy to bed too." Croygen picked up the baby off Ryker's chest, handling him with more care than I ever thought possible. One time he caught me gaping at him and responded, "What? Just because I don't have any doesn't mean I haven't taken care of a lot of brats."

Ryker was the one to tell me Croygen had been raised in a brothel. His mother, one of many ladies of the night, found herself pregnant multiple times. The older he got, the more he was in charge of watching the children born there, while the women "worked."

He lifted Wyatt to his chest, cuddling him. "You guys get some sleep. I'm still wide awake." He rubbed my arm, looking over his shoulder. "Come on, furball, let's go look in the yellow pages for animal adoption agencies."

"Do they have food there?"

"Tons." Croygen smirked. "Especially honey."

"Croygen," I huffed.

He grinned at me. "Maybe there's a circus passing through town."

"Circuses have bananas." Sprig stood on Ryker's chest. "You're trying to kill me. Murder by bananas. It's cruel animal abuse. Someone needs to stop the torture."

I glared at Croygen. He only chuckled, moving for the stairs.

"Wait, that's not the way to the kitchen." Sprig jumped down on Matty, who instantly popped up, ready to play with his buddy. "Go, Matty! We must storm the pantry." He wiggled the dog's collar. Matty took off, but instead of the kitchen, he trailed after Croygen, bounding up the stairs.

"Wrrronnnggg wwayyy, ruff-ruff. You are going the wrong way." Sprig's voice disappeared up the stairs. I shook my head and walked over to Ryker. He sat up, gesturing for me to curl into his side, tucking an arm around me.

"We really do live in a madhouse." He kissed my head.

"Yeah. We do." I melted into him. Everything about this man made me weak in the knees. "You love it."

He snorted. "Wyatt started crying. I didn't want him to wake you."

"He didn't." I tucked my head deeper into his shoulder. "I had a nightmare."

"The same one?"

"No. This one was different. Stronger." I nipped my bottom lip, the fear of the dream rolling back in like fog. Something was coming. I had dreams about the stone all the time, but this one was different. My palm twitched, as though it knew I was talking about it.

"It's calling me."

"You know Lars would have it locked up. Tight. It can't get you. You just have to keep fighting it."

43

"I know." My fingers gripped his T-shirt, feeling the heat of his skin under the fabric. "But I don't feel safe. It's gotten a lot more powerful. It felt as if it could reach out and grab me through the dream." My knuckles rolled, clutching more of his shirt. "I don't know if I have the strength to continuously fight it. What if it never lets up?"

"Then we go to Lars. Ask him to destroy it."

I let out a derisive laugh.

"Right. I can see that happening. The Unseelie King will simply destroy one of the most powerful objects in the world because it's giving me nightmares."

"Do you want to talk about your dream?"

Brief images slid through my mind like vipers, slithering through my head, leaving little drops of poison. I couldn't seem to bring myself to tell Ryker about the monsters I saw. The ones who carried my DNA, who resembled me.

Ryker drew me closer, his arms my safety net. He stayed quiet holding me.

A brief cry came from upstairs before it quieted down again.

"You know we just let a drunk pirate and a narcoleptic monkey take care of our kid," Ryker rumbled against my ear.

A laugh erupted from my chest. "Parents of the year."

"Eh…" He shrugged. "Until we hear a real tantrum—"

"Which will probably be Sprig," I chuckled.

"My money's on Croygen." Ryker's large hand rubbed up and down my bare thigh. "Left alone with Sprig? Croygen will break first." He wrapped me tighter. Merely touching normally led to sex with us, but the fear in my chest wouldn't subside.

"I'm scared," I whispered.

"Whatever comes our way, we will face it as we always do. We're survivors. We fight."

I knew he was right. We had gotten through some unbelievable situations and made it back to each other. I knew what we were capable of, and what we'd do for each other. The lengths we would go to survive for those we loved. We had even more reasons now.

So why did I feel that whatever was coming was bigger than us?

44

"*Bhean! Bhean!* Honey, honey, honey, honey!" A blur of brown fur zipped around the kitchen, a black "cape" trailing behind, catching on everything it could, knocking objects to the floor.

"Sprig!" Ryker tried to grab him with one hand as he zoomed by, but the sprite slipped through. Sprig leaped onto the counter next to me as I packed baby stuff in my bag. My palm still pulsed, like something lived beneath the skin. It did this occasionally, and I had gotten good at ignoring it. This felt different. As though the pulse was a call. Pulling me to it.

"Sweet glorious nectar. Ahhhhh!" Sprig ran in a circle, pulling my attention away from my thoughts. He woke swearing that death was knocking on the door, and his stomach was starting to eat itself. Lexie shoved a full honey bear at him, which shut him up for a total of three minutes. "*Bhean!* Honey goddesses!" He blinked. His mouth parting.

"Here it comes in one, two, three—" I counted. "And out." Sprig crumpled on the counter, falling fast asleep, his honey high turning into a honey coma.

"You have that down to a science." Lexie laughed, kissing my temple. "I'm gonna go get dressed then head to *Casa de la Miel*."

Casa de la Miel, the name for our Peru House, was another place for orphaned kids. We wanted to get them a better education and medical coverage while providing a place where they felt loved and wanted. And I loved Lexie was staying and helping us for now.

"Have a good day." I watched the tall caramel-skinned nineteen-year-old bound up the stairs on her prosthetic legs, her long wavy black hair reaching the middle of her back. Half black and half Puerto Rican, she had turned from a beautiful girl to a stunning woman. She was smart as a whip, but I could feel her restless energy. She was ready to spread her wings and fly. And I needed to be okay with letting her go. Lexie and I had been through so much together. She was my little sister and because of almost losing her twice, it was hard for me to let go again. She wasn't like Annabeth, who loved being home or being in the Honey House with me. Lexie wanted to explore the world. Challenge it.

Be a pirate.

Ryker shifted Wyatt to his other arm, tipping the milk bottle higher.

"You heading to Honey House?" He set the empty bottle in the sink, lifting the baby to his shoulder to burp him. If I ever had a doubt Ryker would be an amazing father, it was squashed the second Wyatt arrived. I didn't know if his natural way with fatherhood arose from a desire to be the opposite of his father or the loss of his first unborn child, but I couldn't have asked for a better partner. I was the one stumbling through the dark sometimes.

I also felt a bit guilty for longing to get back into the fight scene or wanting to go on "jobs" with Ryker. I had started a kickboxing class, but it didn't give me the high I got from my street-fighting days. In the future, I could go back to helping Ryker, but for right now it was too dangerous for both of us to do it. Wyatt needed one of us to be home with him.

With our abilities to jump, Ryker and I were the so-called "Robin Hoods" of the fae world, and Croygen was an excellent thief. We stole from drug cartels or other shady businesses and gave back to the poor. We provided medications, food, and financial support to those who couldn't afford it. It was one form of stealing I had no qualms about. When it came to my kids at the Honey Houses, or those Kate was trying to find cures for, there wasn't anything I wouldn't do.

My full-time job was running the homes for children in Peru and in Seattle. Seattle's house was our newest baby. We had trained and hired enough help at the Peru house that it ran without me. Seattle still needed my attention. It had only been operating a few months.

"Yeah, Annabeth and I are heading there now." I strapped the baby carrier to my front. "You and Croygen getting ready for tonight's job?"

"Yeah." Ryker rubbed Wyatt's back until he burped, then handed him to me. Changed and fed, he curled up against my chest in the carrier and drifted to sleep. Ryker's white eyes glazed over me, heat flaming in them. "I say tonight, after I get back, we go for a drive."

I knew exactly what that entailed. The Chevy we owned had been used more for our "escapades" than driving. We had been in a Chevy the night we admitted how we felt, and we had no problem reenacting the all-night kinky sex that had followed.

"It sounds perfect." I stepped closer to him, Wyatt bumping into his chest. Ryker leaned down, his hand sliding roughly through my hair, his mouth hot and frantic, coveting mine. Neither time nor a baby had ebbed our lust. At. All.

A growl vibrated in his throat, his tongue delving deeper into my mouth, shooting sparks up my nerves. My nipples tightened with need.

"Oh… uh… sorry." Annabeth walked into the room. Ryker pulled back but kept his hands in my hair.

"We'll finish this later." He lifted an eyebrow, kissing me again. Leaning over, he brushed his lips on Wyatt's head before strolling out of the room, giving Annabeth's arm a squeeze.

With long wavy blonde hair, porcelain skin, and blue eyes, Annabeth was so beautiful I'd swear she was part fae. If Lexie held a devilish twinkle in her eyes, Annabeth was sweetness. But looks could be deceiving. Annabeth's past had robbed her of true innocence. She had been captured and forced to be an "escort" when Seattle fell to shit. Then later, like Lexie, she was a victim of Dr. Rapava's experiments. She woke up many nights with nightmares of drowning or being forced to do things which ripped away her innocence at fourteen. Something she and I had in common. There is a high rate of foster homes that are wonderful and loving. Unfortunately, that had not been my experience. I still dreamed about killing one of the "fathers" who had hurt me. It was why I strived to make my foster homes full of love. I never wanted a child to go through what I had.

"You ready?" I turned around to Annabeth.

"I am." Annabeth picked up an apple and bit into it, moving over to Sprig's sleeping form. She grabbed a few honey packets and wrapped him up in her arms, adoration blistering across her face.

"I know. He's so adorable when he's *asleep*."

She laughed, nodding, then stepped closer to me. I stretched out and touched her arm.

Jump.

Wind crashed into us, blowing our hair around. When it stopped, I eased my lids open. The warmth of the Seattle Honey House surrounded us. The sounds of children playing in the other side of the connected buildings echoed through the walls. We had two live-in caregivers who constantly watched over the kids.

A fire already crackled in the fireplace, the sky overcast and dreary. I never got over the thrill of jumping. One moment being in the tiny, tropical town of Barranco, Peru, the next in Seattle, Washington.

The scars engraved in my hand came alive with a burst of fire, pulsing along with my heartbeat. As soon as I felt my feet settle on the wood floor, I knew we weren't alone. My skin prickled with warning. *Danger.* I instantly tried going for the knife I always kept in my boot.

"I'm not here to hurt you." A deep male voice came from the corner.

"Holy shit." I put my hand on Wyatt's back protectively, feeling my heartbeat all the way through him. "You scared me."

"I apologize." The King rose slowly from the chair, sparking memories of the dream from the night before. Something about his movements, the vacancy in his black eyes, had my alarms ringing. I never ignored my intuition.

"What are you doing here, Lars?" I took a step back, pushing Annabeth with me. Lars was dressed in dark jeans and a Henley shirt, looking every bit as handsome as always. But something wasn't right. This was not the King I knew. Even his demeanor felt different. The dread I had felt last night pounded in my chest.

A strange, tight grin pulled at his mouth, looking wrong on his chiseled face.

"What do you think?" His voice was emotionless and robotic. "I came for you, *Zoey*."

My gaze met Lars and I knew...

My time was up. It hadn't been a dream last night but a foretelling.

"I don't want the baby or the human, Zoey. I only want you." Lars took another methodical step toward me. "But I will use or kill them to get what I want."

Terror flushed through my system, inciting the new rage that came from being a mother. To protect at all costs.

Feeling frantic, my fingers fumbled at the straps, peeling the sleeping baby from my chest, my eyes never leaving the King's.

"Take the baby, Annabeth." I shoved Wyatt into her hands. "Get out of here now."

Children and employees were all over this house. I wouldn't simply jump and leave them, but I could only jump with so many at a time.

"No." She shook her head, clutching him to her chest along with Sprig. "I don't understand. What is going on? Lars?"

"We're not dealing with Lars anymore." I gripped my knife, holding it up. It wasn't a question. The creepiest smile pulled at Lars's mouth. "You were always my favorite, Zoey. The one who got away. You tricked me. Insubordinate, girl."

Fucking hell.

"Annabeth, get the kids and go." Until I knew the dozen foster kids playing on the other side of the house were safe, I was staying right here.

"Zoey, I can't lea—"

"Go. Now!" I snapped over my shoulder, her eyes widening to blue plates before she tore off for the stairs, taking Sprig and Wyatt with her to the other section of the house.

"Promise me you won't hurt them."

"Oh, Zoey. We know how promises go between us."

Dammit. Hell. I really hoped they'd be safe. It was me the stone was after.

And it was me the stone finally came for.

SIX
Kennedy

"Kennedy!"

"Someone get Lorcan. I can't wake her," I heard a woman's voice yell out. Everything sounded far away. As if it was happening on a different plane.

Lars.

Zoey.

Wake up, Kennedy! Wake up now. My subconscious screamed at me, but I couldn't pull out. My eyes were still glued on Lars standing feet away from the girl I had met only once but who had imprinted on me strongly. Her large green eyes narrowed, her gaze locked on the King as though she would kill him if she had to, a knife in her hand. She was short, but there was nothing weak about her.

Still, she could not overpower the man standing before her. I could feel it. That man was not Lars. Not totally. The stone was trying to diminish his light, but he was still there. Fighting.

"Kennedy, come on." A voice called to me, trying to pull me out of the limbo I was stuck inside. Fionna. I could feel her, but my mind remained in the living room of the Honey House.

My hand grabbed the sofa I stood next to, feeling the soft fabric under my fingers, fear crawling up my throat. Being able to touch and feel the world also meant I could be lost to it. Everything solidified around me, becoming more real. Magic thumped around me, jerking Lars's head up. Slowly he turned his chin, his eyes landing on me.

"Well, well... look who's also decided to join us." Lars's black demon eyes sparked, his head bowing in false respect. "Druid. What a pleasant surprise."

Holy nerf-herder. He can see me.

Zoey followed his focus, her eyes roaming as if she were trying to find who or what he was talking to.

"Leave her alone." I held his gaze. Even in the vision, I could feel the power of the stone. It radiated off him like a power line.

A smile hitched the side of his face. "What a waste of words." He stood straight like a robot, no twitches or gestures of a normal person. He moved as if he wore a costume and was awkward and uncomfortable in it. "The fae-human tricked me. There are severe punishments for that."

"*Li'l bird.*" My feet stumbled back at a tug, but I fought against it, not wanting to leave Zoey by herself.

"You know what I am. Who I came from." I dug my fists into my thighs, burrowing my heels into the floor. "We made you. We can unmake you."

Lars's head tipped back, a mechanical laugh emanating off the ceiling, sending chills through my flesh.

"You, little girl, are nothing. I can smell how young and inexperienced you are from here. I have *all* the energy from the other treasures. And the Demon King. You think you can challenge me?"

I couldn't. I was nowhere near the level to fight him.

"*Kennedy.*" Lorcan's voice called to me again, forcing me to take a step back, the room wavering. Lorcan was my anchor, my line to reality. If I fought it and it broke, what would happen?

"You don't have the power of a king," I countered. "You are too late for that."

The stone turned fully toward me, taking a step. Zoey raised her knife higher, still confused as to what was going on. His attention left her, giving her a perfect opportunity.

Go. Run. I screamed to her in my head.

"What are you talking about?" Lars's nose flared.

Come on, Lars. I know you are in there. *Fight.*

Over Lars's shoulder I saw Zoey disappear. *Holy nerf-herder.* She vanished in a blink. Not caring how she did it, relief washed over me, my shoulders inching down. Lars strode toward me, forcing me to stumble back. Instinct told me not to let him touch me.

"What are you talking about, Druid?"

"You couldn't tell the man you took over was no longer King?" I shook my head. It was so strange to see the face of the man I had grown to love and respect used as a shell. "And you think yourself so smart and powerful."

Anger tightened his features, dark magic curling off him.

"Then how about I take a Druid Queen?" He lurched for me.

"*Kennedy!*" My name rang from behind me, and I jumped back, shutting my eyes. Lorcan pulled me back from the void.

A guttural roar sounded in my ears, the feel of nails diving into my skin, trying to hold me. Like water, I slipped through, eyes popping open with a gasp.

"Ken." A man's face blurred over mine.

My heart slammed in my chest, confusion suffocating me.

"Focus on me, li'l bird. Just me." He cupped my face, centering my attention on his gorgeous green eyes.

Lorcan.

Home.

Boots danced around my peripheral. A handful of others stood close to me.

"Take a deep breath. What do you smell?" Lorcan's thumb rubbed over my cheek, his voice low and soothing. But I couldn't stop my heart from pounding, knowing something was wrong. I needed to help. Stop something.

Crap times a thousand.

Lars.

Zoey.

"Shit!" I sat up.

"You smell shit?" He tipped back on his heels, adjusting to my sudden movement.

"No... Lars..." My words fumbled around in my mouth, panic clouding my thoughts.

"Lars?" Fionna stepped beside me. "What about him? What did you see? Where is he?"

"Back off, Fionna," Lorcan growled.

"Honey House." I rose to my feet. "He found where Zoey was."

Lorcan's head jerked to Eli, who stood with Ember behind Fionna. I could sense the buzz of them talking through their link.

Ember nodded. "Let's go." Because of a blood transfer, Ember had become part dark dweller and picked up a few of their traits. She could now link with them.

"Zoey got away." I rubbed my temple, recalling the way she disappeared. I had never seen anyone do that. I knew she wasn't quite human, but I had never heard of a fae being able to disappear like that. "But they have children there."

Lorcan, Ember, and Eli were already out the door, Fionna right on their tail.

"Fi." I called for her. She turned to look at me. "It's not him. You understand that, right?"

"He's still in there." Her brown eyes flared with determination.

Barely. I pinned my lips together. She swallowed, understanding my expression.

"I'm going to fight for him," she insisted.

"I know."

"My lady?" Torin ran into the room, severing my moment with Fionna. She took off after the others.

"Torin, I need my unit to go to the Honey House immediately."

He responded without hesitation, sending orders through the walkie-talkie before he was out of the room.

It was beginning... the war I had seen in my visions. I hoped I could stop some of it... or the streets would run with the blood of those I loved.

SEVEN
Zoey

"It's okay, *Bhean*." Sprig patted my shoulder, trying to calm me down. In three groups, I jumped everyone from the Honey House to *Casa de la Miel*. The moment they were all safe, I let out a breath, my heart still thumping erratically in my chest. "You know what might help?"

"Sprig, I swear if you say honey right now..." I pinched the bridge of my nose.

"See, I didn't have to," he exclaimed. "It's like you *know*. Maybe we're mind melding and you can pick up on my thoughts." He put his hands on his temples. "What am I thinking now?"

"Honey."

"Holy toad trolls! You have superhero powers."

"Sprig." Lexie bounced a crying Wyatt in her arms, sending a warning glare at my shoulder. "Shut. Up."

I had known the day was coming the moment the stone marked me. I had felt it in my bones. But I couldn't bear I had put these kids in danger. I gripped my head, my lids squeezing shut.

"I called Ryker." Annabeth walked into the room, moving next to Lexie, stretching her arms out to take Wyatt. Lexie handed him over, probably hoping, as I did, Annabeth's calming nature would soothe him. He had been crying nonstop since we returned, feeling my anxiety like a freight train.

"Zoey?" Ryker's voice boomed through the house. Right on cue.

"Back here," I responded, running my fingers manically through my hair, tangling Sprig in my locks.

His massive form filled the doorway, shoulders knotted with tension. His white eyes scoured the room, settling with relief on his son and then me. As Annabeth bounced Wyatt in her arms, his wails started to ebb, her comforting aura working on him.

"We're fine," I replied automatically but didn't really mean it. Were we fine? Today I got lucky, something drew the stone's attention away from me, but it wouldn't give up. It would come for me again.

It had been so strange to see Lars but know it wasn't him. How did he let that happen? He was the Unseelie King. If he wasn't powerful enough to stop it from claiming him, what chance did I have?

Ryker stepped into the room, Croygen right behind him. Ryker didn't move or speak, his demon filling the room, taking up all breathable space. This was how he handled fear, to shut down emotionally, his demon taking over.

"O-kay." Croygen clapped his hands together. "How about the three of us step out and let them talk?"

"Hey, Swashbucket!" Sprig stood. "There's five of us—oh honey farts, I forgot Pam. Ohhh, honey bears, she's going to be sooooo pissed at me."

"Stuffed goats and banana-loving rodents don't count."

"Whhhhaaaattt?" Sprig screeched. "How *dare* you call me a banana lover."

"Croygen," Ryker growled, his eyes going dark.

Croygen sighed, yanked Sprig from my hair, and marched from the room. Annabeth and Lexie followed with Wyatt as his hiccupped gasps tugged at my heart. I knew I'd only make him worse. My fear was palpable, knocking against Ryker's.

With the door shut, and my son's sobs dying away, I could take a breath. Damn, I felt like a horrible mother.

"What happened?" Ryker seemed twice as big as his hulking size.

"What I have been warning you about for years. It's finally come for me." I faced the Viking.

"How?" Nerves twitched along his jaw.

"I don't know what happened, but it's possessing Lars's body. And it's a hell of a lot stronger than it was. Powerful enough to claim the Demon King."

Ryker balled his hands into fists with a big inhale. "Then we leave."

"What?" That was not the response I had expected. "We can't simply leave. This is our home. Our family. I will not leave these kids."

"Zoey—"

"No, Ryker." I put my hands on my hips. "What happened to fighting? That's what we do, right? We don't run. We fight."

"Goddammit, Zoey," he roared, his arms flying out. "This is not a fight

54

we can win. Don't you remember what happened the last time? You barely survived!" He barely had either, but it wouldn't help pointing that out right now. "And don't say it's strong enough to take Lars?" Damn. He'd come to the same conclusion I did. What hope did I have? None. "We have Wyatt now. I will not put his life on the line."

"You don't get it." I flung my arms right back at him. "There's nowhere I can run. The stone will always find me. And the more I resist it, the more the stone will go after those I love. That's how it works. You know it better than anyone."

Ryker was the one who held the stone for many years, feeling its call, but had been strong enough to fight it. Or maybe he was simply too bullheaded to give in to it. Once I might have been able to resist, but now I was marked. Angry at my betrayal, the rock branded my hand with symbols of remembrance and vengeance. The mark had weakened me to its influence and forged a bond between us. It would always find me.

"Ryker, I know you're scared. But that's not us. We stay and fight."

His head slumped forward, his teeth baring. "I *will not* lose you," he gritted out roughly.

I moved to him, taking his hand in mine. "Then we fight it together."

A rumble came from his chest.

"It's the only way I can see. There's no running. There's no hiding. It's not going to stop."

He lifted his head, taking a deep breath, his gaze on the ceiling. Still full Viking, the demon receded some, letting air return to the room. "What is your plan then?"

"We hide Wyatt until this is done. Kate will gladly take him. The magic Lars placed around the facility is thick." The idea had come to me on my last jump with the kids. "We keep all the kids here for now. Spell it, as well, to keep it protected. We do what we can to guard them... then we go to Seattle."

"Do you know anyone who can do protective spells similar to that?"

"Yeah." I stepped closer to him, his arms wrapping around me, pressing myself against his body. "I happen to know a very powerful Druid Queen."

Ryker exhaled, letting his shoulders drop down, leaning his forehead against mine. "Here we go again."

I rubbed my hands up and down his arms. "We survive, Wanderer. We lie, kill, and cheat. Whatever we have to do to come back to each other, to our family, to our son."

"You better," he rumbled in my ear. "There's nothing I won't destroy if that stone gets its hands on you." His nose skimmed my neck. "You're fucking mine, human."

"And you're mine, Viking." I went up on my tiptoes, my mouth finding his.

I was his… but deep down, I felt the pull.

I was also the stone's.

🐉 🐉 🐉

"Oh, hell no!"

"Lexie." I folded my arms, standing firmly. "You will either stay here or go with Kate. End of discussion."

Kate Geer was the head scientist at Lars's Labs. It was a version of the DMG, except this time no demigod scientist was putting pieces of human, animal, and fae together to create new races. Lexie and Annabeth both had been victims of Dr. Rapava's Department of Molecular Genetics, but I was one of his prodigies. I was born in a petri dish, a fusion of egg and sperm from seers. He created extremely powerful seers, but something went wrong, a fault in our makeup, that ended the subject's life too soon. Most of the other experiments had either died at birth or as young kids. Sera and I were the only ones who had made it to our twenties. Yet even she had died, and I would have if it weren't for Ryker. Receiving his power, becoming fae myself, saved me.

"No." Lexie shook her head, her hair slowly breaking free of the bun she had it rolled into. Her sharp eyes on me. "I'm nineteen, Zoey. You can't stop me."

"Not—"

"And…" She held up her hand, cutting me off. "If you so much as say 'not if you're living under my roof,' I will scream."

Dammit.

"Lexie, we made our decision." Ryker stood next to me, holding a sleeping Wyatt against his chest. The baby had calmed the moment Ryker took him from Annabeth. I understood how safe the world felt in Ryker's arms.

A squeak came from the coffee table. We were back home, getting things we needed for Wyatt, Sprig, and the girls before we left.

"Don't even think about it, Sprig. You're going with Kate too," Ryker declared.

"No, I'm not!" he huffed, stomping his foot. "You need me. You need these magical fingers."

"Guys." I buried my hands in my hair, itching with frustration. "I understand you want to fight with us, but this isn't merely some bad guy. This is one of the most powerful magical objects in the world. I will not risk any of your lives. I have no idea what we're up against. I need to know you're safe. I have almost lost every person in this room... I won't go through that again."

Croygen leaned against the wall, watching us, smug in the knowledge he wasn't part of this fight. He already told us where we could shove it when we asked him to stay back. Unfortunately, I couldn't tell Croygen what to do.

"And we won't either." Annabeth moved beside Lexie. The girls were so different but made perfect harmony. Sisters. Friends. I should have known they'd stick by each other. "You think this is solely your fight? It's not. If this stone wins, it's the world's problem and you know it. We are a family. We love and we fight as one. Isn't that what you say all the time to us? You can't preach it only when it works in your favor."

My head tapped against Ryker's arm with a groan. Leave it to Annabeth to throw my own words in my face. "I didn't quite mean it in that way."

"Too bad." Lexie jumped in with Annabeth. "It applies to everything we do. And in all honesty, we'd follow you anyway. Wouldn't you rather that we were with you, protected, than sneaking behind... exposed and vulnerable."

"Holy shit." I peered at Ryker, my mouth wide. "Hello, manipulators."

"They're good." He shook his head in amazement. "Can I say I'm glad we didn't have a girl? I'm not sure I could handle another in this house."

Croygen snorted. "They twist us until we have no idea which way is up."

Lexie looked over her shoulder, a mischievous smile on her mouth. They held each other's gaze for a moment too long, before Croygen looked away, moving off the wall.

"If they go, I go. I'm needed much more. You wouldn't have made it without me last time! What if someone is chained up? Or puts you in a cell? What if you need someone to call the elevator while you're being shot at again?"

"Not helping, Sprig." I groaned.

"Who wouldn't want a monkey who falls asleep in the middle of a heist?" Croygen quipped dryly.

"Exactly!" Sprig held up his arms, missing Croygen's joke. "I'm the most valuable. You can't go without me. And Pam. Must take her. She is still really, really mad at me."

He sat back on his hind legs, nipping at his lip. "Are we having dinner soon? It feels like it should be dinner time. We haven't been to Izel's in a while. Ohhh, I am craving honey pancakes now. But I could have the honey French toast too. Maybe both. I'm going to die if I don't eat soon."

Croygen rolled his eyes. "Don't tease us unless you're actually going to."

"Stuff it, smelly butt pirate."

"So." Annabeth gave them both a glare, then turned back to us. "We do this together. As a family."

My mouth opened.

"Don't even try, Zoe." Lexie shook her head. "It's futile. We're going. You fought for me my entire life. You've fought for all of us here, never giving up. We're not giving up on you. The stone can't have you. You belong to us. So we either all hide together or we fight together. You choose."

My shoulders fell, my resolve slinking out of me. They were all of age, and as much as I didn't want them hurt, I knew Lexie too well—she would find a way.

"If we do this," my voice became stern, "you listen to everything Ryker and I say. No exceptions."

Lexie clapped her hands together, bouncing. She was so ready for an adventure she didn't get the seriousness of the situation or what was at stake.

"There will be rules." I pointed at her. "You break or even bend one of them, I will send you back to Kate and spell your ass to a chair."

"Okay." She nodded eagerly. Annabeth stood strong, but I could see the fright in her eyes. At least she understood this wasn't some family vacation to Disney World.

"I will be sure they stay safe." Croygen rolled his shoulders back. We exchanged looks. He seemed to understand and nodded. He didn't look any more pleased they were going than I did, but he knew Lexie too. I couldn't keep her locked up forever. She might do something even more stupid if I didn't give her a little rope. When it came to the actual battle, or when I faced the stone, my loved ones would be nowhere near. Croygen would make certain of that.

"So… what's next?" Annabeth rubbed her arms, as though she could feel what was coming.

"I've already talked to Kate. We drop Wyatt off with her, then we go see a queen." There was a good chance Kennedy already knew what had happened to Lars. She was in contact with him all the time and with his compound. She might know how we defeat a treasure of Tuatha Dé Danann. She really was my only hope right now.

"Uh. Is it possible we can have dinner first?" Sprig moaned. "I mean, come on, I'm actually really dying this time."

EIGHT
Ember

Rolling to my side, I flopped my head on the pillow. Five seconds later, I flipped to the other side with a heavy sigh.

"For fuck's sake, woman," Eli grumbled, pressing his hand on my thigh. "Be still for two seconds."

One.

Two.

I shifted into a different position.

He moaned and threw his arm over his eyes as the dawn bled through the split in the curtains.

"I can't stop thinking about Lars." I sat and leaned against the headboard, giving up on sleep. Eli wore me out for a few hours, but once I woke up, my mind wouldn't stop. The constant soldiers patrolling the grounds, moving past our bedroom doors, were like a ticking clock in a silent room, the crunch of stone under their boots, the clink of their weapons hitting their legs.

Fionna and Kennedy put extra protection spells around the castle. We were still on full lockdown, all of us anxiously waiting for the first attack. We needed rest to be at our best, but I couldn't seem to actually do that.

Earlier I visited Marguerite, who was still recovering in the healing room. She was a tough lady, still more concerned if I was eating enough than about her broken arm. She had a line of people out the door waiting to see her. She was loved by everyone: fae, Druid, and human. She loved each and every one of us back with the same ferocity.

"Mr. Lars... he will come home, my *dulce niña*." She gripped my fingers firmly with her good arm. "Love will bring him back to us."

I nodded, blinking back the tears. I wanted so badly for her to be right.

Lars. My uncle. My only living blood family. The bond between us had grown stronger over the years, so much that I hated calling him uncle. He meant more to me. My real father was his identical twin, but every time I looked at Lars, I saw myself: jet-black hair, yellow-green eyes. Sometimes I would catch myself using his same mannerisms. He wasn't easily lovable like Mark, but I loved him just as deeply. We had been through a lot together. Sometimes I felt as if I were the only one who could calm him.

The image of Fionna popped in my head, making me frown. I liked her. She was strong. Someone who could truly challenge him. But I couldn't help a twinge of jealousy, as though my dad was dating someone new and moving on from my mother, forgetting her.

Damn, Em. He's not your dad. She's not some wicked stepmother.

I wanted him to find someone, ever since Rez had taken up with West. He deserved to be happy. His heart had walled up after my birth mother's murder. He'd barely let anyone in. His life was his job. If Fionna gave him even a slice of happiness, I was so happy for them.

But, of course, it wasn't long before they were ripped apart.

"No rest for the wicked, huh?"

I looked down on a pair of deep green eyes burning into me, bringing me back to the present.

"Not in our family."

He grinned, turning me into the pillows, his naked body crawling over mine.

"We'll get him back, Brycin." He nipped my ear, his strength trapping my body under his. I sank into the overstuffed pillows in the guest room, blocking out any view except the man over me.

Sometimes I just stared at him, dumbfounded he was real and mine. I remembered how our paths led us to each other that night at the police station when I saw him for the first time, handcuffed to a chair. Little did I know he would change my life forever, shattering my world. But I'd gotten an even better one.

My fingers laced through his hair, his mouth caressing my nipple, setting me on fire in an instant.

"I know what you're doing." My back arched. "You think you can distract me with sex?"

"I know I can." He grinned at me, moving to the other one.

My breath caught in my throat, my legs opening wider, wrapping around him.

Groans and a knocking on the wall popped my eyes open. Eli paused; the bangs and cries against our wall become louder.

He lifted his hand, pounding on the wall. "Shut up over there; we're trying to have sex here."

A laugh burst from me.

"Fucker." Eli's eyes glinted, gazing hungrily back down on me. "West thinks he can outdo us?"

"Do they not know us?"

"Exactly." Eli winked. "Ready to put them to shame?"

"I'm always ready, Dragen." Hearing them turned me on more.

"You say that now…" A wicked expression crossed his face. Oh crap. I knew that look. Excitement thrilled up my spine; things were about to get rough and kinky. Last time he got that look, I had trouble walking for a week. No complaints, as he struggled along with me. But part of me felt bad, as though this wasn't the time for this.

Lars needed me.

But Eli and I didn't have that inappropriate switch, the same as others did. Sex helped us focus and energize us for missions. It made us a better team.

He pulled me up my knees, folding my hands over the headboard, his tongue gliding down my back, licking. Exploring. His fingers sliding inside me.

"Oh gods." I gripped the headboard.

His tongue broke through the entrance, lighting every nerve ending on fire, stroking me faster and harder.

Our headboard cracked against the wall, my cries exploding in the room. He was ruthless. Making sure I had hit my third orgasm by the time he replaced his tongue with his cock, sending me over so far, so fiercely, everyone in the castle heard us.

Not that we cared. West and Rez seemed to take it as a contest. Their bangs, cries, and moans battering the wall in competition only spurred us on, as though the four of us were on a mission to outdo the other couple, cracking glass and popping bulbs. I knew the energy we created was overwhelming. I felt bad for anyone in the same hallway as us. Particularly Cole, who slept in the room on our other side. Well, he wasn't sleeping now.

He had to hate us. Eli said Cole went out but didn't bring any women back home. He tried to act as if everything was fine, but I could see the loneliness. He seemed to carry the weight of Jared and Owen heavy on his soul.

Sparks crackled in the room as I cried out. Eli groaned as my body squeezed him. The glass vibrated in the doorframes off the balcony, all thoughts of West and Rez becoming a distant haze. He moved over me, his hands gripping mine on the headboard, as he moved deeper and faster. He pounded into me, chasing his own release, and only extending mine.

"Fuuucck!" He bellowed as he slammed into me. As he filled me, my body gripped and pulsed harder, both of us groaning, pleasure thrashing through us.

Sweaty and breathless, we didn't move for a few minutes.

"Dammit, woman," he muttered in my ear. Sex was getting more intense between us.

"And you decided to go easy on me tonight." I huffed, trying to fill my lungs. Last time I did pass out.

"Yeah, I didn't want to completely emasculate West." He nipped my shoulder, smirking, his palm rapping against the wall. West returned the knock, their room also quiet, but energy still churned between the two rooms like the remnants of a storm.

He moved, pulling me back down in the bed with him, holding me against this chest, our heartbeats slowing together. He held me, knowing my fears were still not at rest.

"It's Lars," I whispered into his arms. "He was untouchable. A rock, as if nothing could actually ever happen to him." I dug my head into the pillow, fighting back the dread I'd shoved away. Lars was fallible. It was wrong to think him incapable of weakness, but that's how he came across. Someone you could always trust to be there. Never faltering or lost. Now it was my turn to be his rock.

When Eli, Lorcan, and I had gotten to the Honey House earlier, Lars was already gone. So were Zoey and the children. Board games still lay where they'd been played. Apple slices were half eaten. Everything was left as though they all simply vanished. We searched the area for hours trying to pick up a scent, a direction. Nothing.

At the sound of a loud rap on the door, I jumped out of Eli's arms and sat up. "The Queen needs to see you." Torin's cold voice boomed through the wood. A blast of resentment and hurt flooded through to me, before a wall came down, blocking me from his feelings once again. "Immediately."

I pulled up the sheet, my lids squeezing together. "Dammit." He had heard us. Torin knew Eli and I were mated, but I still didn't like rubbing it in his face. He was good at shutting down our link as much as he could, but I could feel that it would always be there. And sometimes his emotions would blast through our connection before he slammed it shut again.

Torin was a good man. Misguided in love, but still an amazing guy. He deserved happiness. For a moment in time he had believed it to be me. Then Kennedy. Poor guy, both of us falling for the Dragen brothers instead. Dark dwellers and his enemies for so long. I was surprised he could even stand to watch Lorcan, day in and out, while he stood at Kennedy's side. I hoped we hadn't really broken his heart. We weren't his true loves. Someone truly worthy of him would hopefully make him see that.

"Fairy boy will get over it." Eli got out of bed, stretching.

I sighed, getting to my feet and searching for my clothes. We had this conversation a thousand times. He would never understand how much it hurt me to cause Torin to suffer.

We rushed to the library, Cooper catching up with us on the way, smirking at my messy hair.

The library was the perfect place for Kennedy to have her meetings. She loved facts, so a source of information was always close at hand. This room was a lot more relaxed than the throne room, which I knew she didn't like. That was where Aneira had ruled with pleasure, and it was the location of her cruelty.

The buzz of magic lashed at my skin as the murmurs of others grew louder. I was accustomed to the magic of the dark dwellers and my friends. This was new. And strong.

The double doors were open. Castien and another guard, Sturt I think, were on each side of it. The library was already full of my loved ones—Mark, Mom, and Ryan were farthest on one side. Cole, Gabby, Alki were next to them. Fionna, Lorcan, Dax, and Dom were over by the window, hovering near the one who stood center—Kennedy. West and Rez had yet to show up.

"Holy shit," Cooper muttered under his breath, his mouth parting, his eyes locking on something across the room. *She is... wow. Damn. Fucking stunning.* His voice came barreling through our link. *Shit, did I just say that out loud?*

Not exactly out loud, but his entire pack heard. All of us turned to him in shock. Cooper always complained about us mated couples, but no girl ever seemed to entice him for more than a few hours or even minutes. I had never seen him stop dead in his tracks in awe.

Yep. And before the huge guy near her beats the shit out of you, you better shut down those thoughts now. That one looks barely of age. Eli lifted his brow at his brother.

I followed Cooper's enamored stare, my gaze falling to the group next to us until I found the object of Cooper's reverence: a twenty-something, ethereal blonde girl with wavy hair to her waist and huge blue eyes. She was so fair and delicate, you could almost mistake her for a fairy. She stood close to a similarly aged tall, stunning, dark-skinned girl, whose beauty would make you want to weep with envy. But even from here, I could see her legs were not quite right. The way they bent wasn't natural.

The shorter girl standing slightly in front pulled my focus. I knew instantly it was Zoey Daniels. Heart-shaped face, blistering green eyes, toned but curvy, her long brown hair pulled back in a ponytail. I could feel enormous strength radiating from her. Something told me she would not be afraid to throw down. Possibly me.

But it was the two males behind her who made my thoughts jumble.

"Oh. Holy crap." My mouth spilled out my inner thoughts. The man standing behind the two girls was tall, lean, but his ripped body showed through his shirt. He had long black hair pulled back, sultry bedroom almond-shaped dark eyes, which felt as if they were peeling the clothes right off you with every look. Jaw-droppingly gorgeous.

The beast of a man next to him exuded force and power. He looked an inch or so shorter than Eli, but so corded and built, he seemed bigger. Wearing jeans and a black T-shirt, his chin-length blond hair, shaved on the sides, fell to one side, covering some of his bearded face. An axe was strapped to his back. He clenched his jaw; his unnerving white eyes moved over the room, taking in every moment. His attention lingered over each dark dweller.

He. Was. Sexy. As. Hell.

That was all my brain could register. He looked like a modern-day Viking. You wanted him to throw you over his shoulder and drag you back to his cabin. Yet the longer I stared at him, the more I was drawn to him; the pull of his white eyes was strong. There was something about him. Familiar.

"Seriously… just *wow*." I felt a blush heat my cheeks, my gaze still locked on the two guys. "They're sooooo pretty."

"You know I'm standing right here, right?" Eli folded his arms with a smirk.

"Yeah."

"Your *mate*."

I huffed, staring at the men while I fluttered my hand at Eli. "It's not that serious." I shook my head. "I hardly know him."

"I like her." The dark-haired guy laughed, but the other didn't even crack a grin, his expression stone.

"Do you need me to show you again, Brycin?" Eli rumbled, sounding annoyed. It was all an act. This was foreplay for us. How we teased. He knew he was the only one for me.

"No!" The entire room, sans the new group, yelled at once, shaking heads frantically.

"Hmmm, do you get the feeling they might have heard us?" Eli bumped my arm.

"Nah." I shook my head, grinning up at Eli. "We're so quiet."

Gabby snorted so loud, she started coughing, and Alki patted her back.

"Okay." Kennedy held up her hands. "Think we have more important things to discuss than your sex life."

"Not possible." Eli widened his stance with a grin.

Kennedy moved closer to the visitors, introducing everyone to each other. The testosterone in the room grew thick as smoke, the men distrustful as they approached each other, their shoulders rolling back, their chests puffing out.

"Should we let them strut around, fluffing up their feathers?" I approached Zoey, shaking her hand.

Slight amusement danced on her face as she glanced from Eli to Ryker before her green eyes fell on me. I could feel her sizing me up in just a second, studying me. I had been in enough battles and fights to recognize the signs of an opponent figuring out your flaws or weaknesses.

"Guess it's not solely the men." I held my gaze on her, not bowing to the intensity of it.

Her grin widened, her hand landing in mine. "I have a feeling we'll be perfectly fine."

"Or kill each other." I shrugged.

"Or that." She gave a small laugh and her shoulders softened.

"Damn, horny rabbits, get off me." A small voice croaked from Zoey's bag, a furry head popping out. "What? Where are we? Is it lunchtime?"

"What the hell?" I jumped back, my eyes widening at the tiny thing crawling out of the carrier. "Th-that's a monkey? It's. *Talking*."

"Well done." The monkey jerked his thumb at me, hopping up on Zoey's shoulder. "Another one who proves how well the school system works around here."

"Holy shit." I blinked at the tiny brown creature. He couldn't have been more than five inches tall.

"But to be accurate, I'm actually not a monkey. I am a sprite. My name is Spriggan-Galchobhar." He patted his chest.

"Sprigga-a-what?" My tongue tumbled over his name.

"Just call him, Sprig," the blonde girl, Annabeth, said.

"I hate to break it to you." Eli came beside me, looking a little bewildered at the creature. "But I've seen a lot of sprites in my time. You're not that."

"Well, I've had some work done." Sprig huffed, folding his arms. "Kinda like Pam."

"Who's Pam?" I asked.

"Uh…" Zoey muttered. "Long story."

"My girlfriend." The monkey peered at me like *duh*.

"She's a fuckin' stuffed animal." The man I learned to be Croygen spoke up, rolling his gorgeous smoldering eyes. "A goat."

"Shut up, pirate-booty. At least I have one."

"No, you shut up, you fuzzy ass-wiper."

"Ass-wiper? At least I'm not an *ass* face."

"Guys." Zoey dropped her face in her hands, shaking her head. "Do we need a time-out again? I swear my infant son is more mature than you two." Zoey huffed, but a small smile twitched her lips. "Sprig was a lab experiment—"

"Gone wrong," Croygen muttered.

"Gone right." Zoey rubbed the little guy's head. "He was part of Dr. Rapava's research."

"The DMG." Kennedy stepped to my other side. "Yes, Lars told me about it."

I had heard of the DMG. It had been destroyed about six years ago. A horrible government institution, especially for fae. They had hunted and tested them, used them as lab rats.

Ryker moved closer to Zoey, catching my eye. "You're a dae. Half demon."

With that word, I suddenly understood the connection.

"So are you… half demon, I mean?" I tilted my head. He was at least half demon. Our demons recognized each other. "But what else are you?"

Ryker shifted on his feet, his jaw twitching, as if he didn't want to tell me. I knew asking was rude, but my mouth always opened before I thought.

"A wanderer." He grunted so low, I barely heard him.

"A wanderer?" Gabby squeaked from the back wall. Damn dweller ears. They pick up everything. "Are you kidding me?"

Ryker glared at her but didn't respond.

"What's a wanderer?" I glanced between him and Gabby. Not being raised fae, I was still learning things I'd have acquired growing up in the Otherworld.

"They're as rare as you, Brycin." Eli folded his arms, examining Ryker. "Only a handful over the centuries have been born."

"Or made." Zoey winked at the large blond man.

"Made?" Kennedy asked, her eyebrows crunching down. "I've read you can only be born as one."

"Yeah, well throw in a freak electrical storm... and voila." Zoey motioned to herself.

Ice slithered down my throat, a heaviness plunking into my gut.

"An electrical storm?" I croaked.

"Over six years ago now, a crazy lightning storm hit Seattle. You lived around here, right? Devastated Seattle and surrounding areas. Killed thousands. But during that storm somehow his powers transferred to me. Long story short, I became a wanderer too."

My hand went to my mouth, my body curved to the side, acid scorching the back of my throat. Crap on ash bark.

Eli's hand rubbed my arm. "Do you need me to get you a bucket?"

"Not funny." Though I almost said yes. Years of emotions I thought I'd dealt with crawled up and sat in the back of my throat. It was impossible not to cross paths with people I had affected, but I never really knew if the person I passed had lost a loved one or their home because of me.

"What's wrong? What did I say?" Zoey's expression seemed bewildered by my violent reaction.

"Did you lose anyone?" I couldn't look at her.

"My foster mother, Joanna. I thought I lost Lexie too. And my partner Daniel, but he died by a group of fae, not the storm. Annabeth lost her whole family. A lot of people did. It was one of the most devastating catastrophes ever to happen here. And what happened because of it... the aftermath... a lot of damage was done." She looked over at the blonde, sadness and loss passing between them. Zoey didn't mean structural damage, which shoved the vomit higher in my throat. "It was so powerful; I knew it had to be done by fae magic."

My head spun, air sticking in my throat.

"Breathe, Brycin." Eli gripped my wrists, holding me upright. Even after this long, the guilt I felt overwhelmed me. The dead haunted me. Innocent people, who had merely been going along with their lives, had everything taken from them in a blink.

"Em, it was Aneira… not you." Kennedy tried to soothe me, but it didn't help. Aneira might have threatened me by hurting Mark, but in the end, it was still my choice. I chose him. Catching my dad's eyes across the room, I saw the guilt and sadness he still held. He shouldn't. He told me not to, but I couldn't lose him, too, no matter the costs.

Now I was face to face with the consequences of my decision.

Ryker's heavy gaze tore into me, his voice low. "It was you."

Zoey's head jerked to him, her mouth parting, looking back at me. Her lids widened when I didn't refute his claim.

"The reason daes were illegal is because they contain too much magic." Ryker's voice was empty of emotion. "Enough magic to destroy a city…"

My head bowed, my lids squishing together.

"You?" Zoey's face was a mix of emotions, as though she didn't know how to feel or think about the girl in front of her. I didn't look like much compared to the utter destruction I caused. The lives I ruined and took. "You were the one?"

"You did it? You were the reason all that happened to me?" A strangled noise came from Annabeth as she turned away from me. Lexie wrapped an arm around her friend.

I felt like a pariah, even though Eli stood by me. Only I could carry the weight, feel the true burden of what had happened on that hill.

"I am so sorry," I whispered. "I realize nothing I say can take away the pain I had caused." I knew whatever happened to her, it was my fault.

"It's not Ember's burden to carry alone. She had no choice." Lorcan's words startled me, jolting my gaze to him as he stepped up next to Kennedy. "I was there. I was the one who was made to provoke her. The Queen had an amplifier there. She was forced to do it."

Lorcan was defending me? What bizarro world did I step into?

"Wait. You were there? On the old Queen's side?" Croygen stared at our group. "And you're here? Am I missing something?"

"Oh, novels' worth." Kennedy rubbed the bridge of her nose. "But now is not the time. We can't change the past. We have problems right now we must deal with. The stone is taking over Lars and coming for Zoey. And Stavros, who seems to have risen from the dead, is here to claim the throne."

"And the lack of honey." Sprig stood up. "That is the real travesty."

"Honey? Pfffftttt." A winged figure zoomed by my head. "No, what this room needs is to get a barrel full of juniper juice."

"I second it." Croygen held up his arm. The tension in the room dissolved.

"My lady, we were searching for you." Simmons buzzed by my shoulder. "Aaaahhh!" He tipped forward, heading for the ground.

"Pull up! Pull up, you troll twat!" Cal yelled at Simmons, landing perfectly on my shoulder. Simmons brushed the ground, curving his false wings back toward me. Eli reached out, grabbing him before he tried to land again and placed him on my other shoulder.

"Pixies?" Sprig fisted his hands. "Honey bear farts, no!"

"What is your problem, monkey-man?" Cal leaned into my neck, crossing his arms. "Someone glue your furry butt cheeks together?"

"You would do that. Evil pixies!" Sprig stuck his tongue out.

"Sprig?" Zoey tapped his head. "Why are you being rude?"

"As if he knows any other way." Croygen snorted. "But if you didn't know, sprites and pixies don't like each other. Because the little dickheads are too similar."

"Hey!" Simmons's chest puffed out. "How dare you insult pixies? We are nothing like sprites."

"Creatures that are stubborn, obsess about eating and drinking, and love to play tricks on people?" Croygen rubbed his chin. "Yeah, nothing alike."

"Please, sprites don't know how to drink. Can't hold an ounce of alcohol. What kind of fae is that?" Cal snorted.

"And you couldn't consume pure honey as I do. Pansies!"

"Oh. Oh. Oh." Cal hopped up and down on my bone. "Bring it on, monkey man. Not as if you are doing a very good job at being a sprite anyway." He motioned to his fur.

"Ohhhhhh." Sprig's eyes widened. "Challenge accepted. The honey bears will take you down."

"And one drop of juniper juice will have you crying for your mommy."

"Why do I feel I should step in…? But nah, this will be so fun to watch." Eli snickered. "Plus, peanut butter always wins."

"Are we taking bets?" Croygen lifted an eyebrow.

"Now you're talking." Eli grinned.

"Taking bets on what?" West came sauntering in, winked at me, then turned to Kennedy. "Sorry, darlin'. Had a late night."

I snorted with laughter.

Rez strolled in behind him, holding a coffee, looking as stunning as always. Living at the ranch had relaxed her attire and her personality. She mostly wore jeans or cargo pants but somehow still looked stylish. She walked over to me, handing me her coffee to take a sip.

I adored her. "Thank you." I hugged the cup.

"Thought you might need it too." She grinned at me. "What did we miss?"

My mouth opened to catch her up, when movement across the room pulled my attention away.

"Oh. Gods..." Croygen shoved through his group, his mouth open, staring at Rez as if he had seen a ghost. His head started to shake back and forth. "No. You can't possibly be?"

Rez turned her head, searching for whomever this man was addressing, but his gaze was latched on her with a mix of shock and apprehension.

"Morweena?"

Rez inhaled sharply, her feet moving back a few steps. "H-how do you know that name?"

Who was Morweena?

"I can't believe this." Croygen shook his head.

"How do you know her?" Rez's eyes flashed, her shoulders stiffening. "How do you know my mother?"

Croygen blinked, his gaze moving over Rez again, a wildness spinning around his dark eyes. "Your mother... of course." He swallowed, his Adam's apple bobbing. "You look so much like her."

My head snapped back and forth between the two, a strange feeling swirling in my gut.

"Actually, she told me I was the spitting image of my father. I thought that was why she hated me so much." Rez's voice dropped a few notches, defensiveness coiling in her tone. "Answer me. How do you know her?"

"We knew each other a long time ago." His chest began to move up and down. "*Intimately.*"

Rez's pressed a hand to her chest. In that moment looking between them, the dark hair, almond eyes, tanned skin, and high cheekbones...

Holy. Crap. On. Ash bark.

"You're the pirate," she whispered.

"Tradesman."

"Oh gods..." Rez gripped West's arm, bending forward as though she were going to faint.

"Holy shit." West stood strong at her side, staring at Croygen in bewilderment.

"No." Croygen's eyes widened, retreating, but his eyes stopped on every feature they shared, seeming to understand.

You'd have to be blind to not see it. It was like when I first saw Fionna beside Kennedy. There was no way they weren't related.

"No!" He wandered around in a circle similar to a madman. "This is a joke, right?"

"You were on your way to the Orient, correct? When you stopped in Greece?" Rez straightened, her grip still holding tight to West.

Croygen swore, running his hand over his head and neck, not able to stand still, his face pale, as if he were either going to throw up or pass out.

"You met a young siren named Morweena. Took her innocence on the beach, claiming you loved her?"

"No. No…" Croygen took another step back, his head shaking. "This can't be…"

"She fell in love with you, was willing to leave her family, her calling, to be with you. The night she was going tell you she was pregnant with your child, you were gone. Without a word. Like a true thief of the night, you disappeared."

Croygen bent over his hands, grabbing on to his knees, sucking in gulps of air.

"I-I didn't know she was pregnant." He said it so low it was more to himself than anyone else.

"That's because you left before she could tell you." A sprout of anger burst from Rez's words. "You destroyed her that night. Shattered her heart into such tiny pieces it could never be put back together." Resentment lined Rez's face. "I grew up with her bitterness. Hate. She couldn't even love me. Always saw your face in mine."

"Holy fuck." Croygen stood, rubbing his face. Rez seemed to be taking this slightly better than him because she had always known he existed. For Croygen, this was all new. "You, you're my daughter?"

Both were silent, staring at each other, realizing the monumental moment happening while they watched each other.

"Don't worry," Rez finally whispered. "I want nothing from you. Like every young idiot girl, I dreamed of you coming back for us. But those dreams died a long time ago."

Croygen shook his head. "You don't understand. I would never have left if I had known. I didn't want to leave her."

"What do you mean, you didn't want to?"

"I can't believe this." He started pacing again.

"What did you mean?" Rez repeated the sentiment.

Croygen gripped his hand into a fist, anger dancing around him. "I was in love with your mother," he bellowed. "I wanted her to come with me. I asked her to. She was the one who broke *my* heart."

Rez's brow furrowed with confusion. "What?"

"Men were after me. The cargo I was carrying to Asia was much sought after. I left a note for her that I was hiding in a cove down the coast and to come find me there. To run away with me. I waited for three days." Croygen held up his fingers. "Three. A mutiny took place on my boat because of it. I went against code. We weren't even supposed to stay in Greece more than a night to replenish supplies. But I broke every rule. Most of my men left me when we got to the next port." He took a deep breath. "After three days, I realized what a fool I had been. Sirens didn't love, they bewitched you into following them to your death. I pulled up anchor and left and never returned or allowed myself to be played the fool again."

A tear ran down Rez's cheek. She quickly wiped it away, looking at her feet. "She never got the note. She thought you were the one who tricked her. That you left her without a thought."

"No. I didn't," he said quietly back. His anger vanished, face drawn with heavy sadness.

I could barely fathom it. All these years both were broken hearted thinking the other hadn't loved them. A little girl raised without her father because of a miscommunication.

"I can't believe this." He ran his hand over his silky hair. "I have a child."

"Not really much of a child anymore." Rez's voice strained with emotion.

I shifted on my feet, feeling as if we were all intruding on this private moment.

"I hated you for so long. I never wanted to meet you." Rez's eyes shined with tears. "But that was a lie. I always hoped someday I would find you."

"Damn, this is so weird."

Rez laughed. "Yeah, it is."

"In the last ten minutes, I became a father to a grown woman." He motioned to her, his voice going soft. "This will take a while to process. I've missed so much."

"So have I." She took a shaky step toward him. "I don't expect anything. I only want to get to know you."

"Me too." Croygen's voice cracked, blinking back the emotion.

"Hi, I'm Rez... your daughter." Rez held out her hand to him. He stared at it, then back at her. He took her hand in his, smiling at her.

"I'm Croygen, the asshole pirate," he smirked. "And your shit father." Neither went to hug the other, but you could already see a bond forming.

My throat choked with unshed tears.

"Lexie?" I looked toward where Zoey stood, her arm outstretched toward a retreating girl. Lexie's mouth contorted, her eyes creased with pain. "Lexie, stop."

The girl ignored her as she ran from the room, agony crumbling her hard exterior. What the hell was going on?

"Let her go." Ryker grabbed Zoey's arm, stopping her. "She needs a moment. This is a lot for her to take in. She realizes he had whole other lives before her. Loved other women."

Zoey nodded but stared after the girl, worry rumpling her forehead.

Annabeth came up beside Zoey, touching her back. "I'll go check on her."

"Thank you."

Annabeth jogged for the door, reaching it.

Boom!

A loud explosion detonated from outside, blistering my ears. A wave of magic collided into the room, splintering the glass, the floor jolting under us, shoving everyone off their feet. Annabeth screamed, her body flying into the air. I watched Cooper leap for her before my ass hit the wood planks and my head cracked on the floor.

Boom!

Another surge hit. Firecrackers of magic snapped and crackled outside, shaking the castle. Then it died away, the sounds of birds and people squawking outside in terror.

"Kennedy!" Lorcan scrambled over to her.

"I'm all right." She sat up, looking out the window.

"What the hell was that?" I pushed up, looking over the room, seeing if everyone was uninjured.

Annabeth was on top of Cooper, his arms wrapped around her protectively. She looked at him.

"You okay?" he asked, their faces only a sliver a part. She nodded, a deep blush on her cheeks. She pushed out of his grip, rising to her feet, then turned away to check on her family.

Eli helped me to my feet, his gaze roaming over me. No words, no linking. We didn't need to. I gave him a nod.

"Everyone okay?" Kennedy rose to her feet.

"My lady?" Torin bolted into the room, sweat lining his forehead.

"I'm fine, Torin," she responded.

"He's here." Torin rushed to her side. "He's demanding to see you."

"Who?"

"The new King."

"Stavros is here?" Fionna's thick Irish accent filled the room, dancing with fury. Her feet already marched for the door. "That arsehole has my little girl and Nic."

"Fi! No!" Kennedy called after her, but she marched on, determination set along her jaw.

Fionna was the first, but the rest of us sailed after her, sprinting for the gates; it seemed none of us liked being left out of the action.

It was time I met my great-uncle, introduced him to the *whole* family, and hopefully my sword to this throat.

NINE
Kennedy

As though an earthquake shook through the fault lines, chunks of the stone buildings fell to the ground, small hairline cracks zigzagged through the weaker foundation, but everyone appeared to be unharmed. Large groups milled in the streets and courtyards of the village and castle as our group walked by, then followed us to the entrance.

From what Fionna said about Stavros, this was simply a greeting. He enjoyed making dramatic entrances.

Torin, Sturt, Castien, and Georgia flanked me, with Lorcan, Dax, Dom, and the rest of my elite team right on their heels. Torin stood in front of me on our walk out, checking for threats, but the moment I saw Stavros, I took the lead. The closer I got to him, the more I saw the family resemblance between him and Lars. Same dark hair and yellow-green eyes, but Stavros wore his hair long and uncombed. He was dressed in nice suit pants, but they fit him loosely, an untucked white button-up shirt, sleeves rolled up, drooped off his sharp shoulders.

He was wearing Lars's clothes. But Lars's build was tall and extremely toned. Stavros was skinny and slightly shorter. The clothes hung off him like a teenager dressing in his dad's suits. I felt in my gut this was on purpose. He wanted to take everything of the old King's. Demean it. Depreciate Lars's standing in people's eyes while needling those of us close to Lars.

Stavros stood at the gates, where my protective barrier formed around the castle grounds. At least a hundred strighoul stood around him, armed, and howling at our presence, sending chills over my skin. Dread braided with anxiety, my throat clamping shut. Eyes from my own kingdom watched my every move.

Forcing my head higher, I rolled my shoulders back. I could not show any fear. Without Lars, people were ready to see how fast I would fall lacking the King's pillar of strength.

Stavros's mouth broke into a condescending grin at the sight of me, and his scrutiny rolled over my frame, as if he were thinking, *That's it? This is the Seelie Queen?*

"Well, aren't you just adorable." He chuckled, rubbing his hands together. "Not sure if I should bow or give you some candy. Maybe sit you on my knee and spank you."

My jaw cracked, my teeth grinding together. Would there ever be an end to patronizing, narcissistic men?

"Stavros," Fionna snarled, stepping past me. My arm went out, holding her back. As Queen, there were certainties I come to understand:

1. I had to always be front and center. No one could look like they overpowered me, unless it was a guard trying to protect me.

2. I had to make the decisions for everyone.

3. No matter how scared, inexperienced, or angry I was, I could never show it. I had to play the game.

"Wow." Stavros's gaze switched from Fionna to me. "I see it now—the resemblance, Fi-Fi. Little sister is a hottie too. Sweeter and more innocent looking, but I enjoy all types of women. It's a blessing and a curse really." He sighed dramatically, then winked at me. "Can't wait for us to get acquainted."

Lorcan's growl vibrated behind me, his chest bumping my arm.

"Ah, that's sweet. Your little pet is all ready to nip at my heels."

"If I'm so nonthreatening, why don't you come closer and try to pet me?" Lorcan stood still, but his frame puffed up, ready to attack at any moment. The rest of the dwellers crept in closer. When mated to one, you became part of the whole pack. Each one would risk their life to protect me. To guard any of the mates or each other.

"*Boy*, our time will come when either you will become one of my pets or you will be fed to my servants behind me." Stavros flicked his head back to the horde of strighoul behind him, drumming their weapons on the ground, who were cheering at the thought of their next meal.

A throb of magic pulsed through me. Lorcan was losing his temper, his anger bristling off his skin. If Stavros made one move, we'd have a battle right here.

"You made such a grand entrance." I took a step, wanting all the attention on me. "I'm going to assume you are here for a reason?"

Stavros's chartreuse eyes landed back on me. He and Lars were different but similar enough to confuse your head. It was similar to when you saw someone out of the corner of your eye you thought you knew, but when you fully looked, it was someone else entirely.

"I demand you kneel to me." He shoved his hands in his pockets, looking as though he were asking me for the time. "Since your little group is ready to attack me, I'm feeling it might be pointless to ask nicely."

Several people behind me laughed at the idea I would kneel to him.

"And it's probably a waste of my time to ask the same of you." I clasped my hands, trying to act as nonchalant as him. "It looks like neither of us is going to get what we want."

He grinned, baring his white teeth. "You're going to be more enjoyable than I thought."

"The feeling is not mutual."

"Guess it will be my burden to bear." He strode to the edge of the protected line. "That's not going to keep me out for long. When I have the stone, there is no shield I won't be able to tear down as if it's tissue paper." He tapped at the buffer, smiling as it sizzled and crackled against his skin, showing not even a flinch of pain.

"Our deal still holds, Fionna." He indicated to her, withdrawing his hand from the protection field. "You want to see your little girl again? You bring me your boyfriend and that dear great-niece of mine."

My eyes pinched together. Knowing Ember as long as I had, she would not stay hidden. She operated on impulse and heart.

"Only cowards use a little girl to hide behind." Ember's rage laced deeply through her words as she moved beside me. "I'm right here, *uncle*. You want a family reunion or something?"

Stavros's eyes widened, moving over her. "Wow," he muttered, then quickly regained himself, the smug smile back on his face. "Look at you. You couldn't be more of a spitting image of your father and mother. I've never seen a dae in person before. You are exquisite." He examined her like she was an animal in the zoo.

Ember shuffled uncomfortably, narrowing her eyes into daggers.

"Come over and give your uncle a hug." Stavros held out his arms.

"Sure thing, *uncle*." Ember drew her sword, moving forward. I grabbed her, pushing her back next to Fionna. Both were hotheaded and ready for blood.

Seeing me push back Ember made Stavros howl with laughter. "Oh, I can't wait to have you all. Every day will be so entertaining."

It was then I realized he didn't want us to merely bow to him, but to collect us. I didn't even want to imagine how he would do that. *You know perfectly well, Ken.* Even if I had yet to meet her, if he threatened Piper, there wasn't anything Fionna or I would do to protect her. She was my niece. A child. I would do what I needed to save her life.

Even enthrall people.

Horror bubbled in my stomach, churning and gurgling.

"Long live the King!" Voices suddenly shouted out from the expanding crowd who came to watch the spectacle. The ones I was protecting. My head jerked to the horde, heat icing my blood. Stavros's laugh squawked into the air like a flock of crows, clawing and biting at my nerves.

"Even they are ready for a true leader." He held up his arms, turning toward the villagers. "Who is tired of being represented by an incompetent leader? A child? One who understands humans more than your needs and wants?"

Cheers rose along the masses.

"A Druid was never meant to lead you," Stavros shouted. "They should have remained our servants. Now they think they can rise above us. Rule us."

"No! No!" A chant started. My head grew hazy, my legs wobbly. But I forced my chin higher. No matter what, I would not show fear or weakness.

Most of the crowd stayed quiet, but with every word, it felt that Stavros was pulling in another to his side.

"The King who sympathized with humans and welcomed a Druid Queen is gone. I am the rightful King. The true King. Some of you might even remember me. I am back and will return the kingdom to its rightful ways." More shouts and applause picked up; his strong voice seeming to easily sway the crowd.

In the year and a half I had been ruling, I had learned a lot. But I was still new. Young. Every day I discovered more, but I had leaned on Lars too often to guide me through sticky situations.

Now I stood alone.

Stavros's magic was centuries ahead of mine. Aneira, Lars, and even Stavros started out like me once, new to their reign, more vulnerable, but they became almost indestructible. Being Queen, I was harder to kill, but I could in no way challenge an ancient High Demon King. Fionna had more experience to challenge him than I, which did not bode well for the already controversial Seelie leader. Me.

Stavros continued to shout. "The time will come when you will be free of her. Of her manipulation and lies of a better world. But for now, those of you who want to follow me and be on the right side from the start, your loyalty to the crown will be greatly rewarded."

It only took a few heartbeats before more than a dozen people walked to the King as though he would make everything all right.

My nails drove into my palms until I felt drops of blood roll down my knuckles.

"It's already crumbling at your feet." Stavros faced me, a self-satisfied smile lighting up his eyes. "I might not even need another fortnight. You will be throwing yourself at my mercy by the end of this one." He waved to a group of strighoul behind him. "But if you need a reminder of what I will do to the pretty incubus and adorable little girl…"

Six strighoul hauled two objects to the border, dropping them on the ground. Another six dragged only one right behind.

Noooo.

Three bloody and beaten bodies lay in the dirt, auras so dim I didn't know if any of them were alive.

"Shite." Fionna put her hand to her mouth. "No."

It took everything in me to not react, to not go running up to the men.

"There are a lot more where that came from. That big guy…" He pointed at the half ogre laying on the ground, who had been at Lars's side for decades. "My strighoul really wanted to have him for dinner. You should thank me."

Breathe in. Breathe out. Slow.

"Every day you don't bring me what I want… someone dies. Painfully. He's the first. Showing you I am a man of my word." Stavros's relaxed humor had dropped, his focus pointed directly at me. "And Queenie… you think you can fight me? You have no idea what I have coming over land and water. You thought the war with Aneira was bad? I've been gathering my troops for a long time. Preparing for this. Your refusal will merely mean more innocent lives lost. You have no chance against me, the rightful King." With his last statement he swiveled dramatically around, like he was in some cheesy play, and disappeared into the throng behind him.

None of us moved, watching the threat retreat into the forest. The last strighoul slipped away and my guards ran for the protective shield, Fionna shoving them aside and dropping to her knees.

"Goran." She leaned over, putting an ear to his chest. "He's still alive!" She shoved up her sleeves, a spell already humming from her throat.

My feet carried me quickly to Travil, his face so badly sliced up he was barely recognizable, but his aura still sputtered around him.

"Get a healer to him now." I pointed to Travil, then moved on to Rimmon, falling next to the massive brute. He was frightening to look at but loyal and protective of Lars. A few times he had even protected me.

"Rimmon." Ember kneeled on the other side, her face twisted in agony. "No... stay alive, big guy."

I could no longer see his aura, but I still felt the need to try.

"Majesty, we'll do this." Torin tried to pull me back, but I yanked from his grip, my hands hovering over the huge man's torso.

Vacant.

No life buzzed from him.

"No." I gritted through my teeth, panic strangling my throat. An incantation spit over my lips, trying to heal. *No. No. It can't be too late. Not again...*

Jared. My family. Owen. Wizard.

More blood on my hands.

All their images layered over the man lying below me. The horrifying emptiness told me it was too late, but my heart wouldn't give up. Terror shook my arms, my hands pushing down harder, trying to stop the flow of blood.

"No. Dammit... do not die."

"My lady, stop!" Torin grabbed for my arm again. "He's already dead."

"No!" I glared at Torin, shoving him away. "I'm not giving up on him."

I continued to chant, trying to sense any thread of life in him, energy funneling from me like a water hose.

"Hey." Lorcan squatted down, getting in my eye line, his voice soft. "You have to stop, li'l bird. You're just hurting yourself."

Ignoring him, I shoved more energy into Rimmon, feeling the darkness.

"Enough." Lorcan seized my arms, pulling me to my feet and away from the man. "Look at me."

My nostrils flared as I watched Goran and Travil being carried off to the healers. Goran was conscious, his eyes open and narrowed with anger. Fionna stood back, a strange sorrow creasing her features, her head bowed away from Goran's glare.

"Look. At. Me." Lorcan growled. My eyes flicked to his. His voice was hard, but his eyes were filled with love and compassion. "He's not Jared," he whispered so only I could hear. "There's no one you can save who will ever bring Jared back or fill that hole."

A whisper of a cry broke from my lips. He pulled me to his chest, holding me tight. Only a few sobs emerged before I bit the rest back.

Not yet. Don't break down here. There are scared villagers who need your strength. Your guidance.

Lorcan's hands cupped my cheeks, his eyes speaking to mine. *I am here. Whatever you need, li'l bird.*

I know. Thank you. I rubbed my stained fingers over his, then pulled his hands away from my face. My clothes were stained with blood, but I cleared my throat, stepped around him, and hitched back my shoulders. I needed to convey strength and power.

Before my people, I inhaled deeply.

"It is true. Lars is no longer King." I held up my hands to the murmur rushing through the villagers. "But I am still your Queen. Even if you do not believe in me or never wanted me, I will fight for each and every one of you until my last breath. There is nothing I won't do to protect this kingdom." I straightened my back more, my voice carrying over the crowd. "He spoke of a 'better time.' The better times are before us, not behind. Our world is one now. There is no going back. Fae and humans live together. Only dictators use the false ideal of one race being better than another. Even for fae, the freedom he speaks of is false. His good days mean when he sits fat and happy, while everyone else suffers, including you." My voice rang out strong, reverberating against the walls of the castle. "I will not sugarcoat this: a war is coming. Once again, your rights and freedoms are under threat. I understand if you want to flee, but if Stavros wins, there is nowhere you can go that his tyranny won't find you. I know you are scared and still weary from the previous war. But know I will stand by your side. I will not let him win."

Cheers went up in the crowd. "We will fight with you, my lady," a woman screamed.

"I hope it won't come to that, but I want you to be ready. Prepare your homes and families. Whatever you need, my guards will get for you. I extend my gratitude to you all." I dipped my head in thanks to them. Death would come to many, and I appreciated those who stood here with me.

I reached for Torin. "Get a select group of soldiers and as many supplies as you can to last a few weeks at least. It may be months."

"It will be done, my lady." He nodded and moved out, heeding my orders. Stavros would start to tighten the rope around my citadel, cutting off supplies and trade.

I held my head high all the way back to the castle, feeling the strength of my friends behind me. I knew I could count on each one of them, but in that moment, I felt utterly alone.

Every decision I made would take or save lives.

If one of them fell, it would destroy me but might not affect the outcome of the war.

If *I* fell, the kingdom collapsed.

👑 👑 👑

Voices banged against each other in the room packed with chaos and tension.

"Hey!" Ember yelled, trying to get the room's attention. "Everyone, shut up!" Questions and opinions choked each other out. It was not surprising in a room full of alphas.

A piercing whistle sounded through the room, slamming mouths closed.

"Shut the fuck up!" Gabby pulled her fingers from her mouth, nodding at me. "Go ahead, nerd."

"Thanks." I let a brief laugh slide over my tongue. I found it comforting when Gabby called me nerd. Like I could go back to the time I was just a girl, asking her for sex advice. Times weren't simple then, but in contrast to now, they felt like it.

"We have a lot of fights on many sides." I leaned back against the table. Everyone had followed me straight back to the library. It was starting to feel close to a war room.

A spike of sorrow, the memory of Wizard and his war room tugged at my heart. He was my true friend from the DLR. I missed him. I actually missed a lot of the group from the Druid Liberal Republic.

Which gave me an idea.

"Fionna." My thoughts sidetracked. "Do you still stay in contact with the DRL?"

"No, I was kind of locked up." She folded her arms, watching me intently as if she understood where my mind was headed. "But if they are still around, I can get a message to them."

A thin smile tugged up my mouth. "Good. We're going to need every hand on deck."

"Unfortunately, both Wizard and Kenya are dead."

"I know." I frowned. "Does anyone know a hacker? Or someone really good at computers?"

83

"Garrett," a deep voice said from the door. Everyone in the room swung around to see Goran standing in the doorway. "He's the best."

"Goran, you should be resting." Right away I felt something off about him. His aura was a dull gray without sparks of emotion or life. Like he was a zombie or something. I had never seen anything like it. His mouth moved, but lifelessness blanketed his features.

"Garrett?" Ryker sputtered from the corner. "Short little Irish fucker? He's still alive?"

"Yes. He has been a great asset to Lars." Goran grunted in pain as he took a step deeper into the room. "Stavros doesn't know what he does and how good he is yet. It will only be a matter of time. The last I saw, he was locked up in one of the dungeons with Cadoc."

Ryker scoffed, shaking his head. "That asshole is still with him, huh?" It was clear he knew these two men. The life of fae was long, and if you were any kind of player in it, you eventually crossed paths with others you'd known before.

"Nic and Piper are there too." Fionna's meaningful gaze met mine.

"My powers are also there." Rez stepped up to Ember. "Did you hear him? He said troops were coming over land and *sea*. If he has troops sailing to us, then you will need me."

"And me." Croygen added himself to the semicircle around me. "I am a pirate, after all."

"I thought you were a tradesman?" Zoey joined him, bumping his shoulder.

"For this," he lifted an eyebrow, "I'm all pirate, baby."

"You're a banana-munching swashdickler," Sprig said from Zoey's shoulder. "And since we're talking about it, who's hungry? Do you have honey cake here?"

"We weren't talking about food, goat lover," Croygen sniped back.

"Well, we should be. Everyone is so grumpy."

"Here, here!" Cal fluttered from Ember's shoulder to join the monkey. "Crackling crackers, everyone is so uptight. The gods blessed us with the sweet berries for a reason."

"Honey." Sprig all but drooled. "You talking about honey? 'Cause I can eat it on a berry. Mangos are good. Raspberries… oohh, honey apples. But pancakes are best. Have you tried churros? So good."

"Sure, honey… But what if you dip those in juniper juice? Even better!"

"Better than honey? How dare you! Nothing is better."

"Oh, little furball, you have not dipped yourself in a sink full of juniper juice yet."

"Why do I see this going really bad?" Eli rubbed his head.

"But oh so funny." West rubbed his hands together.

"Can we return to the battle, please?" They all snapped back to me. "Rez, do you think you could get more sirens to join you?"

Her mouth pushed together, her gaze going to her feet. "Yeah. I might be able to get my mother's colony."

Croygen's head jerked to her, then away.

"I won't deny she will probably try to kill you," Rez scoffed looking directly at Croygen.

"Yay for me." Croygen's Adam's apple bobbed sharply with his swallow.

"But first we break into the compound." I massaged my temples. Were we really thinking about doing this? "Retrieve Piper, Nic, Garrett, and Rez's powers. And anyone else we can get who is loyal to Lars."

"Sure. That sounds easy enough," Ember scoffed, dropping her hands.

We hadn't even started on what we were going to do about the stone or how to get Lars back. Right now we had to deal with one thing at a time. Rescuing Piper was most important to me. If Stavros didn't have her to threaten us, it would make things a tad bit easier. We were still up against a wall, but those fighting for Lars understood what could happen. They'd chosen that life; the little girl had not.

"I promise, Zoey, we will deal with breaking your link to the stone as soon as we can." I pushed my glasses up.

After a beat, she bobbed her head. "I know. This comes first. If it was Wyatt or my sisters…" She took a breath. "You get us through the protected barrier and Ryker and I will get you in and out of the compound."

"We'll need a distraction." Cole pushed off the wall coming forward. "To pull focus, while a group of you goes in." A proud smile split his mouth. "My family does nothing better than cause chaos."

"Damn right." Cooper and Gabby high-fived each other.

"Okay." A strange relief washed over me. Maybe because it was actually a plan. Even a dumb one. "We're doing this. So Goran, Rez. You two know the castle best. I'll have Olivia bring you plans of the compound and house. I need you guys to show us every entrance and exit. Find the most guarded areas and the least. Anything you think we will need." They both nodded in agreement.

"Dwellers, if you are going to cause a stir, I need it to be good. And time consuming."

"Don't ever doubt the trouble we can create." Lorcan winked at me. I didn't.

"Fionna, Ember, Rez, Zoey, Ryker, Croygen, Goran, and I will go in."

"Don't forget me. I have magic fingers." Sprig wiggled his hands. Eli snorted.

"And us, my lady." Simmons buzzed around Ember. "You will need us."

"You mean to fall asleep and be taken by the enemy again?" Eli mocked.

Simmons's mouth dropped open. "I will have you know, sir, I was never taken by the old Queen's men. Nor did I fall asleep. I fought by Sir Torin's side. By my lady's."

"Cool your britches, Simmons; he's talking about me." Cal landed on Ember's shoulder, crossing his arms. "And if I must sacrifice and be put into a coma by juniper powder, then I will do it. For the team. I'm a team player."

"Thank you, Cal," Ember said, grinning evilly at Eli. "Your heroism knows no bounds."

Cal stuck out his tongue at dark dweller. "Watch it, dweller. I've got a whole new sheet of glittery dick stickers."

I walked over to a call button on the desk I used when I was in here. "Olivia, can you bring me plans of Lars's compound? And coffee. Lots of it." I let go and then pushed the button again. "Oh, and bring honey."

"I like her." Sprig rose up on his legs. "Honey tits for all the kingdom!"

👑 👑 👑

After five hours of planning and then arguing about the plan, I called it a night. We were exhausted and going around in circles.

I'd had a quick shower to wash off Rimmon's blood, but I still felt dirty, coated with the grime of Stavros. The terror he was already causing was overwhelming. I was so far out of my element, terrified that whatever choice I made, it could be the wrong one. One that would kill those around me.

"Hey, li'l bird." Lorcan's body pressed against my back. Brushing my hair off my shoulder, he pressed his lips to my neck. "You okay?"

A grim laugh stumbled from my chest. Was I okay? No. Not really.

"You were amazing today." He towed me in closer, his lips moving across my shoulder blade.

"I'm holding on by my fingertips." I touched my forehead. "I have no clue what I'm doing. And any choice I make could end lives."

He was quiet, his mouth trying to comfort me ways words couldn't.

86

"I feel so alone," I confessed.

"You aren't. You have us. And I will be at your side every moment."

Frustration built up in me, and I pushed away from him. "But *your* decisions don't possibly get thousands murdered." I swung around, weariness from the day spiraling through me. "I can't do this alone. I need Lars. And he's one of the forces I have to fight. How can I do this?" I held out my arm waving outside my patio doors. "I am everything Stavros said. Inexperienced, weak, scared…"

"You are not weak."

"Tell that to the hundred or so who walked away to join him. Who mistrust and hate me so much they will jump to any other side but mine."

"They are weak, not you. They need someone to tell them what to do and believe."

"It doesn't matter," I exclaimed. "My own people think I'm not worth following. They question if they should be standing beside me. Don't you think there will be more who have left by morning?"

Lorcan rubbed his nose, exhaling, staring at the floor. "I feel there is nothing I can say without you skewing it."

Weight pressed down my shoulders. I turned to face the windows, staring over the lake, which was hidden by the night.

"I can't do this."

"Yes. You can, li'l bird." He moved behind me again, his arms wrapping around my waist. "And you will. We all will. There is no other choice. I will be here every step."

His attempt at comfort was nice, but it felt like a bandage. No matter whether Lorcan walked next to me or not, the burden fell on me. Being Queen at twenty-three came with a heavy crown.

I didn't realize how much I had depended on Lars as a mentor and a friend. It felt wrong without him. And the loss of him wouldn't only affect me. What would happen when others around the world learned he was gone? So many who supported me did so because of Lars. Without him? How many would turn on me? Run to the new King?

Stavros might be full of lies, but he spoke with conviction, strength, and power. Even if people didn't know why they were following him, they would do it anyway, caught up in the certainty of his speeches. The rhetoric of fae compared to human was potent.

The visions I had were more feelings than images, but I knew death and war were coming, a fight for Lars and our kingdom. I didn't know if we would win.

87

Most people could focus on one step at a time, but I had to look at the whole picture. Try to perceive future situations and how to handle each outcome. See the big picture, the future, and plan for it. Pain thumped through my head around the knots tied up there.

"You can't do anything more tonight," Lorcan murmured in my ear, his breath gliding down the back of my neck. "You need to rest."

"I can't sleep." I was exhausted, but my mind swirled with plans and lists.

"Let me handle that." He laced his hand with mine, tugging me toward the bed. My feet followed him, wanting to disappear beneath his body, to pretend for one moment I wasn't Queen, and that horror and devastation weren't awaiting me.

Lorcan laid me back on the bed, stripping my clothes and removing all barriers between us. His tongue and mouth evaporated all thought except the pleasure he brought. When he thrust into me, with our bodies moving together and our moans piercing the air, nothing existed in the room except us.

But outside the door, I could feel it waiting.

My crown drenched with blood.

TEN
Fionna

Metal objects littered the floor around me. Empty. Cold. Useless.

My fingers wrapped around the smooth edges of the cauldron, trying to feel a pulse. Anything. Only a hollow ring echoed back. My hands squeezed the black metal till my bones moaned with the pressure.

Shite.

The one thing we needed was obsolete because of me. Because Lars couldn't let me go. My fate had been to die, to sacrifice for the greater good. I had been ready. Lars made the ultimate sacrifice, for love. The exact thing which saved my life destroyed all hope for him.

Greedily and mercilessly, the stone claimed the man I loved. I wasn't someone who had believed in love. I didn't have starry-eyed dreams of someone saving me or true love conquering all. That wasn't me. I saved myself. And I certainly didn't need love. Especially with a fae. A demon.

A King.

Not with someone I had spent years hating and plotting to kill. Yet here I was, my heart cracking over the floor like a broken egg. My soul ached as if it lost a piece of itself.

Then there was Piper. My heart and thoughts had to shut down at the idea of what she must be enduring; the pain and dread so deep, I could barely move. My baby girl. I'd failed her again. My worst fear had happened.

With a grunt, I shoved black magic at the cauldron, my lids squeezing shut, discomfort stabbing me like darts. Desperate, I would try anything, do anything, to get her back.

My energy slammed against the cauldron, akin to running into a cement wall. The bounce shoved me backward, my arse landing on the hard stone floor.

"Fuck." Tears blistered behind my lids, my anger flaring. I crawled back, fury shoving more magic through my words, grabbing the cauldron. "Come back you frickin' piece of shite!"

My body skidded and rolled back into the wall with a harsh thud.

Our family had made this damn thing. I would bring it back. I *had* to.

Scuttling back to it, I cried out in frustration, seized the pot, and dug my words into it through gritted teeth.

"Fionna." My sister's voice drifted from behind me, her body crashing next to me. "Stop!" She covered my hands with hers, trying to pry them off.

"No." I tried to push her away with an elbow, but she wiggled around, still trying to remove my hands.

"Black magic isn't going to help bring this back."

"How do you know?" I barked.

"Because." Her fingers moved from my hands to my face. She forced me to look at her. "It wasn't made from black magic."

"So? I can bring people back from the dead. Why not this?" I tried to wriggle out of her grip, but she grabbed my face tighter. "I've done it before. I'll do it again."

She dropped her arms, her body leaning back. "You've brought someone back from the dead? Are you serious?" Her soft brown eyes were wide with shock and fear.

A wash of shame turned my crumpled brow toward the floor.

"Fionna?"

Silence.

"Look at me." Kennedy's voice tightened. "Tell me you are not serious."

Rolling back my shoulders, I looked at her defiantly. "I did."

"Oh gods..." Her eyes widened. "Goran."

"How did you know?"

"His aura. It's gray. Not one bit of life or emotion." She shook her head. "Like he was the walking dead."

"I had to." A reflex defense popped from my mouth.

"No. You didn't. Do you understand what you are playing with? Death is the one thing no one should tamper with. You do not mess with the laws of death. You know that!"

I felt like a child being reprimanded. I did know. But it hadn't stopped me in the moment. "Don't tell me if you could go back in time, you wouldn't have saved your little boyfriend," I snapped.

She jerked back, anguish flooding her eyes.

Immediately, I felt awful. "I'm sorry, I didn't mean that."

"You don't think I don't relive that moment every day?" Her lips pressed together, holding back her anger. "That I don't wonder if I could have tried to save him instead of standing there watching him die? I've spent countless nights imagining bringing him back from the dead."

"I know. I'm sorry."

"No, you don't know." Her eyes flamed. "It's been two years, and there isn't a day I don't think of him, of what I could have done differently. It haunts me. Along with my family and all the other people who died. You do not understand for a moment what I've been through."

Shite. Leave it to a sister to cause you to feel like a wee thing. "You're right, I don't." My shoulders sagged, the anger dissipating. "And I'm sorry you carry so much on your shoulders. So much pain and responsibility."

We both stayed quiet for a few minutes, as though reliving the painful reality of what we had gone through and what we were about to do.

"I'm scared." A whispered breath whisked off my tongue.

"I know." Kennedy wiggled closer, lacing her fingers in mine again. "So am I."

"I love him, Kennedy." I gripped her hands, trying to fight the wave of emotion flooding me. "It's so deep I can't even breathe. What if I lose him?"

"I'm not going to lie to you. I have no idea what we are going to do, but I promise this—I won't stop until we find something. I have Olivia looking through anything mentioning the stone." She pressed my hands in comfort. "You are not the only one who loves him. We will fight to get him back."

I nodded, none of my fears ebbing. "And Piper." I blinked rapidly. "She is my entire world. My heart... if anything happens to her."

"We will get her back."

"My life has been revenge. War. Hate." I gulped, my throat twisting. "I don't know how to handle this." With one hand I motioned to where my chest was clogged with overwhelming fear and love. "If I let myself think for a moment, I won't be able to move or breathe."

Without warning, Kennedy wrapped her arms around me, pulling me into an embrace. I had not been hugged a lot growing up. It still felt uncomfortable to me. Lars had broken that barrier quickly, but to be hugged by my long-lost sister was odd but also lovely. Shoving through the peculiar feeling, I hugged her back.

"I haven't met my niece yet, but I already know there isn't anything I won't do to get her back." Kennedy pulled back. "You ready to go get her?"

It was so dangerous, bordering on stupid. But I didn't care; I would claw and dig my way down to the dungeons if I had to.

I was walking out with my daughter.

Rising to my feet, I picked up the Sword of Nuada. It no longer held magic, but it was still a sword, a Druid-made weapon no less.

Kennedy took a step back, her eyes locked on the blade.

"Right, you two have a past." I held it out to her. "It's technically yours. It yielded for you."

As if I were tempting her with candy, she took a step closer, stretching to touch it. Her fingers almost grazed the blade before she jerked back her arm.

"No. You take it." She laced her hands together.

Kennedy wasn't a fighter, but this object still seemed to hold temptation for her. Even magicless, it was deadly. Beautiful and lethal.

"For now." I retracted my arm. "But it's yours, Kennedy. It's meant for a Queen."

She turned for the door and glanced back at me. "It's meant for a warrior."

Leaves swayed overhead, exposing the stars above, the signs of summer licking the air with warmth. The cover of the forest hid the huge group of us moving through the brush with silent speed.

I had not spent much time around dark dwellers, especially in their natural form, so I was unnerved by how those huge beasts could creep up on you without a sound. I thought my skills were attuned and ready for anything, but a dozen times on the journey over, a dweller had come up beside me so quietly I'd jumped.

A few of them seemed to love to take the piss out of me. Startling me by sliding next to me, their slick fur grazed my leg or arm, then they'd disappear into the shadows before I could do anything.

"Wankers," I growled under my breath, only to hear a strange hiccupped growl, as though they were sniggering at me.

But not all of us were quiet.

"*Bhean?* Are we there yet? It's been forever. It has to be dessert time. I need sustenance." A small voice cried from Zoey's backpack. A small brown head poked out. "Pam says she's hungry too."

"Sprig," Ryker snarled. The two girls, Lexie and Annabeth, had stayed back, but the pirate/Viking guy jogged beside Zoey, like her own bodyguard. "Be quiet or I'm going to do more than stuff that tail down your throat."

"Oh, the *Viking* is out in full force tonight, I see," he quipped back, sticking out his tongue at Ryker.

"There is a granola bar at the bottom," Zoey said low over her shoulder.

"What?" Sprig squeaked. "You've been harboring a granola bar here the whole time. Are you trying to starve me to death?"

"Sprig, are you going to make me wish we left you with Kate?"

Zoey pulled the bag around to her front, digging into the pouch and pulling out a bar, unwrapping it.

"Givemegivemegiveme! Giiiiivvvveee meeeee!" The monkey bopped around the bag, his hands open and closing, reaching for the snack.

"Now eat and be quiet."

"Grumpy! Thought after the noises of the two dying animals I heard in your room earlier, you'd be pleasant."

Zoey pinched the bridge of her nose.

"Actually, why don't you pass out? That would be great," Ryker muttered under his breath.

Sprig shoved the granola bar into his mouth but glared at the wanderer. Holding up his fingers, he pointed them at his eyes then at Ryker.

"Yeah, furball, you have me quaking in my boots," he scoffed.

Simmons's motored wings buzzed over my head, drawing my attention away from them.

The other pixie followed his friend, weaving and bobbing in the air.

"Heeyyy, giiirrrrlllyyy?" Cal hiccupped, flying toward Ember. I could see her ponytail dancing around the sword strapped to her back in front of me. "Goood pow-pow-ner. Thiiss stuffff." He patted the little bag around his waist. "Whhere are ya monnn-key man? Show ya…" Hiccup. "Better thannn honn-ey."

"I told him not to eat any, my lady." Simmons danced around Ember's head. "But he didn't listen."

"I'm shocked," Ember replied dryly.

"Really, my lady? This is exactly something he would do."

"Sheeezz pullin your leeg, Simm-mm-on." Cal swayed over my head, forcing me to dodge out of the way. "Clo-thez are heavy."

"No. No taking your clothes off, Cal," Ember chided him.

"But me weeee bitz?"

"Clothes stay on."

"Phhhhffftt." Cal swished his hand at Ember, faltering in the air, struggling with his coat. His head dipped, as though he was falling asleep.

She reached up, plucking him from the air as the pixie passed out in her hands. Ember glanced over her shoulder at Zoey. "Have room for one more?"

"Why not? What's one more at the zoo hotel?" She laughed quietly, taking the pixie from Zoey. "Hope he enjoys sharing space with a farting sprite and a stuffed goat."

"That would be a Tuesday for Cal."

"Guys?" Kennedy held a finger to her lips, and the rest of the trip passed in silence.

We knew we were getting close when all of us began to feel the pull to turn around and leave the area. Stavros had placed a new spell around the border, extending it to the place where Fionna and Marguerite escaped.

It was our way in, but we couldn't unless we could break the protective barrier. All we needed was a moment. Kennedy and I worked hard, mixing our magic within the explosive. Druid magic was the only kind which might give us that chance. We came up to the property line, the house quiet through the trees in the far distance. For some reason, I had a hard time picturing Stavros ever sleeping, as though that were too human, boring, and common for him.

"All right." Kennedy turned to face us, her eyes scanning the group. My skin felt as if it were crawling when a few enormous beasts pawed past me, the glare from the stars gleaming off the poisonous spiking blades down their backs. A shiver ran along my spine, my teeth clenching together. I still wasn't terribly comfortable around fae, and dark dwellers were the epitome of terrifying and unnerving.

"Dwellers, you know what you have to do. We move on your signal," Kennedy said. A dweller with green eyes moved up to her, rubbing against her leg, her fingers running through its coat. Lorcan. "Which I doubt will be subtle."

The beast rumbled, like he was laughing.

"Be safe and link to Ember if anything goes wrong," she said to them. One with hazel eyes, Cole?, stepped in front of his group, roaring softly, before the two groups took off into the dark, disappearing without a sound. Alki went with them, carrying a bag and trailing after Gabby's beast. Our whole plan was set on the items in the bag. If they didn't work, we were screwed. Alki moved with stealth and speed that almost matched the dwellers. He knew every corner of the compound property and exactly where to attack to draw the attention away from us.

Kennedy's eyes tracked the darkness for a moment before she snapped back to us. "Ember, Croygen, and Ryker, you will follow Rez. Zoey, Fionna, and I will follow Goran."

We'd split up to make sure we each had someone who knew the compound well and a person who could jump. Though I warned them that once in the dungeon area all our powers were null and void.

Sprig was there to break the locks, and the pixies to put any remaining guards to sleep.

Kennedy had ordered Torin to stay behind. She wanted her soldiers to stay and protect the castle and the defenseless people among its walls. I thought Torin was going to burst all his blood vessels. Defy her. They fought for a bit before she declared it an order, and he receded to it. Not happily at all.

"Now we wait for—"

Boom!

Kennedy's words were ripped away by an explosion that shook the ground with tremendous force. Fire billowed into the sky. Green magic zapped at the barrier, cracking it like a thousand bones.

"Holy shite." Gasping, I grabbed my chest, staring up at the balloon of the blast on the opposite side of the grounds. It resembled a mushroom cloud from a nuclear bomb. A dome of smoke and fire reached for the stars, Druid magic lashing at the defense with its claws.

The shield around the land flickered. We needed more time to cross it. A second blast wasn't going to get all of us past the force field.

Shouts and commotion erupted within the compound. None of us could hear specifics exactly, but I knew an alarm was going off, warning them of intruders.

"My man does nothing small." Ember grinned.

"Not the dweller style, I'm imagining," I said.

"Understatement," she chuckled. "Small is not in their vocabulary."

"Same for demons," I smirked. "Nothing small there."

"Ugh." Ember dropped her head forward. "I don't want to know that. It's my... uncle you're talking about." I heard the slight hesitation before she said uncle. Did she also feel, as Lars did, they were more than that?

Another boom thundered a little farther out from the other, the ground trembling with its force. The spell sizzled, blinking out.

We only had a short time before it came back.

"All right, everyone. It's go time." Kennedy gripped the gun hanging from her belt, running forward.

Piper, I'm coming. My heart thumped.

We all joined Kennedy, jumping over the defense line. We had gone over the plan a dozen times, but that was hypothetical. This was real and was dangerous. Everything could go as planned or go terribly wrong.

ELEVEN
Ember

The sound of our boots crunched down the gritty stone steps as a sharp, musty smell filled my nose. I held my sleeve to my face. The oppression of the tight narrow space curled around my throat like rope. *In through the nose and out the mouth*, I commanded myself. *You've been through worse. It's the same as the caves in Greece, when we were crawling on our stomachs.*

Dressed in black clothes, we all blended into the shadows. We rushed through the tunnel like some black ops team, sneaking into a place I once called home. Memories of the smells from Marguerite's cooking floated from the kitchen.

During my time living here, I had never thought about secret exits and tunnels. Thinking back, I realized how stupid that was. I had gotten so comfortable with Lars, so secure in his power and rule, I never thought about needing to escape in the night. Even now, this place still felt like coming home. Lars kept a room for me upstairs for whenever I visited. Now I was sneaking up on it like an intruder. And the man I would usually run to, forcing a hug on him, was gone.

It felt strange, wrong.

"There are a handful of the secret exits from below, but only three from the actual house. Lars wanted to limit the chance of enemies actually getting into the upper part of the home. There is only an entrance from the King's private chambers, hall closet, and his office on the other side of the house. The tunnel has several exits leading to different sides of the property," Goran said, his voice void of anything. He seemed off, with jilted movements. It was as though the part of the brain which held emotion was

97

shut off. Losing Rimmon had to be hard, but he hadn't even flinched when his comrade's body had been carried away. Goran wasn't known for his emotions, but this was different. A robot in his stead. "There is minimal protection if we meet with them head-on in the tunnels. If they attack us inside, there is a good chance we will all die."

Holy crap. O-kay.

Lars was always prepared. He thought of circumstances no one else would. But I doubt even he had foreseen this future.

Goran pushed our group ahead quickly, only pausing to check a corner as if to sense an attacker.

We weren't far into the tunnels when I picked up on traces of iron. High fairy's kryptonite. Every species had some weakness. Goblin-made metal worked against all fae, but for some reason, iron was also another weakness for fairies. Since the Seelie were the Unseelie's true enemy at one time, I wasn't really shocked Lars had embedded iron in his walls. I was the only one who could feel it in this group.

"My lady, are you okay?" Simmons, who sat on my shoulder, must have felt me tense.

"Fine." I gritted my teeth, my skin itching, wanting to slither off my body and crawl back to the exit. I tensed in the too quiet passage, ready for something to jump out at me at any minute.

We came to a fork in the passage, and Goran motioned our group to go ahead. This was where we would split up. Past these walls anything could go wrong.

Cal flew from Zoey's bag, completely sober, and landed on my other shoulder. Both he and Simmons gripped my ponytail, staying quiet. I wasn't afraid of danger, but I was no good at living in the unknown. Were there a hundred strighoul waiting for us on the other side? Two hundred?

"Human," Ryker rumbled, striding to Zoey and grabbing the back of her head.

"Viking." She barely got the word out before his mouth crushed into hers with a brutal force, their kiss so passionate my toes curled.

"You stay alive," he muttered to her.

"Ditto," she replied, her eyes glistening with raw love and passion.

"I'm going with her," Sprig said, his head and arms hanging out of the bag. "Magic fingers, remember?" He wiggled his hands. "Though I'm a little upset I had to leave my cape behind... and Pam. Holy honey possum— what she called you two when I told her she had to stay." He clicked his tongue.

Ryker chuckled then kissed Zoey again. Rubbing Sprig's head, he wheeled around, his muscles locked, his expression severe. He was ready to go.

Croygen eyed Sprig. "Keep her alive, rodent, or I will make banana pudding and bury you in it."

Sprig's eyes widened in horror. "You wouldn't."

"I *so* would."

"Can you make juniper pudding and bury me in it?" Cal raised his hand, offering himself.

"Quiet," Goran stated, his tone and face not showing a single emotion. The more I looked at him, the more forlorn he appeared. His eyes were distant, as though his mind were somewhere else. What had happened to him?

Kennedy clutched my hand, then Rez's. "Good luck."

"You too." I swallowed back the knot of nerves in my throat.

Goran waved them forward, and I watched Kennedy, Fionna, Zoey, and Sprig disappear down the dark tunnel. Dread burned in my gut. What if this was the last time I saw them? Shaking my head, I turned to our leader. Rez was already stepping in front of our group.

"This way. Keep close." Rez nodded for us to start down the other side. She knew every inch of this property. Lars had made sure she was one of the few people who knew every entrance and exit in case of an emergency. This was definitely an emergency.

The deeper we went, the more the iron content in the walls bowed my shoulders. Gnashing my teeth, I took in harsh breaths. If I was full fairy, I would have been on the ground, compressed with pain. My demon and dark dweller parts helped me push through the metal's power although my heart still walloped in my chest as iron siphoned my powers away.

Rez paused at a section of stone wall, which appeared no different than the rest. Scurrying around Aneira's castle, trying to break in, I learned that passages could blend into the walls, or a solid tunnel could lead nowhere. Lars's setup probably wasn't much different.

She sucked in a breath, flipped up a hidden keyboard, seamlessly blended in the stone, and typed in a code. The chances were slim Stavros hadn't changed these, but we had to try.

The red button flared up, denying us access.

"All right, ladies, move aside." Croygen brushed past me, pulling some small tools from a satchel. Electricity and computers were never a sure thing, so the hidden doors contained a manual lock.

Croygen went onto his knees, tinkering with the latch as we circled him, keeping guard. I drew out my sword, my muscles tense. Only one encounter with Stavros and I knew he was a formidable enemy. Crazy and unpredictable, which made him every more dangerous.

"The moment we're in, my lady, we'll go ahead. See if there is any trap," Simmons whispered in my ear, turning on his wings which buzzed slightly. He rose into the air, coasting close to the entrance.

"We got this, girly." Cal patted the bag on his hip. "We'll have them sleeping like babies."

"Or you will be," I quipped.

"I resent that." Cal straightened to full height.

"It's true."

"Yes, but I still resent it," he huffed. "I can control myself."

I snorted.

"Okay, I can't. Not around this scrumptious, beautiful, delicious gift…" He peered into the pouch dreamily, licking his lips. "Who am I to turn down such a thing? I am merely a pixie."

A click triggered behind me, as Croygen scooted back. "We're in."

"Cal, come on." Simmons motioned to his friend. Cal glided into the air, following Simmons into the tunnel.

"Shit, I'm having *déjà vu*," I mumbled to myself.

"Done this before?" Ryker herded me in before him, taking the rear guard.

"You have no idea."

"I probably do."

Yeah, I had a feeling he did.

Firelights along the walls ignited as we stepped in, sensing our presence like automated lights, allowing us to see a few feet in front of us. It wasn't much different from the tunnel we'd just left. Same cobblestone, but a lot wider, and there were wooden doors along the way.

"What are in these?" Croygen's eyes glowed with interest. "Anything I can *borrow*?"

"This section is extra food and supplies. Lars has the weapon and collection rooms better guarded," Rez whispered over her shoulder, the firelights reflecting the sharp angles of her beautiful face. In this light the resemblance between Croygen and her was striking. "We're headed to the collection room now."

Collection room. That sounded interesting.

Rez led us along a long path. "It's right around this corner." She pointed at a heavier bolted door when we turned down the hallway.

My heart was in my throat, my ears tuned to any threat. Was there anyone still walking these corridors? No leader I knew would completely leave an area abandoned. But maybe Stavros didn't realize what he had here. Or never imagined we'd come for a siren's powers. He hadn't been here long; maybe he didn't know about this room.

As Croygen went to work, a trail of sweat trickled down his temple. His expression remained relaxed, as though he were picking a lock for fun.

"My lady." Simmons came flying through the shadows. "We went all the way down. There's no one."

"That *should* be good news." Ryker ran his hand over his hair, his feet shifting, his eyes examining every inch of space.

"Yeah." My gaze snapped to every dark corner, tension rising, clenching my lungs. "It should."

But it wasn't.

I could feel both our demons were unsettled, as if they were cohorts, working together. Something was not right.

Anxiety curled around me the longer Croygen struggled with the lock, his serene demeanor giving way to a pinched forehead.

"I'm hurrying," he bit at Ryker. "Stop dancing around me like we're in a Zumba class."

"You know what Zumba is?" Rez looked down at Croygen in shock.

"What?" He shrugged. "I might have taken a class or two."

"Seriously?"

"Being the only guy in a room full of barely dressed, easily stimulated women…" He shrugged. "I'm okay with your judgment."

"I should be disturbed by this, right?" Rez cocked her head at me, a mix of humor and distress winking in her eyes. "I feel as if I should be deeply distraught by my fath—" She stopped, letting the rest of word get caught in her throat, the air expanding with tension.

"Guess you're never too old for parents to embarrass you." Croygen smiled awkwardly at Rez.

"You're not my father and you embarrass and disturb me all the time," Ryker said dryly, his gaze still searching the hallways.

"Zumba's fun." Cal dropped to my shoulder. "And I like wearing the little shorts."

"*You've* done Zumba?" I choked. "In shorts?"

"Yeah." Cal wiggled his hips, bouncing his butt up and down. "Sinnie likes it… but the shorts were all my idea. She can't resist these sexy legs and the way the spandex shapes my ass." He slapped his butt.

"Croygen, please hurry." I rubbed my head, the images of Cal in spandex shorts doing Zumba troubled me on so many levels.

The pirate grunted, picking up another tool, working it in.

Click.

The latch gave way and I sucked in a breath. With a creak, the door slowly swung in on the dark room. Rez took a step in, a torch blazing alive on the wall, painting the room with deep shadows.

As I walked in, my mouth dropped open. The room was the size of a large living room but full of shelves and boxes stuffed with items: paintings, jewelry, coins, art sculptures, and other collectible objects.

"What is this?" I stumbled over a box.

"My heaven." Croygen sighed dreamily.

"Money isn't the only thing Lars took as payment. A lot of this stuff is from those who tried to negate on a deal or deceive him," Rez said. "He took revenge on those who did him wrong. Death isn't everyone's greatest fear." Rez moved to the farthest wall of the room, staring at a shelf. "And death certainly isn't the cruelest way to punish those who did him wrong." She blinked, tears filling her eyes. I followed her gaze, fixing on an almost empty shelf. Six clear jars sat upon it. Multicolored liquid moved around each one similar to a lava lamp. I could feel they were alive. Magic.

Souls.

"Oh gods, powers are in there." I nodded to the jar. "Fae essences."

"Yeah." Holding a hand to her chest, her throat bobbed with unshed emotion. "Though, he only took from those who have done the worst of crimes." She tilted her head. "You think I was the first Lars did this to over the centuries?"

"No. I guess not," I replied. Over the *centuries* only six had defied him so grievously he took their souls. No stranger to Lars's wrath, I couldn't imagine what they could have done to deserve that. A handful might not seem a lot, but taking someone's magic, their soul, away from them... that was *extreme*. Most would opt for death.

That Lars had taken Rez's powers only proved how much Rez had hurt him. What she did was probably the worst of all of them on this shelf. He had trusted her, loved her, in his way, and brought her into his family.

"Which one is yours?" I stared, mesmerized, at the different-colored magic flexing inside the jars.

"That one." She pointed to the last one on the end. Her eyes were damp as she stared at the jar not unlike a long-lost love. Blue as the ocean, her powers circled the glass like a pod of dolphins, swimming through the water with grace and beauty. Intoxicating.

I wanted to stand here and watch it forever. Follow it wherever it went.

"Wow," I muttered. I was immune to the full blast of fae powers, but I could still feel her magic pull me in, wanting to grasp the jar, listen to the music inside.

"Grab it and let's go." Ryker gruff voice broke my trance. I snapped to look at him. He guarded the door, his axe in his hand.

Rez rolled her shoulders back, her trembling hand lifting the vessel. Her powers swam inside excitedly, as if they knew their owner was coming back for them. When she cracked the jar open, the room filled with song.

Heartbreaking. Exquisite. Joyous.

The most beautiful voice rippled over my skin, drawing tears to my eyes and chills over my skin. The music sank deep, like claws, consuming me, tears slipping down my cheeks.

Out of the corner of my eye, I could see Ryker and Croygen moving in closer. Drawn to her call as well.

Rez opened her mouth, humming, and tipped the jar into her mouth. Her magic twirled and dove down her throat, thrilled with excitement. I dropped to my knees, the beauty was painful, the craving to follow the sound. Humans would have no fight against a creature like her.

Rez slumped to the floor with a cry as the intense magic pummeled her body. I hadn't been in the same room when they were taken from her, but I heard her screams from across the house. It was the most gut-wrenching, heartbreaking sound. I had tried to reach her, but Goran and Rimmon had held me back from getting into Lars's office. It seemed to be almost as painful going back in.

As the powers returned to her, her skin and eyes glowed bright, charging the room with electricity that bent her forward over her knees. It crackled up my spine, too, my bones wiggling with excessive energy.

Then she shut her mouth, the glow dimming, the song falling silent.

"Rez?" I moved to her, watching her chest move up and down, her body shaking. "Are you all right?"

"Yes." She nodded, quiet sobs rattling her chest. "I feel whole..." Her eyes turned to me, glinting with pure joy. "I've been pretending, for West, I was fine without them." Tears rained down her face. "It was a lie. I wanted him to be okay not turning into a beast... that being without your powers was okay." Guilt and sorrow filled her face. "But all I can think now is thank the gods I'm me again. Am I a horrible person?"

"No." I crouched next to her. "You did it because you love him. If he got his powers back and you didn't, would you begrudge him?"

"No." She sniffed. "But he hasn't lied to me about missing them or being lost without them. I am the one who pretended all was okay."

"Girls, this is not the time." Ryker pranced toward the door again. "Therapy session later."

Rez nodded, grabbing for a shelf filled with old coins and gold to help her stand.

"No, Ms. Rez, stop! A wire! It's a trap!" Simmons yelled behind us, but it was too late. Rez's fingers grasped a ledge, crossing an unseen snare.

Boom!

The surge blasted into me, picked me up, tore the sword from my hands, and tossed me across the room. The back of my head cracked against the stone wall. My bones slammed into the ground, debris raining down, bruising and cutting my skin. A cloud of smoke filled the room, obscuring my vision, my body screaming in agony. Ringing ricocheted in my ears.

Don't black out. Stay awake.

With every breath, the pain in my body rose. I felt as though someone were flipping my skin inside out. The edges of my vision darkened as bile rose up my throat.

I couldn't see anyone else as the fog rolled thickly around me. "Rez?" My voice sounded muffled and distant. "Cal? Simmons?" Oh gods. Where were they? Were they okay? "Ryker? Croygen?"

Silence.

A gulp of air sent more torture through my body. I tried to sit up, but nothing happened; my brain and muscles ignored me. My magic was trapped deep inside me, hidden away from the claws digging into them.

Holy crap on ash bark.

I knew what this was… goblin metal so finely ground it was used as a gas bomb. No fae or human could breathe it without it affecting them. With every intake, I was sucking in tiny slivers of poison, and I couldn't do anything about it.

The perfect weapon. Panic had me gulping for air, which only infected my body faster.

A silhouette appeared against the white cloud, the haze thinning around the figure. Green-yellow eyes burned through the mist as the man stepped closer, his face coming into view. I jerked back with a hiss, ramming myself into the wall, stabbing more discomfort through me.

"Look, my great-niece has come for a visit." Stavros put his hand over his heart. "I feel so honored. You're my first visitors. I hope I'm a good host. I do want to accommodate all my guests." He peered over his shoulder. "If they are still alive."

Acid pooled in my stomach. *Be all right. Please.*

Fighting against the weight of my lids, I tilted my head back. I didn't have long to stay conscious. The poison was seeping into every pore, the goblin metal shards ripping at my throat.

How the hell was he standing there unaffected?

"How?" My voice scraped with the effort to talk, cutting off the full question. It also sucked more energy from me.

"How am I still standing here, while you are shutting down? Dying a painful death?" He squatted next to me, a smile pinned unnaturally to his face. "I had a long, long time to become immune. It took over fifty years, but what else do you do while you wait for your comeback? Don't get me wrong, I still get sleepy and such a sore throat." He rubbed his throat mockingly. "But I'll put up with the discomfort for you. We're family, after all."

The humor dropped from his face. "Did you think you could get the jump on me so easy? You have no idea what you are up against. I will always be ten steps ahead. I have every possible outcome planned. Blame it on your grandfather; he gave me plenty of time to scheme and prepare my revenge."

The smoke was dissipating, letting me see lumps over the ground. My friends. Ryker's massive frame was face-first on the floor only a few yards from me. When he groaned and struggled to lift his head, I felt a surge of relief.

"Ember, you have brought me some wonderful housewarming gifts. Wanderer? Thief? Siren? How did you know what I wanted for my birthday?"

I could now make out Rez buried under the items dislodged from the shelf.

"Except I'll regift the two pixies. Useless things."

I tried to snarl, but nothing but a whimper came out, my eyes dropping to half-mast.

Fight, Ember. Fight it.

"Oh, and as for your other friends. They've already been captured. You all failed." He stood up, looking down at me. "I warned the Druid. She should have taken my threat a little more seriously."

His boot kicked my head.

My neck snapped back, but I didn't feel anything; blackness swallowed me whole. My last thought was of Eli. I tried to call for him, then there was nothing.

My lashes fluttered open. Blinking, my head jerked around. *What the hell?* I was in the castle. Kennedy's castle. Or was I in some sick nightmare and Aneira would step around the corner at any moment?

I took a tentative step and glanced around, recognizing the area I was in. The doors to the dungeons sat before me, reminding me of the time I was yanked through them, becoming Aneira's prisoner.

Footsteps clicked across the floor, and I instinctively retreated against the wall. A figure strode around the corner.

"Torin!" I exclaimed with relief, moving to him. He didn't look or respond to me.

"Ah, crap," I muttered, tugging the end of my ponytail. My head fell back, feeling pain from the explosion. I was in a freaking dreamwalk. It had been so long since I'd done one I'd almost forgotten what it was like. As a royal-blooded fairy on my mother's side, I could both dreamscape and dreamwalk. Dreamscaping was pulling someone into a dream, usually only another fairy. In it I could fully interact with people, and it felt as real as if I were awake. In dreamwalking, I put myself in a place in real life and actual time, but I could not be seen, heard, or interact with people. I was a ghost. Why was I here? I needed to be helping my friends.

Torin walked past the dungeon doors, then paused, turned, and walked past them again. A low rumbling sparked from his throat, and his face creased with frustration.

He paced back and forth a couple more times, his anger seeping into me, his emotions clogging my chest. Anger. Hurt. Frustration. Sorrow.

Our link would always be there, and sometimes when he let down his walls by accident, I felt him. He had brought me here, unknowingly. His heightened emotions were a call I could never ignore. He was in pain.

"Dammit!" He bashed his fists against the wall, causing me to jump back. He rarely let his anger get the best of him. When he did… watch out.

"Torin," a woman called to him, coming around the corner, looking as if she had followed him down. Georgia. I recognized her as one of Kennedy's personal guards. The tall Scottish-looking guard, Sturt, followed right behind her. "Calm down."

"Calm down?" He shoved off the wall, glaring at her. "Our Queen is probably getting herself killed, and I have to stay here, twiddling my thumbs. I should be with her. Guarding her."

"She wants us here. Protecting the castle."

Torin shook his head, grinding his jaw, his annoyance spiking through me.

"Lass, why don't we do another walk around the walls?" Sturt grabbed Georgia's arm, giving her a pointed look. Her lips bunched together, her gaze still on Torin.

"Go see her." She let Sturt walk her back a few steps.

"See who?" Torin's torso went rigid.

Georgia slanted her head, shaking it with a look like *come on, we're not idiots*. "You don't have to forget, but maybe if you forgive…"

"I will never forgive her." His chin rose. "What she has done is unforgivable. A dishonor on us."

Georgia sighed. "Torin, your stubbornness and unwillingness to accept people's flaws blinds you. That is *your* weakness."

"Aye. Come on, lass. Now, before you get thrown down with her." Sturt tugged her closer to his body and steered her along the path, leaving the First Knight seething.

Torin watched the vacated hallway for more than a minute, a vein thumping along his temple.

I imagined Torin would walk away, so his turn for the doors surprised me. He put his hand on one, but it was as far as he got. Minutes ticked by without even a muscle twitching. He stood there, his head bowed, his lids squeezed shut.

He needed to do this. Thara was his best friend, their relationship thicker than anything he thought we could have had. He tolerated Eli and me, but he had not forgiven us. Same with Kennedy and Lorcan. Anger and hatred were building in him. Someday it might override duty and allegiance.

"Go, Torin," I whispered to him. He couldn't hear me, but maybe he could feel it through our link.

His fingers curled, and he gave a strangled cry before he yanked the doors open. He moved down the stairs into the darkened hallway. Following him through the labyrinth of passages, we reached the dungeons, but turned down a different row than I expected.

"Well, crap! Conditions have changed since I've been here," I exclaimed with a huff.

The cells we passed were empty, but each contained a cot and a side table. A curtain hung from above to give the sink and toilets privacy. A far cry from the urine drenched hay in my former cell. These cells were for the upper-tier prisoners.

Torin paused, then twisted as though he were about to turn around, but he took a deep breath and pushed forward. Every sliver of emotion was locked up, his expression hard.

We came to the last cell, where a woman sat on the bed. Her legs were folded, a book in her hand, and an uneaten snack sat on the stool next to her bed.

"Snacks? Books?" I exclaimed. "Crap, this would have been a vacation for me." I turned to Torin. "I want to submit a grievance concerning my stay here."

Torin stopped in front of the cage, hands tightening into fists.

Thara lowered the book, showing no sign of surprise. Her violet eyes locked on Torin. Dressed in pocketless cotton pants and a T-shirt, her dirty brown hair hung limply down her arms. Her cheeks were sunken in from lack of food, the glint in her eyes gone, but somehow she still looked stunning.

"For the first few weeks, every time I heard footsteps coming along the path, I feared it was you. Then I longed for it to be you." She set the book on the stool. "Now, I feel neither. I wish I'd felt that a long time ago."

Torin flinched, but the reaction disappeared swiftly behind his façade. "I had nothing to say."

"And you do now?" She leaned back against the wall, pulling a knee up and laying her arm on it.

"No." Torin glanced down the row, away from her. "I do not know why I am here."

"Then I cannot help you."

"Oh my gods, you two." I curled my hands in frustration, wanting to knock their heads together. Talk about stubborn to the point of causing their own misery. Kennedy told me she had been down here a lot, talking with Thara. It would be a long time before she could release Thara or ever forget the betrayal, but she had forgiven her. That was Kennedy, though. If I were in his shoes, I would probably be just as stubborn. It was easy to see something when you were outside and not in the center of it.

I waited for Torin to walk away, but he surprised me again, stepping closer to the bars, gripping them. "Why?" His voice was soft, a touch of agony winding through it.

Thara's cheek twitched.

"Tell me. How could you do that? To me? To the Queen, who did nothing but treat you with kindness? How could honor mean so little to you?"

108

Thara's head jerked up, her eyes firing with anger. "Honor?" She popped off the bed, her nose flaring. "Honor, respect... I lost those years ago." She walked to the bars. "For myself."

Torin dropped his hands, but held his ground, a snarl rising on his lips.

"I blame myself for that. I was blind. Hopeful. Hanging on to every speck of attention you gave me. A smile, a touch, a shared look... I clung to them. We shared *everything*. And still you turned to anyone other than me, and I did not feel worthy of your love. I was not enough." She stated these as facts. "Am I ashamed for what I've done? Yes. I twisted into something I did not recognize, but now I see myself again. And I see her clearly now too. A true Queen. She is a gracious person."

"Majesty has been here?" Torin rocked back on his heels.

"Many times," Thara stated. "I understand she cannot let me go now, but her forgiveness means everything to me."

Torin grunted, fidgeting with the bars. "I am not as good as her," he snarled. "I cannot forgive you."

"I did not expect you to." She raised her chin. "But I no longer need you to."

His brows furrowed.

"For too many years your opinion meant everything to me." She stared at him without humiliation. "It is mine that matters now."

Go girl.

Thara had formerly come across so self-confident and sure of herself, it was hard to think she had any weaknesses. As awful as her actions had been, they made her more real to me.

"Accepting what I've done and finding the person I want to be..." She licked her lips. "For once it has nothing to do with you. It took too long, but I am free of you. Finally." She turned her back on him. "Go, Torin. There is nothing for you here."

He stood there, his mouth locked tight, not moving. As though a hammer knocked him on the head, clearing his vision, a wave of emotion flooded our link. I gasped, taking a step back, his emotions drawing me in so sharply it was as if I was looking at her through his eyes.

Strength. Beauty...

So much beauty. His heart started to drum against his ribs, tightening his lungs. He didn't realize how much his chest had ached without her. How off he felt when she wasn't there. Little flashes of memory flickered through: her laughter, the times she sat next to him, or held him Aneira had abused him. Even without speaking a word, she knew what he was thinking.

Her smile.

Her mouth. Lips...

Holy shit. Torin's thoughts wrapped around me. *What the hell?* His breathing picked up, fear slinking into his realization. *No! I do not feel that. I only miss her. The girl I thought I knew. This girl is a traitor.*

The feelings did not subside, and panic shot through him like adrenaline. His lids narrowed on Thara as he shook his head, blaming her for his feelings.

"You're right. There's nothing here for me." He whipped toward the exit, marching down the tunnel. His boots stopped halfway down, looking back over his shoulder, as though she were a magnet, tugging him back.

Thara stood in the same spot, her head bowed slightly, but her stance was proud. Strong. She did not need him.

That's what bothered him and made him view her in a new light.

I could feel Torin's heart leap in his chest, his gaze moving over her, taking her in. Terror ballooned through him and, like the fog of the poison, immobilized him from letting him acknowledge what he'd probably known forever.

He turned back around, clenching his teeth and hands, and shunted all his emotion back. Still not understanding why he subconsciously pulled me in, he unknowingly shut down the link between us. I was tossed back to my reality with a crash.

The reality where the witches were good and the great Oz was a real bastard.

TWELVE
Zoey

Goran led us to the dungeons, the smell of urine, vomit, and feces making me gag. It was creepy being here, but our guide freaked me out the most. I had met him in my prior dealings with Lars. Something was different about him now. Wrong.

Kennedy and Fionna walked in the middle, and I kept watch behind, my trained instincts twisted tight, ready to act. Sprig held on to the rim of the bag, playing with his tail, watching everything silently. The nervous energy bouncing around the group coiled tight like violin strings. All I could think of was Wyatt. My nerves were tied into knots with the unspoken belief Stavros would probably not keep the kids locked up with the others. Hope and doubt rolled like acid through my stomach.

Goran held up his hand, halting us as he peered slowly around the corner. It was eerily quiet and as much as I should have preferred that fact, I didn't. It jumped up and down on my nerves and batted at them similar to a cat after a mouse.

Fionna gripped her knife, her teeth sawing into her bottom lip. By the way Fionna moved and held herself, I could tell she was highly trained in combat. She took in everything around her as I did. Assessed and calculated her response to it. She was sure of herself and used her fear to keep her on point. She was a good one to have by your side in a fight. She could handle herself.

The Queen, on the other hand, might be strong in mind and backbone, but fighting was not her forte. Not like Fionna and me. Her words would be her fists.

"This way." Goran slunk through a doorway to a long room filled with dark and dank cells, one after another until they disappeared into the shadows, goblin-iron bars caging half the room. Most of the cells held those

111

who were once Lars's guards. I gagged and covered my mouth and nose at the fetid odor of sweaty bodies, blood, and piss.

"Oh gods." Kennedy dry-heaved, shaking her head. "These poor people."

"You thought the dungeons were going to be a day at the spa?" Goran leveled his gaze at the Queen, his words and face empty of any reaction. Weren't these his men? His friends?

"Goran?" A thick-accented voice came from down the row, stopping the air in my lungs.

I knew he was here. He was why we were coming, but the sound of his voice after so long squeezed my lungs.

My boots squeaked over the cobbles as I strode closer to the cell, spotting the familiar ginger-haired man leaning against the cement wall. His buffed sidekick stood right next to him as usual.

"Feck me arseways." Garrett snorted, wagging his head back and forth, peering at me through narrowed eyes. "Look, Cadoc. My long-lost 'sister' has come to save me. Miss me, sis?"

"What?" Fionna jerked her head to me.

I shook my head back. "Thankfully, no actual blood links us. When he was hunting for Ryker and me after the disaster in Seattle, he took my picture around conveying a sob story that he was looking for his 'sister,' who disappeared in the storm, trying to find a lead on us."

"Come closer and I'll show you how much I've missed you." I twirled my knife in my hands. I was there when Lars took on Vadik's lackeys years before. I was impressed Garrett and Cadoc were still with Lars.

"Wait... what?" Sprig squeaked from the bag. "Him? Banana toad farts. No. Way. I will not help that dingleberry. Nor that muscle for brains." He pointed between Garrett and Cadoc.

"I see you still have your pet weasel." Garrett pushed off the wall, strolling up to me.

"P-p-pet *weasel*?" the sprite sputtered.

"Sorry, I meant mole rat." Garrett winked.

Hell.

"Dry up, carrot nuts!" Sprig climbed out of my bag. "I know some flesh-eating bunnies who would love to snack on you."

"Think I already had them for super." Garrett picked at his teeth. "Tasty."

Sprig gasped, folding his arms. "I hope you drown slowly in boiling banana pudding."

"Bananas are the best fruit, don't you agree?" Garrett smirked. "Wish there were *only* bananas."

"Whhhhhaaaatttttt?" Sprig's mouth dropped open, his eyes wide in disbelief. "How… what…"

I sighed.

Garrett looked up, winking at me.

"We don't have time for this." Goran stepped beside me. "We need to release them and all get out of here."

"I'm not helping Agent Orangenut." Sprig waggled his finger at Garrett. "No. No way."

"Please?" I rubbed his head.

"No. He almost killed us, *Bhean*." He peered up at me. "How can you want him out?"

"We need him," I grunted.

"I am no longer talking to you." Sprig crawled back in the bag.

"What if I let you watch soap operas and eat honey all day?"

An eyeball appeared at the opening of my bag.

"Nice parenting skills, Zoey. Bribery?" Garrett folded his arms, curving his eyebrows.

"I'm close to agreeing with him and leaving you here. Better if you just shut it." I lifted the flap of my bag, turning my attention to Sprig. "And we'll go to Izel's when we get home."

Sprig came back out, still not looking happy. "Fine. But I want *double* the pancake order *and* churros."

"Deal."

He huffed and leaped onto the lock, sticking out his tongue in concentration as he worked.

Goran moved down the path to keep his guards from answering the cries from his old comrades wanting freedom. We came for Garrett and the kids. It was harsh, but we couldn't take everyone today.

"Hmmm." Sprig tipped his head.

"What?"

"This one is tricky… something feels jammed in here." He closed one eye, examining the hole. "Oh wait… think I got it…" The lock clicked.

The moment Sprig cracked the lock, a machine cranked on, whirling wind through the vents.

"Oh. No." Kennedy scanned the room, my gaze following hers. From a handful of vents, white clouds billowed out, expanding like a wildfire through the room.

Right away I could feel the heaviness of the air, dread tingling my toes.

"Shite! It's goblin gas!" Fionna stumbled back, covering her mouth.

The gas moved quickly, feeling similar to shards of glass stabbing my skin, throat, and lungs with every breath or movement.

"Sprig!" I grabbed him, shoving him in my bag to protect him.

"Run!" Garrett shoved through the open cell door, Cadoc and him running for the exit. I plastered a hand over my mouth, I could still feel the gas seeping through, clouding my vision and dragging my legs with fatigue. Pain soon pierced my lungs and I closed my lids. My body was shutting down.

No, Zoey. Keep fighting.

But my body wouldn't listen to my mind. The vapor coated me, digging into my skin like the bites of a thousand red ants.

Garrett, Kennedy, and Fionna dropped to the ground, their bodies squirming in agony. I staggered, reaching down to help Kennedy back to her feet, but my muscles gave out. With a cry, I crumpled next to the Queen.

Goran and Cadoc were the last to fall, but none of us could fight the attack. Darkness slithered in at the edges of my vision. Every breath felt the same as knives slicing through my chest, ripping my throat.

My lashes fluttered closed, sleep beckoning me into its arms. Like a faraway dream, I heard the fan shut off, followed by pounding of feet and the chilling cries of monsters.

Stavros had known we were coming. The cell was set to detonate when we unlocked it. He let us believe we were getting ahead, then ripped that hope away. He let us know who was in charge.

My last thought before I tipped over into the blackness: We were fools.

ༀ ༀ ༀ

"Move it." Rotting flesh and sludge whisked across my cheek—the breath from a strighoul behind me crinkled my nose. He shoved me forward, my feet struggling to keep up with his momentum. The goblin metal coating my skin caused my legs to wobble every few steps.

I scarcely drifted off before my body was violently shaken awake. The air vents pushed in clean air as the strighoul descended on us like the plague, unarming and apprehending us. The poison hung to our clothes, affecting us enough that it was a struggle to fight the lethargy.

I hoped Ryker's group had better luck than us. Yet I knew it was wishful thinking. Stavros was not only prepared for us now but seemed several steps ahead.

The patchy-skinned creature shoved me toward a room, almost tripping me again. My thigh bumped the bag, feeling Sprig stir inside. Sub-fae didn't have the same extreme reaction we did to goblin metal, but they also couldn't fight it as we could. Not in doses like that. Their bodies were so much smaller to handle the onslaught of poison as they breathed in the slivers.

Please be all right. I looked at my bag. *Please.*

The strighoul herded us toward a room. A tiny wheeze came from next to me, and I glanced over to see Fionna, her jaw locked but her eyes wide.

"What?"

"Room." She croaked and mumbled the word, flinching in pain, her eyes watering from discomfort. I also swallowed razor blades with every word.

"Should I be worried?"

Fionna gave me a look.

"Hell," I muttered.

"Shut up!" The strighoul thrust me into the chamber, its nails digging painfully into my skin.

"Zoey."

No.

My heart swelled at the sound of his voice and then dropped into my stomach. Hope of his escape vanished like the vapor that had rendered us powerless. I wanted them to be safe, the ones who made it out.

I craned my neck to the side. "Ryker." My eyes found him, my body wanting to run to him. He looked like hell. His skin was pale, he struggled to hold himself upright, and his face and arms were covered with dried blood. His axe was gone. Scanning the space, I spotted an unusually large strighoul wearing it on his back. Strighoul were usually lean, but this one was brute size and muscled.

Croygen, Rez, and Ember stood next to Ryker, also ragged and ashen, alleviated of their weapons. Ember's face was the worst—bloody, black and blue. One eye swollen closed as though she had been punched.

"Goody. The whole fucked-up family is here." Garrett exhaled, rolling his eyes, his voice raw.

Ryker's gaze went to Garrett and Cadoc, a snarl vibrating the room.

"Ach. Good to see ya too, Ryker," Garrett grumbled.

"Asshole and cock sucker. What's up?" Croygen jerked his chin; he also sounded as if he had swallowed glass. "Or is it the other way around? Always get you guys confused."

"Feck off, Croygen." Garrett scowled.

"Oh, I do love reunions." Croygen winked at them.

Ryker turned to me, ignoring them. "Furball?" he mouthed, the corner of his eyes lined with worry.

My gaze dropped to my bag and I shrugged, trying not to imagine the worst. I had no idea if he was all right. I hoped he was only sleeping.

Ember caught Kennedy's eye, winking at her. "Together again, huh?"

Slowly, a grin played on the Queen's lips, as though she were in on an inside joke.

"Wouldn't miss it," Kennedy said as if she were repeating a line from a script. Her vocal cords sounded as if they'd been through a cheese grater.

"How we doin'?"

"Same as always."

"That bad, huh?" Ember smirked, her head shaking.

"Damn, I wish I thought of that." Croygen snorted. "But, Em, I think I'm the Han Solo here. Sexy swashbuckling rebel." He nodded over at Ryker. "You're my Chewie."

"What the fuck are you talking about?" Ryker glared at him. "Who's Chewie?"

"Dude, how have you survived this long not seeing *Star Wars*?"

"Looks as though I've survived just fine without seeing it."

"That might run out today."

The strighoul moved around us, turning us toward a darkened wall. It was the first time I really took in the space. It was a large empty room with one side made entirely of glass, though I couldn't see what was on the other side. We were far below ground, so I doubted there was a nice pastoral scene outside.

Footsteps clipped against the stone floor behind me. My back faced the doorway, and my spine tensed instantly.

Fionna's head jerked back as she stared at the person entering the room.

"Margo," her voice broke, barely audible, but hatred contorted Fionna's features.

"Holy shit," Ryker and Croygen both said, open-mouthed.

"Shite," Garrett scoffed, shaking his head, a strange chuckle coming from him.

My head snapped around, and I wiggled until I could see the figure standing in the entry.

My eyes ran over the woman. Her hair was cut in a black bob with hints of the true violet shining under the light. Her trim figure was dressed in black jeans, boots, and a formfitting sweater, with a constant cruel smile on her face. A sword hung from her waist.

Holy hell.

"Amara?" I blinked as every moment the goblin metal eased off my throat, making it easier to talk.

Her malevolent grin curved higher on her mouth. She rocked her hips as she strutted into the room, her eyes glowing with delight.

"Oh, Zoey. It's been a while. Can I say how much I *haven't* missed you?" She walked past Garrett and me and moved straight to Ryker, placing her hand on his chest. "You, I've *really* missed."

"Shocker," Garrett muttered. Croygen rolled his eyes.

"Funny, because I've dreamed about strangling you to death," Ryker snarled, his shoulders tensing.

"Well, we did prefer it kinky." She winked, rubbing her hand over his torso, moving lower. "And maybe you shouldn't tell Zoey you're still dreaming of me."

"Get your fucking hands off me, Amara," he snapped at her, also trying to free himself of the strighoul's hold.

"What a waste you have become. You were *magnificent.* You could have been a legend. Now you change diapers. Pathetic, Ryker. Half demon, half wanderer and you play house with humans."

"Guess I'll have to bear my failings."

"Wait." Fionna's brows drew down, still hoarse. "How do you know Margo?"

"Margo?" My eyebrow went up. "Is that what you go by now? What was wrong with deceiving, lying, malicious bitch?"

"I couldn't get that all on a business card." She looked at me, but her body remained pointed at Ryker. Then her attention moved to the man next to him. "Croygen, good to see you're still sniffing around Zoey, hoping for a handout."

"Fuck you."

"You tried. Over and over, remember?"

The muscles around Croygen's neck strained, coiling with rage.

"Garrett. It's never been a pleasure." She waved off the Irishman next to me. "Always someone's bitch."

"Better than spreading my legs and being a hussy to the top bidder," Garrett shot back. It looked as though he finally learned his lesson with her as well. It took Croygen long enough.

117

She glared at Garrett, spreading her distaste onto Cadoc next. He didn't react to her.

I twisted my face to Fionna. "Let's just say we all go way back," I replied to her question. "She's like an STD that won't go away." The woman had plenty of enemies in this room. By Fionna's daggered scowl, it appeared the list was getting longer.

My astonishment at seeing her quickly evaporated. I was only shocked I'd been surprised at all. This was exactly something Amara would do—keep attaching herself to power, moving up the ladder, going for the top rung. It was who she was: a deceiver. She would lie, cheat, and manipulate to get what she wanted.

"Missed your chance," Fionna gulped, pushing through her pain. Her voice became stronger. "The stone's gone, Margo, Amara, whoever the hell you are."

Of course. The stone. "Seriously?" My head dipped back. "You are still trying to get it? Girl, give it up. It's just not that into you."

She swung around, glaring at me. "Why, Zoey? You took everything else from me. I am *owed* that."

"As I told you before, you can't take something which was never truly yours," I snarled. Ryker. This always came back to him.

Her mouth opened to speak again, but Stavros strolled into the room, and we all went still. Amara became an afterthought.

My eyes tracked his every step. I hated to give him props, but the goblin-metal smoke bombs had crippled us, even after the blast. It had covered us in its poisoned ashes, keeping all of us as threatening as kittens.

"Welcome! I am so happy to have you all." Stavros pulled his hands to his chest in false sincerity. He moved to Goran. "You lived… well, sort of."

Goran's face stayed blank, as though he didn't even notice Stavros.

"You're a cheery one. Happy to be alive, huh?" Stavros tapped his face. Only Goran's irises moved, looking through Stavros.

The King snorted, walking back to the middle of the room. "I have a few house rules for all of you, you understand." He looked at Amara. "My lovely, can you show my guests what they will lose if they try to attack me?"

"Gladly." She leered at me and Fionna, moving past us with smug intensity. She reached for a set of switches on the wall.

"No. No… this isn't happening again," Fionna whimpered to herself, understanding what was going to occur far more than I did.

"Oh, did Lars do this before?" Stavros snapped his fingers. "Dammit.

I thought I was being original." He put his hands on his hips, sighing deeply. "I guess I'll have to try and be more creative then."

With that, Amara flicked the switch, lighting up the room behind the glass.

A cry broke out next to me, but my gaze was locked on the figures behind the glass.

My world.

Everything.

Collapsed.

I lurched forward, a shrill scream breaking from my tender throat. "Wyatt!"

Kate sat in a chair holding him, but she looked drugged, her eyes rolled back into her head, the baby fussing on her lap. Oh gods. What did I do? I thought I was protecting them.

Desperation to get to Wyatt vaporized all logic, my limbs whipping around like a feral animal. A dozen hands pinned me in place, preventing me from moving, the goblin metal coating my skin, working deeper the more I fought against their hold.

A roar broke from the other side of the room, Ryker shoved through the strighoul like a linebacker, making them screech and howl in excitement, biting him. He crumpled to the floor but still tried to crawl forward, reaching for his son.

"Nic!" Ember screamed.

Fionna fought next to me, screaming the name "Piper" over and over.

My gaze breaking from Wyatt for a moment, I noticed the little brown-haired girl with bright blue eyes in the room next to Wyatt. Piper. She couldn't be more than four or five. A gorgeous man, presumably Nic, wore an eyepatch over one eye was chained to a chair next to Piper, sweat pouring down his pain-etched face. His eye was on the girl, his mouth muttering words I could not hear.

"Silence!" Stavros yelled. "Or I cause more pain to them."

The room went still, our labored breaths the only sound in the space.

"I have placed goblin-metal bombs in the air ducts above them. You all experienced how agonizingly painful it is. Even if they're not fae, breathing in metal slivers will cause internal bleeding. Even the little Druid will not be able to heal herself fast enough. Behave and I won't have to use them."

Kate was human; she couldn't heal herself at all. And a baby? His powers to heal or do anything wouldn't kick in until he was much older. Wyatt would die along with Kate. I couldn't let that happen.

"You wondered, queenie, what I would do if you didn't willingly bend your knee to me." He waved back at his hostages. "How I could collect you all and have you work for me without question?"

"You fucking bollocks," Fionna seethed.

"Uh-uh." Stavros wiggled his finger. "Watch your mouth, Fionna. You're speaking to the King."

"King?" Ember's face was damp with perspiration, her bruised eye drooping and swollen, but she still wrestled against the strighoul's hold. With the constant exposure to the metal and the lack of magic in the room, none of us could truly heal. "Is this what you think a King does? You aren't even near the same realm as a true King."

"No. Lars was soft and weak. You all got comfortable and entitled. Benign. He was too lenient and indolent. People like false freedoms. They want someone telling them what to do, providing the illusion they are free. But humans take it too far, get big ideas and try to fight against us. I respect what Aneira was trying to do. The humans will know their place again. And so will all of you."

He stared at us for a beat before he let out a howling laugh, goosebumps rippling down my arms.

"You should see all your faces." His green eyes danced. "Wow! It's as though I kicked your puppy or something."

Oh. Hell. He is crazy.

"You guys are going to be so much fun to have around." He motioned at our group, his chuckles petering out. "Okay, I'm sure you're all tired and want to rest up for the day's activities. First day at camp is always the most difficult. Exhausting." His humor died away in an instant as he turned to the strighoul. "Show them to their rooms."

This was not unlike when I'd been taken by that gang in Seattle that my instincts sprouted like weeds. If they locked us up, probably separate, it was game over.

"No! No!" Fionna bellowed hoarsely. She rammed herself forward, trying to get to the glass. Thrashing, she wormed away from the strighoul's hold, falling on her knees in front of her daughter. "Piper!"

"Mummy. No." The little girl put her hand to the glass, as if she could see and hear us. "Don't fight. He will hurt you."

Fionna whimpered, leaning her head toward her child's hand.

"I'm supposed to be here. I can't leave yet. I will protect him. He needs me."

The strighoul wrenched Fionna back to her feet and hauled her toward the door.

My focus landed on my son and the white-haired woman who had become my family and his grandma. I would not lose either of them. Or anyone in this room. Yet each of us were powerless. There were a dozen strighoul for each of us. My hands flexed in back of me, my thumb running over the scar in my palm.

Fuck, Zoey, you really can't be thinking of doing this.

Yet at the sight of my weakened comrades around the room, the children and loved ones tortured and held as leverage… I knew I had no other choice.

There was a good possibility it wouldn't even work. I was going to try anything. For Wyatt, Kate, Piper, and Nic, at least.

Hands pushed me to move, but I stood my ground, shutting my eyes, and directed all the energy I had left into the two symbols carved into my hand.

Stone! I screamed in my head. *Come for me. You want me. Come get me!*

Silence, but I thought I felt a tingle in my hand.

You get us out of here, I paused, terrified I was making an even worse decision, *and I will go with you.*

Again, nothing. Shit.

I crumpled to the floor, succumbing to the crushing defeat. Stavros had us squarely in his hands. There wasn't anything I wouldn't do to protect Wyatt.

Sickness like thick, chunky soup swirled in my stomach. I fought so long to never be a victim again, no matter what happened to me. But if anything happened to Wyatt… there would be no coming back from that.

༺ ༺ ༺

The strighoul shuffled us to the other side of the underground quarters, pointing us toward a different area of the dungeon where we had found Garrett and Cadoc.

A line of metal doors led down the hallway almost stacking up against each other, but each one of these were built into the foundation of the ground. They were tiny, dark cells with heavy bolted doors.

"For you, my dear." Stavros opened the first one, waving Kennedy to enter. Goblin metal and something else I couldn't put my finger on coated the door and room. Shit. Once they put us in, the chances of escaping were nearly impossible.

121

"What is this?" Kennedy shoved back into the monsters holding her. She glanced briefly at Fionna. "How are you doing this? Blocking our magic?"

Fae could not usually control Druid magic, which was one of the reasons fae feared and targeted them.

"I learned a thing or two in South America from the Kalku," Stavros replied.

My stomach dropped. Living in South America, I knew of the Kalku of Chile. Kalku were malevolent sorceresses who used black magic and spirits to wreak havoc. People talked about them in hushed tones and with heavy doses of fear. They believed that even a word about them would guide their evil eye in your direction. They were supposed to be more of a superstition. Fantastical. But similar to all superstitions and fantasies in the fae world, folktales were real and none were sweet fairy tales.

"Black magic." I cringed, nodding in understanding. "Kalku perform black magic."

"Very good. Someone here studied." Stavros clapped his hands. "Druids aren't the only ones who dabble or are extremely proficient in it. It is pathetic that over centuries fae have failed to find ways of controlling Druids. But leave it to me to be the first to realize how to do it."

Experimenting in dark magic always came with a price. The precise talent Druids had adapted to protect could also hurt them.

"After Scotland, I brought a Kalku sorceress here. She did all the enhancing. My encounter with dear, sweet Fionna here," he winked at her, "prepared me. I hadn't taken Druids very seriously before. So, Queenie, you should thank your sister for your accommodations and limited powers. Our meeting in Scotland opened my eyes to my shortcomings." Stavros glanced over at Fionna. "Also, Lars had a few spells already in place against Druid powers, didn't he, Fi-Fi? Your so-called *great* leader also wanted to muzzle you Druids."

Fionna tipped her head back, staring at the new King, ignoring Kennedy's wild gaze on her.

"Fi?"

"You think I would have stayed imprisoned here if he didn't safeguard my cell?" Fionna snapped to her sister. "Don't be naïve. He was King, and I was his prisoner."

"As you are all mine." Stavros nodded at the thing behind Kennedy. It shoved her forward, her heels digging into the stone, her tiny frame sliding across the barrier, the door closing on her.

Booooom!

A blast from above jarred me from the top of my head to my toes. We all tumbled to the ground like dominos. The house shook, moaning, the joints and hinges creaking and breaking under the force. Dust and debris sprinkled down as our bodies scattered, the taste of magic bitter on my tongue.

Then a pause. We had only a moment before our only chance would be gone.

"Get up, imbeciles!" Stavros yelled at the strighoul as he climbed to his feet.

Goran, Ryker, and Croygen jumped up, leaping for Stavros, but a handful of the flesh-eaters sprang up as a wall between, snapping their teeth at them.

Chaos broke around us like putting a bunch of cats in a bathtub. My fight instincts kicked in, hungry for action. I may not have had my powers, but I was still a bad-ass fighter. Summoning the Avenging Angel, I swung my arms out at the patchy-skinned freaks. Spinning, kicking, and jabbing my fists into flesh, the world beyond a four-foot perimeter disappeared as my muscles zinged to life.

Strighoul were easy to read. They weren't especially smart. Unlike a lot of people I had fought in my time, I didn't need to gauge their habits or fighting cues.

Daggered teeth snapped at me, and nails dug into my clothes. Spinning, my knuckles smashed into the gut of one beast, my boot making contact with its groin, where it dropped it to the ground, but three more climbed over it and came for me.

Cadoc slammed his shoulder into them, dumping them onto the ground.

"Thanks."

Cadoc nodded and returned to fighting. Wow, I never thought one day Cadoc would not only help me, but we'd be on the same side of a fight.

Circling around, a strighoul carrying the knife which had been procured from my harness earlier, came for me. I dropped down and swept my leg out in an arc, the creature crashing onto its back.

"This is mine." I snagged my dagger back between my clasped wrists, slicing its throat without pause, blood spewing up over my face. Its howl stabbed my eardrums. I'd grown up in a brutal world where everything came down to survival. You didn't hesitate. If you did, you were as good as dead. There was a reason I had lived this long. This was only an extreme version of it.

"Enough!" Stavros bellowed. Pressure slammed into my head. With a scream, my knees buckled, striking the floor. Pain froze my muscles, locking the air in my lungs. Cries and high-pitched squeals echoed around me as the commotion of the room quickly silenced.

I could feel it—a thumping of magic from outside the walls.

"You," he yelled. I peered at him as he pointed at a group of his men. Everyone, including his toadies, were crumpled on the floor except for Goran. He didn't appear in any kind of pain. He bent his head, but his expression looked bored, his finger idly rubbing at a bloodstain on his jeans.

With the focus on the other side of the room, I slipped the knife in my hand into my boot, though even that slight movement seemed to aggravate my brain matter.

"Go check what is going on. Why have your idiot brethren not already killed those dwellers?"

Still holding their heads and whimpering, the group rose and limped from the room. Stavros watched them for a while, his nose flaring.

"Did some of you already forget?" Stavros held up his arms, sending another wave of magic through the room. I groaned, bending over farther, clutching my head against the pain. He strolled between us, working his way through the room. "I am immune to all fae weakness. Goblin metal does nothing. I will always overpower you. I am a demon. The King! The more you fight, the more I hurt your loved ones, and the worse jobs I will force you to do." He clutched the back of Ember's head, yanking her ponytail, forcing her face to look at him. "Your dwellers were a nuisance before. A tiny distraction. But now?" He growled, getting close to her face. "How did they have the power to break through my barriers?"

Is that what happened? Did the bombs created by Fionna and Kennedy break through the shield? With Druid power, it was possible, but something in my gut said what we felt was far more powerful than a bomb.

"Huh?" He wrenched her head farther back. She didn't so much as flinch. Was she smirking? Damn. I was starting to really like her.

"Well, why don't we go upstairs and you can watch each one of them being torn apart and eaten? They would have been fun to have around, but I can do without feral kitty cats around the place." Stavros hauled her to her feet by her hair. Her teeth sawed into her bottom lip, but she made no sound of distress.

The pressure in my head lifted, and I fell slightly backward, my muscles shaking from the tension of holding them taut.

"*Bhean?*" Sprig whispered from my bag. Taking a deep breath and closing my eyes, I held in my relief at hearing Sprig's voice. My hand went to the bag, patting him softly, telling him I was here. *Please keep quiet and stay hidden.*

"Get them up." Stavros motioned to us but glared at his men. A few strighoul bodies didn't rise when we did. They wouldn't be missed.

Nails dug into the skin around my neck, and two strighoul moved me through the house. Ryker was in front of me; he turned his head, his gaze finding mine. I gave him a nod. *I'm okay.*

We stepped outside and my knees almost gave out again, magic was so thick it stifled the air, the barrier clinging to it in chunks. Kennedy said Druid magic could split holes into the protective shield, enough to get through, but it would pop it like a balloon, leaving scraps of it around similar to plastic. This was different.

Then a chill zigzagged down my spine.

"Come out, come out!" Stavros called out to the forest surrounding the house. "The game is over. I've won!"

Silence followed his claim, only the cracking from burning foliage sizzled the air.

"You are only making it worse." A cackled laugh came from him. "They know!" He pointed back at us. "The more you fight me, the worse it is for *others*…"

Nothing.

"I guess I shouldn't be surprised. Dark dwellers love death and blood. Family doesn't mean as much as I thought it did to you." He walked backward, finding Ember again. "Just imagine how good she'll taste." He grabbed for Rez. "Or a siren. Her blood has to be so sweet."

The strighoul cheered, smacking their lips together.

A sudden growl emerged from the forest, loud enough to make the ground rumble beneath our feet again.

A huge grin engulfed Stavros's face; he knew he was getting to them. He pushed Ember in front of him, pulled out a knife, and put it to her throat, digging the blade into her skin. "I think it's time we get this little standoff going." With one swift swipe, he sliced her throat. Ember gasped, blood spurting out.

A roar shredded the forest, booming over the land. Stavros shoved her down on the ground, his arms splayed wide as though he begged them to come and get him.

Giant black bodies leaped from the trees with a piercing explosion. Strighoul yelled, running for them.

For one second I watched Ember—one hand pressed to her throat, the other clawing the earth. Fae could heal quickly, but we were all coated in the goblin metal, which slowed that down immensely. I hoped enough of her powers could at least slow the bleeding.

But none of us would live if we didn't fight.

Kennedy ran for Ember, but the rest of us turned on our enemy, attacking with everything we had. Out of the corner of my eye, I saw Ryker climb over a strighoul, heading for the burly one who held his axe.

Stavros stood in the center, untouched. He circled around, like he was enjoying a show from a comfortable living room.

That man had taken my baby. He needed to die. I took a step toward him, when another figure jumped into my path.

"I don't think so." Amara winked, pulling a sword from her waist. "Think you can still beat me now that you can't jump and run away?"

Shucking the knife from my boot, I grinned back. "Without a doubt."

"Wait. Wait. Wait." A head pushed out of my bag. "Banana poop in my Honey Nut Cheerios, are you kidding me? Medusa is here?" Sprig's face twisted into disgust. "This is a nightmare, right?"

"And I was hoping that *thing* had been stuffed with bananas and shipped off to a taxidermist." Amara glared at Sprig.

"Hey, purple broomstick with a bob, why don't you ever close that hole?" he sputtered back. "And I'm not talking about the one on your face."

Rage flashed through her features. She rolled her shoulders back and brought her sword down toward me. Dipping, I slipped to the side, our blades clanging together. Mine was tiny compared to her sword, but it meant I could get a lot closer.

"Is that all you got, human?" Her waiflike figure might look fragile, but it was only an illusion. I had fought her before and nearly lost. But I was barely trained then. Over the years, I had honed my skills.

Stavros's laugh crackled through the air. "It's as though I'm back in the Roman times. I should bring the gladiator games back. They were so much fun." This fight was entertainment for him, but it was a matter of time before he got bored and brought us all to our knees. We would lose. And some of us would die.

Dodging Amara's swing, I felt the same chill from earlier flood over me, going straight into my palm. Flaming to life.

I've wasted enough time, Zoey. You promised me.

I stumbled back, my heart slamming into my chest, my eyes darting around. "No," I whispered to myself. Everything around me went distant, as if I were on another plane. Then I understood, the dwellers didn't break the barrier; the stone did. He came for me...

"Zoey!" I heard Ryker scream in the distance, felt Amara's blade swipe so close to me that wind brushed against my cheek, but she didn't hit me. I could see her pause, her eyebrows furrowing in confusion.

Now, Zoey. I am growing impatient, the deep voice said into my head.

My hand pulsed and then my feet moved without thought, walking past Amara and through the pandemonium of fighting bodies, completely untouched.

The shell of Lars leaned against a tree, his arms folded, as though he had been waiting there for hours. Air only grazed my lungs, every step bringing me closer to my nemesis. I had always known I would have to face it. I had called it. Now I had to deal with that decision.

"I said if you got us out, I would go with you." I clamped down on the handle of my blade, still hanging from my fingers. "*Us* means *all* my friends. Not just me."

It was eerie to watch the stone use Lars's body, a grin curving unnaturally on his mouth.

"You certainly act like a fae. Constantly trying to use tricks and ambiguities."

"I won't go unless you help them."

The stone sighed, pushing off the tree, gazing over my head. "Fine. But this is the last favor I do for you."

"It's not a favor. It's part of the deal."

"You have to go with me, Ms. Daniels. No loopholes."

I swallowed. For a brief moment I felt Wyatt's soft downy hair against my breast, Ryker's lips warm on my throat, but I shoved it all away. They would live, and it was all that mattered. "That is what I said."

The stone nodded at the group, and in an instant Stavros and his men froze. My friends were now free to move. They all stumbled, glancing around, unsure of what was happening.

Hell. The stone could play with the High Demon King like a Barbie doll.

"I'm only holding the illusion for a moment. Tell them not to waste it." The stone turned to walk away, the pull to follow him yanked on every muscle painfully. "Let us go."

"Zoey?" Ryker called out.

"Run." I glanced over my shoulder to stare into white eyes. "Now." I lifted my bag from over my head.

"*Bhean*... what are you doing?" Sprig crawled out. "No, let me go with you."

"No, little buddy. You stay with Ryker." I gulped back the tears. "I won't be myself anymore. Wyatt, Lexie, Annabeth, Ryker... even Croygen, they will need you. Please do this for me."

He stared at me, his eyes wide, his hand reaching for me.

"Zoey! No!" Croygen bellowed, but none of them could get near me. The stone played with everyone's mind, making them believe they had no control. The stone could give you all you desired or make you feel like you had nothing... the mind was a powerful weapon. Especially when it was used against itself.

Tears burned down my throat and I raised my chin, trying to blink them away, and started to walk.

"Zoey! Don't do this. You can fight it," Ryker howled, his voice moving around me. I took a few steps. "Human... you fight. That's what you do. Do not give up on me."

I glanced over my shoulder, feeling the tug to move clawing at my skin. Ryker stared at me, pain etched deep in his eyes.

"Get our son... tell him sometimes fighting is about protecting those you love." My voice quaked. "I love you, Viking." With that I ran into the forest.

"*ZOEY!*" My name shook and rattled through the trees, heartbreak dripping off every leaf like acid rain, burning into my soul.

I let one cry escape my lips before I shifted back into myself. The stone greedily took control of my body, feeling my withdrawal. I was still there, could see and understand, but I was a passenger. A ghost haunting my own body.

Time seemed to have lost meaning. I almost drifted a few times as my legs kept moving over terrain. My muscles quaked with fatigue, but I did not slow or falter keeping pace with the false Lars.

We ran on and on. Finally, the stone slowed, went down a ravine, and approached the entrance to a cave. Torches burned at the entrance. Fresh and old ash were piled on the ground, suggesting this place was used frequently.

We're home, the false Lars said into my head.

I felt a spike of surprise inside me but almost laughed it off. This person looking at me wasn't Lars. He wouldn't need hotels or fancy dinners. This was an inanimate object, incapable of feeling things like fatigue or hunger.

He handed me the second torch, and I followed him without hesitation into the dark cave. But inside, I could feel the stone's control growing like thorny weeds, circling and digging into my soul.

Hell. Hell. Hell.

Phantom chills ran down the spine I could no longer feel. It was strange to not feel your body but have all the same sensations, or the hallucination of them, comparable to people who had lost limbs. This wasn't my limb, but an entire body.

My eyes tracked the passage as it led into a giant underground cave. Torches and a huge bonfire in the middle lit the space enough to reflect deep shadows off the walls.

The smell of cooking meat, dirt, and piss filtered around me. Obscure figures moved in the space, building or sharpening weapons, talking or eating. They looked human from what I could see, but something felt way off. Wrong. Some had heads too big for their bodies, others with crooked limbs. One looked as if it had a daggered tail.

Gazing over the cave, my heartbeat thumped against my ribs. Dread looped around, cinching tight. I felt the answer already skimming the surface.

Nononono. There was no way. They were dead.

"They've been waiting to be reunited with you for a long time." The stone jumped on top of a large rock above the blazing fire. A tug in my brain, and my body joined him on the rock. "Look who is here, my creatures."

Every one of them went still, their faces turning slowly to me.

Oh gods...

Green eyes, brown hair, some with heart-shaped faces, some looking identical to Sera.

No. This can't be true.

But it is, Zoey. Aren't you happy to see them? the stone responded to my thoughts.

Happy? These monsters should have died with Rapava.

Some are hurt that you abandoned them so easily, but I'm sure after spending time with your offspring your maternal instinct will kick in.

Fuck you, I seethed. *Stavros took my eggs while I was unconsciousness and "created" them. I had no say.*

Be nice, Zoey, or you will find yourself the same as Lars.

Why? I know you want your revenge. Is this what you had planned? Keeping these things alive?

Merely because they are not pretty doesn't mean they're not useful. I have found them exceptional. A new breed. A better, stronger species, but pliable, easy to control. Still willing to do another's bidding.

The stone turned away from me, holding up his arms.

"Let us give a warm welcome to your mother. She has finally come home to you."

As though he stung them with an electrical current, they all jumped to their feet, piercing roars filling the cave. Their weapons and feet stomped the ground, drumming along with my heart. It was not in excitement or joy, but pure hate. In their rage, a few stepped toward me, snapping at me, their mouths full of thousands of needlelike teeth.

The bubble I inhabited jerked back, but my actual body didn't move a muscle, standing strong against the threat.

"Oh dear... guess some are going to take a little more time." The stone quirked Lars's mouth up.

My body moved to the edge of the boulder.

Stop. What are you doing to me? I yelled at the stone. False Lars's smile lifted higher.

My mouth opened, words coming out without my say.

"Stop!" I held up my hand, my voice filling the room, hushing their cries. "I am your creator. Your master. Not only do you have a King to follow, but you have a Queen. My bidding is law. Now bow, my children."

There was a tense moment before the throng of monsters went onto their knees.

"Our mother. Our master. Our Queen!" A half-strighoul called out, bending his head. I remembered him. The infant who had begun his life in an incubator at DMG was now a man. His green eyes flashed with hate as he peered at me from bended knee. But the rest followed his lead, repeating his mantra until the entire room chanted and pounded their weapons on the ground.

My head turned to the stone, and I felt a smile curl my own lips.

"You are master of them." False Lars moved closer to me. "But do not forget, I am master of you. I own you now, Zoey."

With a shove, I felt my grip on myself slip into the darkness.

THIRTEEN
Kennedy

My grimy boots paced over the stone floor of the castle, drowning out the commotion around me. Absently I brushed back strands of hair from my face. Dried sweat, dirt, and blood crusted on my skin like ancient wallpaper, my skin still itching with the slivers of goblin metal. The desire to wash it all away caused me to skim my hands continuously over my hair and arms. But nothing would wash away the sickness in my stomach or the terror shaking my limbs. The black spell which had neutralized my magic was gone, but I felt weakened by the attack on my body. Drained.

"I won't simply sit here. My son and mate have been taken," a voice boomed through the room, fury riding it like a rodeo bronco. I looked toward its source. "You assholes may not care that thing has her, but..." Ryker's chest inflated, several nerves along his cheek and temple twitched, and his white-blue eyes were fierce and glowing. A Viking about to attack, to battle against the world.

"Does it look as if we don't care?" Eli whipped around, growling, his pupils elongating. "The stone has one of ours too."

Ryker took a step, his shoulders rolled forward, his hand reaching for his axe. "And you've done nothing to get him back."

Eli and Lorcan both curled forward, rumbles vibrating the ground. *Dammit by a thousand.* This was going to go bad fast.

"Stop," I yelled, none of the men heeding my warning.

"Watch yourself, Wanderer." Eli tilted his head, almost daring him to make another move. "I just watched my mate's throat being sliced in front of me. I'm not in a very good mood."

Ember stood next to me, her neck still pink and healing from Stavros's blade. The cut appeared deeper than it actually was, and she had been quick to use the earth's energy to heal, but she still lost a lot of blood. She was sure Stavros wanted to cause a scene, chaos, get the dwellers to act, not kill her. Yet. We all knew with each one of us it was only a matter of time.

Ryker leaned into Eli's face, his mouth twisting. "What would you do if it was your mate?" Veins in Ryker's temple throbbed against his skin. "Don't tell me to back down. I will not let that stone have her. Not before and not now." He flipped around, barreling for the exit.

Lorcan inclined forward, but it was Eli who advanced. In a blink, his hand grasped Ryker's throat, his claws digging into his skin, slamming him back in the wall with a vibrating thud. The ferocity of alpha energy discharged off them, hitting my chest so powerfully it knocked me back a step.

"You're not doing her any favors, Wanderer." Eli clamped down firmer on Ryker's neck.

Bursting waves of anger shot off Ryker. "Get your fucking hands off me." His nose flared.

"Then get hold of yourself." Eli using his weight to push into him. "You think rushing out there without a plan is a good idea? It's suicide. Do you think Zoey would want you to do that? Do you understand what you are up against?"

Ryker's shoulders hunched up, his hands colliding with Eli's chest, shoving him back.

"Ryker, stop!" Lexie tried to reach for him, but Croygen stopped her, pulling her back into him. Streaks of tears still lined her face from when Croygen told her and Annabeth what happened... that their sister was gone.

"I know more than anybody here." Ryker pushed off the wall, getting in Eli's face. "Who do you think carried it for centuries? I was strong enough to fight it, ignore the constant pull. So don't get righteous with me, dweller. I understand it better than anyone."

"Then use your fucking head instead," Eli bellowed back.

Fury swelled over the wanderer's chest, tension cramming into every corner.

Crapping nerf-herder.

"Enough!" I yelled, jumping in between the two men, pushing their chests, which was as effective as trying to shove back a brick wall. Neither inched back a smidge. "We can't have fighting among us as well. We have far too many enemies outside these doors for us to be at each other's throats." I took a breath, letting them ease back before I turned to Ryker. "I understand you are scared and angry. I may not know Zoey well, but I already grasp that she would not want you to act foolishly, get yourself hurt or killed, because you didn't take a moment to think. What if your actions get yourself or her killed?"

"Man, you know she'd kick your ass," Croygen said from his spot against the wall with Lexie.

Ryker huffed air through his nose, side-eyeing Croygen.

"You know the stone, so help us think like it. Brute strength is not going to help us here." I hesitated, but then touched his arm. "You are not alone in this fight. Not only do I care for Zoey, but we also want to save Lars, if there is any chance he is still in there."

"He damn well is." Fionna folded her arms, appearing ready to take down anyone who opposed her. "And I'll get him, even if I have to drag that demon out by his dick."

Snorted laughter scattered through the room. That was my sister. No filter.

Slight amusement simmered briefly on Ryker's face. He took a step back, exhaling. Sprig crawled out of the bag Ryker wore, the one Zoey had left behind.

"Viking?" He got up on his shoulder, Ryker automatically started rubbing his head. "We'll get *Bhean* and *Buachaillín*." He patted Ryker's cheek softly. "We have to. *Bhean* is the only one who knows where to order that supersized honey jar. Oh, since we're on the subject of food."

"We weren't."

"Yeah, we are. I just brought it up." He rubbed his belly. "Do you hear it? I won't be of any use to anyone without sustenance."

"You're not any use to anyone, anyway." Croygen approached Ryker.

"Shut it, bootleg-humper." Sprig stuck out his tongue at the pirate. "Oh, I want some churros. *Bhean* and *Buachaillín* need me at full capacity, so maybe pancakes. Honey mango chips to hold me over until the pancakes. I can settle for donuts or waffles."

"Douse those in juniper syrup and you got yourself a partner." Cal flew over to the sprite. "I'm open to trying honey-infused juniper juice."

"Ohhhhhh." Sprig's eyes widened, his lips smacking.

"Shit." Croygen chuckled. "I'm open to that too."

I rubbed my neck, disgusted by the coat of dust. "Stavros will be coming for us soon. His pride took a hit today." After Zoey had walked away, it took us a moment to realize what happened. When I felt the stone's power dwindle over Stavros and his men, I ordered everyone to retreat.

Fionna and Ryker fought me, trying to get back into the house, to go after their kids. It was my decision. A choice no one else had to bear. My mind quickly scrambled down the pros and cons lists. There was no chance we could get the children out without another huge fight. And the gas bombs in the rooms had confirmed my decision. Stavros could hurt them at any time. I wasn't willing to risk their lives or ours. Not yet. Not without a plan.

Olivia walked into the room, carrying a tray full of coffee and biscuits. The rich aroma filled my nose, making my mouth water.

"My lady." She set it on the desk. "Thought you might need a pick-me-up."

"Thank you, Olivia." I almost hugged her; the small act almost broke me. She was always a step ahead, always thinking of my needs before I even knew I wanted something.

Cole leaned against the desk, peering down. "No chocolate biscuits?"

"I'm sorry, do I look like *your* servant, dweller?" Olivia whipped around on him, her hand pressed to her hip. "I don't remember you signing my paychecks."

"You want me to pay you to bring me cookies, fox?" His lifted his eyebrows, expression neutral.

Olivia's cheeks heated, her lids narrowing.

"If you want chocolate biscuits, then walk your ass to the kitchen yourself." She flipped back around to me, her tone shifting. "Anything else, my Queen?"

Actually, I wanted chocolate biscuits, too, but shook my head, letting her stride out. She glared back at Cole before leaving, his amused grin inching farther up the side of his face.

Olivia came from Lily's fox skulk. It was Lily who recommended her to me, for which I was grateful. It was no secret foxes and dark dwellers weren't crazy about each other, but Olivia had been one of the first to accept my relationship with Lorcan. She liked him and was not upset at all when she found him naked in my office, which was more often than not.

Lily had grown immune to them, being around them all the time, but I could see having so many dwellers in one place might make Olivia a little uneasy.

Or maybe it was solely Cole who did.

"I suggest we all relax, get something to eat, and meet back here in an hour." My shoulders slumped down, the weight of what was ahead of us bearing down on me. "I'm tired of Stavros being one step ahead. And as far as the stone… if any of you have ideas or anything that might help…" *I need Lars. I can't do this by myself.* "All right. One hour."

Only a few reacted, stepping toward the door. Ember came and stood beside me, taking my hand.

"I know," Ember croaked out, her fingers touching the wound lining her neck. "You think this is all on you, Ken, but it's not."

I tried to smile back. Her sentiment was nice, but it *was* all on me. "Aren't you glad I picked up that sword about now?" I clasped her hand.

"Hell, yeah." She breathed out a laugh. "If I were Queen, this place would have burned down the first week, everyone running around, probably naked and drunk. Chaos. Mayhem."

"I'm saving that for the holidays."

Ember's face grew serious. "You are an amazing leader. No one could do any better than you have." She squeezed my fingers. "I am so proud of you."

"Thank you." I didn't feel amazing. Not even close. I felt scared. Inexperienced. And extremely tired.

"Brycin," Eli yelled over his shoulder, walking toward the doors. "We have an hour."

Ember turned to retort when Torin rushed into the room, his eyes wide. "What is it, Torin?"

He didn't answer. Just grabbed something off the desk and flicked the screen on. Images flashed on the TV, his thumb jabbing at the volume button.

"Riots and protests have broken out all over the world." A woman's voice came over the speakers, the TV flashing groups holding signs and chanting. "Violence is springing up between the two sides, between the Queen and new King. Fae and human police are trying to stop it, but there have already been four deaths."

Everyone in the room went still. Those who were almost out the door came back in, staring at the monitor in horror.

Signs marked with quotes like:
1) Off with her head!
2) No vote, no queen.
3) Time for a true leader.

Sprinkled in were a few pro-Queen posters, but all I saw was hate. Rage. Distress that I was in charge.

"The response in the streets has been swift after the allegedly new King broadcasted live only moments ago," the news reporter said as the screen flashed to Stavros standing before a throng of people. Some I recognized as individuals who had lived here in the village under my protection.

"Crap on ash bark," Ember muttered next to me, stepping closer to the display.

Wearing one of Lars's suits but foregoing the tie, Stavros stood in front of a crowd with the first three buttons of the shirt undone. Despite his shabby fashion, his presence was undeniably formidable. Charismatic. Maybe even approachable. All of it lies.

"Today I come forward as the true Seelie King. The rightful leader. The *only* leader. It is time for a single ruler. No more of this division that is ripping the country in half." He held out his arms, projecting power. Cheers responded to him.

"Who here believes a *girl* of twenty-four can do anything for you? That she has any idea about your wants and needs? Most of you are centuries older than her, have lived and seen things she could never possibly imagine. How can she lead you? A child… and a Druid."

The crowd roared with applause. These were people already following him, who believed humans and Druids were lesser than fae. But as a viewer, would you understand it was staged? Or would you start questioning your own beliefs?

"Fuck," Lorcan grumbled on my other side.

My heartbeat and breath were stuck in my throat, acid burning holes in my stomach. I could feel my crown crashing into dust at my feet, maybe hypothetically, but every word he spoke shoved me further off the throne. My fists rolled so tightly my nails cut into my flesh.

"Druids were never supposed to rule us fae. It is a disgrace. I am ashamed to come back to see how badly we have fallen." He placed his palms on his heart, looking pained, shaking his head.

He wasn't even a good actor, but the audience gobbled it up, responding with boos at their present state.

"And humans, if you think she has your rights in mind, why don't we take a look at the team helping her make decisions on your behalf? All fae! Not one human."

I wanted to change that. It had always been at the top of adjustments I aspired to make. But I wanted the dust to settle after my ascension to the throne. I didn't want to displease the fae and cause a revolt right out of the gate. It was my mistake for not pushing it. And now I would take the brunt of that choice because no one knew about my good intentions.

It also didn't matter his intentions were less than honorable for humans; he just had to declare mine.

"There are a lot of you still in favor of the old King and Queen. You're scared. I understand that." He again brought his hands to his chest, as if he could sympathize.

"Seriously? Is anyone believing this crap?" Lexie threw up her arms, looking around the room.

"Unfortunately, it looks like a lot are, little shark." Croygen stood so close to her their arms brushed together.

"I hate being the messenger of bad news, but Lars is dead. My dear, kind nephew. We shall miss him," Stavros went on.

"Fuckin' bastard," Fionna growled behind me. "He's not dead, wanker. And he will come back and kick your bloody ass."

"I hope I cannot only be as good as him, but better. For all of you. Get us off this destructive downhill course and set it right." His voice rose along with one arm. "Who is with me? Who will fight for what is right, push against an insolent spoiled child, and take back our position in this world. We need to remove the Queen, by *any* means. Let's rip her off the throne she should never have had."

Holy fuck. Did he just subtly tell them to kill me?

Roars thundered over the mass like a rock concert. Every cheer or clap was a knife stab into my gut. Bending over, I groaned, feeling each pierce.

"Turn it off!" Lorcan touched my back, yelling at Torin. "Now!"

Air strained to get through my airwaves, burning up my nose, searing my eyes.

"Shit." Lorcan rubbed at my back, running his hand up my neck to my tattoo. "Breathe, li'l bird."

No stranger to panic attacks, especially during the last two years, I knew what was happening. But having Lorcan beside me, hearing his voice, felt like stepping into a warm bath.

Don't let them see you this way, Ken. Stand up. They are all scared, too, maybe even thinking, deep down, you can't handle this either.

My spine went board-straight, as I stood to my full height. I felt Lorcan's hand fall away.

"Torin, double the guards around our borders. There will be no days off for anyone. We need every guard we can muster on duty around the clock." If not Stavros himself, it would be his fanatics who would try to get in, probably dreaming of being the one who took down the appalling Druid Queen.

Torin was already scrambling from the room yelling into his walkie-talkie before I even finished.

I turned to the room. "Rez, I need you to contact all the sirens now. Lily, I want you to do the same for your skulk. Fionna, get word to the DRL, whomever is left to fight. Don't use phones or anything that can get tapped until we get our system locked down. Garrett, how long before you can get our servers protected?"

"I have to look." Garrett stepped closer.

"Castien will take you to our computer room. While you are safeguarding our system, see if Stavros is communicating with anyone. Can you hack into the camera system in the compound?"

Garrett flicked his eyes in annoyance. "I fuckin' hope so. I created it."

"Good. Go." My voice sounded like someone else. The Queen had stepped in and she wanted things done now. "Dwellers, you will rotate shifts patrolling the outer forest. If anyone is coming near, I want to know it way before they do."

Cole and Lorcan both nodded. "I won't ask for your permission to kill if that moment comes." Lorcan's green eyes met mine with the same determination as mine.

"Do what you need to." I knew it must be so, but my gut twisted at the coldness in my own voice. This wasn't me. But I could no longer be the kind, sympathetic Queen. I was getting stomped on, crushed into the dirt with a twist of Stavros's claims.

I needed to become the same as Lars. Think like him, act like him. Without him, I realized how much I had leaned on him and felt comfort in knowing he was there that nothing bad could happen because he would come to fix it.

Now Lars needed me to be ruthless in protecting this kingdom.

I am trying, Lars.

Don't try, Ms. Johnson. Just do it. I could hear his voice in my head.

"What can I do?" Annabeth moved past Ryker and Croygen.

"Uh."

"Please, Majesty. I may not be a fighter, but I can't sit. I will go crazy thinking about Wyatt and Zoey."

"Me too! But I wouldn't mind a sword." Lexie held up her hand, stepping next to Annabeth.

A snort came from across the room. Cooper covered his mouth.

"Oh no you didn't." Lexie swung to the blond dweller, but Croygen jumped in, putting his arms around her and pulling her into his body.

"You can come with me, li'l shark. I need to get my ship ready and recruit a few more *tradesmen* down by the docks."

"Tradesmen, my ass." She rolled her eyes, but let herself fall into him, calming instantly.

Annabeth still stared at Cooper. She wasn't glaring, but he shifted uncomfortably beneath the intensity of her gaze. His head jerked around as though he was fighting something before he looked at the ground, his head bowing.

It took me a moment to realize the severity of that minuscule moment. My eyes widened, going straight to Lorcan. *Did I just see Cooper submit?* I tried to hide my shock.

Yep. Lorcan rolled his lips together to stop the grin forming on his face. *He'll be on his back soon, waiting for a belly rub... Speaking of rub...*

I turned around before he could finish, hearing a snort of laughter from him.

"Annabeth." I pulled her focus from Cooper. "You can get refreshments to the soldiers on duty."

"Thank you, my Queen." She dipped her head, looking relieved to have a task. In the face of terrible anxiety, nobody wanted to be idle.

"I'll show you to the kitchen. Was going to grab something to eat on the way out." Cooper jerked his head for her to follow.

"Sure you were, brother." Gabby leaned against the wall, smirking at him when he walked past. He punched her arm, knocking her into Alki. "Asswad!" she yelled at his back. He responded by flipping her off.

"Wait!" Sprig yelled at Annabeth, rising. "You're going to the kitchen? I mean... since you're heading that way and everything."

Annabeth grabbed Sprig from Ryker's shoulder and turned to follow Cooper.

"Do you think they'll have the whipped honey I love so much? What about honey-glazed muffins? Diggle berries, I'll settle for those corn nuts... but of course dipped in honey. Oh, do you think they'd make me fries?"

"Hold up, monkey boy. I'm coming!" Cal flew after them. "Think we need to start testing this honey/juniper concoction. Might need a lot of sampling to get it right."

"Yeah. Lots and lots of sampling." Sprig nodded eagerly at the pixie. "I really should get Pam. She's already pissed I left her behind. You'd like her. She's has an amazing sense of humor. But don't mention the work she's had done. She's still sensitive about that..." Sprig's voice carried down the hall before it disappeared.

"My lady?" Simmons spun to address Ember.

"Please, Simmons. Go. I think they are going to need a babysitter."

"I will do my best, my lady." Simmons saluted her.

"Yeah, because you're a stellar babysitter. Cal never gets drunk on your shift." Eli came up next to Em, slipping one finger into her belt loop.

"I am a pixie, Sir Eli, not a sorcerer."

Ember laughed, grinning at Eli. "It's true, no one has the power to stop that." She waved at Simmons. "Go, I can already sense the kitchen staff losing their minds."

He bowed, flying out of the room.

"Come with us." Eli tugged on her belt loop. "You know you're craving a run."

Her eyes glinted with yearning, her tongue slipping over her bottom lip. I had grown used to Lorcan "hunting" and sometimes tasting his kill, but Ember craved it in the same way a dweller did. She couldn't shift into one, but her senses, her lock on prey, were all dark dweller. She looked back at me guiltily.

"Go," I encouraged her. "I'm going to check on everything, contact the nobles, and take a shower."

"Okay." She stepped into me, her arms wrapping around me. "I'll be back in an hour."

Lorcan kissed me saying he'd meet me in the shower in forty-five minutes before he took off, and at last the room was empty. I took a deep breath, shutting my lids to drown out the fear inside me.

"I say screw the meeting and we get drunk." A voice came from the corner, making me jump. I twisted around to see Ryan. My best friend. My other soulmate.

Our friendship had been struggling a bit because of my time spent with Lorcan, but I hoped every day it would get better. Before he seemed to avoid being left in a room alone with me. He seemed to want Ember there to buffer the tension.

"You scared me."

"I know; we humans fade into the background after a while."

"The way you dress?" I teased softly, not sure how far I could push a joke with him.

"Are you saying my clothes are loud and obnoxious?" He gasped, patting his pink-pinstriped gray jacket rolled to his elbows and green designer jeans.

"Noooo." I shook my head, a grin tugging at my mouth. Ember and I loved to razz him about his clothes, but the boy dressed better than anyone in the castle. "I would never say obnoxious… offensive, maybe?"

"Ohhh! You did not say that." Ryan put a hand to his mouth. "You know those are fightin' words."

"What are you gonna do, pretty boy? Go change your outfit?"

He tried to look aghast before a guffaw went through his nose. "I've missed you, sweet one."

Tears burned through my eyes, forcing me to blink. "I've missed you more, salty one."

"Never," he whispered. "I felt as if I lost my soul."

My legs bolted forward, both of us crashing into each other with a laughing sob, my arms squeezing him, not wanting to ever let go. He was my home. My heart.

"Your mate is going to have to deal with the fact another man claims you as his soulmate," he whispered, choking out his words.

"He knew that before he even started anything with me. I don't work without you…"

"It might make the bedroom awkward."

I snorted loudly.

"I know you, Ken." He cupped the back of my head, keeping me tight in the embrace. "I can see the weight you are carrying. I can feel it, because when you hurt, I hurt."

I squeezed my lids tighter.

"I realized no argument in the world should stand between us, keeping me from being there and carrying the burden with you." He leaned back, searching my face. "Plus, I really have nothing better to do than look fabulous at your side."

Even with the horrors we were going to face, the dangers heading straight for us, I felt a tiny bit of relief. I stared back at Ryan, understanding it was only him who could do that, because some of my fear and sadness had been the loss of him. Of us.

"I love you." I gripped his hand.

"I love you too." He wiped his face, quickly brushing off any sentiment. "Now, if you want to take that love to the bedroom, I really must insist on two hot males joining us… Because I love you, but I don't want to kiss you. Again." He wrinkled his nose, shaking his head.

A laugh bubbled up my throat, lightening my heart and soul. Ryan was always able to ease my serious nature.

"Of course. Sure, Lorcan and Castien will be fine with that."

"Oh, did I say them? I meant *any* two hot-bodied males." He winked. "Preferably with exceptionally loose morals."

FOURTEEN
Ember

Twigs and foliage crunched under my boots as I ran through the forest, my senses tasting everything like a buffet. A few deer were close by and after what I had been through earlier and the loss of blood, my dweller craved food. Raw and bloody.

"This way," Eli muttered ahead of me. Deep aromas of musty dirt and decaying vegetation crowded my nose, but the smell of people and warm-blooded animals overpowered them, especially when they were scared. Terrified humans smelled somewhat sour, similar to sweat, and their hearts hammered in their chest, thumping in my ears like a drum.

My tongue slid across my bottom lip as I took a deeper whiff of the fear exploding through the forest. The majority of it came from the village right next to the trail where we ran. I could control it but couldn't deny the taste of terror excited my dark dweller side.

My legs pumped a steady rhythm trying to keep up with the boys. Eli and Lorcan treaded ahead of me, staying in their human shape. The rest shifted, prowling the other sections of the forest, circling the castle right outside the protected line.

"Look." Lorcan stopped, his finger pointing to the streets of the village. Dozens of citizens ran around, the atmosphere filled with fear and restless anxiety. Automobiles and horse-drawn wagons moved down the lanes, some already parked in front of houses, people loading their belongings with rushed movements.

"Crap." My shoulders sagged, feeling crestfallen for Kennedy, which stirred up anger with my need to protect and defend her. I wanted to fight these faithless asses. Did they not realize how much she had sacrificed for them? What she had done to keep them safe? To keep the kingdom standing? "What a bunch of fickle, disloyal, dickhead, bagnuts sacks!" I yelled toward the hamlet. Each second I watched another person fill a wagon with their possessions, getting ready to run, to either join Stavros or hide like cowards, my fury rose. My powers began to spark through the layer of dust still coating my skin.

"Easy, Brycin." Eli nudged me. "Setting the village on fire is not going to help."

"Why not?" I spit out. "They deserve nothing better than to be zapped in the ass with lightning. To suffer for their disloyalty."

"I'm all for watching that." Lorcan folded his arms. I had little doubt he felt how I did, probably more so. "Go for it, dae. Let's watch them squeal."

I was that angry; it only took a little push. I stomped forward, my teeth grinding.

"Whoa. I don't think so." Eli grabbed my shoulder, pulling me back as he looked between his brother and me. "Shit, how am I the reasonable one here?"

"Scary times are upon us," Lorcan replied evenly, his focus on a few fleeing into the forest, running on foot with only the bags on their backs.

A baby wailed. Its mother and father led their brood into a car and peeled away, abandoning their cottage. My nose told me they were human.

Lars kept his compound small, so everyone had a blood link to the shield protecting it. We could go in and out without worry. Kennedy did not have that luxury. There were far too many people inhabiting the village around the castle. She could only erect a general protection from outside threats. There wasn't anything to protect against inside threats.

"I don't understand how they can so easily be swayed by Stavros. Especially the humans." I tossed up my arms. "Do they really believe what he said? Didn't they notice he singled out Kennedy for not having their ideals in mind, but he never said he did? He will be worse than Aneira. And does the average fae, who can do anything for him, truly think he will care what they want?"

"I've learned the power of words actually is stronger than actions." Lorcan glanced over at me. I knew exactly what he was talking about. Because of Kennedy, we learned the truth about Lorcan, what he sacrificed for Eli, why he'd done the things he did. But I could never forget the day he tried to kidnap me. His threats had chilled my soul. Now I knew he never planned to go through with most of them, but at the time, his words had terrified me. "And sadly, a lot of people want to be controlled. It means they feel they aren't responsible for their own lives. All that happens is someone else's fault."

Still, it was hard for me to see how anyone could look at Stavros and think he was the better choice. With fae I knew Kennedy being a woman didn't really come into play, but with humans, sexism was still alive and strong. They would walk headlong into their own demise because they'd rather have a man leading them than a woman.

At least there were a lot of villagers staying, yelling at those leaving, standing up for their Queen.

Guys. We have a problem, Cole's voice boomed into my head through the link, jarring both Eli and me out of our thoughts. Lorcan cocked his head to the side, as though he were trying to listen to a faraway noise.

What? Eli responded.

A large group of fae in the north part of the forest are headed for the castle. Looks like a renegade party, Cole declared.

There's also another group coming from the east, Cooper stated.

The three of us shot off, the boys shifting into their dweller beasts, their clothes shredding into scraps, which they left along the forest floor like breadcrumbs. Trying to keep up, my body flew through the woods, bounding off rocks, and scrambling over fallen trees. Roars in the distance signaled the location of both attacks, but we were closer to the east side.

Dax. Dom. Head to Cole. I'm heading to Cooper. Lorcan's voice was vastly distant compared to Cole's. Separating from our clan, Lorcan was alpha of Dax and Dom, having lost Samantha in the war. We could all still link, but theirs was close to a radio call from a remote island.

The boys found Cooper and Gabby and jumped into the fight. A hunting party, more than two dozen fae—some human-looking, some animal shifters, and a few trolls—pounced on the dark dwellers, slashing with axes, swords, and spiked clubs. Dark dwellers were killers, their claws, teeth, and spiked backs slicing through their prey with poison, but there were a lot of attackers.

Cursing that I hadn't showered off the goblin metal, I tugged out my sword, swiping at a figure leaping for me.

The creature's arm transformed into a cheetah's paw, sharp claws swiping at my face. I dropped to the ground, rolling out of the reach, and pulled the knife Eli gave me for my birthday and sliced at his legs.

"You bitch," he bellowed, stumbling back.

"You come to kill the Queen, to hurt my friend… and I'm the bitch here?"

"She is not Queen. She is a Druid. She should have been slaughtered, and her bones scattered the same as the rest of her brethren. As you should be, *dae*." He spit out the term in utter disgust.

Daes didn't have any better reputation than Druids. Thanks to Aneira, almost all my kind had been extinguished along with the Druids.

Rage discharged from my pores like steam, and my vision locked on my prey. I knew my pupils had elongated and gone black.

Kill. Kill. Kill. Spotted kitty cat was going to die.

With a cry, I leaped for him, my teeth snapping for his neck, both of us smacking to the ground. Underneath me, he shifted into full cheetah, hissing and digging his claws into my arms.

When I was like this, I didn't feel pain—too much adrenaline pumping out the need to kill. Once a dark dweller locked on its prey, it was nearly impossible to get their attention off a target.

Deep scratches tunneled through my clothes into my skin, the sensation of warm liquid rolling down my arms. The cheetah's teeth went for my neck.

I bit down first, going straight for the carotid artery in its neck. The cat screeched, howling into the air, its body wiggling violently underneath me. His front and back legs dug into me, trying to push me away. My mouth only locked down firmer; the taste of blood cloaked my tongue in a tangy warmth.

My sword and knife stabbed its arms into the dirt, pinning them back from clawing at me, but I continued to saw my teeth into his neck, my dweller wanting this kill.

Anger over our situation with the stone and Stavros filled me. I thought of the people being held as leverage. The loss of Lars and Zoey. The attack on Kennedy, who only wanted the best for her people. The shifter took all my rage.

Brycin. I heard Eli's voice in my head, but I ignored it, feeling the dying kicks of the cheetah. *He's dead, Ember. Let go.*

A touch brushed my back and a snarl vibrated through my throat. *Mine. My kill.*

"Brycin. Back off," Eli growled back. An order. He might not be second anymore, but he was still an alpha, and I would always be the bottom of the pack. "Now."

My sharp tunnel vision broke, and I pulled away from the man, blood dripping from my mouth. The first time, I gagged after tearing into a throat, though it was a disgusting strighoul. That sensation had passed long ago.

Now I was as much a killer as any dweller. This was who I was. And I liked it. The power, the taste.

The rush intensified all your senses, which was why dark dwellers craved sex after a kill.

My gaze roved to where he stood over me, naked, his green eyes glinting with desire.

"Shit. Remind me not to get in her way." Lorcan stared at me with awe a few yards behind Eli, also naked, but that was normal. Bodies of the hunting party were strewn across the ground in bits. "I don't think I've ever seen her in full dweller mode. Impressive."

"Yeah. She's a force." Eli reached down, helping me to my feet. The cheetah's head fell to the side, the hole in his neck still spouting blood. I wiped my chin with my sleeve. Now I felt the throbbing pain from the scratches the shifter left on my arms, and the older wound Stavros left on my neck as a display of how far he'd go. He was unpredictable, which made him truly frightening.

Cooper and Gabby plucked weapons and anything else important off the bodies before dragging them into a pile to burn. They would be used as a warning to others.

"Cole?" I continued to rub my mouth.

"They're starting their own bonfire over there." Gabby flopped another torso down on the growing mound. Long ago, I had lost all disgust and shock of this kind of scene. The day I met Eli my human world, my reality of right and wrong, slowly changed.

"Do we tell Kennedy?" I leaned into Eli, the exhaustion of the day catching up with me. "I don't want to lie to her, but there is only so much one person can take."

Lorcan heaved out a sigh, pinching the bridge of his nose. "I don't know. Honestly, I want to keep this from her. She has so much going on. And she's holding it all on her shoulders. This might be the thing that makes her snap, but..."

I nodded. Kennedy was strong, but there were some things no one person should have to bear.

"I agree, we don't tell her," Eli said firmly. "It's already done and taken care of. We'll just let Torin know to be extra vigilant. We don't need her focusing on something she can't control anyway."

Lorcan and I hemmed and hawed.

"Fuck, brother. You think you have a hellion? Kennedy may appear sweet and quiet, but have you seen her pissed?"

"I have." I lifted my hand. "Not pretty."

"Exactly. And if she learns I'm keeping something from her..." He appeared to be weighing his options. "But you're right. I know her. This will keep her awake all night. She already can't sleep." Lorcan let his head fall back, his hands on his hips. "We're doing this for her sanity. She doesn't need to know that on top of everything else she's being actively hunted."

"Yeah." I rubbed my hand over my hair, turning my gaze to the ground. I was used to seeing the guys and Gabby naked, but even I had my limit. It was a human trait which would probably always be there.

"We should head back soon." I leaned more heavily on Eli, wanting to sleep.

"We'll stay." Cooper walked over, letting Gabby light the pyre. "Do a few more runs around. See if there are any more coming. Gabby can check the forest, and I can scope the area close to the wall."

"Thanks, man." Eli bowed his head to the second.

"Hmmm. I wonder why you want to do the wall area of the castle and not the forest?" Gabby snorted, folding her arms over her bare chest. "Because I'm sure there is more danger there with all the guards around..." She snapped her fingers. "Oh right, they have snacks there. Being served by a tiny blue-eyed blonde."

"Shut up." Cooper lifted his lip at his sister. "As if you don't want an excuse to go find your demon-fighter."

"Where is Alki?" I scanned around, realizing he wasn't there.

"He's with Goran on the south rim." She frowned. "What the hell is up with Goran anyway? He gives me the creeps now. Something is not right with him."

I couldn't disagree. He moved the same as an automaton, and his speech was void of emotion. Even the disgruntled, uptight guy I knew had something of a personality. Now there was nothing.

"Hey?" Eli whispered into my ear, and I peered at him. "Race you to the showers?" Before I could even respond, he took off running toward the castle.

"Damn you, Dragen!" I yelled, running after him, his laughter trailing back to me.

He beat me to the shower by only ten seconds, but he gloated his win. He walked me backward into the shower. "You know what I want for winning?"

"What?" The spray of water trailed down my body.

He picked me up, and I wrapped my legs around him.

"You." His mouth brushed mine with a smirk. "And a jar of peanut butter. Together."

"Damn. You know just what to say, Dragen, to make me hot." I nipped at his lip. I considered peanut butter its own food group. It was one of my favorite things, besides him. Many times we combined the pairing. "Too bad we don't have any here."

"Guess you'll have to bring the rest of my prize to me later. Naked."

"If I don't eat it all first," I teased.

"You know the rules, Brycin. *Never* mess with a man's peanut butter," he growled.

It was really me who won in the end as he shoved me back into the wall of the shower, entering me with fervor, pounding the thrill of the hunt into me. Already humming with peaked adrenaline, it didn't take long for us to find our first release, but Eli didn't stop. Not after the second or third either. Sometimes it took us all night to calm down, taking our excess energy out on each other.

It looked like this was one of those times.

The door to our bathroom rattled. "Why is it always me who has to get you two out of shower?" Gabby's annoyance slithered through the door.

"Go away," Eli growled, his mouth running down my neck, nipping at my skin. "I thought you were patrolling anyway?"

"That was an hour ago."

What? My head went back onto the tile, looking into Eli's eyes. Had an hour really passed? To confirm Gabby's claim, my skin felt the icy water running over us. When did the hot water run out?

"What the fuck do you want?" Eli's movements slowed, but he continued to rock into me, hitting me so deep, my nails dug into his arms.

"To present you both with parents-of-the-year award, of course," she said dryly. "Really, your parenting is stellar. Your kids are drunk and running amuck, scaring the kitchen staff."

"They're pixies!" Eli's head fell into my neck, halting his movements. "What can they possibly get into that you can't handle?"

"Those two?" I dropped my legs, touching back to the shower floor. "Everything. Okay, really, one of them can get into enough trouble for a dozen pixies."

"We can put them up for adoption. It's not too late." Eli stepped back with a sigh.

"They'll follow us. You know we can never get away," I whispered glancing around with feigned nervousness, as though they could hear me.

"Maybe you can't, but I could make a run for it."

"You'd leave me by myself with them?"

"To be free of them? In a fuckin' heartbeat, woman." The side of his mouth hitched up and his hands pushed me back into the wall, his mouth finding mine. Neither Eli nor the pixies would ever admit it, but they loved each other. We were family. Warped as it was.

"Oh, for fuck sake!" Gabby hit the door again. "Seriously, you need to get to the kitchen." Gabby's footsteps dwindled away from the door.

"We finish this later, Brycin," he growled in my ear. "I am nowhere near done with you."

It took everything I had to leave the bathroom, get dressed, and head down the hall, already fearful of what I would find.

"Holy shit." I stopped at the entrance, taking in the destroyed room. Eli stopped at my side as well. White flour, honey, juniper berries, and bits of pastries covered the walls, ceiling, and tables. The matter spilled onto the floor and dripped off the ceiling in globs. It looked as though a science experiment exploded in the room.

A handful of the kitchen staff, armed with brooms and mops, waved them in the air or at the tables, yelling. Others filed in to watch the spectacle.

"My lady! My lady!" Simmons darted from his hiding place in the timber, zooming for me. "I tried! I told Cal it wasn't a good idea."

"What the hell happened?" I caught Simmons as he tried to land on my shoulder, slipping off the other side.

"All idiots." A squawk came from the window where Grimmel, the raven, sat. "Stupidity lives."

"The raven is not entirely wrong, my lady..." Simmons didn't have time to finish his thought before I saw a furry body zip across the table, a hand towel wrapped around his neck. "Ahhhhhh! Honey Hero!" He jumped from a table to a shelf, missing a swiping broom by inches. "Super Sprig! Honey! Honey! Honey! Ahhhhhh!" He jumped for a pendant light, swinging on the lamp. "Wheeeeee!" The towel flew behind him as he rode on it like a swing set.

"It's a pixie." Sprig pointed at the lamp next to him, giggling. "It's a bird. No, it's dah-dah-dah… supersprite!"

"Let ya wee bits freeeee, suuuper spit," Cal called from another pendant light, his naked bum pressed into the translucent lampshade, his arms and legs spread open.

"Dingle my berries, they're free." Sprig cheered, swinging the lamp higher. "I don't feel them. But they're free."

"Gooood on yer!" Cal cheered.

"What the fuck?" Ryker came up beside Eli and me, gazing at the state of the room.

"Viking! Viking! Viking! My weee bits are free!" Sprig leaped to the table, stumbling and tripping over the towel. "Super-Sprig-duper!" He hiccupped, falling over.

"Are you drunk?" Ryker's eyebrows went up.

"Juniper nuts dingle."

Ryker coughed out a laugh, the first hint of a smile I'd ever seen on his face. "Holy shit, you're lagered."

"Sorry, it looks as if my kid has been a bad influence on yours." I winked at the large man.

"Nah." He shook his head. "We have Croygen for that."

"I liikee ya, monnkey mann." Cal slurred from above, his arm going up in the air. "Youz cann hang wit me aaannytimme. Simmons iz no fuunn."

"Hey!" Simmons put his hands on his hips, stamping his foot into my shoulder. "I'm fun!"

"Pfffftttttttt!" Cal snorted.

"Warrior's nectar sweet we are." Sprig fisted the air before he went face-first onto the table, snoring.

Some of the staff started clapping and cheering, as though this had been a play. Most of the women and men working in the kitchen smiled, but Bess, the lead chef, turned her severe temper on me.

"You!" She pointed a ladle at me. "I told you what I'd do the next time that pixie made a mess of my kitchen."

"You know when I said I'd abandon you in a heartbeat?" Eli muttered next to me, backing away.

"Don't you dare," I growled at him.

"It's been a nice ride, Brycin. Maybe our paths will cross again someday." He took another step back as Bess barreled toward me.

"Coward!" I yelled as he slipped into the shadows with a smirk. Bess was scary; she was as wide as she was tall, with a sour face and stern expression. She whacked the ladle against her palm, as though I were some child about to be paddled for bad behavior.

"You got this, right?" Ryker moved back.

My hand clamped down on his. "No you don't. I'm not facing the gargoyle by myself."

"Damn, that was exactly what I was thinking she looked like." He chuckled.

"You two!" She pointed at the mess and the two snoring troublemakers. "You get my kitchen sparkling clean, or I'm roasting you on the pit for dinner."

"They have all the fun, and we get the punishment," I grumbled, taking the mop she shoved at me.

"Fire should know better." Grimmel tilted his head from the open window. "Surrounded by imbeciles."

I flicked the mop at him, and he flew into the air. "You'd be good on that roasted pit as well, turkey."

He squawked at my insult, flying into the room, and pooped all over the table before gliding out with what sounded like a guffaw. The cook shrieked at the fresh mess splattered over the fruit bowl.

"Could you stop pissing everyone off?" Ryker grabbed a bucket with a sigh. "Plus, that's really my job."

"Great. You and I are never getting out of detention then."

Another slight smile hinted on his mouth. For a second I could see the man underneath, the one Zoey fell in love with. In many ways he wasn't much different from a dweller. He showed his family his real self, but no one else.

I wasn't sure if it was a good premonition or a bad one, but I sensed by the end of this journey we'd either become family or mortal enemies.

FIFTEEN
Zoey

Firelight flickered off the walls and ceiling of the cave. Elongated and shadowy figures moved around or worked by the fire, constructing weapons. A mass of weapons. Far more than the amount of people here.

I pulled my legs to my chest, my backbone grinding into the stone. I tried to make myself as invisible as possible. Disappear into the corner of the cave.

Was it day or night? I didn't know. Nor did I know how much time had passed since the stone brought me here. A couple of days, maybe? Enough time for me to figure out a few things.

I'd learned the stone didn't have endless energy, and it occasionally needed to rest, replenish its grip on us. Controlling both me and Lars took a toll, and it would release its hold on me for brief spells, let my consciousness surface. Sometimes I was semi-aware of what I had done and sometimes my memory was blank, as though the stone wanted to keep its plans a secret from me.

In brief moments, I would see the real Lars, his chartreuse eyes staring at me, as if he wanted to tell me something. Then the stone would shove him back again, silencing him, those empty black pits filling his pupils. Lars was strong and did not like being out of control. The man I knew would be constantly trying to find a way, a weakness in the stone.

Grunts sounded across the area as figures sharpened and welded weapons. The leader of them, the half-strighoul, half-seer called Zeke, walked around, overseeing their work. My "son."

Even when I had seen them as children at DMG, I understood they should not exist. I had felt nothing for them. But watching them during the last couple days, a slice of doubt shivered down my throat. Zeke was the most unsettling. With his mouth closed, all I could see were my green eyes, brown hair, and heart-shaped face. Even some of his mannerisms were similar to mine. The way he adjusted and moved his body, constantly watching and ready for anything to come at him, was exactly like me.

It was more disturbing to see Sera's annoyed expression flitter over a few of the dark-haired creatures' faces. It frightened me that I was starting to feel sympathy for them. What Rapava did to them was not their fault any more than what he did to me was mine. I could have easily been one of them.

My eyes caught on one facing away from me, his long brown hair tied in a braid hanging down his bare back. He bent over, sharpening a scythe with long precise strokes. His spine protruded from his back, gray scales covering his torso. His arms and legs were so big he waddled when he moved, but his clawed feet and hands suggested that when he really needed to move, he went down on all fours like a Komodo dragon.

Feeling my gaze, he peered at me over his shoulder, his green irises piercing mine. With a snarl, he snapped back to his weapon.

They may have bowed to me, but I sensed they would rather kill me. Serious mother issues here. And Sera's group had no allegiance to me. Their "mother" was dead, and I was a poor substitute.

The stone kept them in line, but I wondered how long before they either ignored its order or the stone let them tear me apart.

"Faster," Zeke growled through his needled teeth, his pitchy, nasally voice reminding me what he was: a Frankenstein monster.

What did they need all these weapons for?

"I feel your curiosity." A deep voice emerged from the darkness beside me, flames reflecting off the demon's black eyes.

I jolted and rose to my feet as the stone strolled closer to me, feeling it slither around inside me. It never fully let me go, keeping my ability to jump just on the shelf above my head.

"Why so many weapons?" Lars's boots hit mine. At first it was difficult to not see the King, to not associate the demon as the thing standing before me. This thing was not Lars.

Lars held himself with an elegant arrogance, with the confidence of a king. The stone didn't understand how to be in a physical form. It was awkward and jerky in its movements, only playing the part of a man.

"Did the Dr. Rapava ever tell you how truly special these creatures are?" When I didn't respond, it continued. "I am not even sure he realized what he created. They are unique and by far superior in strength, magic, and even intelligence to their blood relations."

I counted about twenty of them.

"Do not let their number fool you," the stone replied to my thought. "One of them can kill dozens of fae, humans, and even dwellers." It poked its chin at the one I had been looking at. "You are right about that one. A Komodo dragon. And precisely like its ancestor, with one bite, one lick of its tongue, poison lodges into its victim, paralyzing them immediately. The death is extremely painful."

I would remember not to get within licking distance of him.

"I've been planning this for a while, Zoey. Do you think I would not try to expand my army?" A crooked, eerie smile twisted its lips. "I did my own experiments, finding them exceptionally fertile... and you know how fast they mature. Too bad I couldn't recreate the procedure like the doctor, but I worked with what I had. Even slightly watered down by human and fae women, they are still by far superior."

Bile rolled in my stomach, forcing me swallow. "What are you talking about?"

"Let me show you." The stone turned with an unnatural jerk and strode away. My body moved without my say. A dog on a leash. I trotted after the tall figure down a passage of the cave I didn't even know was there.

My time "awake" had been limited to the main room, waking up on the ground or in the middle of an activity before the stone would sense me fighting for dominance, and clamp down, harnessing me.

Fight. Suddenly I heard Ryker's yell at me in my head. *Fight, human.*

I was trying, but every time I did, it sucked a little more life from me. I had watched it do the same to Rapava, until there remained nothing left but the dust of his bones. The stone would make sure my death was even more painful. Now with each step, I felt like I was walking to my death, my stomach coiling with terror.

Torches lit the way along the long corridor, and I realized this part was man made. A military bunker. We walked for more than ten minutes when I heard distant cries and wails.

Women.

I shoved energy to my legs, digging my heels into the ground, my body pulled in two directions: the power of the stone and the needs of the women.

"You are only tiring yourself out, Zoey. Every time you fight me, you are only hurting yourself. Draining your own life."

"What is down there?" My instincts knew, but sadly I still hoped I was wrong and that once again my nightmare wasn't crawling up from the pits of blackness and wrapping around me.

You know, his voice came into my head.

"No." My voice cracked. "Please…" I didn't even know why I said "please." I felt if I stopped now, I wouldn't have to deal with what I knew was down there. It wasn't like me to act on fear, but how could I fight this?

"You can't, Zoey." The stone tugged on my brain, forcing me back into the passenger seat as it compelled me to walk down the hall.

We passed a room and sounds registered into my head, but I spit them back out, not wanting to put images to those noises. Groans of women echoed through the door.

"Not all are against this. Some volunteered and even enjoy this immensely." The stone nodded toward the closed door.

If it was possible to throw up internally, I did. My limbs held steady, but I trembled inside, or rather, so did the little girl inside me who fought so many devils. She huddled in the corner, begging not to be pulled back into the dark. I had fought so hard to heal her, to let her know peace. While Annabeth was dealing with what happened, I had to relive it. Not simply accept it, but really let myself heal and forgive. We leaned on each other through that time.

Now, that nearly closed wound was being ripped open.

"You're raping women to build an army?" I seethed.

"Do those women sound as if they are being forced?" The stone stopped in front of another door, twisting the knob.

"What about the ones who didn't volunteer, you vile piece of shit?"

"Do not upset me, Zoey. I can take so much more from you than merely your life." I ached for my son then, for Ryker. I couldn't do anything that would threaten their lives. He opened the door on a grocery-store-sized bunker room lined with beds. Hundreds of figures moved through the room, dressed in dirty rags, their bodies skin and bones, like victims of a refugee camp. All women. Human and fae. Some held babies, some were in various stages of pregnancy, a few chained to their metal cots. But most seemed docile, eyes glazed over.

Drugged.

Ohmygodsohmygodsohmygods. Breath hiccupped in my chest as I took in the room.

No. Fuck. No.

The stone had created its own sex trafficking/birthing ring to produce more of Sera's and my offspring. All of Rapava's creations had been male. Of course, he had only thought about men for strength of war, not caring about breeding. He could do that in his facility. But the stone wanted an army of its own. The only way to do that was to have them reproduce.

"These children can't grow in time…" I trailed off, watching a young brunette sob as a baby with razor-sharp teeth, identical to Zeke, breastfed from her, blood soaking her top. With every ounce of control I could gather, I twisted my head away.

"When they reach a month old, they are put into a nursery. After six months they are mature enough to train. These different babies grow up faster than any mortal children—a month is the same as a year to their development."

It's been five years since I walked away from DMG, when I thought they all had died.

"Some did," he responded, reading my mind. "Not all those out there are first generation. Some are sons and daughters."

"But?"

"The genes they carry are dominant, especially over the humans or lower fae, which is why they will look more like you than other seers and their fathers."

This was a nightmare. *Please say I am asleep and all this a dream.*

"The humans don't usually live, but a few like that one," he nodded at the brunette, "are surprisingly strong. This is her third birth from Zeke."

Sensing the stone was talking about her, she looked up, meeting my gaze. Behind the veneer of the drugs, I saw the depths of her hell. I knew that look. The feeling of utter despair. Retreating so far inside yourself you wanted to let your brain break and feel nothing anymore.

A door slammed on the other side of the room, making my gaze jerk away from her. A bald, tall, willowy frame stepped in, his back to me, but I could see his clothes hung off him like a hanger.

"Medicine time, ladies." The man's voice was hollow and scratchy, but something about him corkscrewed into the base of my neck with familiarity.

The women reacted, getting up and shuffling over, their lips smacking. Their next high must be their only escape from this hell.

"My assistant here has helped make them extremely compliant. He's quite the expert in dens not unlike these and how to make individuals submissive. Over the years he has perfected a special magic-infused opium concoction, crushed into a little pill. Easy, clean, and just as addictive as heroin for both fae and human."

I heard every word, but my gaze was still locked on the man, mostly blocked by the flock of girls. My heart thumped against my ribs. The stone's mouth twitched, his eyes on me, watching my every move. He eased back, letting me step forward.

The man lifted his head, his navy-blue eyes finding mine.

With a hiss, my legs stumbled underneath, my feet backpedaling.

"No." I whispered. "No. It can't…"

An eerie smile crept across the man's mouth, hollowing his cheeks even more. He might have been a twisted shell of the man I had known, but I'd recognize those eyes and that evil smile anywhere.

"It's been a long time." He set down the tray, stepping from the throng of girls toward me. "Aren't you going to give your dear father-in-law a hug?"

Holy crap.

Vadik.

He was alive.

🐉 🐉 🐉

I struggled for air. The shock froze me in place.

Vadik. The demon who tricked Ryker's mother into marrying him. He abused both her and their son until she decided to free them from the demon by sacrificing her own life to veil her baby from Vadik.

It wasn't until centuries later that the rumors about Ryker having the Stone of Fáil drew Vadik after his long-lost son, using Amara as enticing bait. She fell for Ryker, but at the end, money and power ruled her more than love.

Lars gave Ryker the chance to kill Vadik, but instead, the Viking cursed him to live on the light side, thinking it would rip him apart in a slow, agonizing death.

Less than five years later, the wall between worlds fell. Vadik, not unscathed, had somehow survived. His blond hair and muscular build, once like his son's, were gone. Now his shoulder bones poked from this shirt, his frame hunched forward, his skin pale and scarred, and a few teeth were missing.

He would be a horror movie's version of Igor, acting as the mad scientist's assistant, but what they were doing here went way beyond any horror movie.

"I hear I have a grandson. What's his name? Wyatt? Little disappointed you didn't name him after me."

My muscles clinched around my spine, strangling my nerves. "Do not say his name. Don't even think his name," I growled.

"But I have gifts for the boy. You would deny a grandfather a chance to meet his only grandson?"

"I know your type of gifts. You get anywhere near him, I will rip you apart piece by piece."

"A mother with such rage issues." He lifted an eyebrow.

I lunged for him, getting farther than I thought I would, my fist colliding with the soft part of his neck. His eyes widened in shock, as though he hadn't expected me to be able to touch him. He leaned back, grappling for this throat, trying to breathe.

My gaze shot to the stone. Its head was down, its feet shifting, its body jerking like some internal battle was going on.

"Lars?" I whispered, ignoring Vadik hacking and gasping for air. *Lars, if you are in there, fight.*

His physique stilled, his head slowly rising up, black pits meeting mine. "Lars is dying. Soon he will have no strength left to fight me. I will miss his demon. What true power and darkness he once had."

Vadik took in a gulp of air, straightening, glaring at me. "That is too good for that bastard. I would love to string him up and peel his skin from his body, sprawling his internal organs on the ground... akin to how it felt when he banished me to the Light side. Then I will do the same *to you*, extra slow, while Ryker watches."

This time, my bones were held firmly in place, so I couldn't respond with my fist.

"Return to your duties," the stone ordered Vadik. "Some of the fae women need higher doses."

Vadik snarled but turned back, snatching the tray, and headed through the door he had entered.

Without a word, the stone strode out the doorway, ordering me to follow with a tug of my mind.

Rage bubbled inside, and it was hard to not want to drive a knife into the man in front of me. But this wasn't Lars, though I doubt any woman in this room saw anything but the King causing their suffering.

We traveled along the hallway again before he went through another door. The large room was set up the same as a training facility. The space crawled with these chimera children ranging from five to fifteen in age. Hundreds of them. There were a few older men in the room helping to train them with weapons and brutal Krav Maga-style combat.

The children looked all wrong: disproportioned bodies, needle teeth, spiked tails, and claws. All of them a product of their fathers. Similar to the original group, they weren't shape-shifters. Even in the fae world, they would be considered abominations and killed. If the creatures didn't kill you first.

A girl of around nine stood in a fighting ring, her brown hair tied back. Her forehead and nose protruded comparable to a wolf's, and her mouth was open in a snarl, her fangs dripping with her opponent's blood. A group surrounded them, cheering and bellowing. She twirled her long stick with an arrow at the end, dancing toward the black-haired boy. He was around the same age, with eyes and tongue like a snake, brown scales over his face and neck, carrying a pitchfork, the ends like knives.

She feinted to one side, and the boy fell for it. As she twirled, she swiped her stick around her, knocking him off his ass, then jumped on him, her mouth snapping down on his neck and thrashing her head. The boy screamed, a high-pitched, inhuman sound, blood gurgling from his mouth.

Holy shit. She was going to kill him.

"Survival of the fittest. It is the law of nature. Only humans have tried to bend that rule, keeping their sick, old, and weak alive on machines. It is not natural," the stone spoke into my ear while I watched the wolf-looking girl howl into the crowd.

The roar of noise, the kids cheering for another's death, resembled a version of *Lord of the Flies*. I hated that book. This was ten times more disgusting and vile.

Vomit burned in my stomach as the boy tried to dig his nails into her skin and push her away, but she only bit in deeper. He stopped struggling, his body going limp before she rose, her arms rising in the air in a show of victory.

"Stop. I can't watch this anymore."

"I forget how fragile you all are." He twisted himself toward me. "This is only nature, Zoey. A wolf killing a snake."

"They are still children."

"They might look the same as children, but I guarantee there is nothing 'human' in them. They've known nothing else but fight, kill, and train like monsters."

A girl of four or five brushed past us, her long brown hair pulled half off her pretty heart-shaped face, showing her freckles and green eyes. Even though I knew she was related to me, she reminded me of the little girl locked behind the glass at Stavros's. Piper, Fionna's little girl. The same age, build, and brown hair.

The stone turned its head, gaze glued on the little girl. Tension moved down its shoulders, rolling his long fingers into a ball. Emotion flashed in its eyes.

My head jerked up. Dark green eyes snapped to me. "Zo-ey…" He struggled to say my name.

"Lars." Holy hell. What could I do? How could I keep him here? "Lars… please fight. Stay with me." I grabbed for his hands, needing to touch him, have contact with the actual man.

"I—I am weak…" He spit out every word, his fingers clinging to mine, as though I were an anchor. "I am trying." Sweat beaded his brow. "It. Won't. Be. Long."

"No, the hell with that. You are a King. A demon. If we both keep fighting him…"

"You are much…" He grunted, a shiver running through his body. "Stronger… you… fight."

"No, Lars. I can't do this without you." I looked around at the horror show. This was so much more than I could handle, especially when I had limited access to my body.

"I apologize for my weakness," he huffed, taking a few jagged inhalations. "It can't ever truly have you." His grip crunched down on my hand. Hell. I was losing him; I could feel it. He yanked my hand, lifting my attention back to his eyes. His gaze burning into mine. "Hear me."

"What do you mean?" The stone was doing a pretty good job, and I didn't even think my punishment had started yet. He was merely playing with me right now.

"It. Can. Offer. You. Nothing." Lars sucked in, bending over in pain.

"No. Please, Lars… don't leave me." It was crazy; I was begging the King who had one time bent me to my knees, scared the piss out of me, to stay with me. But over the years, I came to respect and care for him. He was the reason I had my second Honey House and why Kate could keep doing research.

His hands dropped away from mine, the air in the room stilling.

"Lars?"

Suddenly, a battering ram of energy heaved from him, shoving me off my feet and slamming me to the ground with a painful crunch. I gasped for air, my tongue tasting something bitter and stale.

A robotic chuckle shook Lars's shoulder, his shoulders rolling back, his chin slowly rising.

Black pupils stared back at me. The stone was back, but something felt different. Crawling back on my elbows, I stared at the man.

160

"You should be scared, Zoey. What I just did to him... I will eventually do to you." It bared its teeth. "After I force you to watch yourself destroy all those you love."

"Wh-what did you do to him?"

"The old King is dead. I got bored of his moping presence." He took a step toward me, looming over me, then bent down and grasped my jaw painfully. "Squashed him like a bug. Do not try to fight me, too, or you will join him in hell." His grip tightened. "Let us get to work, slave."

He jerked my head back, standing to his full height.

"Long live *this* King."

SIXTEEN
Fionna

"Fionna," a voice bellowed into my head, the sound striking me like a chunk of ice. I bolted awake.

"Lars?" I sat up with a gasp, choking on dread.

Emptiness scooped out my belly, spreading over my torso like a disease. I grasped my breastbone, trying to find the hole. My throat tightening, panic rising through my shoulders.

"No. No." I stumbled out of bed, my knees buckling as I slid down to the rug. "Lars!" I screamed, suffering a tear in my soul where we were connected. I pushed against my chest trying to stop it.

"Nooooo!" I wailed, my heart understanding what was happening. Pain hacked a hole in my heart and dampened my head with perspiration, which drenched the back of my neck. My screams tore through the room.

"Fionna?" Kennedy's voice filtered in from outside. Then Lorcan crashed through my door, my sister right on his tail. "Fionna!" She ran to me, falling beside me. "What's wrong? What happened? I had a vision you were in pain. Calling me."

Buckling forward, a wail screeched from me as I wrapped my arms around myself, trying to protect the precious thing connecting us.

My bond to Lars.

I cried out his name over and over. Kennedy curled herself over me, rocking with me. Lars was dying, I could feel him slipping away, peeling away from my soul, leaving me empty. The agony cleaved through me, and the fissure of my soulmate being taken from me nicked the air from my lungs, stealing my breath.

I couldn't move. Breathe. Think.

I love you, Druid... I felt his words as a sensation against my soul.

162

A goodbye.

No. Please. Don't leave me, you bastard, I yowled, not sure if I said this out loud. Nothing felt real or right. *Don't you fuckin' dare, demon. I will hunt you down myself and kill you.*

It was as if I could feel him smile. Then everything went numb.

"Nooooooooooo... Lars!" I screamed, tears rolling down my face, and my fist crashed against the floor. I was vaguely aware there were more people in my room, but I could see nothing beyond the hollow pit in my gut as pain clouded my vision.

"What? What about Lars?" Ember's voice was full of panic and fear.

I stared at the rug, my eyes trailing the elegant diamond print, my chest heaving. No one spoke or moved, but I could feel each of their stares drilling into my head, as though they could split it open and take out the answer. In that moment I would have gratefully let them, anything to end the pain. I was drowning in the emptiness, and sorrow gripped my legs and pulled me down underneath, where it would consume me.

Piper. She was the only reason I took another breath, forced my body to rise from the floor. A handful of people were stuffed around the entrance, but it was Ember I locked onto. Fear and grief danced in her irises like fire, as if she simply needed me to say the words. Confirm what she already knew.

But the words would not form on my tongue. My eyes watered. I turned my head, staring at the moonlight glistening off the lake. Misery silenced my thoughts and voice.

"No," she snapped, her voice cracking. "Nooooo!" Eli grabbed her, her body fighting against his hold.

Kennedy's mouth parted. "Lars?" She shook her head in disbelief.

It seemed impossible that the invincible, indestructible High Demon King was dead. Lars, the man, was ruthless and cruel, but you found yourself admiring and loving him in spite of it. The man who taught me unconditional love that no prejudice or hate could transcend. Our time together so brief, but so deep and true, nothing would ever come close to it.

"Let me go!" Ember wiggled against Eli, her words heavy with anguish. He pulled her to his chest until her fight turned into sobs, her body collapsing against his.

"Fi." Kennedy cupped my face, twisting me back to look at her, her voice soft. "You're sure? He's gone?"

My lips bunched together, swallowing back the blockade in my throat, the river of anguish ready to flood out and submerge the room.

I nodded, my tears dripping onto her hands. Her mouth wobbled, liquid slipping down her face. She pulled me into her and held me tightly.

My body automatically stiffened.

Olwyn never let me show grief. She didn't hug me or coddle when I came home with a black eye or broken heart. She would tap my chin and tell me to turn the hurt and despair into action.

Don't cry, girl. Tears are useless. Use their strength here instead. She'd pat my temple.

Looking back, I could see she was trying to make me tough, knowing my destiny would never be an easy one. My fight would bring constant loss and devastation. As the DLR leader, Olwyn's discipline helped me survive, to do what I needed to do. But none of that prepared me for this. My body curled into Kennedy, wanting to shut down. To disappear.

Piper. You have to keep going for Piper. Lars's voice hummed in my head, like he was still there, pushing me to go on.

Pulling away, I got to my feet. Eli had Ember pinned to his chest, his arms engulfing her as he rubbed his hand soothingly over her hair. Lorcan crouched next to Ken, holding her. Cole, Olivia, West, and Rez filled the rest of the room, all of their faces reflecting mine: Grief. Shock.

Rez's watery brown eyes found mine, a strange understanding linking the old and new lovers of the King. She didn't hesitate to yank me into a hug. I didn't fight it. Most in this room could sympathize with losing a "mate," but Rez, having shared that intimacy with Lars, made me feel she could uniquely understand my grief. Even as an ex-lover, she didn't push me away, but brought me closer to her. I felt our shared understanding in our hug of the man we'd lost.

Eventually, I stepped back from the siren, peering at Kennedy. "Lars would not want us to wallow. He'd want us to fight. The way we can best honor Lars is to kill Stavros, get our loved ones back, then destroy the stone until it is dust. It will not take Zoey too."

Kennedy rose to her feet, setting her head high. "I agree."

"I'll get coffee." Olivia tugged at the thigh-length T-shirt she wore to bed. Cole glanced over at her, his eyes skimming her legs.

"I'll help."

"I don't need help, dweller. I'm perfectly capable of getting coffee."

"I'm sure you are capable of a lot more than that," he said, scouring his head before he pushed off the wall, heading out without another word. Olivia stared after him for a moment, scowling, then shook her head and followed him.

"I need to check in with Garrett, see if the messages have been received." Kennedy fiddled with the hem of her *Stargate Atlantis* shirt, her teeth digging into her bottom lip. Everyone stepped for the door, following her lead.

On autopilot, my emotions dead inside, I reached for a pair of leggings off a chair. I was alive but dead at the same time. Cold. Empty.

My fingers wrapped around the cloth, and I felt something flutter inside my stomach.

As if a dozen daggers were thrust into my gut, digging to the hilt, pain rocked through my body, arching my back. My mouth parted, but only a gurgle escaped as my shoulder hit the floor with an echoing thud.

"Fionna!" Kennedy screamed. I sensed figures moving around, talking, touching me, but the pain cut off all my senses, my system responding to the unbearable agony.

The claws dug in deeper, as though they were trying to hold on for dear life.

Druid... A brush of the word stroked against my soul.

Holy shite.

Lars? Everything in me reached out for him. I felt him pull himself deeper into me, latching on to my soul. The pain transformed into something else, as his soul buried itself in mine, curling up. Seeking safety. Mine leaped and rubbed all over his like a cat welcoming him home.

"Fuucckk." I rolled onto my back, my nails digging into the floor, my limbs shaking, my teeth digging into my bottom lip. Since Lars and I had "bonded," I'd always felt a link to him, a piece of him connected to me, but nothing similar to this. The intensity of completely carrying it, not having him buffer it, ripped away my vision. The brutal attack on my senses hit excruciating levels. For a moment I couldn't see, hear, or smell, but once I could, the pain became pleasure. It reminded me of the time we performed the blood ritual. The exquisite throbbing was too much. I heard the moan come out of my mouth.

"Fionna, what's wrong?" Kennedy's hands touched my arms, zapping an electric jolt through my arms.

"Don't. Touch," I gritted out, sweat trailing down my temple.

Struggling, I tried to take a slow breath to ease the intensity. *Relax*, I demanded my body. *Breathe in. Breathe out.* Over and over my chest moved methodically, easing the tension in my muscles. Slowly the pain eased, my soul winding protectively around Lars. *Mine*, it purred.

My lids opened, my vision hazy, but gradually I could make out faces hovering over me. Brows furrowed, concern crinkling the corners of their eyes.

"Fi?" Kennedy hesitated to touch my arm.

"I'm okay." I groaned, my limbs stiff as I sat up.

"What the hell just happened?" Ember grabbed my other hand, helping me to my feet. "Seriously, I didn't know if you were dying or having the best sex of your life."

Fatigued, I leaned against the wall, touching my head to keep the room from spinning. "Both." My hands went to my chest, feeling the weight of his presence. "This is going to sound really unbelievable and strange."

"Nothing is ever too strange here." Eli snorted. "That's what we deal with best."

"Well. Um." I sucked in oxygen like it was helping me prepare. I pressed my shoulders back into the stone. "Lars is here."

"Where is he?" Ember looked around.

"He's not here floating around the room, but here." I tapped at my belly and rib cage.

"Come again, darlin'?" West folded his arms, cocking an eyebrow.

"You're pregnant?" Kennedy's eyes widened.

"No!" I responded. "Ah feck, I hope not." I shook my head. I was not ready for something like that. I needed to be a mother to Piper first. And look how well I was doing with her.

I cleared my throat, I was usually pretty blunt, but this was personal. Private. "Lars and I aren't simply together. We… *linked*… you can say. Found our match. And I guess when demons do that, their souls connect. And I don't mean figuratively. The bastard is using me as a vessel. I think when he died just now he… entered me." I smiled, my heart beating in my chest again, the sense of him soothing me. I didn't want to think about whether this was permanent. If we could get him out or if he would fade away. I was simply happy he was fighting. If he couldn't do it in his body, he could sure as hell have mine.

"So… there is a chance he's still alive." Ember blinked rapidly, face pointing to the side, her hand going to her necklace, running it back and forth.

"I think so." I pushed off the wall. "I will find a way. Whatever I have to do. That demon thinks he can squat here without paying rent?"

A tiny laugh escaped Ember's mouth. "And whatever you need. I will do *anything* to bring him back to us."

A strange pulse of love flickered inside me.

"Okay, that's going to be frickin' weird." My eyes widened.

"What?" Em asked.

"Pretty sure Lars just sent his love right back." Feck, if it *didn't* feel as though I were pregnant in some twisted way.

Everyone eyed me as though I were a freak then dropped their eyes to my stomach.

"Stop staring at my belly. It's not as though his head is going to pop out like in *Alien*." I stabbed a finger at my gut. "You better not, arsehole."

The tension in the room eased, but most looked confused or dazed, as if they were trying come to terms with what just happened. A turmoil of emotions.

Lars's sudden presence inside me calmed me. It didn't feel as odd as it should have. He was home with me. That was all that mattered at the moment.

"My lady?" Torin stepped into the doorway. "Olivia woke me and said you might need me."

"You never get a night off." Kennedy waggled her head.

"I took this position to protect you, not to have a night off." He stood up taller. "Plus, it is almost dawn. My shift starts in a couple of hours anyway."

Kennedy stepped for the entry. "Breakfast. Coffee. And planning in fifteen minutes?"

We all nodded; no one was going to get back to sleep now.

"Oh, and Fionna?" Kennedy peeked over her shoulder at me. "Bring Lars if you want."

"Hilarious." Like I had a choice.

"Good morning, Uncle." Ember touched my stomach with a wink before walking out, emptying the room.

Another pulse responded inside. This time I could fully feel how Lars felt about her. He wanted her to be his daughter. They both wanted that, but neither wanted to step on any toes or disrespect those who were dead.

Fuck that, I said. *You're her father. Stop being a wanker and just admit it.*

Pulse.

"Stubborn arse."

Pulse.

"Okay, you're getting awfully lippy. Isn't it time for your nap?"

I took a step toward the pants I dropped, the room swaying. I gripped the bed frame, keeping myself from falling over again. My legs wobbled with fatigue and my head spun.

It had been a tough night, emotionally and physically draining. I had slept terribly since the evening the stone took over Lars.

To rest, I needed Stavros dead, the stone destroyed, my daughter back in my arms, food, Lars returned to his body, in my bed, and a swimming tank full of coffee.

Nothing out of the ordinary.

I rubbed my throbbing head. The crisp bite of air kissing the icy lake and surging up to the castle walk filled my lungs but did very little to wake my knackered body.

The gathering of minds went into the afternoon, planning, plotting, and getting the fuck nowhere. We went around and round, scheming ideas we had no way to control or confront, and planning for alliances' help we had yet to hear from.

Lily's skulk was the only group that responded to the plea and was heading our way from Canada. Rez had yet to hear from the sirens, and there was only radio silence from anyone left of the DLR. Not that I blamed any of them who survived. They'd been through so much loss and anger, much of which was probably pointed at me. Me, the leader against the fae, the one trying to give Druids their voice back, had since fallen in with the exact beings the DLR used to fight against. A traitor to my own cause.

No matter what I felt for Lars, it still bothered me how easily I had fallen in with the fae. I liked them. I could see now how quick I was to lump them all together. To blame wholly for the atrocities of a few. Hating them was easier—no lines, no gray area.

Now everything was gray.

I traveled along the wall, the sky spotted with threatening clouds. The late-spring sun only took a nip off the chilly afternoon air, not that I minded the cold; I was Irish, born and bred. Dreary, rainy, and cold were embedded in my DNA. It usually woke me up, made me feel alive. Today fatigue trailed after me like a shadow.

Piper.

Lars.

The stone.

Stavros.

Every one laid upon my shoulders.

Sounds of men training pounded from the valley. I could feel the tension of guards milling around on constant watch, their hands on their weapons, their bodies alert. The castle guard was wound like a clock, coiled to near snapping.

All of it ticked inside me as if a bomb were ready to explode. My body was knackered, my mind unable to shut down, my skin itching, as though my bones were trying to dig their way out.

Gulping in air, I moved across the cobblestones, seeking a place of refuge. A figure in the distance caught my eye as he stood on the bridge, overlooking the deep lake below.

Goran.

He stared longingly at the gushing water, his hands gripping the railing, as though at any moment he would impel himself over it.

"Goran?" I took slow steps toward him. He did not respond to my call. "Goran." I tried again.

His fingers tightened around the bar, but otherwise he didn't react. The aura around him swirled like a melancholy fog—only one emotion I experienced coming from him. Gloom.

I stopped beside him, peering over the bridge to the distant churning waterfall; sharp rocks cracked over the surface, slicing the cascading water.

"You did this to me," Goran said, his voice low and detached.

Responsibility for what I had done settled heavily upon me like a weighted blanket. "Yes." I continued to watch the water. "I did."

He was silent for a long time before he spoke again.

"I long to die. I dream of it. It calls to me every second. With each passing day, the invitation becomes stronger. Every second of life is painful." Though his statements were intense, no emotion existed behind them, which chilled me. "I am not supposed to be here. I breathe, but I do not live. I should have died next to Rimmon, but I cannot have the thing I desire."

I covered my face with my hands. There was no apology card for bringing someone back to life. In the moment, I thought I was doing the best thing. I hadn't wanted Lars to deal with the fact he had killed his own man. His friend.

"I live in hell. Every moment."

I had kept Olwyn alive decades past her natural life. I had also saved people from almost death, but I had never actually brought someone back from the dead. I didn't understand the repercussions until now or how the people would suffer.

"I am sorry."

"Your apologies are nothing to me." He tipped closer into the railing. "I wish you had let me die. At least then it would have been on my own terms."

My lids blinked, shoving back the tears filling them.

"I have tried to end the agony. But I wake up again. My hell does not let me go."

"What?" I swiveled to him. "You tried to kill yourself?"

"To end this nightmare, I would do anything." His empty blue eyes met mine. "But you have linked me to the earth. To you. I cannot end my own misery."

"Shite." My hand went to my mouth. "I-I didn't realize."

"No. You. Didn't."

Black magic, the art of bringing back a life already lost, was unnatural. Wrong. It went against a Druid's nature. Yet my family had raised me in black magic, justifying that we had to use every tool to survive when the world tried to destroy us. At the time, I cared very little for the repercussions, especially against fae.

"I still owe my King what is left of my life, to return him home. Then we will be even. My debt paid." He turned back to watch the water. "You will kill me after. You owe me that, Druid."

I swallowed and nodded. "I do."

Goran let out a small breath, as though it were the first bit of relief he had felt in a long time.

"I see him," he said absently, his gaze tracking the falls.

"What?" I squinted over at the huge guy.

"My King. His aura is around you." A single nerve jumped around his eye. "And he is killing you."

"Sorry?"

"I walk with one foot already in the grave. I can see death all around me. He is dragging you into one as well… My liege is too much for you to bear. You are not meant to hold two souls, especially one as heavy as his." He gave me a vacant glance, then his gaze returned to the water.

A distressed pulse filled my stomach as if Lars validated Goran's words. "Of course." The lump in my throat expanded, my head bowing down.

"Find a way to get him back to his body, or he will destroy yours," Goran said, then abruptly turned and walked away.

I watched him go, the weight on my shoulders becoming boulders.

"Shite!" I screamed into the water, one hand pressed to my stomach. If I die, he dies. "What do I do?" I asked over and over, hoping for anything to answer me: the universe, Lars, the fae gods. I didn't care. "Please…" My legs grew weak, bending me to the cobblestones, my hands gripping the curved design of the stone railing, placing my head on it.

You are strong, Fionna. You can do this, I imagined Lars saying to me.

How? How do I get the stone out of power and you back in before it's too late? I asked back. Even if I couldn't actually talk to him, it helped. Anything for me to not lose my bloody mind right now.

Think. Use that incredible sharp mind of yours, Druid. You have the answers right in front of you.

What? I can't seem to find my own arse presently.

Come on, I know you have more ability than that. You had the power to outwit a Demon King. You can figure this out too… I conjured his soothing sexy voice in my head. *What does the stone fear? What is its biggest weakness?*

The cauldron… But it is dead, useless. We broke it.

Perhaps. However, if anyone has the power to reconstruct it, it would be a Cathbad, the bloodline that created it. Your blood is in it, Fionna. Your family's magic.

I jerked my head up. "Holy shite." Could it be possible? Could I bring it back to life? Rebuild the only weapon which could fight the stone? The treasures were so old; it was as if they were created from some mystical family before time. But they weren't. They were created by Druids the same as me, from my family blood. Why couldn't I restore it? I had to at least try. It might be our only hope to beat the stone and get Lars back.

I felt Lars rub against me, his pride thumping against my soul.

I would fight to the death to get him back.

"Probably the only time you're going hear me say this, demon, but it's time to get you the fuck out of me."

SEVENTEEN
Kennedy

"Fuck. Shite!" My sister's Irish poured through the corridor like syrup, sticky with anger. "Bloody rubbish."

I was learning the thicker the accent, the more pissed off she was.

"Fi?" I poked my head around the doorway of her room. "What are you doing?"

Fionna stood in the middle of the room, the Treasures of Tuatha Dé Danann strewn over the floor, as if she played a game.

"Are you using the most powerful weapons in the world as soccer balls?" I stepped into the room, my mouth dropping.

"Footie." She put her hands on her hips, glaring at the objects. "You Americans are the only ones in the world who name a sport football that has hardly any contact with the foot, and we're the odd ones."

"Pretty sure that was not my point." My gaze followed her glower, which was poised on the cauldron. "Why are you tossing them around?"

They were all devoid of magic, but I still felt cautious and nervous around the items that at one time could destroy the world.

"I am trying to bring the cauldron back to life. The other ones just had the cheek to be in chucking distance."

My mouth parted. "Y-you're doing what?"

Fionna's turned her face to me, her lips pinched, determination setting her jaw. "I have to try. For him. For my little girl."

"You think bringing back the cauldron will rein in the stone?" I glanced at the black metal bowl. It appeared so harmless, like an old pot from the past being used to cook soup or something mundane. Not something that had the power to control magical forces beyond your comprehension.

172

Fionna licked her lip and stared back at the vessel, sadness brushing against her aura. My eyes narrowed, taking in a deep gray color bleeding around her edges, consuming the color of her life.

"Fi?" I whispered. I blinked, making sure I was not mistaken.

"I'm dying." She sighed, her shoulders dropping. Weary. "Guess there's a price for carrying a demon's soul inside you."

My hand went to my mouth as I tried to absorb her statement. It didn't take long for me to gain the truth of it. A human body, even with a Druid's powers, could not contain two souls, especially one of Lars's magnitude.

"If I get him back to his body and bring the cauldron back," she rubbed her forehead, "we might have a chance. It's our fault we are even in this mess. Our selfishness to not let go of each other."

"No." I bolted to her, touching her arm. She had told me how she was supposed to die in that cave and strengthen the cauldron so it could fight the stone. But Lars had made the ultimate sacrifice—love. In doing so, it splintered the cauldron, nullifying its powers. I couldn't be more grateful to Lars for choosing Fionna. "I don't care. You are meant to be here. For Piper, for Lars." She swallowed. "For me. I do not want to lose you, Fionna. Not when I just found you."

Fionna's lashes fluttered as she tilted to look at me.

"A Cathbad made the cauldron. Our family bloodline is woven into it. Blood, sweat, and tears. If anyone should be able to bring it back, it's me. I must keep trying to pour everything I have left in it. To save us."

"Seriously?" I set myself in front of her, my head shaking.

"What?"

"You are not the only Cathbad in this room. That blood runs through me too. My magic might help." I gripped her hands. "The power of two is better than one."

"I can't let you do this," she responded. "You have enough to worry about… And this will drain you to nothing. You need to lead."

"Yes, but our chances suck nerf-herding ass as of late. If there is a possibility we could negate the stone and get Lars and Zoey back, I'm willing to take the chance."

Fionna's lips tweaked into a frown. "You know it still might not be enough. Two is better, but it's not the power we need."

Unfortunately, three was the rule in Druid magic. Three was a dominant and powerful number in nature.

"Unless, you want to bring Grandpa Cathbad back to life, we're working with what we have here."

"This is really going to be shite. Agonizing."

"You can stop trying to sell me on it, big sis." I squeezed her hands. "I'm already in."

♛♛♛

Did I take her words to heart? No. Not as much as I should have.

Magic swirled around the room, our hair billowing, the power of the spell scraping, leaching the strength from us. But still we pressed on, sitting in the middle of the floor, both of us gripping the sides of the pot, pouring what felt like our blood into it.

Every muscle and nerve of mine felt shredded. Sweat poured down my back, and my throat was raw from chanting over and over. Exhaustion shook my body as I tried to keep from falling over.

And still the cauldron sat lifeless. One moment, I thought I felt a pulse, a beat of life. That could have been more wishful thinking on my end.

"Take a break." Fionna wiped her brow, sitting back. "You need to rest."

"No, I swear I felt something last time."

"No." Fionna batted my hand away from the rim of the cauldron. "I won't let you hurt yourself. You still have millions of people to protect. You are Queen."

"And as Queen, I order you to stop bossing me around."

"You're not my Queen." She winked. "Simply my annoying little sister."

"You know I have dungeons below." I tilted my head, sitting back on my heels.

"Damn, playing dirty." She grinned, falling back on her butt, her face lined with fatigue. "Sounds like a true Cathbad."

It still felt strange to think of myself as a Cathbad and not a Johnson. I was both. I knew that. But it also felt good to think I came from such a powerful family, born in Ireland to Keela and Reghan. My mother was the daughter of the infamous Cathbad, a Druid who gained such favor with the gods and royals he became more powerful than them.

That favor eventually became a threat. He was killed, along with millions of other Druids. Aneira created fear and hate which drove remaining Druids underground. My parents, deep in the black arts, hid my sister and me from Aneira, separating us for our safety. I grew up in Olympia, Washington, as Kennedy Johnson. A nerdy human girl.

It wasn't until Lorcan and I infiltrated an extremist Druid group called the DLR that I was led to their general, my sister, and the truth of my biological family.

"Kennedy?" My name rang down the hallway, picking up my head. His voice was an instant energy boost to my heart. "Li'l druid?" Lorcan stepped in the room, a grin hooking up the side of his mouth, then it quickly dropped, his eyes moving over me and the cauldron.

"What are you two doing?"

I leaned over the pot to hide it.

"Nothing." I blinked innocently, knowing he wouldn't buy my crap for a moment.

"Ken…" He growled, putting his hands on his hips.

"She started it." I pointed over my shoulder.

"Tattletale!" Fionna shot back. "Feck… you held out for what, a half second?"

"Nah-uh."

"Uh-huh."

"Is this what it would have been like to parent you two?" He rubbed his forehead. "Note for the future: have boys. I can't handle girls."

"Excuse me?" My eyebrows went up into my hairline. An arrow of panic stabbed my chest.

He gave a lazy, sexy grin. "Purely hypothetical, li'l bird. Unless you want to work on that right now."

Fionna groaned, leaning back into the bed.

"It's staying hypothetical." I tilted my head in warning, but a strange warmth filled me. Lorcan, a father? Even with his past, I knew he'd be a great one. Me, on the other hand? I was not sure I could fathom being a mother. My attention was on my kingdom. I couldn't handle anything more. Not that I had to worry about it. Fairy birth control was bulletproof.

"Answer my question." He approached me, nodding at the cauldron. "Actually, don't. I think I can figure it out."

"We're running out of choices. I'm going to do what I have to save my people." I grasped for him. He helped me to my feet, my legs wobbling with weakness.

"I get it, but if it starts to harm you, then Project Cauldron is over."

"I'm sorry?" I tugged from his grip. "You do not tell me what is over or not."

He stepped up to me, looming over me.

"Puff yourself up all you want. You do not dictate what I do." I met his eyes, not backing down. "I am—"

"If the next line out of your mouth is 'I am Queen," he leaned his face an inch from mine, "I'm going to take you over my knee and paddle your ass."

Heat flared up my thighs, my spine tingling with a mix of fury and desire. "Do not treat me like a child."

"Believe me, it would be for adults only." He gritted his jaw. "You are my equal, not my Queen. You need to stop acting as if you can rule me too. What you do involves me as well."

Had I been doing that? "And what *I* do affects thousands, if not millions. I'm sorry I am not the sweet, docile girl you fell in love with, but I cannot afford to be."

"You think I fell in love with a sweet, docile girl?" He snorted.

"*Everything* rides on my choices... on my decisions. Not yours. Not anyone else. Not even Lars. *Me*." I stabbed my chest, trying to bite back the tears. "So if I decide hurting myself to restore the cauldron or sacrificing myself to Stavros or the stone to save my people is the right decision, I will do it. Not you."

He leaned back, his eyes trailing over me, his head bobbing slightly. "Yes, Your Majesty." He stepped away, turning for the door, then stopped and turned back to me. "You think you are sitting by yourself up there, but you're not. You have a lot of people sitting with you, ready to fight at your side." He drummed his palm against the doorjamb. "You seem to forget I know what it's like to be leader. You aren't the only leader in this castle who feels the weight of each of their decisions, to know their choice may have gotten people killed or hurt. Maybe you should be using them instead of pushing them away." He inhaled. "And call me selfish, but I will do everything in my power not to lose you." With that, he strode from the room.

I closed my eyes and tipped my head forward. "Dammit," I muttered, feeling the pull in my gut to run after him.

"Wanker's got a point," Fionna said, causing my head to snap to her. "You know me. I would never defend a fae, especially a dweller, but I've learned with Lars that they're not being masochistic. Simply protective. And you can't deny you feel just as possessive of him. I know when Stavros almost killed Lars, I was about to take out the entire world. Don't tell me you wouldn't do the same for Lorcan."

"Of course I would." My response came out softly.

"He's also right that you aren't alone, Kennedy. I was a general of the DRL, and you have two alpha dark dwellers. Everyone here is a leader in their own right. Don't play into Stavros's hand."

"What do you mean?"

"I know him better than anyone here. He would love nothing more than for us to break ourselves down. Make it easy pickings. We isolate each other, turn on each other… then we have no hope."

"I really am in *Star Wars*, aren't I? Except I don't have a smart-alecky robot as a sidekick."

As if on cue, I heard a squawk from the windowsill. Fionna and I jumped.

"Grimmel." My hand plastered against my chest.

"Light. Trade winds bring more idiots." The black raven's talons clicked along the ledge.

"Never mind, there's my R2-D2. Or are you more a C-3PO?"

Grimmel tipped his head from side to side, as though I were nuts. Which was highly possible.

"Light is hazy. Too long around witless."

"Yoda!" I snapped my fingers. "You're a Yoda."

"Wow, you really are a geek." Fionna pushed herself onto the mattress, her legs shaky.

"A proud one." I scrubbed my head, trying to rouse some energy. "I better go find Lorcan and apologize."

"Uh-huh." Fionna grinned. "Apologize, huh? I know how that goes."

I stared at my sister, aware she was touching her stomach. Lars.

"Besides this being really weird right now," I nodded at her hand, "did I tell you how happy I am for you? For Lars. I'm still shocked… but ecstatic you guys found each other. You both deserve love."

"*You're* surprised." For the first time ever, a deep blush coated Fionna's cheeks, her gaze going to the bed, a joyful smile playing on her mouth. "Do you think I ever thought I would fall in love with any fae, much less the frickin' Unseelie King at that?" She chuckled. "Fate really wanted to bite me in the arse with that one."

"My lady?" Torin's voice hollered into the room. My First Knight poked his head in with a slight bow.

"Yes, Torin?"

"We have guests of pirates at the dock."

"Thank you." Ah… the "idiots" the trade winds brought.

"If Light listened. Already told." Grimmel fluttered up in the air with annoyance, flying off.

"Bird hunting is legal here, right?" Fionna clutched the poster bed, pulling herself up to her feet.

"I would call it open season right now, if my lady would let me," Torin replied, a ghost of a smile on his face.

"Holy nerf-herder. First, was that a joke? And second, is that a smile I see?" My mouth parted. "What is going on?"

"Nothing, my lady." He cleared his throat, dropping the grin, but I saw a lightness I hadn't seen in his eyes in a long time. Something was up with him, but I didn't have time to figure it out.

My castle had been invaded by pirates.

Excuse me—tradesmen.

👑 👑 👑

"No! No, there can't be more of these swashbuckets." Sprig hugged his arms to his chest, stomping his foot into Ryker's shoulder. "One buttaneer is enough."

"I think our friendship just came to an end, monkey man." Cal flapped around. His eyes were wide and dazed, like he was meeting his favorite rock band. "These are my people. Do you know how much juniper juice they have? Barrels and barrels of it. They are gods."

Sprig's eyes grew enormous. "Ohhh, do you think they brought honey too?"

"No." Ryker shook his head. "No more for you."

"Oh, look who is the Viking parent now." Sprig stuck out his tongue at Ryker, then turned to Cal, fake whispering, "*Viking* is code for *dickhead*."

"Then that dweller is a *massive* Viking." Cal nodded at Eli.

A large group of us had descended on the docks, welcoming the new visitors. There weren't as many as I hoped, only eight ships, about twenty men on each boat, but it was more than we had before.

"Croygen, how the hell are you?"

The tall man had long, wavy, dirty blond hair, tattoos covering his arms, and wore aviator sunglasses, leather pants, and a dark blue shirt. He peeled off his glasses, showing his vivid blue eyes, winking at Annabeth as he passed by. He looked more like a rock star than a pirate. He was good-looking and he knew it. He even walked with a swagger and a permanent smug smile.

I rolled my eyes at his pretension, so obnoxious compared to the dark dwellers who didn't have to try and be sexy and alluring. They simply were. They'd eat him for breakfast.

"Jack!" Croygen gave him a hug, patting him on the back. "Been a long time."

178

"Yeah, since the Orient. Man, did we have good times… The women we went through—"

"Yeah. That was a long time ago." Croygen cleared his throat, cutting him off. So quickly, I almost missed it when his gaze slid to Lexie, then back to Jack.

Irritation washed over Lexie's features before she shoved her feelings back, folding her arms.

"Please, you haven't curbed your ways. How many women do you have just in *this* port?" Jack laughed, slapping Croygen on the shoulder. "I already see a dozen here I'd love to be introduced to."

"Times have changed." Croygen shook his head, standing tall. Unconsciously or consciously, he took a step in front of Lexie, which only directed Jack's attention to the girl.

"Holy shit, aren't you exquisite?" He stepped past Croygen, taking Lexie's hand in his and kissing it.

"Not here. And not her." Croygen growled, moving until he was barricading her.

Jack's eyebrow's shot up, looking between the two.

"Whoa, has the notorious womanizer settled down?"

"Jack, let me introduce you to Her Majesty. You know… the reason you're here." Croygen yanked Jack's arm, directing him toward me.

"Majesty." Jack's eyes lit up, moving over me. "So much beauty for one Queen." He took my hand, his eyes locking on mine as his lips brushed the skin of my knuckles. Quickly his attention flickered to Ember, Rez, and Fionna next to me, his eyes bugging out, like a kid locked in a candy store.

"Damn…" He shook his head, reaching for Ember's hand. "Shit, I've never seen a dae in person before. You're *so fucking hot*."

"You touch me and you will truly become a pirate." She smiled flakily. "Your girlfriend becomes a hook…"

Too bad for him, not only was the candy unreachable, but it would kill him.

He jerked upright, taking a step back from Ember.

"He's just the type I enjoy." Rez leaned into Ember, a smile growing in her face at the pirate. "Maybe we can go for a swim later? Won't that be fun, Jack?"

He started to shake his head back and forth as he realized what Rez was, and he walked backward away from us.

"Girlie, don't scare the pirate away." Cal flew near Jack, guarding him. "He's brought nectar from the gods. He's a floating distillery. A giant sink of happiness."

"Sweet nectar of the golden gods." Sprig rang out, making Jack swear and jump back.

"What the fuck is that?" Jack's mouth dipped open.

"I asked the same thing looking at your face." Sprig glared at the new guy, nudging Ryker's neck. "We can vote this one off the island, right? There should be a law against too many buttlickers in one place. We already have one, and I'd love for you to take him back."

"I'm all for it," Ryker replied gruffly.

"It-it talks." Jack glanced around at all of us, as if we should be shocked too.

"Very good," Sprig replied. "I also poop on pillows and in boots. Ask that boot-humper." Sprig pointed at Croygen.

"He does." Croygen nodded. "Watch your socks too."

"Missing the point here." Cal waved his arms. "He. Has. Juniper. Juice."

"Was that a point?" Ember smirked.

"All the point I need," Cal responded.

"Besides being an asshole," Croygen patted Jack's shoulder, "do you have any news? Underground mumblings?"

"Mumblings." Jack laughed. "It's more like screams. Everyone is talking about Stavros and the fight coming. The Eastern bloc is getting even more restless to cut all ties to this. They don't want anything to do with any of it, but our biggest concern is the reports of a fleet coming from the south. Lawson, the captain of the ship coming in now, said he saw over two dozen more heading this way."

"How far?" I stepped up to Jack. I noticed all flirtation was gone. His expression serious.

"In three days. Less if the winds change."

My hands rolled into fists. Stavros had told us his forces would be coming by sea and land, but I hoped we'd have more time. We needed more fighters... on our side.

"I'm gonna go talk to Garrett." Rez turned. "See if I can get another message to my mother."

I nodded, Rez jogging away to run her errand. West watched her go but stayed with his brothers.

"Majesty, many are fleeing; no one wants another war. They're ready to go into hiding and deal with the aftermath of the results. I tried to get more ships... few were willing to volunteer for this battle." Jack's sober tone only piled weight on my shoulders. What he didn't say was that no one believed

180

in me enough to fight or thought I couldn't win. They'd rather be neutral and deal with whomever was leader when the dust settled than pick a side.

The pirates might hate Stavros, but they didn't care for me either, so why fight? Didn't they understand what he would do to the world? He would settle for nothing but being a complete dictator. Rights, even for fae, would eventually disappear.

"Okay," I set my shoulders, "I'm sure your men need rest and refreshments. But in an hour, I want all the captains to assemble and go over the plan."

Jack bowed his head.

"That last ship better hurry, we'll be closing the shield soon." Torin pointed to the water, where a small ship slipped through the channel from sea to the lake.

Jack shielded his eyes from the sun, staring back at the vessel, his eyebrows crunching.

"It's not one of ours."

My head snapped to the boat, sailing quickly toward the port. "What?"

"Not any flag I recognize." Jack continued to stare. "Doesn't belong to us."

Crap times a million.

Torin responded instantly. Yells and orders bellowed around me to stop the vessel and close the harbor. Guards ran to boats, jetting them out to the unknown vessel.

"Fuck." Lorcan moved in next to me, his gaze on the craft.

"What?" I looked to him, then back out to the water, panic rising in my chest.

"No... no..." Ember ambled forward until her boots hit the edge of the pier. Her eyes squinting and locked forward.

"What!" I exclaimed, but after a moment, I didn't need their response, my sight had been getting better, along with my powers. I hardly needed the glasses but wore them more from habit than anything.

Tied to the mast of the ship, two figures were bound and gagged.

"No! Kate!" Annabeth screamed, her body lurching forward. Cooper grabbed her, dragging her back to him.

Kate and Nic struggled against their binds as Stavros stood at the hull, his arms open, as if he were being welcomed home.

He had the audacity to come here to claim my territory as his, bringing "gifts" to solidify his stance in the kingdom.

EIGHTEEN
Ember

The ship sailed in, so close to the pier we could see everyone on the deck clearly, but far enough away no one could board it. Boats with Kennedy's men surrounded it, pointing their guns at the King, waiting for the Queen's word.

My great-uncle stood at the hull, his long black hair flowing in the wind as if he were in a modeling shoot. It looked like a strong family resemblance from afar, but the closer you got to Stavros, you saw he was a poor man's version of Lars. Nose and face longer, not strong and fit like Lars, and he was skinny. He wore loose pants, a black button-up shirt, and a colorful sash around his waist, as though he were trying to play the part of a pirate but got the outfit at a costume store.

He wanted to be the focal point, but my eyes kept drifting to Nic and Kate. Nic's one dark eye stared out wildly as he fought against the binds. Amara stood next to Nic, keeping a knife pointed at his gut. Strighoul circled around them both.

Dread gripped my chest, knowing nothing good was coming our way.

"Hello, all. Such a beautiful day for sailing, isn't it?" Stavros clutched a rope, leaned out to us, not even acknowledging the guards surrounding his ship. "Thought I'd stop by and visit. Been a while since my great-niece and I spent time together."

I ambled to the front, glaring at him. "You taking me to the park? How about Disneyland? I've always wanted to go there. You'd fit in there perfectly."

"Hop on, my dear. We'll head anywhere you'd like." He raised his eyebrows, motioning for me to join him on the boat.

"I have to get a parent permission slip before I go off with creepy old men," I countered. "Especially ones related to me."

"I thought you had no parents left. Little Orphan Ember." He grinned, but something about his demeanor iced my blood, as though he knew something. "Do you actually let yourself pretend that human could play your daddy… or the fox-shifter your mom?"

"What do you want, Stavros?" I growled.

"Well, I've come to realize after taking inventory of the prisons, something I love to do in my spare time, my hostages were only second rate." Stavros strolled causally, curving around Kate, pointing at her. "I mean, a human. Ugh. How boring. She's spunky, but damn she prattles on and on." He batted his fingers together to simulate someone talking his ear off. "So annoying."

"Yes. You are." I put my hands on my hips, curving my eyebrow at him.

"What are you talking about? My voice is a dream. You haven't even had the pleasure of hearing me sing yet. Famous opera stars told me I was in a category all my own."

"Yeah, I'm sure they did." I snorted.

Stavros glared down at me. "They said I was magic to listen to."

"I'm sure you had to douse them with a lot of magic for them to believe that."

"Dear niece, I'm starting to feel you do not support my talents. Your own family." He tsked, then pointed at Nic. "Now this one is hot, granted, but really, unless I want to get some horny human in bed, what use is he?" He stepped around Amara's knife, and sidled up to Nic. "Though he does make a great babysitter. You should see him try to protect that little darling girl when she's screaming in pain."

Fionna moved like a bull, shoving through people until she was at the end of the pier, her teeth bared. "You touch her—"

"You'll what, Druid?" Stavros's laugh cut her off. "Hex me again, as you tried in the cavern? I am a lot stronger now, witch, and your child is a prisoner. At my word she will be cut into little pieces." He plucked a device out of his pocket. One of Lars's walkie-talkie phones. "So you will sit there like the pretty, useless thing you are and continue to do nothing. Even though I have given you things to accomplish, you have done nothing." Suddenly the figure and face of Stavros disappeared, shrinking to a brown-haired, blue-eyed little girl. I gasped. Fionna told us he was capable of doing this, but to see it in person? *Crap on ash bark.*

183

"Mummy." Piper's voice cried out, reaching for Fionna. "Don't you love me? Why haven't you saved me?"

Fionna made a heart-wrenching cry and turned her head away in anguish. We all knew it wasn't really Piper, but that didn't make the pain any less real. This was psychological warfare.

"Fuck you." Fionna spat at Stavros, her eyes narrowing in pure hate.

Piper disappeared, Stavros's image returning. "Your daughter will receive punishment for your failings… I told you, Fionna. Did you think I would not follow through?"

Fionna's chest sucked in, fury spitting off her in dark tendrils. She didn't speak; she couldn't do a damn thing.

"Good girl." He smirked, winking at her. "Now, if you want to finally be useful, why don't you run off and retrieve my nephew? Is he still too much of a coward to show his face?"

A collective rage grew like a sudden wind on the pier, clotted between all of us, stirring our magic.

"Ooooh," Stavros cooed. "Do you feel that, Mar?" He winked at Amara. "Think they might be a wee bit upset with me? I have no idea why. I am always so generous. Look, I'm willing to give *these* back to them." He motioned to Nic and Kate. "Any volunteers to take their place?"

No one moved or spoke, only because we knew it really wasn't a question. He just loved the theatrics of it all.

"Wow." He shook his head at his two hostages. "No one is willing to step up and take your place. That really speaks volumes of how they truly feel about you. I mean, with friends like these…" He laughed motioning to us. "Think it might be time to get new ones."

"Enough, Stavros." Kennedy addressed him, her head held high. "Get to the reason you're here."

Stavros spun to us, all playfulness dropping from him, maliciousness darkening his eyes.

"You really are mind-numbingly dull." His nose wrinkled with disgust at her. "This is all on you, *Queenie*. This could end right now if you kneeled to me. You are dragging this out. Starting a war. Killing all those innocent lives. For what? Your pride?"

"I'm sure their lives would be much better off in your care. Especially the humans." Kennedy's voice was thick with sarcasm. Ahhh, I felt like a proud parent. Ryan and I really had rubbed off on her.

"Humans." Stavros snorted. "The laws of nature are simple: the weak are always controlled and used as food for the stronger. They are less than us. Their true place was *never* supposed to be above fae. *We* feed off *them*, and it's time they understood the true hierarchy of this world."

"For this, and so many other reasons, I will never kneel to you," Kennedy fired back with the authority of a true Queen.

"Then you die." Stavros took a step toward the hull. "All of you do. Or maybe become my personal servants." An eerie grin curved his mouth. "I know, Amara here would love to have that blond wanderer back as a plaything. It will be fun to watch her break you. I might even join in." He winked at Ryker. "Speaking of, I have a message from your son." Stavros clicked on the device, holding it out. Instantly the sobs of an infant in distress wailed over the monitor.

It was a blink of an eye. Ryker was standing next to me one moment, the next he was on the bow, reaching for his axe.

"Ryker! No!" Lexie screamed.

Holy shit. I hadn't seen the wanderer use his transportation powers yet. In an instant he could transport himself somewhere else. Damn. I was jealous.

Ryker lunged for Stavros, his axe swinging at the demon. Stavros stepped to the side with a bored sigh. A scream tore from the Viking, and his huge form dropped to the deck with a thud, his hands gripping his skull. The axe tumbled from his hand, sliding over the edge, water splashing up as the huge weapon hit the water, leaving the Viking unarmed.

"Did you really think you could take me?" Stavros bent over, whispering hoarsely to Ryker. "I can pop your brain in a matter of seconds."

Ryker heaved, his face and eyes scrunched in agony, his hands digging into his skull as he curled over his knees.

"Looks as if we have our first volunteer." Stavros stood fully, holding his arms out. "Do you not see how kind I've been? I can destroy you where you stand. Tear through your tiny brains like paper. You should be thanking me. Instead, I get attitude and disrespect." He grabbed the knife from Amara's hand and walked straight for Kate.

Shit. Shit. Shit.

"All of you think you are so powerful, but you cannot challenge me. You want war?" He sliced through the ropes holding Kate, shoving her to the edge. "You got it." With the slightest motion he buried the knife in her side. Her scream echoed in the wind. With a shove, Kate's body splashed into the water below.

"No!"

"Kate!"

Annabeth and Lexie both darted for the dock closest to where she fell, shrieking her name as her body sank below the waterline. Croygen shoved past us, diving into the water, swimming for her. Stavros only laughed.

Shaking his head in annoyance, he strolled to Nic, whose eyes found mine.

Crap.

"This one's special to you, right, Ember?" Holding the bloody knife to Nic's neck, he stared at me. "You had a little fun with this one, I suspect. Oh, I hope your mate is aware of your little fling with the incubus?" He gasped in fake shock. "But really, dweller, can you blame her? He is a sex god, after all. And a lot more skilled in bed than you."

Don't let him provoke you, I sent to Eli through our link, feeling him behind me.

Provoke me? Brycin, if you *haven't been able to make me lose my mind yet, then I doubt this two-bit actor can.*

I grinned to myself. That was my man.

And it's not me he wants, Eli added, his fingers brushing my back. *Don't let him get to you.*

Stavros's watchful gaze drifted to me then Eli when he didn't get the response he wanted. The knife dug into Nic's neck. Nic tightened his jaw, spit flurrying through his teeth.

Dammit. I couldn't let him hurt Nic. Not if I could stop it. Stavros wanted me. He would easily kill Nic to prove he could and not even bat an eye.

Blood gushed down the incubus's neck, his nose flaring with grunts of pain.

"Stop!"

No. Eli's stern voice shot in my head, his grip wrapping around my arm. *Don't you dare.*

I have to. I pulled away, stepping forward.

Stavros propped the knife an inch away from Nic's throat. "Are you volunteering?

"Yes."

"Fuck," Eli hissed behind me.

"Let him go first." I pointed to Nic.

"No, Ember. Don't," Nic grunted out, but neither I nor Stavros were listening.

"Not until you are standing in his place, niece. I am no fool."

I turned to Eli, not speaking through our link, but my eyes told him everything. This was not a choice for me. I fought for my loved ones. I wouldn't let them be used as bait or a lesson. He knew that about me.

My hand touched his scruffy cheek. *I love you.* My eyes said to his. *Dammit, woman.*

I knew he would let me go. I could never live with myself if I didn't. Plus, I was dae. I would figure something out.

Hopefully.

My lips barely brushed his before I turned around, catching Kennedy's eyes. I knew she couldn't hear my thoughts, but we had known each other a long time. She understood my expressions. Her eyes were pained, but I knew she would have done no different.

One of the strighoul with Stavros laid down a plank, and I walked onto the boat.

"Good decision." Stavros grabbed me by the shoulders, my gaze roaming over my two comrades. Ryker was still hunched over his knees, his face still pinched in discomfort, but not agony. He made no indication of moving.

"We don't need him anymore." Stavros waved a man to Nic. Two strighoul gripped the incubus, his neck badly bleeding, and his face was puffy and swollen with older bruises.

"Little dae." Nic stared deep into my eyes before he was tossed over the side, water splashing up as he hit.

I let out of a tiny breath of relief. He would be okay. That could have totally backfired on me.

The ship pulled up anchor quickly, curving for the exit out. I stared back at my family and friends. Commotion from the dock drew my eye to Croygen dragging Kate's body onto the pier, pumping at her chest. After a few times I saw her body convulse, like she was hacking up water. She was alive. For now. Blood still poured from her wound.

"All right. Let's head home. It's been an eventful day," Stavros sang to Ryker and me.

Ryker's white eyes darted to me, no longer filled with pain. He kept his eyes locked on mine. My eyes narrowed in question. It only took me a second to realize why he hadn't jumped. Wyatt. He wanted to be taken prisoner.

"Now, I know there are rules when receiving new guests. But let's be honest. *Guest* is such a formal word. And I prefer my company to be relaxed."

As if a vise reached into my brain and clamped down, pressure coiled around it, filling me with unbearable, stabbing pain. Screaming, I crashed onto the planks, cradling my head, sweat pouring down the back of my neck.

Ryker grunted and groaned next to me, curling forward.

"Did I say *relaxed*? I meant passed out." Stavros's voice filtered through the agony, the pressure inside intensifying.

Consciousness seeped from me, my body needing to defend itself against the agony, bile rolling around my throat.

In the distance, sounding more like a dream, I heard a roar, the call of a dark dweller, before blackness submerged me, taking me to its deepest depths.

My lids blinked open. My gaze stared right at the familiar wooden doors leading down to the castle dungeon. The torches were low, suggesting it was late at night, that time had passed from when I was taken, this part of the castle quiet. After what happened, I doubted anyone was sleeping. I didn't want to think about where my physical form was, but I knew it was nowhere near this castle. It was with Stavros, probably already at Lars's compound, stuffed in a room way below my old bedroom.

"Damn! Not again," I muttered, very aware who brought me here. The tug of Torin, the flux of his emotions, raked along my spine, so I turned to stare down the hallway. Anger. Fear. Frustration. And something else he was trying to deny... excitement. I could feel it pulsing under the rest.

Gazing down the corridor, I waited for the sound of Torin's boots. He was the only reason I was here, his defenses receding enough to pull me in. A smile curved my mouth when I heard him turn the corner, his jaw set rigidly. He walked past the doors and stopped, his head rotating back, but the rest of his body didn't follow.

Huffing he rubbed his head and stared at the ceiling as though he searched for an answer, then he took another step and stopped.

"What's wrong, Torin? Something bothering you? Hmmm?" I asked, knowing he couldn't hear or see me. Dreamwalks were fun. I could dance around him, taunt him, and he'd never know. I walked over to the doors, holding my hands similar to a game show host. "What's behind door number one? Could it be a tall, dark-haired goddess who is driving you a bit mad?"

I could sense something had shifted in Torin. He saw Thara differently. But he was so stubborn. Set in the black and white. Right and wrong. Rules. Obligations. Blah-blah...

It would be nice to see him follow his heart one time and not his moral code. The work Eli and I did had taught me life was much more complicated than black-and-white extremes.

Dragging his hand down his face, he stared at the door.

"Oh, come on. You know you want to," I teased. "I'm not here to watch you pace the hallways. You dragged my ass here for a reason."

His boots squeaked as he turned to face the twin doors. He sucked in, rolled his shoulders back, and reached for the door, yanking it open. Following him down the path, he took every step with a cool aloofness, as if he was doing this because he was ordered to.

"Thara knows you too well. She'll see through that."

His eyebrows creased, as though he heard me, a little murmur in his subconscious. We moved along the same corridor we took before, reaching the last cell.

Thara sat almost in the same position as last time—on her bed, her knees pulled up to her chest. This time she leaned her head back into the wall, her eyes closed, deep in meditation.

Torin cleared his throat, running his hand over his hair, his feet bouncing slightly. Nervous? Wow. I could not recall a time I had ever seen him anxious like this. Not with me. For once he didn't seem sure of himself... and he was not comfortable with it.

"As if I didn't know you are here," Thara said, keeping her eyes closed. "I could hear your meticulous strides the moment you entered."

"You knew without a doubt it was me?"

"I have studied the weight of your steps, the length of your stride. If you were angry, worried, determined, sad, happy, even scared. What each breath you took meant. I could pick you out in a pitch-black room, solely by the sound of your breathing." Her brow furrowed, her lids still shut. "When we were in training, I used to close my eyes at night, listen to you walk in, climb into bed, and determine what mood you were in. It was a little game I played. Before long, it became second nature."

Torin frowned, looking at his boots. "I did not know that."

"Of course you didn't." Thara's eyes popped open, her gaze centering on him. "When it came to me, you never saw. You simply assumed I would be there. And I always was, letting you take me for granted, just so I could be close to you... You never saw."

Torin shifted to his other leg, glancing away.

"What are you doing here, Torin?" Her voice was strong, but her gaze fell to her knees. "I thought we already covered this. I have nothing new to say."

He gritted his teeth, irritation flexing his hands. But I could feel it wasn't annoyance with her. It was pointed at himself.

"I've made my apologies to the Queen. To you. I will not grovel if that is what you came here for."

"I don't want you to." He gripped the bars of the cage.

"Then what do you want?" She pushed to the edge of the bed, her feet touching the floor.

"I-I..." He scoured at the space between his eyes. "I came here..."

Her eyes tracked him, watching Torin flail and stutter. "Yes?"

He grunted. "I wanted to see you."

Silence followed. Her face remained impassive.

He scuffed his boots along the floor and puffed out his chest, bracing his head to look back at her.

"Why?"

I could see and feel his struggle, the need to look away from her intrusive gaze, feeling she'd see right through to the feelings stirring inside him. Emotions had been growing since the moment he walked away last time. His entire world had been altered in one moment. She was the comrade in training, the partner in duty, the companion on their nights off, the friend who held him without a word after rounds of Aneira's abuse. Who would patch him up, let him talk or not talk. He had always been the one who dictated their relationship.

Now looking at this woman, he felt sensations... attraction... need... desire he had never experienced before. He had never been nervous around her. Why would he? He had never seen the woman. Only the colleague.

Now all he saw and dreamed about was her. Her intelligence, her loyalty to him, her reliability. But also her curves, her mouth, deep, dark eyes, the feel of her silky hair sliding through his fingers. The woman who was a conspirator against the crown, convicted of sedition, had entered his thoughts, torturing him until he had to relieve himself.

I had no idea what to do. Torin's thoughts entered my head, letting me get a peek of some of the visions he had of her. Images of kissing her, of slowly undressing her body, laying her back on a bed, the feel of her bare skin, her moans.

"Okay. Awkward." I shook my head. "Hot. But awkward."

"Why?" She stood and strolled to the bars, never once backing down from him.

"Damn, boy... You have so met your match." I folded my arms, respecting Thara even more. Because of Torin, I never had the chance to get to know her. The more I watched and listened to her, the more I liked her. What she did was wrong. If Kennedy got hurt, I would have torn her apart, but I couldn't stop myself from respecting her. Kennedy told me she spent a lot of time here after she returned from Ireland. Talking to her. Trying to understand. Ken said within the first week, she had already forgiven her. At the time I chalked it up to Kennedy's unflappable kindness and big heart. Now I agreed with her.

"I-I... don't know."

"That is not an answer. A captain knows his every move." She wrapped her fingers near his, not letting up. "Look at me."

He flicked his eyes to her, then glanced away quickly.

"Look. At. Me."

Torin snapped his head to hers, a nerve in his jaw twitching. "For once I do not feel like a captain."

"Why?"

He exhaled, struggling with the emotions flooding through him to me. Fear dominated. He was terrified to feel something truly real. What he felt for me, for Kennedy, was dim compared to the sprout that had started in his heart for Thara, tangling thickly into his core.

"Ouch." I feigned hurt at the realization he mostly loved the idea of me. At first he was awed by me, but later those qualities aggravated him. I was too reckless. Free. I spoke and acted from my emotions first and my thoughts later. We wouldn't have been a good match.

"Why, Torin?" she challenged.

"Because." He paused, swallowing. "War is coming again and when I looked to my right, you weren't there." He inhaled. "Because everything is out of my control, and I can't stop any of it."

She tilted her head to the side.

"My lady was almost taken today. Ember was..."

"What? Ember?" Thara's posture went stiff. "What happened?"

"Stavros. He simply sailed in here." Torin waved his arm in the direction of the lake. "And I could do nothing to prevent it. Ember and a fae named Ryker went in exchange for Nic and a human woman, Kate." He gulped. "They sacrificed themselves, and I stood back and watched it happen. Watched Stavros take Ember."

191

"What could you have done?" Her brows furrowed. "You protected the Queen. That is your job."

He nodded.

"Oh." A realization flickered over Thara's face and she took a step back. "You are still in love with Ember."

Torin snorted, scrubbing his face. "That's the ironic part." He slicked back his dark hair, lifting his gaze to Thara. "She'd been taken prisoner, the woman I was supposed to marry, spend the rest of eternity with, but she was not who I kept thinking of, not the one I pictured at my side, not the one whose advice and thoughts I wanted to hear."

Thara's chest heaved with tiny pulses.

"I am falling... and I don't know how to make it stop."

Thara tilted her head. "You were protecting Her Majesty. It is all you can do. Whatever comes, I know you will die to keep her safe."

"No. You don't..." He shook his head. "That's not what I meant."

Thara scowled, confused by his statement.

"Oh, for crap sake!" I tossed my arms, yelling at no one. "He likes you."

"Torin?" She said his name defensively.

He picked up his head, his gaze fully meeting hers, his violet eyes full of emotion. "I see." His declaration came out in a whisper. "I see you."

A wave of bewilderment flickered over her features. I could see a wall going up, as if she was trying to protect herself from hope. From being clobbered again if his meaning was not what she yearned it to be.

"Kiss her already!" I swatted Torin, but he of course felt nothing, though I saw his tongue slip along his bottom lip, as though he heard me.

"I better go," he said quietly.

"Yes." Her wall locked into place. "You probably should."

He didn't move, his gaze tracing down her neck to the fingers wrapped near his. One hand raised and he softly brushed his fingers over hers, as though he was caressed her entire body.

A groan came from his chest before he turned and walked away. This time he did look back at her. Thara stood staring at the hand he had touched, then her hands fell to her sides.

His feelings pounded down on me, along with his thoughts. He didn't simply see her... He was in love with her.

And for once he didn't think about the honorable thing or what was right or wrong.

He just wanted.

My lids flew open and I had to blink through the grit, my eyes watering and burning. When they cleared enough to see I could make out a dark cell, the only light streaming in from the slit on top and bottom of the door. Goblin metal saturated the room, coated the walls, and wrapped around my ankle, keeping me pinned to the icy stone floor.

The safety of my dreamwalk, the familiarity of Torin's head, slithered out the door, leaving me cold and alone. Reality stomped in the room and bitch-slapped me.

All my energy and magic siphoned out with every breath, robbing me of my will to fight or even move. My tongue slid over my chapped lips, and I tried to lift my head. Someone must have filled it with cement, because it tipped forward, smacking back down on the unforgivable stone.

It was no surprise to wake up here. This was what I had expected. Nic and Kate were safe, away from harm. This was all I wanted in that moment, but like typical me, I hadn't thought much passed that.

Two down, two to go. The kids were my first thought, and I had no doubt it was Ryker's too.

Shit. The Viking.

"Ryker?" I tried to call out, his name grinding in my throat. I twisted, lying on my back, drawing in a long breath. "Ry-ker?" I shoved the word from my gut, but it barely floated in the air like gauze. Air stumbled into my lungs, my head spinning with even the tiniest effort. Crap. Stavros was determined to make certain whomever was in these cells was minimally conscious.

A rumble slipped through the wall near my head, the sound of chains and a moan.

"Ryker?" I twisted my head, tossing my voice to where I heard the noise.

"Ye—ah…" Ryker's voice strained, more a sigh than an actual word.

Knowing he was close ignited a flash of energy through me. My nails dug into the grout as I tugged myself the few feet to the wall, my limbs sagging with exertion.

"You okay?" I pressed my words against the stone.

"Sure." The sarcasm dripped from him. No doubt he was chained the same as me, probably with twice as many chains, because he was a big muscular guy. Never one to do well with being helpless, my exhausted brain wheeled around any ideas for a plan. We were useless, chained up and stuck in these cells. Stavros would not risk losing us or letting us get out. If the war would begin in a few days, I had a feeling he would leave us here until then.

Until he needed to use us... to destroy.

I jumped at the sound of squealing metal, realizing I must have dozed off. I curled my body into the corner, staring at the window cut from the top of the door where Stavros's face grinned at me.

"My dear niece, I hope you enjoy your accommodations. I picked them out especially for you."

"You have crappy taste." I spat out every word. "I prefer the ones upstairs."

"Oh, you mean the room with the soft gray duvet and beautiful view over the grounds?" His grin widened. "Oh, I hope you don't mind, I gave that room to Amara. We've fucked in it several times. It has nice springs. She is relentless. I think we've already screwed in every room. The office was the best though. Right on his desk."

Bile burned up my throat, but my only response was to blink and sag back into the wall. Like a child, he wanted to degrade and deprecate everything of Lars's. Taint it. Defame his sanctuary.

"You will need your rest. My ships are coming in tomorrow, so by dinner, I will be back here, watching TV and planning the remodel of my newly acquired castle."

"Tomorrow?" A cord of fear laced around my lungs, strapping them together.

A cruel grin tugged at one side of his face. "Don't you know not to trust pirates?" He shook his head. "Not when money or treasure is concerned. They told you what I wanted you to know."

Crap on ash bark. "They work for you?" Shit. Shit. Shit. We had let a snake into our house, lying in wait to strike.

"Pirates like to believe they work for no one, but they will soon see. I will reign over land, water, and air. Nothing and no one will be out of my reach."

I didn't respond, my eyes never leaving him.

"The war is coming tomorrow, and your side won't be prepared. The Queen is first, and those who don't follow her to their knees for me will die."

"You think she will simply kneel to you?" I snarled.

"I know she will," he responded. "When she sees how many are dying in her name. She will choose to bow to me instead of letting innocents get killed. Especially those sweet children and defenseless humans."

He was right. Kennedy would sacrifice herself if it came to people's lives, children's lives.

"Don't look at me that way. I do what needs to be done to win. You have never known what true leadership is."

I snorted. He thought this was what true leadership looked like? I had seen it before, and her head was no longer attached to her body.

"You know what will happen if you don't do as I say tomorrow?" He stepped closer to the barred window and turned his face to the side. "And you too, Wanderer. I know you can hear me."

There was no response from next door, but I could have sworn I felt a surge of magic leak through the stone wall into me. Angry and familiar... demon energy.

This was something all three of us shared, though Stavros had us beat. Ryker and I were only half and no match for the new High Demon King.

"I thought about rehearsing with you guys but decided it would be better to improvise." He bounced on his toes, rolling his head back and forth. "Go with the flow. It makes it more organic. Exciting. You two rest up, come prepared to play tomorrow. Nighty-night!" He wiggled his fingers at me then slammed the plank of metal over the square opening, shutting me into the darkness again. His footsteps bled away into silence punctuated only by the sound of my own labored breaths humming against my ears.

What were we going to do? I wanted desperately to get to Kennedy, warn her what was coming. How would I stop Stavros from using me as a puppet? That was another reason I needed to escape. Tonight.

"Ryker?" I pulled down my sleeves, pressing my covered hand to the wall. It didn't matter, every inch of this place was painted with goblin metal, but bare skin against the surface increased the torture. "We need to get out of here. Warn them. Please have an idea, because I have nothing over here."

Silence. Was he awake? Dying? Too much goblin metal in our system *could* kill us.

"Ryker?"

Nothing.

"Dammit, Ryker, answer me." I weakly hit my fist against the wall.

The thud of chains clanking on the floor told me he was, at least, alive.

"Hey, Wanderer? Talk to me." A jangle of metal, but still no response.

Twisting my neck, I pressed my naked ear to the wall, the cursed substance sucking more energy from me as if it were draining my blood.

"Ry-ker…" I barked.

"Stop calling for me." Light streamed into the room from the door window. An outline framed the space. *How the hell?*

"Ryker?" My mouth parted.

"Stop talking." His white eyes narrowed on me, then his focus went down.

"But how?"

"Hi!" A tiny brown head poked into the window. "The amazing, magical fingers at your service, *suile-aisteach.*"

"Sprig?" I blinked my lashes a few times to make sure I was seeing the little sprite-monkey.

"I prefer to go by Super Sprig."

"You're gonna go by Flat Furball if you don't hurry up," Ryker growled, peering around him.

"Someone is being extra '*Viking*' today." Sprig curled his fingers into air quotes, rolling his eyes.

"Sprig…"

"Fine, but I deserve a *sink* full of honey when we get back. Having to stay quiet and packed away next to your not-so-honey nuts."

"*Sprig,*" Ryker rumbled.

Sprig rolled his eyes and disappeared down his arm.

"Sink?" Ryker peered at me.

"Sorry, my boys are a bad influence." I pushed myself higher up the wall.

Clank. Clank.

The door swung open to my amazement. "How?"

Sprig dropped to the ground, scrambling across the cell to me.

"High fae always forget about us lower fae… We are powerful in our own way." Sprig climbed onto my ankle, working the lock as Ryker stood guard. "Sprites have a talent for picking locks."

"I have two pixies. I never underestimate how mighty you guys are."

Sprig grinned, his chest puffing up in pride. "I like you, *Suile-aisteach.*"

"What does that mean?"

"Strange eyes."

"Oh. Okay." I shrugged. I had far worse nicknames.

"Sprig, hurry it up." Ryker repeatedly swiveled his head down each side of the hallway.

"This takes time. Leave the master to his work."

"I'm surprised they didn't find him." I glanced over at Ryker. "You'd think they would have searched us."

Ryker's eyes met mine, a snarl frozen on his mouth.

"We're not going to talk about it. Or think about it." Sprig shivered, wiggling a finger back at the wanderer. "Actually, I don't think I want to talk to you right now."

"Promise?" Ryker huffed. "Like I wanted you there either."

"I'm scarred for life."

"Oh." I pinned my lips together, trying not to laugh. This reminded me of several nights when Eli woke up to a passed-out Cal snuggling up to his cock, thinking it was Sinnie.

"When no one was looking, I crawled into his pocket," Sprig whispered to me. "I figured you guys would need me. He always does. Can't take him anywhere."

"I thought you weren't talking."

"I'm not talking to you." He stuck out his tongue at Ryker before returning to the lock. "Her, I like. She called me mighty."

A handful of seconds later, the lock dropped from my ankle, a river of relief rushing through my system. The metal in the room still fatigued me, but without it touching my skin, I could rise.

Scooping up Sprig, I stumbled from the room, grappling for clean air once I stepped out. I knew it would take some time to get my full energy back. What I really needed to do was go lie out in the forest, letting the plants and earth heal me. Not possible right now.

"My son." Ryker took a few steps, staring back at me. Sprig leaped from my hands to his shoulder, gripping onto his shirt. It was similar to Cal and Simmons claiming Eli was an asshole, and despite obvious love for everyone to see, Ryker was Sprig's asshole. I learned no one messed with *their* asshole.

"Don't worry, Viking, I am not leaving this place until we have Wyatt and Piper."

He nodded, his shoulders lowering in relief.

"But we need to warn Kennedy. We cannot let them be ambushed... or even attacked by those pirates in the middle of the night."

"I agree." His attention curved to Sprig.

"What? Me?" Sprig pointed at himself. "But you guys will need me."

"We need you to do this more." He could easily slip out; we could not. "Please, Sprig."

"But..." Sprig threw his arms down like a teenager.

"You know Zoey would want you to do this." Ryker rubbed his head. Sprig's eyes narrowed.

"You're throwing out the *Bhean* card? That's mean!" He folded his arms. "I thought you were the fun parent."

"We have to get her back so I can be again."

"Please, Super-Duper Sprig?" I pressed my hands together, pleading. "The mighty one."

"Ohhh, I like that." He placed his hands on his hips as if he were a superhero. "The mighty one. Savior and guardian of the honey gods."

"Sprig..." Ryker rubbed his temple.

"Fiiiinnneee." He sighed. "But if I miss any of the fun or you get trapped in a vault of honey jars, I'm gonna be so Viking mad."

"Why would we be locked in a vault with honey?"

"I'm not the only one with that fantasy."

Ryker set him on the ground.

"Follow the tunn—"

"Please." He swished his hand. "This isn't my first rodeo. The vents will take me straight to the surface." His mouth went into an O-shape, his eyes widening. "Are there rats in those vents?"

"Probably." I shrugged.

He turned to Ryker, glaring, tapping his foot.

"You'll get the sink full of honey, I promise."

"I swear, Viking, if one of those wingless pigeons tries to mate with me, you're dealing with my woman's wrath."

"Who knows, you might become king of the vermin." Ryker nudged him with his boot.

"Oh, I am so not talking to you." Sprig grumbled, but jumped to the vent, easily slipping in. "Adieu, may the forces of the honey gods be with you."

"And you, sir." I winked.

He crept deeper into the darkness, disappearing from sight.

"Let's hope he gets to them in time," I breathed, turning in the direction where we last saw the kids. Chances were Stavros kept them elsewhere, but we had to start somewhere, and we could be caught at any time.

"You know you just sent a narcoleptic monkey-sprite, who gets distracted by anything resembling food or shiny objects, to save us all?" Humor glinted in Ryker's slight smile.

"We're so screwed."

"Pretty much." He turned and stopped short, his body going rigid, hissing. "Fuck."

I swung around, my stomach bottoming out. Before the word *what* could leave my lips, I saw the reason for his response.

Oh shit.

"Come on, Ryker." Amara leaned against the archway of the passage, a smug smile tilting her mouth. "How long were we together? You don't think I know you?"

Neither one of us moved, our gaze locked on the beautiful, lethal woman. She had model good looks, but you could feel the emptiness behind the pretty face. Smart and conniving but lacked any fire.

"At one time we shared that. We knew what the other was thinking and could finish each other's sentences, we knew each other so well."

"I never knew you." Ryker shoved back his shoulders. "You were always deceiving me. Working for my father. Playing me for the fool."

"You can believe that." She looked at the ground, a flicker of sadness rolling over her face. "But you were the only one I ever loved. Still do."

"Betraying and swindling someone is not love."

Her gaze flicked to his, a mix of hurt and anger in them. "It's who I am. This is my nature. You knew that and still fucked me every night. Stayed with me for decades." She wrapped her arms around her stomach. "And I did love you. Even *I'm* capable of it."

Ryker's jaw strained, but he said nothing, the tunnel filling with awkward silence.

"What are you going to do, Amara?" Ryker finally spoke low. "Are you here to catch me? Prove yourself to your master?"

Her body flinched back, her lids blinking.

"Fuck you, Ryker," she whispered.

I didn't like her at all but, for a moment, I felt sorry for her. Only Ryker seemed to bring it out, the human in her. Someone who wanted to be loved too. She just went about it all wrong.

Amara pushed off the wall, her long, lean legs strutting past us.

"They're down the passage. Look for the sconce that's out." Her face remained blank, her words monotonous. "And hurry. I'm only giving you a ten-minute start before we come after you." She curved one dark eyebrow then swished back around, disappearing down the opposite hall.

Ryker and I both gaped after her, stunned with the realization Amara had helped us.

"Holy shit," I muttered, peering up at the wanderer. Deep in his strained expression, I saw a glimpse of sadness. As though he saw the girl he once knew. Possibly loved. But it was gone as quick as it arrived.

"Let's go." He grabbed my arm, swinging me around for the other passage.

The clock had started.

And with every second that passed, our chance at escape dwindled.

NINETEEN
Zoey

Women moved around the room, almost seventy of them, but I could barely hear a whisper. The only murmurs of noise came from the babies, but even they seemed to understand the necessity of silence. Better to become washed away in the sea of beds and bodies.

The longer I watched, the more aware I became of the subtle hierarchy and system these women had developed. Clusters of groups stuck close to each other, quietly helping each other. A definite division stood between species—human and fae. The fae women were more dominant, probably because they lived longer and had been here from the beginning. But the longer I watched them, the more I saw even that line disappear. The real separation was those who perceived this life as an honor and those who understood they were in a forced drug/sex ring.

All were in fear and awe of me. They bowed their heads, scurrying around me against the far wall, giving me a wide berth. Was it because they knew I was the original "mother"? The originator of their torment? Or was it because at any moment the stone might return? They looked at me through narrowed lids like I was a spy, the watching eyes of the head monster.

In moments, glitches of time, when the stone was away from the cave, it released its hold on me a little, and I emerged from the dark. This was the only time I had control over my body again and when my mind was clear. But there was always a string linking me to him; I was never fully off my leash.

It was hard to fight the sensation to curl back into myself and hide. I was plagued by wounds from my childhood, where I was forced to do things against my will, locked in dark closets. I wanted to close my eyes and disappear into myself.

"Oh, are we mourning Lars?" Vadik's voice slithered into my ear, generating a chill to shiver my bones. "Good riddance to that fucker. A constant thorn in my side. All he did was make my life hell, ruining my business, taking my best workers from my clubs." Vadik rolled his bony shoulders. "I feel so free knowing he's gone for good."

Don't react, Zoey. Don't let him get to you. Hell, this man was asking for an ass-pounding and in his current state, I knew it would be easy. He might be a demon, but he was weak, and I no longer played in the human world.

Vadik chuckled, leaning against the wall next to me, his arm brushing mine as he whispered into my ear. "How things have changed for the old fae hunter." He clicked his tongue. "At one time were you any different? You hunted us, brought us in to be lab rats. We were nothing to you. We were beneath your kind. At one time you were completely fine letting fae be tortured and killed for experiments. No difference here."

"This coming from a man who turned over his own kin to be tortured and killed."

"Yeah, but I never claimed to be doing something honorable."

"Believe me, if I knew what was really happening, I would have done things differently."

"You wouldn't have done shit and you know it." He shook his head with a laugh. "Don't give me that, Zoey. You are not any more honorable than I am. You merely pretend to carry that righteous flag."

My gaze locked straight ahead, watching the woman who'd borne Zeke's child, staring off in space, disappearing from life. Was I any different? At one time, I would have hunted these fae women and taken them to DMG to be tested on. I thought I was helping find cures for human disabilities and diseases. I wasn't fully aware of what Dr. Rapava was doing. But honestly, would I have stopped if I had known? At one time to me, fae had deserved to die. As I gazed over the room, I preferred to believe I would have stopped something like this, and not purely for the human women.

Vadik leered at me. "What's wrong? Am I hitting too close to home?"

"Get. The. Fuck. Away. From. Me." I snapped each word, avoiding his gaze penetrating into the side of my face.

"Is that how you speak to your father-in-law?"

In human terms, Ryker and I weren't married, but in the fae world, we were. A sheet of paper declaring you are "legally" married was silly to the fae. When they found their mate, it was a connection beyond any marriage humans could fathom.

"How is my grandson? I bet he is a spitting image of his father. Of me."

I whipped to him in a blink, baring my teeth. I only came up to his chest as I rose onto my toes, but I got into his face. "I told you to *never* mention him. And let's make this extremely clear. You will never, ever see him. I will not hesitate to kill you; do not doubt it, old man." My gaze ran down his skeleton frame with disgust. "It would not take me long. I am not someone you should mess with."

"Right, Zoey. Because you are fae now." He grinned, his yellow teeth showing between his lips.

"No." I tilted my head with a twisted smile. "Because I am the fucking Avenging Angel." I rammed my shoulder into his body as I stomped past him, leaving the room.

I took only nine steps before I fell against the corridor wall, my breath burning down my esophagus. There were too many truths to what Vadik had said. For years I'd captured fae, despised them.

Things only changed because of Ember. That one storm she inadvertently caused had changed my whole life. Truths became lies and certainties became doubts. And I couldn't be more thankful.

Ryker would have never come into my life if not for that freak accident. Magic tied us together until we both saw each other as people. And fell in love.

"Ryker," I whispered his name, tipping my head back onto the cool cement. "I'm trying. I'm trying to fight. For you. For us. For our family."

Burning tears licked behind my eyes, grief grating at my lungs. Saying the words didn't take away the knowledge this would not end well for me. The stone would never let go. It would punish me for eternity or kill me the moment revenge was no longer fun. The loss of Lars was profound. Knowing he was there, even buried underneath, had been a chain keeping me linked to possibility. To hope. When he died, possibility and kinship fractured, letting excruciating loneliness and despair smother what was left of my soul. The darkness leaking in so deep, there were no tears. I went numb.

To stare into the face of the man, but know he was gone broke another piece of me. Not only had I grown to respect and care for him, he was my tether—I wasn't alone so long as he was here.

The torches spread deep shadows down the darkened barracks. The muted sounds of children's voices screaming and wailing from the fighting room chilled me.

Zoey Daniels, the Avenging Angel, had fought her way out of a lot of situations, but this was past surviving or fighting. The stone's words came back into my head: *You should be scared, Zoey. What I just did to him… I will eventually do to you. After I force you to watch yourself destroy all those you love.*

Right behind the stone's declaration, I heard Lars's voice wrap around my chest, whispering softly into my subconscious. *"Remember, Zoey, it can't ever truly have you."*

What did he mean by that? The stone had claimed *him*! The most powerful fae I knew. What fight could I have against it?

A swirling sensation filled my chest, coiling into my gut like a lasso tugging me back to the cave, calling me to my master. The stone was back.

Sometimes it kept me "awake" to play with me. To show me all it was doing, knowing I could do nothing but let it happen. It would take my soul bit by bit, until nothing was left.

Come join me, Zoey.

No longer fighting, I made my way back to the main cave, the fire enlarging the shadows of the monsters frantically moving around the space. Zeke yelled commands through his daggered teeth at the rest.

Something was happening.

"Zoey." Lars's figure moved to me. I tried to fight calling the stone, Lars, or even a man, because it wasn't, but the more the stone stretched under Lars's skin, the more it looked like a person. A man. He even wanted me to call him "Stone." I noticed him staring at some of the girls with a glint in his eyes, as though he were coming into a sexual awakening and getting to participate and feel things it only watched before.

"What's going on?" I tracked a group that grabbed weapons and headed down the tunnel to the outside world.

"The time is upon us," Stone replied, motioning his hand stiffly at his first in command. "Zeke has just reported a string of ships heading along the coast, full of fae. They are only hours away now. The war has started, precisely as I hoped. Human or fae, their brains are so simple to understand and foresee."

The two sides would be so concerned about fighting each other they wouldn't notice the third party moving in, demolishing them both.

"The deceit of your tricky words… The years you made me wait for you. It is time for you to pay up." Stone leaned closer, fire flickering off the black of the pupils. "I will take everything from you while you watch… You deserve no less. I've dreamed of nothing but revenge upon you."

His gaze dropped to my mouth and every molecule of air vanished from my lungs. I tried to pull back, but his will locked my limbs in place. His brow furrowed, and he looked down, my gaze following.

Fuck. No. Terror gripped me. His pants pitched out, showing off his arousal.

"W-what is happening?" He growled.

The thought of the most powerful weapon in the world getting his first boner and not understanding what it signified almost made me want to laugh. But then I realized what it meant. The idea of hurting me turned him on. There was nothing humorous about that.

I said nothing as past trauma froze me in place. I'd worked hard to overcome what I'd gone through, to not be a victim. I promised myself I never would let anyone make me feel that way again. But it didn't stop the icy claws of terror from scraping across my spine. He had full control over me and could do anything he wanted.

"It can't ever truly have you," I repeated Lars's statement over and over in my head.

"Master. Mother." Zeke walked up, bowing to both of us, hate flicking at me with a quick glance. "The children are ready."

"Great." Stone backed away from me, clearing his throat. "Prepare everyone in the next few hours. We head out at dawn."

"Yes, sir." Zeke dipped his head and took off down the tunnel.

"Are you ready, Zoey?" Stone faced me again. "You ready to watch everyone you love die?"

"I'm ready to watch you die."

The stone tried to smile, his lips curving oddly. "I cannot die."

He was a weapon of magic, but he was also a man now… susceptible to weaknesses of men: power, lust, greed.

"We'll see about that."

TWENTY
Kennedy

Impressions of the soles of my shoes were worn into the rug from my constant pacing. Dawn hinted at the horizon, yet my eyes had not closed, my hurting heart and weighted mind did not allow me rest.

"Ken, please." Lorcan scrubbed his face, a yawn stretching his lips. "Lay down for two seconds." He rolled his head on the pillow, patting the empty space next to him. "You are exhausted; I can feel it. You need to sleep."

"No." I wagged my head, starting my cycle over the rug again. "I really shouldn't be sleeping. I need to figure out how to save my friends. My people. To win this battle."

"Have you?" Lorcan propped on his elbows, curving one eyebrow.

"Have I what?"

"Figured all that out. I mean, you had all night." He shook his head in disappointment. "Really, Ken, you should have broken into the castle, defeated the dragon, and found the meaning of life by now."

I paused and glared over my shoulder at him. "You're not helping."

"Come on." He patted the bed again. "You are only hurting yourself. You need to rest. You've gone long past the point of figuring anything out. Now you're just going in circles. Figuratively and literally." He nodded at the indentations on the rug.

My shoulders slumped, and I walked over to the bed, sinking onto the mattress. Watching Ember sail away with Stavros, sacrificing herself, had added another block of concrete onto my shoulders. Should I have let her? Was it the right decision? Not that I could ever order Ember to do anything, but I still felt as though it would be my fault if anything happened to her. Ryker as well.

Nic and Kate were not helpful with any behind-the-scenes information at the compound. Stavros kept them drugged and barely coherent the entire stay. Marguerite, who was now up and about, had shooed away the healers and was hovering over the two invalids like a mother hen, stuffing their bellies full of love and healing powers. I swear her food had a magic component to it. Whatever was going on, it somehow made you feel better.

"She chose to go. You couldn't have stopped her." Lorcan brushed strands of hair from my face. "Hell, my brother couldn't do shit to stop her." After Ember's departure, Eli went berserk, shifting into his beast and roaring into the forest. As far as I knew, he hadn't returned. Lorcan, West, and Cooper went after him but returned muttering something about the ass needing space.

"I know." I bowed my head.

"Then let it go. I know it sounds harsh, but you have enough to try and figure out. She is strong and stubborn as hell. I have no doubt that between her and the Viking, Ember will be the one who walks out."

A small smile wobbled on my mouth.

"We have two more days to devise our battle plans. A few hours of sleep will help that, not hurt it." His hand dropped to my shoulder. "We've been to war before. We survived and we'll do it again."

Staring into his green eyes, I swallowed before responding. "Dying is not my worst fear."

His mouth pinched together, understanding my meaning. He wrapped his arms around me as I curled into his body, inhaling his scent. An ointment to my soul. "I have this sick feeling in my gut, as if something horrible is about to happen."

Lorcan's lips brushed my forehead. "Because it is."

A worm of fear kept wiggling in my stomach, my intuition sensing doom. Immediate doom… as though this moment was the calm before the storm.

"You are so wound up." Lorcan pulled me tighter into him. "Every muscle is tense. I can help with that."

"I'm sure you *think* you can." I grinned into his chest.

"You purposely trying to challenge me?"

"Maybe."

In an instant, Lorcan flipped me on my back, pinning my body under his, naked and wanting. His mouth found mine, parting my lips in a deep kiss, which swiftly turned desperate and wild. I needed to feel him. Now.

Time felt so short, darkness looming at the edge of the bed, and I didn't want to waste a moment of it.

I wrapped my hand around his shaft, pumping my hand up and down. Lorcan rumbled against my mouth, his fingers flicking my nipples. I locked my legs around his waist, twisted us over, and climbed on top of him. I ripped off my T-shirt, the rest of me already naked. His irises shimmered with red as I took lead, leading his cock inside me as I slammed down, gasping.

"Fuuucck." His head curled back into the pillow, his hands grabbing my hips. I had grown more aggressive in the bedroom, but tonight I felt even more fearless. The world was about to end and nothing else mattered but this moment with Lorcan. Rolling my hips, I began to build a ruthless rhythm, taking what I wanted. My need for him, to drive so deep inside me, felt different as I ground my teeth together, grunting in desperation.

"Shit, Kennedy." He hissed, thrusting into me with abandonment, hitting the spot that had me grabbing the headboard, picking up my pace. A cry ripped from my throat, words I knew to be Latin, barked from me, but I didn't think about what they meant or why it was coming from my mouth without thought. Sweat trickled over my back, our bodies slapping together. I rode him mercilessly, the tingle of an orgasm heating up my thighs.

A deep growl rumbled through the room as his eyes turned fully red. He grabbed me and pulled me off him, his teeth bared. He quickly had me bent over the side of the bed on my stomach, plunging back into me from behind. Using the curve of the bed to get traction, his thickness pounded into me. My nails dug into the sheets, my body tightening around him. His hands slid into mine, lacing them together, slamming even harder.

"Oh god..." I wailed, pleasure hitting every nerve, sending flames through my muscles.

He leaned back, changing his position slightly. The tip of him struck my G-spot and my body tightened around him. I could feel his cock pulse inside, and my body exploded, my eyes shutting as more Latin curled off my tongue in choppy bits. He drove into me a couple more times before he roared and released into me. Unbelievable pleasure tore at every nerve, stealing the air from my lungs. He pulsed as he continued to empty himself inside me, causing bliss so raw I cried out another string of Latin words.

Sparks of white blinked behind my lids, ripping me from reality.

Oh. No. Not now!

Flash.

Ships sail for the harbor, the King's insignia on the masts.

Flash.

My office. My desk. A calendar. Today's date.

Flash.

I was standing outside the castle in a courtyard of the village. Crumbled building. Charred cars and wagons. Dead bodies were sprawled and shredded in lumps all around me. Tap, tap, tap. The sound of blood dripping down into the gutter echoed in my ears.

I had been in a vision like this before. But this time I wasn't in a field, ready to fight Aneira. This time I was Queen, inside my own castle walls, fighting for it against another mad leader.

Something tickled my feet, and I knew before I even looked what I touched this time.

Everyone I loved and cared for lay in a heap around me. Dead.

I was here again.

My heart raced in my chest, devastation welling in my eyes. Who would I lose in this war?

"Time's up." At the sound of a squawk, my gaze bolted up. Grimmel was perched on top a burned-out car.

"Grimmel."

"That is what you call me."

I sighed. I wished just once he would tell me what I needed to know. But that was not Grimmel's way.

"Is this a vision I can change?"

"Only you know."

"Always helpful."

"Hurry, Light." Grimmel flapped his wings.

"Hurry, what?"

"What can fly without wings?"

Flash.

Ships. A loud clock ticking. Bodies.

Flash.

"Hey, li'l bird. Come back to me." A voice pulled me back, blinking up at deep green eyes.

Pillows and blankets were strewn around my naked body. My gaze wandered around the room.

"What do you feel?" He ran his fingers between my thighs. Lorcan. Home.

Crap times a million. He had literally screwed me into oblivion.

"What do you see?" He leaned over, kissing my neck. "Smell?" He bit my earlobe and the jolt of pain jerked me fully awake. "I take it as a compliment I can make you pass out from an orgasm, so don't ruin this for me."

Clock. Blood. Ships. My desk.

"What can fly without wings?"

This vision had been more obscure than most. It jumped around, but my brain kept hearing the loudly ticking clock, flashing to my desk.

"Ken?" Lorcan flipped hair away from my face.

"I need to go to my office." I climbed off the bed, heading for the closet.

"No 'thank you, Lorcan, for the best sex of my life'? Really, you should get medals and have a holiday named in your honor." His sarcasm reached me in the large walk-in. I grabbed leggings and a sweater, strolling back into our room.

"Thank you, Lorcan, for the best sex of my life." I smirked, pulling on my clothes. "I will ask the nobles if I can get a day named after you."

"Oh, ask for statues to be *erected*." He slipped from the bed, walking proudly to me.

"Cute."

"Make the women jealous in all the land."

I laughed, pulling on my boots. I wasn't about to admit that a naked statue of him would do exactly that. Also, the sex we just had was so incredible my legs still wobbled.

"What was your vision?" He grabbed his T-shirt off a chair, his expression losing all humor.

"It was odd." I zipped my last boot and stood. "It was different from usual. Incredibly jumbled. But it kept showing me my desk. As if it were hinting at something I was missing there."

I went to the door, hearing Lorcan slip on clothes. I swung open the door to see Torin pacing around my outer chamber. Since Lorcan had moved in, Hazel, the personal attendant who came with the castle, had decided retirement wasn't such a bad thing, which couldn't have pleased me more. She had scared the hell out of me.

"Torin?" A flush coated my cheeks. How long had he been there? How much had he heard?

His head jolted up like he was surprised to see me there. A wild, perplexed expression showed in his eyes. His hair was ruffled and untied, his clothes rumpled, as though he'd slept in them. Instantly, I felt unsettled, and scared. This was very unlike him.

"What's wrong? What are you doing here?" I stepped out of the room, Lorcan following close behind, thankfully dressed in a shirt and jeans.

210

"I-I…" He ran his hand over his hair, tweaking it even more. "No. I shouldn't do this. It's reprehensible." He shook his head, turning to leave.

"Torin. Stop." I jogged up next to him, my brows dipping down. I had never seen him like this. He was always in control and disciplined. "What is it? You can talk to me." I grabbed his arm, halting his fleeing steps.

"No. I'm sorry I bothered you, my lady. Forget it." Pain clouded his expression before he shook it off, pushing forward.

"No." I cut him off, stepping in front of him. "Tell me." I could order him, but instead I reached out, touching his hand. "I am your Queen, but also your friend. If I can do anything to unburden you, please let me. I can tell something is bothering you."

"I can't believe I'm going to ask this of you, my lady." Anguish shone brightly in his eyes, his tongue running over his bottom lip. "I understand by law you must say no, but I still feel I have to ask, to try. Beg for your consideration."

My eyes widened, hearing the desperation in his voice, my heart rate picking up. What could possibly have the stoic First Knight begging? "What is it, Torin?"

"Uh." He exhaled heavily. "It's Thara…" He briefly shut his eyes, his Adam's apple bobbing. "I would like to ask for a pardon on her behalf."

Okay. Wow. I was not expecting that. Not from him. The last I had known, he wouldn't even go see her. I had long ago forgiven her, but he said he never would.

"Have you gone to see her?"

"Yes." He bowed his head. "I've been down there several times now."

"And you have forgiven her?"

"Forgiven?" He shook his head. "No. Not fully, but I want to. I understand her motives a bit more." He swallowed. "Things have changed."

It was an instant, a bloom of his aurora, the sensation fluttering at the edges, but enough for me to see what he was trying to hide.

"You're in love with her." I tried to hide my smile.

"Love?" He wagged his head fervently. "Absolutely not, my lady. I care about her. She has been my comrade for centuries." His protest was as thin as parchment. Even he knew it.

I stepped closer, my mouth curving. "I am happy for you, Torin. You don't know how much I wish you happiness. You deserve that more than anyone I know, but pardoning her will be almost impossible with the nobles."

"You are Queen, and we are going to war. We need all available warriors possible. She is a fighter. An excellent one. It is *your* decision to make."

My smile grew. "You mean *break the rules*," I whispered conspiratorially.

I thought he would react to my words, try to deny he would break code, but instead he picked himself up higher. "Yes, my lady. Screw the nobles."

Wow. This was serious.

"Screw the nobles." I nodded. "I hereby pardon Thara of the wrongs she enacted against the crown."

"Really?" Torin looked shocked at my statement. "You truly are all right with this?"

"Anyone who makes you say 'screw the nobles' is more than all right with me." I held up my hand. "But she can never be a private soldier for me. You understand that, right? She has to stay in the general army, without close access to me. She has a long way to go to prove herself."

"Of course, my lady." Torin bowed, grabbing my hand and kissing it. "Thank you."

"Go." I tipped my head to the side. "Go free her. Get her prepared for what is coming."

He nodded, turning to the hall.

"Oh, and Torin?" He turned back to me. "Do not take her for granted again. Every day you should feel lucky you have an amazing woman like her who still loves you."

He didn't talk but bowed his head before he turned around and ran down the hall.

"I think I'm really going to like Thara." Lorcan came beside me. "Anyone who can make his ass even a tiny bit tolerable has to be fucking awesome."

"Some might say the same about you."

"Oh, I know I'm fucking awesome." He nudged me. "Hence the statues in my name."

"I meant being more tolerable." I winked at him. "Actually, never mind. That's impossible."

"Okay, li'l Druid, you're getting lippy again." He smacked my ass, herding me along the passage. "Might have to discipline you again. Office spankings?"

A few minutes later, I stared at my desk, trying to find anything of significance. Maps, notes, and paperwork were strewn over it, but nothing new, nothing that was important.

"Night out, but light is still off." A squawk came from the window. I craned my neck to the side.

"Grimmel, you were there. Help me. What am I missing?" I placed my palms on the top of each sheet, hoping for a flashback to kick in.

"I know not. Only bringer, not prophet." He huffed snidely, hopping onto the desk.

"Ahhhh! Why can't you ever be helpful?"

"Can only lead. You must drink."

Lorcan snorted coming next to me. "What about stuffed raven for the holidays?"

I eyed my feathered friend. "Not a bad idea."

Grimmel flapped his wings, a low raspy hiss coming from his chest. "What can fly without wings?" I jerked toward him. This was the same riddle he spoke in the vision.

"Easy." Lorcan snorted. "Time."

Grimmel huffed as if he were upset Lorcan figured it out. "Brain cell still left in dweller."

"Time," I repeated. My hand slid over the contents of my desk, touching everything, my fingers grazing the propped-up calendar.

Flash.

The vision I had earlier slammed back in as I zeroed in on the date. The clock sounded like a time bomb about to go off. Today's date, before the sounds of screams echoed in my ear. Blood. Dead bodies. Ships sailing in.

Flash.

I jerked back to the present. The vision didn't take me fully under. I peered at the calendar, then swung around to the peaceful lake, but my gut rolled with the impending storm, understanding what was coming.

"Oh. No," I said at the same moment Lorcan went rigid beside me, his head snapping toward outside. I felt the buzz of energy, the link between dark dwellers.

My mouth opened to ask as he bolted for the door, running out of the room. Padding after him, I got to the hallway when I heard the sounds of doors slamming, muttering in the hallways. West, still tugging on a T-shirt, was the first one I spotted.

"What is happening?"

"Eli." He jogged past me. "Something's wrong, darlin'."

Staying close behind him, I followed West outside. Cole, Lorcan, Dax, and Dom were already there watching Eli's dweller sprint from the forest toward us, something hanging gingerly from his daggered mouth. I squinted, trying to see what it was.

"Sprig!" Annabeth's voice cried out behind me, swinging me around. She stood in only a thigh-length men's T-shirt next to Cooper, who wore no shirt at all. Both looked flushed, hair a mess. Annabeth bolted forward, her bare feet striking the debris of the forest bed, crashing to her knees in front of Eli, her hands stretched out for the tiny monkey.

Her ethereal appearance reminded me of Belle from *Beauty and the Beast*. Though, that was the wrong beast she was taming. I glanced over at Cooper, who stared at her as if she were a dream come to life.

She gently picked Sprig from Eli's mouth, laying the unconscious sprite in her hands. He was slimy, but otherwise appeared unharmed. Annabeth curled him to her chest, stroking Sprig's head.

Eli rumbled, his body shifting back to human. As many times as I'd watched Lorcan do it, it never ceased to amaze and disturb me.

His body curved and twisted, forming back into his human shape. The sleek black fur receded, defining every solid toned muscle underneath. His razor-sharp teeth and spine lined with sharp, spiked horns disappeared in a blink. Eli stood before us, naked.

"What's going on, Eli?" Cole tossed him a pair of sweats. "You didn't make much sense."

Eli pulled on the pants, his chest still heaving from running.

"I was prowling around Lars's property, seeing if there was any way I could get in." Where Ember was, he would be there. "I smelled him. Escaping from the compound." He nodded to the bundle in Annabeth's arms. "I was only able to get a few words from him before he passed out." Eli licked his lips.

"What?" Deep down, I felt I already knew.

"Pirates. Trap. And honey bears wanting to eat his brains. I got the feeling that was not really related."

A few of my private guards stayed on the outer ring, ready for a command. It was strange how I almost stopped realizing they were there. Sturt, Georgia, and Castien hovered close by.

"Castien, go get Torin. He should be in the dungeons. Tell him to get the men ready and then retrieve Croygen. Georgia and Sturt, lock down the docks. No one goes in or out. And bring all the captains to me... in handcuffs."

"Yes, Your Majesty." The three of them bowed and dashed off to execute my demands.

"Croygen wouldn't betray you." Annabeth stood, tossing her blonde hair over her shoulders as she shook her head. "He is my family. I know him. He wouldn't do that."

"I've been deceived by those I thought closest to me. A friend. I want to believe you, but I can't afford to risk my people's lives." The statement came from my mouth, empathy and strength holding up each word. In that instant, I realized how much I had changed. I used to be like her. I could tell she carried her own demons, but there remained an innocence to her. I wanted to believe I still had a little of that, but with all that happened, those I'd lost, and becoming a leader had ripped idealism from me. Yet each scar had made me be a stronger person. And they all led me here. To be Queen and to be with Lorcan.

"Let's gather in the throne room; I think we've been betrayed." Anger whipped inside me. I turned back for the palace, a place I had never considered home until now when my home and everyone in it had been threatened. Now I wanted to protect it with everything I had. "War is coming today. We must be ready."

TWENTY-ONE
Fionna

Staring up, the lights from the sleeping village in the distance grazed over the timber, strange designs winding over the ceiling. Dawn nipped at night's heels, and I had yet to get my lids to shut. The soft bed curved around me, but my restless limbs made it feel more like a torture device.

Guilt and shame dwarfed all logic. I wasn't the one who'd gone with Stavros to save my daughter.

I should be there trying to protect Piper, but here I lay, useless, scared, and sick to my stomach. Stavros's threats looped in my head.

Ember's pointed look to me, the unsaid *I will get your daughter,* only ebbed my fear a smidge. But nothing took away the sensation I'd failed Piper. Again.

Pulse.

"And another bloody reason why I can't sleep." My hand grazed my stomach. "Carrying your arse around."

Pulse.

The warmth of him spread farther across my abdomen. I didn't want to admit out loud that the weight of him had tripled, fatiguing my muscles and mind. The longer I held his soul, the faster mine suffocated under his power. I was dying. And if my body failed, he would die too.

Pushing myself up, I stared at the outline of the object in the corner. The cauldron sat there, taunting me. Sliding down the bed, I crawled to it, running my fingers over the lip. "Please," I whispered. "Tell me how to bring you back."

The power of two Cathbads didn't bring it back to life, but I still couldn't give up on the idea. There had to be a way. It was part of me. It came from my family's magic. Our blood.

Shite.

Blood.

Was it possible? "It would be something like that, wouldn't it?" I spoke to the treasure. "Druids and the gods are that twisted."

One of the most powerful forms of magic was a blood ritual. I should know; I had done one recently. With Lars.

Technically he was *still* with me.

I pressed my fingers into my gut. "You ready for another round, demon?"

Pulse. Pulse. Pulse.

Each felt like a jab of anger. *No.* I could practically taste his refusal. *Don't even think about it, Druid. You barely survived last time.*

"That's going to happen anyway." I shrugged, holding on to my last thread of hope. "I'd rather try. We did it once and it worked. This time we're not searching for the cauldron, we're bringing it back to life."

Pulsepulsepulsepulse.

"Feck off, demon. You owe me this. You destroyed it to save me... now I must bring it back to life to save you. Only fair." Fury burned through my stomach, rising up my throat.

"Stop being an arse," I muttered, not fazed in the least at his fury or that I was pretty much talking to myself. Picking my heavy bones off the floor, I went to my boot and pulled out the dagger I never returned to Travil. It was mine now. It chose me, holding too much energy and memory from my sacrifices to ever be held by another. It had been there for the first blood ritual and would be even more powerful for this one, already carrying my blood and Lars's within its metal.

The pulses turned to stabs, but I ignored his tantrum, knowing I would get my way. He needed to throw his alpha-king authority around for a bit before realizing who he was dealing with. Someone who equaled him and would not bow down.

There were no candles, but I had chalk in my bag. Every Druid carried chalk. You never knew when you needed to do a blood ritual at the drop of a hat. Shoving back the rug, I drew a circle on the wood floor, not closing it completely. Slipping out of my underwear and tank, I picked up the cauldron and stepped into the ring. Lars's demon still prowled heavily inside me, stomping around, holding on to the fringes of his objection.

"Lars. Focus. I need you. I need you to hold on to me," I practically whispered, sitting down. I placed the cauldron next to me. The anger vanished, his presence expanding inside me. We both understood that "me" meant my soul. It almost drifted away last time, the ritual too powerful for it to hold on to my physical form. He saved me. Brought me back.

This time he was in his purest form, powerful and strong, but I had no clue if this would even work without his physical body here. Never in a thousand years did I think I would be doing another blood ritual. I tried to shut out the dread I felt knowing what I was getting into.

"Here we go." I exhaled, shaking out my arms and legs, letting go of all my thoughts. Closing the circle, I lay down and shut my eyes. Meditation cut off the world outside the circle, and the spell hummed from my lips. The handle of the knife warmed in my hand. The blade sliced over one wrist. With a hiss, I cut at the other. Stinging pain folded over my chant, weighing down my throat. Pushing through, I carved quickly at the tops of my thighs, a small cry filling the gaps between my words. *Don't stop, Fionna. You can do this.*

Lifting my free hand, I dipped in the pooling blood, painting symbols over my skin, then duplicating them onto the cauldron's surface as I continued to chant and slice wounds into myself.

Shite. This was a lot harder to do to by yourself.

My head began to spin, my lids struggling to stay open, the pain throbbing over my body. Hissing out more of the spell, I felt the magic barrel down on me, pinning me back into the floorboards. A scream broke from my mouth as the pressure slammed me down, stealing my air and mindfulness.

The knife dropped from my hand, fresh agony tearing through me. This time the pain pulsed between my thighs. Every touch only flamed the fire under my skin, burning me from the inside out. Tears flooded down my face; whimpers and cries came out the same way a wounded animal sounds.

I gripped the cauldron, pouring my life essence into it. Slipping further and further away from consciousness, sexual need filled its place. *Make it stop. Please!* Instead, the aching increased, forcing another cry from my lips, my bones cracking as I gripped the cauldron.

Please. Please. Please. Someone, make it stop.

Suddenly I felt the sensation of hands slipping over my skin. Inside my mind I saw him. Black demon eyes, hungry and devouring, hovered over me. A mischievous smile curved on the demon's mouth as he brought it down to my body, his tongue licking at my breasts, his sharp teeth nibbling my nipples.

The gods could never simply let you suffer with one kind of pain. They were horny shites who loved to flood sexual agony into every cell as well. To the point you wished for death or to be screwed until the pain ebbed.

Most of these rituals ended in orgies. I no longer judged those still practicing the old ways. If anything, I was now an advocate.

"Lars," a whimper sliced upon my tongue.

He showed me his full demon, his presence taking up every molecule of space in my head and underneath my skin. His form grunted, dragging his mouth and body over my scorching skin.

"Lars," I cried out his name again, his touch flooding me with pleasure. More tears slithered over my face as the heartache of missing him rocked me.

"I'm here, Druid." His hands and mouth moved over my stomach, my neck curling back into the floor. The pleasure of his touch, of feeling the weight of him on me, was so intense I gasped for air. "Conclude your incantation; I am here to take care of everything else." It was like I could feel him take one hand, placing it on the treasure.

The spell sobbed from my chest, the pain of desire cooking me alive. My legs spread, begging for him to fill me. To end this agony. He bit my inner thighs, skating his tongue between my folds.

Anguish.

Torment.

The moment I finished the spell, commanding life into the cauldron, knives daggered my skin like the teeth of the strighoul. My body bucked as though possessed, trying to get away from the unrelenting pain.

"Lars! Please..." I wailed, my free hand burrowing into the floorboards. "End this... please... hurts... so much."

"Stay with me, Druid." He gripped me. "Don't leave me. Fight it, Fionna."

What the hell was he talking about? I wasn't going anywhere.

"Fuck me," I begged.

"Will that keep you here with me?"

"Yes! Yes... just do it! Please!"

"I am at your will." He smirked, sliding up my body. My skin was unblemished and clear of blood, nothing surrounded us but shadows, which grew darker, reaching for me. A string of consciousness told me I was no longer in my physical body, but the anguish kept any thoughts really reaching my brain. It was only need. Desire.

"Put me in my place, demon." I clawed at his flesh, bringing him down on me. He leaned back, and then I felt him thrust in hard, pleasure rolling through me. He roared, his claws digging deeper into my skin. He started to pump his hips. Every cell in me blistered with unbelievable pleasure. It reminded me of the moment when his soul first touched mine—another plane of sensation, where physical forms didn't exist, only energy.

Pure bliss.

The pain eased as euphoria took over, our grunts growing louder and more primal.

"Fuck, I've missed you, Druid." He hissed, slamming into me so hard I skidded deeper into the blackness. "No!" he bellowed, rocking even more reverently. "Do not let go. Do not leave me. You are strong. Fight, Fionna! Fight for Piper."

Why was he yelling at me?

Why was I so tired?

"Promise me." He poured more of himself into me. As I parted my lips, my muscles locked in pleasure. My body spasmed, clutching around him. "Promise!"

"I promise!" I screamed, blackness curled around me, creeping in like mist, making it harder to even see or feel him.

"Now, Druid," he demanded. "Fucking *come* for me."

I let his command take over my mind and body, moaning with relief as the pain drained from me, euphoria stealing my vision. I no longer felt attached to anything. Only pleasure, warmth, and serenity blanketed me. Darkness. Peace.

"No. Fionna!" Lars's voice sounded distant.

Then I heard a scream, one that sent chills along my spine. A banshee call. The sound of death.

Through the murk I heard my daughter's voice calling me. Then Lars shouted into my soul, pulling me back with the fear in his voice.

But it was so quiet here. Peaceful and calm.

Don't you give up on me. Or your daughter, Lars growled, the sound curling around my body. *Wake up. Now.*

Piper. Lars. Kennedy. Marguerite. Nic... my family—their faces filled my mind. I never had much family; how strange to have so many needing me.

"Fionna?" A voice I didn't recognize slashed into the peaceful void. "Oh my god! Get help! Fionna? Fionna, wake up!"

People were so fecking demanding today. Couldn't I rest for a little longer?

You're dying, Fionna. Get your ass up and fight, an inner voice whispered. Shite. I was. I could feel my soul slipping away.

Images of my little girl, her smile, and laugh flooded me. I recalled Lars dropping the King façade and really looking at me, the feel of his touch on my skin. I could picture the three of us curled on a sofa, watching a movie, like a real family.

I gave a deep grunt as I pushed forward, swimming back to life. To the ones I loved.

Bolting up, I hissed in a gulp of air, my lids ripping open only to flinch back at the light in the room. My head spun and every muscle shook, my naked body still drenched with blood, the cauldron tipped over a few feet away from me painted with my sacrifice.

With the back of my hand I wiped away blood on my lashes as I looked over to the person squatting next to me. It took a few beats for me to recognize her.

Flawless caramel skin and dark curly hair. Dressed in tiny pajama shorts and a tank, Lexi's mouth moved frantically, her expression anxious, but I didn't comprehend anything coming out of her mouth, my brain slow to catch up. The sexy pirate, Croygen, with dark eyes, his ripped, lean abs on display, leaned over, staring at me with curiosity. What the hell was going on?

I shook my head, clearing away the fuzz in my mind.

"Are you okay?" Lexie peered down my body, taking in the cuts and symbols shrouding my skin, then to the blood-covered black pot. Croygen stood beside her, staring at me.

"What the hell were you doing?" he said. "I've seen some twisted shit in Asia, but you, Druid, might take the prize."

Lexie peered over her shoulder at him, then back at me, gazing at my naked skin with a frown. "Why don't I get you something to cover up." She grabbed the shirt I left outside the ring, handing it to me.

"What are you doing here?" I pulled it on and tried to stand up, my legs wobbling underneath me. Lexie reached for me, her mechanical legs clicking with the movement of her rising.

"What are *we* doing?" Croygen snorted, waving down at me. "My room is next door. We heard screaming and moans as if either someone was having sex or was being murdered… we took a chance on the last one after you screamed like the dead."

Dead…

I spun around to the cauldron, the motion making me nauseous. Kneeling again, I placed my hands on it. Nerves thumped my heart loudly, and I took a deep breath to relax.

"What are you doing?" Lexie asked.

"Shhh," I snapped. My energy was practically nonexistent, but I

221

pushed away all distracting thoughts and focused what little strength I had left onto the vessel, tuning out the others.

Was that a beat I felt? I placed my palms on the vessel. For several moments I stayed quiet, feeling nothing. It was just my own heart thumping in my chest, working hard to fill my veins and heal me.

"Shite!" I bent over as a frustrated, heartbroken sob surged through my chest. I'd given it everything. My magic, my blood, practically my life... and it still wasn't enough.

It wasn't enough. It wanted all of me. My life. To fulfill the prophecy and claim me like it was supposed to. I tried to run from fate, and it had still found me.

My forehead hit the edge of the vessel, another soft cry leaking from me. Piper. Lars. Kennedy... I would do it for them. If that's what it took to protect the ones I loved. Uncle Isaac had been right—my death was already foreseen. I had changed the script a little, but not the outcome.

Ignoring the people behind me, I started to cry. The enormity of this loss stripped me of any pride or barriers I'd been holding up. I would not get to see my daughter grow up, or see those important moments in her life, or truly have the chance to be her mum. I probably would never see Lars again, not in his body. My sacrifice would have to wait until we were face to face with the stone, Lars's body ready to be taken back, but I would die before I got to feel his touch one last time, the cauldron needing all my power to take on the Stone of Fáil.

"Fionna?" A hand touched my shoulder. Lexie's fingers squeezed my muscles. I dropped the cauldron, wanting to toss it out the window into the lake. I hated it. I hated having no choice; it went against everything I was. I bucked against authority, challenged it, and designed my own future.

But I couldn't fight this. Wiping away the tears, I stared at the drying blood on my arms and hands.

Sudden shouts echoed through the hall, twisting my head around. Croygen and Lexie both turned, the sound of feet pounding toward us.

"What the hell is going on?" Croygen's eyebrows furrowed, and he took a step to the door. Torin, Castien, and a few other guards I recognized but didn't recall their names, passed my open doorway. Torin peered into my room, his eyes landing on the pirate. He stopped short.

"He's here!" Torin twisted, blocking the doorway. "Seize him." Castien and two other men pushed past, circling Croygen.

"Me?" Croygen took a step back, but the soldiers surrounded him, their weapons drawn.

"What is going on? What are you doing?" Lexie yelled, her eyes wide with confusion. "Stop! He didn't do anything. Why are you arresting him?"

"By declaration of the Queen, we are taking him for questioning."

"Why?" Croygen bewilderment rode over his features.

"Treason."

"What?" Lexie screeched.

My mouth dropped open as I slowly pushed myself to standing, my gaze bouncing between Torin and Croygen.

"Treason?" Croygen shook his head. "Are you kidding me? I haven't done a fucking thing."

"That is not for me to decide." Torin eyes finally drifted over to me, his eyes widening. "Are you all right? Did he hurt you?"

"Oh." I looked down at my body, realizing what this might look like. "No—"

My explanation was not fast enough, for Torin jerked his head to the door with severity. "Move now, pirate."

"Wait! No… he didn't…" My words fell flat as the group rushed out my door, shoving Croygen with them.

"Torin. No!" My bare feet stumbled forward, my legs quivering severely under my weight. Lexie screamed his innocence, trailing after the troops. Forgetting I was caked with drying blood, I scampered after them as well, my legs wanting to give out with each step.

Croygen peered over his shoulder as they hurried him down the hallway, his gaze catching Lexie's, something intimate transpiring between them. Something deep and profound.

Ready to defend Croygen of any wrongdoing on my behalf at least, I matched my steps close behind Lexie. I couldn't believe he would deceive us. If he did, wouldn't that be betraying Zoey, Ryker, and Lexie as well? And the way Croygen looked at Lexie told me he would never hurt her.

We entered the throne room, and I jerked back in shock. The room was filled with people.

Croygen was shoved up to the front to Kennedy, who sat on the raised throne. As long as I had been around, she barely used this room, and not when speaking to us. She was doing this on purpose. Showing her authority.

What the hell happened in the few hours since I last saw her?

I stepped up to Lexie, not looking at her, but letting her know I was there.

"Let him go." Kennedy nodded at Castien. "I don't think he will flee. You can get back to your post."

"What the hell is going on?" Croygen ripped his arms out of the soldier's hold. "Why am I here?"

"Croygen." Kennedy addressed him. Her voice was strong, but her eyes were softer than her tone. "I apologize if you are innocent in this, but right now I can't be too careful. Too many lives are at stake."

"What is this about?" He looked around the room, trying to find some explanation.

"Your friends." Kennedy waved her had toward the window, the docks far below. "Betrayed us. Lied to us. They came here under my protection and told us Stavros's ships were three days out. When in truth, they are here now."

"What?" Croygen stilled, his annoyance draining away. "What are you talking about?"

"Stavros bought your acquaintances." Kennedy stood, her tiny frame full of strength. "And because you were the one to vouch for them, I have to suspect you as well."

Croygen's mouth fell open, words dying on his lips.

"No." Lexie shook her head next to me. "Croygen would never do that. He's innocent."

At Lexie's declaration, Annabeth came to her side, grabbing her hand, the other hand holding the small monkey. "I also vouch for his innocence."

Before anyone could respond, the doors banged open, startling me. A mass of Kennedy's guards swarmed in the space, delivering the Queen a handful of pirates—men and women. The only one I recognized was Jack, the one we'd met on the dock earlier.

"All the ships are accounted for, but we only found individuals on the *Black Revenge*, Your Majesty." The large redheaded Scot shoved Jack forward, his feet scrambling, his expression twisted with anger. He, too, was dressed only in pants, his feet and chest bare. Lipstick marks dotted his bare torso.

"Is this what you call being accommodating to your guests?" Jack wiggled his tied hands, his eyes blazing. "I enjoy kinky sex in my cabin, but being tied up by the Queen is giving me flashbacks to the previous leader, Your Highness."

Kennedy's eyes narrowed on the pirate, her aura sparking with anger. Comparing her to Aneira was one of the worst things you could do, not to mention untrue.

"Let's skip the denials and untruths; I don't have time for them." Kennedy lifted her head with indignation, her raven tattoo showing on her neck. "I have a castle to defend and kingdom to save." She took a step down, coming even with Croygen and Jack.

Lorcan, standing by the window to her side, moved forward, his eyes flashing red in warning to the men: Don't fuck with the Queen, or you became a dweller feast. "People always say don't trust a pirate. Lesson learned."

"You fucking bastard!" Croygen surged for Jack, but guards quickly grabbed him, pulling him back.

"What are you talking about?" Jack looked around, stopping on Croygen for a beat before peering back at Kennedy. "You asked me to come as a favor to the Queen. I was happy to stay far away from this fight."

"I know pirates have no honor, but there was an unspoken code between us. I saved your life," Croygen seethed, leaning into Jack's face.

Jack's mouth parted, his eyes wandering back to the few crew being held around him. "Where's the rest?" His head snapped to the Queen. "Why only nab us?"

"There was no one else," Sturt growled back. "Seems some of your crew took off."

Croygen and Jack both gaped at the Scot.

Mutiny was a cardinal sin with pirates.

"No. No way..." Jack's voice tapered off. His attention flew to Kennedy. "My crew wouldn't do that."

"Were you the one to get word about the location of the ships?" Kennedy took another step closer.

Befuddled, Jack stared around the room, taking in each one of his stunned crew. His head bowed, a vein twitching in his forehead. "No. My second relayed the information to me."

"Bellamy?" Croygen snorted. "Yeah, that's a shocker."

"He's been faithful to me for fifty years."

"Fifty years he's been dreaming about taking your ship." Croygen leaned into Jack's face. "I warned you years ago about him, but you didn't listen."

"Why would I listen to you? You were the one who wanted my ships," Jack snarled back.

"I was open about it." Croygen didn't back down. "He was the weasel. The one slowly taking over the crew, questioning their alliance to you." Croygen's toes knocked into Jack's. "I swear, if your mistake hurts any of mine, you're dead."

With arms tied behind his back, Jack bucked his chest into Croygen, shoving him back. Fury strained Croygen's features. He bared his teeth, diving for Jack.

"Stop!" Kennedy's hand rose, her authority ringing through the air. Both men stopped, but didn't look at her, their chests heaving with rage. "We don't have time for this. It can wait until the real battle is over." She rubbed her head. "I'm going to have to take the risk and believe you were deceived as well."

"You'd think I would stick around here if I were lying?" Jack said to Ken, but kept his gaze locked on his fellow pirate.

"No, I don't think you would." Kennedy stared at Jack. "Actually, I know you wouldn't. I can sense your truth. You would run like the coward you are."

Jack scoffed. Croygen's mouth parted in a grin.

"It's the one thing you can trust about a pirate. He'll charm you, rob you blind, but won't ever stick around."

"True." Jack chuckled. "Sorry, man."

"Sorry I didn't believe you, but you know, you're a fucking pirate."

"Seriously, boot humper," Sprig's voice exclaimed. We all turned to the monkey leaping from Annabeth, to Sturt, to Croygen, where he settled at last, pointing at the rock-star pirate. "You trust him?"

"Trust?" Croygen tipped one eyebrow. "Pirates don't trust. But we do have a code. And he owes me."

"But…" Sprig folded his arms in a huff.

"Right now, that's the best I can hope for. We can't worry about those already gone." Kennedy's voice filled the space. "We have to worry about the ones coming for us now. The fight is on our doorstep. Do what you need to do. Meet back here in an hour ready for battle." She waved a dismissal to the room. The guards let the remaining pirates go, watching them closely.

"I don't have the crew anymore to get all the ships prepared," Jack said.

"Hey!" Croygen opened his arm. "What the hell am I?"

"One man." Jack replied.

"Don't underestimate me." Croygen winked.

"Or me." Lexie stepped up, moving next to him. "He's taught me a lot. I can help."

"So can I." Rez pushed through the throng of people, moving beside her father. Croygen smiled at her with warmth and love. "Sirens know a lot about sailing. By ship or by sea, I can help."

"Georgia will help you get the rest of the crew you need from around the docks." Kennedy motioned to the pretty guard. "Not to be cheesy, but all hands on deck. Every single person is to be put to work. We are greatly outnumbered, and this is only one of our fights."

226

We also still had to fight the stone. Fight for Lars and Zoey. As far as we knew, Stavros had no idea Lars was no longer, that there was something more powerful in his place ready to take over.

The stone could destroy Stavros, but at what cost? Were we making a deal with the devil to beat another devil?

Fionna, you could end this. Your sacrifice would give the cauldron enough power to fight the stone. Put the stone back in its old cage. Save Lars. Zoey. Possibly end the war.

It was the worst plan in the world with more holes than swiss cheese, but I couldn't think of another way this would play out. As Kennedy said, we were outnumbered and outpowered with no other choice.

This time I would not hold back. It was my only choice left. It had to work.

Pulsepulsepulsepulse. I felt Lars screaming his refusal. As usual, I ignored him. We denied the fates my death the first time and brought this on ourselves. This time he couldn't stop me.

I slipped out quickly, before my sister saw the blood covering me. Turning the corner, I gasped at the figure lurking in the shadows. "Shite." I took in a breath. "You scared me."

Goran stepped forward, his skin pallid, his eyes dead. "I will help you."

"Help me with what?" I shifted on my feet, trying to act innocent.

"Die." His stiff form moved forward. Every day he appeared less humanlike. It was so creepy and heartbreaking, but I did this to him. "We are connected, Fionna. You are the one who ties me to the earth. You are my puppet master. You called for me. Even if you don't realize it."

That was unsettling.

"I will help you save Lars," he stated. "Your death will unlatch me from this hell while saving thousands."

Feck. That was direct, but it was also true.

My lips rolled together and I nodded. "Okay. But I need a shower and trousers first."

He stared at me, no response.

"And knickers." I motioned to my bare legs.

Abruptly he turned and walked away without any kind of acknowledgment.

Even if I had to leave it behind, I wanted to make this world safe for my friends and family... and most of all my daughter. She made this all so much harder for me.

But it was time to face my fate.

TWENTY-TWO
Ember

Ryker's massive physique slipped silently down the corridor, his head swiveling around, his shoulders tight and pulsing with tension. Like the patter of rain on a rooftop, our boots tapped softly over the stone floor in unison. My eyes darted into every crevice and hallway we passed, waiting for something to jump out at us. I hated being weaponless, literally and magically, leaving us vulnerable and open for hunting season.

We passed several hallways that led off to other passages, but we stayed on the main one, leading us past the room where we had last seen the kids, the room within a room. If I ever saw Lars again, we would have a serious talk about why he even had this room. I understood he had done a lot of things I neither wanted to know about nor would agree with, but even more than the dungeons, this space unsettled me. How many times had Lars brought a loved one here to torture his captor with? Lars was different from Stavros, but only in degrees.

At least Lars strived to be fair, to be equal to all.

"Do you think she's setting us up? Some sick cat-and-mouse game to her?"

Ryker's jaw clicked, his teeth grinding as if he had no clue if Amara was toying with us. Determination and anger set his brow. I could feel rage pumping off him, the ferocious need to save his son. Protect him.

I didn't have kids, but I still understood that feeling. I'd watched too many of my loved ones get captured because of me… had seen some of them tortured or killed. There was nothing you wouldn't do to save them. No law you wouldn't break, no line you wouldn't cross.

Scouring the hall as we stepped out, we sank deeper into the underground maze. Even though I knew the house, I had no clue how vast the world was down here. The farther we went, the more my chest clenched at the sensation of being trapped far underground.

"Wait." Ryker's hand shot out, grabbing me, adrenaline soaring through me. He stopped, tilting his head. The thump of my heart pounded in my ears, blocking out all other noise.

"What?" I croaked, spearing my vision around, ready for the attack. "What do you hear?"

His eyebrows furrowed, his head twisting even more, trying to catch something.

"What?"

"Shhhhh." He stepped past me, every inch of him on alert.

Swallowing, I tried to ease my thundering heart, forcing my ears to switch into dweller mode. The moment I let myself and zeroed in on the noises around me, it slammed into my ears.

Singing.

"Look!" I pointed at a sconce hanging from the wall. No flame burned inside. Shit, Amara was really helping us?

The singing was soft, and I didn't recognize the tune, but the soft little Irish voice whispering the rhyme gave me a rush of hope.

"Piper." I stumbled forward, following the sound, my nose trying to pick up her scent. It was challenging down here with all the smells, and I wasn't near the level of a true dark dweller, but my senses were super strength compared to a human. Turning a corner, we came to a short hallway lined with a dozen barred doors. More dungeons.

Piper's smell was blocked from me, but her little voice bounced off the stone, echoing her presence from every chamber.

"Piper?" I whispered hoarsely, running along the doors, looking into the cells. They were pitch-dark, damp, and held the same chains mine had. She was a child, and he kept her locked down here. How scared she must be. I bit back the bile curling my stomach. "Piper?"

Ryker flipped the window guards open on the other side, both of us making our way back.

She went silent, probably unsure who was coming for her.

"Piper, it's okay, I'm Ember and I'm a friend of your aunt and mommy." I glanced into a cell. Empty. "Please, talk to me so we can find you."

Nothing.

Almost at the end of the hall, I swung open a window door, shining light into the small cell. I almost missed the tiny pair of boots scrunched into the corner, the rest of her hidden in the shadows. "Piper! Ryker, she's right here," I squeaked, gripping the bars, feeling the goblin metal licking at my skin. "Hey, sweetie, we're here to get you out. Can you move into the light?" Ryker's hands already fiddled with the lock bolted over her door, probably wishing as I was that Sprig was still here.

"Piper, are you okay?" I forced my voice to stay soft and calm.

Like a breath of wind, her small voice floated to me. "Yes."

"Do you know where my son is? Wyatt. He's just a baby," Ryker asked, his hands twisting at the bolt trying to break it off the wall, his voice tense. I could make out the sound of clothes brushing the wall, her shoes sliding on the stone, her body rising as she stepped into the shower of light across the floor. Only dressed in leggings and a short-sleeved top, her arms were coated with bruises, as if she had been gripped and manhandled with force. But lying in her thin arms was Wyatt, wrapped in a dirty blanket, asleep.

Ryker sucked in sharply, veins straining in his neck, his muscles vibrating.

"I protected him. They didn't hurt him." She adjusted his weight in her arms, bringing him closer to her chest. He was little, but she was so tiny for a five-year-old I was shocked she didn't drop him.

"Did they do that? Did they hurt you?" I nodded toward her marks.

She lifted her chin, looking identical to her mother with her little defiant expression.

Ryker's shoulders bumped into me, almost as though they grew, his entire body bulking up, eyes glowing with fury. More veins popped up from his skin, his nose flaring. He seemed to occupy the entire hallway with his rage. His teeth bared, his fingers gripping the deadbolt, twisting it with a deep vibrating growl. I stepped away from him. A whine of metal pulled my eyes to his hands, flakes of dust chipping off the wall. Trickles of sweat glided down the side of his face, his shoulders rising with the strength he exerted to bend the lock.

Crap on ash bark. It was the first time I'd seen the true demon in him. Anyone else probably would be frightened, but it didn't scare me at all. If anything, my demon side felt very comfortable with him, as though it wanted to come out and help too. But mine was locked away by the goblin metal, and I had no clue how Ryker was able to muster his.

A roar ricocheted off the walls, Ryker's body bowing forward, fatigue creeping up on him.

Snap!

The bar ripped off the wall, swinging the door open. He was inside in an instant, reaching for the baby. I went next to Piper. She gently placed Wyatt in his father's arms. The baby stirred, his lids blinking up at his father, wiggling with recognition and excitement. Ryker's expression softened, his eyes full of unequivocal love, his rough fingers brushing over Wyatt's chubby cheeks with a choked sigh. He brushed his lips over the baby's forehead, his blond lashes blinking away the emotion in his eyes.

"Thank you," Ryker whispered, glancing at Piper. "Thank you for protecting my son."

Piper tilted her head, her hand palming Ryker's arm, her face appearing so wise for her age. "I protect him. I saw it. He will also be my best mate." She touched Wyatt's face. "When he gets bigger, of course."

I smiled, turning Piper toward me, running my hands over her bruised arms.

"Are you hurt anywhere else?"

"No." She shook her head. "But I am *very* hungry." She rubbed her belly, her accent dancing in my ears.

Noises reached us from down the hall, yells booming throughout the corridor, my head perking up.

Time was up.

"Shit. We've got to go." I got back on my feet, grabbing Piper's hand. Ryker rose, folding Wyatt into his chest, his mouth tight with power, all earlier emotion locked back inside.

"Do you know another exit out of here?" he asked while we scampered back to the main hallway, looking both ways for any enemies.

"No."

He grunted with annoyance.

"Sorry. Lars never gave me the super-secret map of his torture labyrinth down here," I snapped, keeping Piper close to my side.

We heard more shouting from the path behind us and swiveled our heads that way. Only one choice existed.

"Let's hope there is a way out." Ryker moved first. Keeping low, he crept along the path, Piper and me close behind. The shouting reached a fever pitch. They knew we were gone, and it wouldn't be long until some were coming down this path for us.

Ryker and I picked up our pace, though I constantly swung around, sure I felt strighoul teeth caressing my neck. The thud of their footsteps pounded along the back of my spine.

We came upon a split in the hallway, a wrong or right choice before us. "Which way?"

"I... I don't know." My head swiveled. In both walkways, nothing hinted at what lay beyond the dark passage. The group behind gained on us. "Crap!" I rubbed my head, the hair on the back of my neck standing up. Every second we wasted...

"This way." I took the lead down the left one, Piper jogging next to me, her little hand tight in mine. After a while, her weak legs started to falter, slowing us down. I swooped her up on my back, her arms strangling my neck, but I pushed forward, sprinting down the endless corridor.

Then I sensed it, the rise in the path, my muscles fatiguing at the ascension. An incline meant we were closer to the ground level. To freedom. But the stink of strighoul skulked up my nose. If I could smell them, they were too close.

"Faster!" Ryker barked, nudging me with his elbow as Wyatt began to fuss. They were coming anyway, but his cry would be a beacon straight to us. Sweat clung to my skin, my legs kicking through the lethargy.

I saw it before my brain could register the truth.

"No. No. No," I muttered, hoping my eyes were playing tricks on me. But the solid brick wall stood only yards from me, a dead end, shutting off access to the world. "No!" I ran to it, slamming my fists into it. "Nooooo!"

"Fuck!" Ryker slammed his hand against it, bouncing Wyatt in the other, scanning the space for any other way out. I couldn't see any escape. No doors to even hide behind. Wyatt's face was scrunched up, a howl bouncing inside in his chest, preparing to come up, as he burped up unhappy whimpers.

Piper wiggled off my back and dropped to the ground, her brows crushed down in a fierce expression. I glanced at Ryker, our eyes meeting, both of us realizing this was literally the end. We were screwed. The beating resonance of feet filled my heart with lead. We had gotten so close, but still we failed. Whatever Stavros had planned for me, for all of us, now he would make sure we suffered even more.

As if Wyatt absorbed our predicament, a wail broke from his mouth, piercing the air. I rubbed the back of my neck in frustration.

"Auntie Ember?" Piper's voice was so soft I barely heard her.

"Take him." Ryker stretched out his arms, delivering the crying baby into my arms. The piercing howls stabbed my eardrums. "And stand behind me."

"What the hell are you going to do? Fight them all?" I scoffed.

"I will go down protecting you guys if necessary."

"Auntie Em?" A tug on my arm.

"Don't be stupid. We're caught either way. Don't waste your energy." I was usually all for jumping into a fight, but this one seemed pointless.

More tugging on my arm. "Auntie Em!" Piper shouted, jerking my head to her.

"Wow, did we just step into *Wizard of Oz*?" I quipped.

She stared at me, not getting my reference.

"Never mind."

"I dreamt this. A tiny woman helps me. I remember now. I save him." She held out her arms, asking for Wyatt. "We're small enough to get through."

"What are you talking about?" Tiny woman? Save him?

"She helps me. She knows the way." Piper tugged at my arm.

High-pitched yells rode over Wyatt's sobs, the shadows of their figures reflecting off the walls.

"Shit." Instinctually taking a step back, my heels knocked into the wall.

"We escape. I've seen it." She tilted her arms up higher, reaching for the baby. "I save him."

"How Piper?" I glanced at her then to Ryker, who stared at her with as much confusion. "There's no way out."

"There they are!" a nasally voice cried, his lance pointed at us, a herd of strighoul behind him howling like a frenzied mob.

"Yes, there is." Piper pointed to the corner, almost impregnable with darkness, but my dweller eyesight picked up the outline of a large vent. Only big enough to fit someone her size, but not an ounce bigger.

"Get them!" another strighoul roared.

"Trust me, Mr. Viker." Her huge blue eyes drilled into the wanderer, not flinching as shouts and figures moved in on us.

Ryker's jaw clenched, his chest rose with panic as his eyes slid to the group bearing down on us. He touched his son's cheek, then tickled his head. "Go." He whirled around to the oncoming monsters, running for them like a crazy man.

He was distracting them. Giving Piper a chance. I practically dumped Wyatt into her arms and darted for the corner. Strength that came from sheer desperation coursed through my veins as I ripped off the cover from the vent.

A tiny familiar figure stood deep inside the vent, hiding back in the shadows, watching us.

233

Sinnie.

A burst of happiness at seeing her, realizing she was who Piper was talking about. Sinnie knew every inch of this castle. She would help them get out of here.

"Go!" I pressed my hand to Piper's back as she crouched down and climbed into the space. "Please get them to safety, Sinnie." My gaze connected with the blonde, foot-tall house brownie, and she gave me a curt nod. Once again, I was so grateful for the supposed "sub" fae. If anything, they were the true heroes in this story.

"Come, girl." Sinnie waved Piper forward, vanishing deeper into the tunnel, the blackness gobbling up the tiny woman.

Wyatt relaxed in Piper's embrace, his cries calming, his wide eyes tracking the activity bustling around him. "Go fast and stay safe. Please."

Piper nodded, giving my hand a last squeeze. "I will protect him with my life, Auntie Em. I promise." Then in a blink her figure disappeared into obscurity, scurrying deeper into the vent, following Sinnie. Damn, she was so strong and fierce. What an incredible person; to think she was only five blew my mind.

Please let them get out of here.

Needing to believe Sinnie would show them the way and Piper would succeed, I jumped up, throwing myself into the brawl next to Ryker. It was all for show, but we needed to buy the children time to escape before Stavros realized what happened.

His ultimate leverage had just slipped through the drainpipes.

TWENTY-THREE
Kennedy

Sun streaked through the thick murky clouds. Rain hinted on the horizon, bringing more gloom upon the castle. Swallowing the lump in my throat, I fought the urge to vomit all over the floor. It was the calm before the storm, these moments we would hopefully look back on, if we survived, shaking our heads thinking "if we only knew what was ahead."

I was dressed in dark, flexible pants and a long-sleeved top thick enough to slow a blade from cutting into me like butter. I strapped a harness holding guns and knives to my back. But it was my magic that I relied on; the one thing I hoped would not fail my people or me.

The entire kingdom rested on my shoulders, each life as important as the next. Many people in my kingdom would not see another day. This might be their last morning and last sunrise they would ever see, and I could do nothing to prevent it.

"Hey, li'l Druid." Lorcan's arms wrapped around my waist. His mouth brushed my ear, pulling me against him. "You can't think like that. Everyone here understands the sacrifice." It was still strange that Lorcan could feel my emotions, grasp my thoughts when I looked at him. "You can only do so much. You can't save every life today. You just have to fight for the ones who do make it today, because if Stavros wins, those are the ones to pity."

"I know." I laced my hands with his, falling into his strong chest, the weapons on my back making me lean against him. "I can't believe we are here again. And you know it's not only Stavros we're fighting." I gulped, liquid stabbing behind my lids. I wasn't sure we had any hope of winning against the stone. "I'm scared."

"Me too." Lorcan kissed my temple. "But you use that. Turn it into anger. You are Queen, no one should threaten to take that away from you."

235

"Maybe I shouldn't be. No one wants me here anyway." I broke from his embrace, twisting to look at him. "Look how many joined with Stavros because I am a Druid. They will take a cruel dictator simply so they don't have me as their leader."

"Stop." Lorcan's lids narrowed, gripping my hips. "Do you know how many love and support you? Don't just see what's bad. There are a lot of people in Europe and right here standing by your side. There are more who love you than don't. So stop those thoughts right here. It is what will make you weak. There will always be haters who prefer the old ways, who want fae to be in control. You stand for everyone. Even the voices that can't hear you right now."

I stared into his green eyes, passionate, strong, with awe.

"What?" He lifted an eyebrow when I continued to gape at him.

"You." I shook my head softly, my ponytail brushing my shoulders, and cupped his cheeks. "You are my strength. My rock… thank you." Emotion clogged my throat, and my eyes filled with tears. "Thank you for challenging me, for always cutting through the bullshit. Thank you for wanting a life with me no matter how chaotic and frustrating. For picking me."

"Well…" He smirked. "*I* didn't pick you…" He drew me in tighter against his body. "I have to thank my beast for that. He gave me no choice."

"I plan to." I went on my tiptoes, kissing him softly. "If we get through this, I will show him my gratitude over and over in whatever way he wants."

Lorcan grinned against my mouth. "Now there is a reason to survive," he muttered before his mouth claimed mine, his hand grabbing the back of my head, deepening our kiss. It was the same kind of promise we made to each other before the last big war, the first night Lorcan and I were together.

"Don't you dare die, so you can deliver on your word." He pulled back, his eyes fixed on mine, his hands now gripping my face. "Because I will follow wherever you go. I will haunt you and drive you mad for eternity if you leave me; that I can promise you."

My fingers brushed his lips. "Same."

Lorcan brought his lips to mine again, our mouths saying everything else we couldn't.

A throat cleared behind us. "Excuse me, Majesty." Torin's voice drifted from over Lorcan's shoulder, drawing me away from the hunger growing between us.

"As usual, fairy boy interrupts." Lorcan sighed, shaking his head. He stepped away, twisting to look at Torin. "Is that your superpower? Cockblocking me?"

236

"Believe me, it's not something I enjoy either." Torin frowned, but it was the first time I didn't hear the disgust or biting jealousy behind his words. He looked more bored than anything.

"Go ahead, Torin." I stepped around Lorcan, walking closer to my First Knight.

"Ten ships have been spotted in the outer port, but so far no movement on land." Torin gripped the sword attached to one hip; on the other he held a gun. This kind of battle was new to fae. They still preferred a fair fight, but since the human and fae worlds had blended, they were adapting to other ways of fighting. Humans used weapons against fae, so the fae felt they had the right to use them as well. Now humans and fae could die easier and faster in this new combined world.

"The troops are ready for battle, the ships are ready to go out, the villagers are armed and organized. We are just waiting for your word to lift the spell."

"Okay, thank you." I remembered Lars's ardent speech in the war with Aneira, revving the troops into a frenzy. Could I inspire the same? Get them bloodthirsty and ready to battle whatever came?

Nerf-herder, I hoped so.

"Also, I wanted to let you know I saw your sister and Goran in the hallway." Torin shifted on his feet, his brows drawing together. "Overheard them talking."

"And?"

"She's going to do a blood ritual at the old Druid circle." Torin rubbed his lips together. "You do know the blood rituals one does there are sacrifices?"

"What do you mean?" Panic clotted my esophagus.

"Death sacrifices."

"What?" I darted closer to my knight, my mouth dropping open. "Are you serious?"

"Yes, my lady. I didn't hear it all, but I heard enough to determine she plans to give her life over to the cauldron to fight the stone."

"No. It is the stupidest plan. What is she thinking? She can't kill herself. I won't let her."

"I'm solely relaying what I heard." Torin lifted his chin. "If that is all, I want to go join my troop."

"Yes, that's all." I nodded. "I need to find my sister, then I will be out."

"Travil is waiting with the bird-shifter. It is easier for the soldiers to hear you from above."

Crap times twenty… Flying? Up high? Not my favorite thing.

Torin stopped and turned. "Also, Thara has joined my unit, I hope that is all right with you."

"Yes. Everyone who is capable and willing; we need them out there."

"Thank you, Majesty." He nodded, a tiny smile tugging at the side of his mouth before he stalked from the room.

I didn't even look at Lorcan before I hurried out of the room, heading for my sister's accommodation, but I could feel him right behind me. Yes, we were outnumbered and in deep trouble, but I wouldn't let her do this. There had to be another way. And what if it didn't even work? She'd leave her child motherless on a chance? There had to be more to her plan.

What are you up to, Fionna?

Halfway to my room, boisterous yells rolled through the corridors, luring me to a window that looked upon the bridge. I pushed up my glasses, squinting down, trying to recognize the objects.

Sturt, Rowlands, Vander, and Georgia hustled around a young guard running along the path yelling, holding something in his arms. A female guard walked behind him carrying something else.

A baby's wail pierced the air, stabbing me in the chest.

"Oh my gods!" I cried out, already moving toward the exit. My brain registered what I'd heard, but I was still dazed and needed to see for myself.

Lorcan stayed close behind me as we skipped half the stairs and ran outside, through the courtyard where the assembly had stopped.

Sturt had taken the baby away from the woman, letting her catch her breath, and was now bouncing the little boy while singing comforting hymns. Georgia, Vander, and Rowlands squatted around the barely conscious little girl they laid on the ground.

My niece.

"Piper!" I rammed my knees onto the cobbled path, crawling to her, my hand reaching for her face. I brushed bloody, greasy, filthy strands away. Every inch of exposed skin was covered in dirt, cuts, and bruises. "Piper?" I cupped her face, her lashes fluttering. I had only seen her once, from behind glass, but every part of me felt the bond to her. We shared blood, even though I was a stranger to her. We'd never had the chance to meet before the world went to crap.

"There was no one else with them, Majesty," the young guard who brought her in told me. "She was barely walking, or coherent, but wouldn't let him go until we told her she was safe. I think she carried him all the way here on her own."

I peered at her then at Wyatt. He was a baby, but he was the Viking's baby, and a lot to carry for a five-year-old, especially over a long stretch of time. The baby's sobs were quieting down as the big burly Sturt sang softly to him, rocking him as if he were the most precious thing in the world. I noticed Georgia staring at him, her lips parted, eyes soft, her normal guarded expression melting away as she took in the hunky Scot calming the child.

"Wyatt!" A female voice rang across the courtyard. Annabeth's blonde hair fell out of her bun as she ran for Sturt. She scooped Wyatt from Sturt's arms, burying her face into the baby's neck. "You're all right... You're all right." She wept deeply, her shoulders shaking.

Cooper came up behind her, touching her back. She peered at him, then back at the baby. A happy hiccupped cry broke from her throat as she brought Wyatt closer to her, rubbing his back. He cooed and gurgled with excitement, recognizing her.

"Wyatt?" Piper muttered, stirring under my hands. "He's okay?"

"Yes, sweetheart. He is safe and so are you." I choked on an unbearable feeling of what bound me to her. "I am so proud of you."

Her eyes fluttered open as she looked at me. Slowly a tiny grin ghosted her mouth. "Auntie Ken." She reached up for my face. Her fingernails were black with grime, as though she'd had to dig her way through dirt.

"I'm here. I will never let anything happen to you again."

Her teeth peered through her lips. "Can't promise that." She said it like *"Duh, Auntie Ken."*

"Piper! Oh my god, Piper!" My sister's Irish accent bellowed from the castle entrance. She soon appeared with Goran standing next to her. They both were dressed in the same battle uniform as the rest of us, loaded with weapons, looking to be headed out. A backpack filled with something heavy thumped against her spine as she ran for us. I scooted away, giving Fionna clear access to her daughter. She fell next to me, already sobbing, her arms wrapping around her little girl, pulling her into her lap. "Piper..."

"Mummy, I did it. I told you. I saved him."

"Yes, you did, baby." Fionna rocked, both of them swaying together. "You are so amazing."

Piper snuggled into her mom, who hugged her back, both lost in the reunion. Fionna kissed and brushed Piper's hair soothingly, continuing to rock them back and forth. "I am so sorry."

"Mummy, I told you. It was supposed to happen that way. I knew." Piper tapped at her head. Then her little head jerked around, looking for someone. "Where is Uncle Nic? Nana?"

"I'm right here, Squirt," Nic rumbled, using a cane as he ambled down the path, a smile growing on his mouth. He still hadn't fully recovered from Stavros's torture, but the healers felt he would eventually. The incubus was definitely a favorite in the ward, thanks to his charm. "Heard someone calling your name and couldn't get here fast enough."

"Uncle Nic!" Piper screamed, barreling for the Spanish god. She knocked into him and wrapped her arms around his waist so fiercely he stumbled back.

"Whoa, Squirt." He regained his feet and picked her up, settling her on his hip. She wrapped her arms around his neck, squeezing him tight. "Nana is in the kitchen, and when she hears you're back, she's going to be so happy. She'll probably make the biggest cake."

"With sprinkles?"

"Do they come any other way?" He scoffed, shaking his head. Piper curled into him, hugging him even tighter.

Fionna stared adoringly at Piper, but I saw a speck of hurt she must feel at seeing the pair together. It probably wasn't jealousy, but guilt. She had barely two full days with her daughter before she'd been taken again. I wasn't a mother, but I could relate to the guilt of feeling that you'd failed those you loved.

Piper lifted her head. "Mummy, where is Mr. Darz?"

The speck of pain turned to full-blown agony on Fionna's face, and her hand automatically pressed to her stomach.

"Remember, sweetie, he went away?"

"Yes." She nodded. "He hasn't come back to us yet?"

Fionna sucked in, covered her mouth with a hand, and tears flooded her eyes. "Not yet. But he really, really wants to, sweetie." She rubbed her abdomen. "I can tell you that for sure. He *really* wants to."

I tipped one eyebrow at her.

"The arsehole won't stop *talking*." Fionna tried to look annoyed but smiled instead. She patted her stomach and stood up.

"Piper?" I rose with her. "How did you escape? Did anyone help you? A big blonde guy and a girl with two different-color eyes?"

"Auntie Em and Viker?" She nodded, wiggling off Nic's hip to the ground.

"Auntie Em?" Fionna echoed, sounding surprised Piper already called Ember auntie.

"It's what I call her. I saw." She marched right up to me, raising her hands. "It's what they'll call her too." She placed her hands on my stomach, tapping on it lightly.

I stared down at Piper in bewilderment.

"Honey, what are you talking about?" Fionna stepped closer, watching her daughter curiously.

"The twins." She patted at my belly. "Me, Wyatt, and the twins become the best of friends. Always."

"What. In. The. F—hell." Lorcan swiftly changed his wording, moving to my side. "Are you talking about?"

Piper rolled her eyes. "The babies."

"What babies?" I swallowed, feeling my throat close in.

"Yours." She kissed my stomach, whispering into my shirt. "So excited to play with you guys. Though sometimes we fight... Wyatt always makes me feel better. And we always forgive each other." Her blue eyes looked at me. "Can't you feel them, their energy and power, Aunt Ken? They're already so ram-bun-ctious." She tsked, the huge word stumbling over her tongue.

I froze, the blood running through my body clotted into ice, while lava poured over my skin. "That-that's impossible." I shook my head, glancing at Lorcan for confirmation. His eyes were as wide as mine, his muscles locked in place.

"Actually, it's not," Nic spoke up. "As an incubus, believe me, I know everything there is on birth control. It's rare, but because you're a Druid, it might be possible. You guys have the power to break the fairy spell."

"What? Why didn't anyone tell me? That should have come on the warning label! No. It's not true." I shook my head. Kids were the furthest thing from my mind, especially today. We were going into war. I had a kingdom to save, and the chances of us living were thin at best. To be pregnant on top of that? With freaking twins? No—just no.

I pressed my hand to my stomach, concentrating on it, recalling that last night when Lorcan and I had sex, the Latin bubbling out of my mouth I didn't recognize, the intensity I had never felt before. The sensation of him claiming me inside and out. Dots of life and warmth pulsed under my hand. I didn't need to take a test; I knew what Piper said was true.

Holy nut-cracking nerf-herder!

"Damn," Lorcan whispered, like he had come to the same conclusion. His eyes darted to my stomach, where he pushed aside my hand and laid his own upon it. "Seriously? Damn... I have super-sperm."

I groaned, palming my face.

"Come on." Lorcan grinned at me, joy dancing in his eyes, the shock already seeming to dissipate from him. "I have a right to brag about my superior sperm. Both of us on tree-fairy protection and I can still knock you up with twins?"

"I'm going to kill you in your sleep."

His mouth parted in a bigger smile, pulling me into him. "With pleasure." He kissed me. I gave in for one moment, letting a drop of excitement overshadow the daunting fear. But there was still a war on our doorstep, and I was still Queen.

"Okay, wow. Well, I can't deal with this right now." I stepped back. "Nic, get the kids inside." He couldn't fight on the field, but I knew he would fight if anyone got into the castle, threatening those children. Marguerite would probably bash them with a rolling pin.

"But I'm supposed to help," Piper responded, shaking her head at Nic's call. "You need me."

"No!" Fionna insisted. "You have been put in danger too much already. I need you to stay with Nic and Marguerite."

"But, Mummy…"

"No, Piper." She crouched down to Piper's eyeline. "Please, I need you to be safe. Darz would want that too. Please do this for me."

Piper scrunched up her mouth, not replying. Fionna took that as a yes and walked her to Nic, giving her a kiss and hug before wiping her eyes and turning back to me.

"It's time. Let's end this." Her expression hardened—reminding me she'd once been the DLR leader who took no prisoners.

I nodded and turned for the field, spotting the ships on the water captained by Croygen and Jack. Lexie and Rez stood on the decks, ready to fight with the rest of the crew. The field was filled with Light and Dark fae, as well as humans, all armed and ready for battle. Fighting for me.

So much blood would soak the grass.

Grimmel flew overhead squawking, something on his back flapping in the wind.

"Wheeeeee!" Sprig yelped. He wore what looked like a pair of black underwear around his neck, gripping the bird's feathers. "You're right, my wee bits feel even freer. Honey droppings, this is amazing. Super-Sprig to the rescue!"

"See, monkey man!" Cal whizzed by, winging in closer to the raven, stark naked.

"Cal, my lady would be so mad at you. You left very little for us to sprinkle over everyone." Simmons trailed behind.

"It was an emergency. It had to be done," Cal replied back.

"No, it's just because Sir Eli left and there was no one to stop you."

"Come on, Simmons... or should I say Mr. No Fun?"

"Flying honey biscuits dipped in honey, fried, and soaked in honey! Wheeeeee! Though I think I would vomit if I wasn't drunk. Ahhhhhh!" Sprig yelled out before Grimmel swooped closer to me.

"Idiots. Surrounded by imbeciles." Grimmel grumbled, circling around to me.

"What do you mean Eli left?" Lorcan asked Simmons.

Simmons's face went red, and he pressed his hand to his mouth, as his mechanical wings brought him down to us.

"Ohhh, Simmons, you're so in trouble. Mr. Asswipe told you not to tell." Cal sniggered.

"Tell. Me. Simmons," Lorcan demanded.

"Well... um... he told me he'd take away my wings if I told."

"I will take them away and stuff them up your ass if you don't."

"Actually, he pretty much said that too."

"Simmons," I spoke softly. "Will you tell me, your Queen?"

His face twisted as though I was torturing him.

"Don't do it, Simmons," Cal warned.

"I have to." He pointed at me. "She's the Queen!"

"Simmons." Lorcan growled. Time ticked by. Any moment we could be attacked.

"Sir Eli, Cole, Ms. Olivia, Lady Lily, and that Garrett guy went to get my lady and the wanderer."

"What?" I gaped. I could understand Eli, Cole, and Lily, but Olivia and Garrett? What trouble were they getting into?

"I'm sorry, is this a bad time?" a familiar voice robotically rumbled from the entrance. Fear slid down my bones, whipping me around, a gasp coming from my lips.

Fionna went rigid next to me.

"Darz!" Piper leaped forward, but Nic grabbed her, holding her back.

Lars and Zoey stood before us, but their bodies were mere costumes, their eyes vacant of life.

"I think our invitation got lost in the mail." The stone tried to appear relaxed but was stiff and awkward. "I hope we're not too late."

None of us moved or spoke.

"And I brought my own guests." He motioned behind him where figures moved in behind the pair.

"Holy. Nerf. Herder." I jerked back, watching the creatures move protectively around Lars and Zoey. *Oh my god. What are those things?* The huge one next to Zoey had the face of a human with green eyes, but his mouth was all strighoul, actually a strighoul on steroids.

"Noooo," Annabeth cried out, her eyes wide, her head shaking. "No... it can't be. They died... we killed them!" Annabeth shrieked, tripping backward, holding Wyatt tighter to her, terror contorting her features.

The stone stared at Annabeth. "Zoey's children are a lot stronger than you give them credit for. And I hated to see such wonderful work go to waste."

Zoey's *children*? I didn't know what was going on, but I knew we were in much more trouble than we thought.

These things weren't only monsters, they could be our end.

TWENTY-FOUR
Ember

My knees hit the floor with such force my teeth clattered together. I felt the bruise all the way to the bone. A strighoul dug its nails into my shoulder, holding me in place. Ryker's form fell next to mine, his shoulders heaving with fury. Blood dripped from both of us, still trying to heal from our little scrimmage with the flesh-eaters. By the time they dragged us to Stavros and he found out the kids were missing, I hoped Piper had cleared the property. She still had a long way to go, and the strighoul would be hunting her. Her chance at escape was slim, but hope was all I had to hold on to.

Stavros paced in front of us, his rage scarcely contained by the thin parchment of white skin. His demon scraped away at his façade. Like Lars when his demon was out, his eyes were black, skin sunken into his skull, but he somehow seemed larger, stuffing the room with his power. It raked over my skin with such intensity I curved forward beneath its biting rage. My lungs struggled to expand, his magic stealing the oxygen.

"Emmy... you've been an exceptionally bad girl," he seethed, his bony nose flaring. "Unlike Lars, I don't put up with bad behavior. He should have taught you manners. I guess it's up to me to make you obedient."

"Good luck with that," I snarled back, trying to lift my head.

Magic slammed into me so hard I slid a few feet back. In a blink, Stavros stood in front of me, an invisible hand gripping my throat, squeezing down, forcing choked gasps through my teeth.

"I guarantee I will break you. Like a wild horse, you will be my pet in no time." My image reflected off his black eyes. Stavros's magic was powerful and old, twisting around my bones. Lars could be scary, but I had

245

never truly been afraid of him. He could get angry to the point of losing control, but I was still his niece. His family.

I felt no such allegiance from Stavros. Similar to my aunt Aneira, Stavros only wanted to use me. And if I did not oblige, I would join other resisters in an unmarked grave.

A knock tapped on the door and Amara stepped in. Her chin-length black hairstyle was now a deep violet color. Two strighoul followed her into the room.

"Yes?" Stavros jerked his head to her, his sharp fangs snapping.

"We searched everywhere." She stood strong, but her throat bobbed with nerves. "They were nowhere to be found."

"What?" Stavros's chest bloomed. "You are telling me a five-year-old child carrying an infant outsmarted all of you?" Stavros could come across as theatrical and almost carefree most of the time. But this was not the man before us. The role of the crazy dictator King had been cast. And I did not envy Amara as deliverer of bad news. "Let's try this again. Tell your King that you let two small children slip through your fingers."

"I have scouts out there following her trail. We will get her, Majesty." One of the strighoul bowed, his speech slurred and babylike.

Ice pricked over my back. Oh holy crap… I looked harder at the strighoul, my stomach dropping. Crap. His broken teeth left me with no doubt.

Vek.

He had no teeth because of *me*.

He was a far cry from the last time I'd seen him. He once had led a strighoul pack, avenging the old leader Drauk, whom I also killed. But a strighoul without teeth was useless and could not provide for its pack. It would be shoved out, turned against. Ousted.

Now he was barely skin and bones, one hand crippled and twisted, wearing paper-thin dirty rags. His broken teeth gaped from his mouth, creating a more frightening and pathetic image.

Sensing my gaze, his head lifted slowly, his red eyes finding mine. It was a beat before full recognition set in. A guttural wail pitched in my ears as Vek leaped for me.

"You ffffuuccing vitch!" he squealed, his dirty nails swiping for me. "Youuve veduced me to fishhhh! Kill yoouuu!" Vek lunged as if to jump on my back, but he collapsed to the ground squealing like a stuck pig, his form withering on the ground in agony.

Stavros stepped up to him, peering down. "How dare you." He spit on Vek, fury vibrating throughout the demon. "You do not come into my home. *The. King's. Home.* And touch anything of mine. You are nothing. Imps have more worth to me than you do." Stavros bent over the creature. "I was so kind to bring you in after you were abandoned and rejected by even your own mother. You don't even have a right to even breathe in my presence. You attack my prisoners without my approval... and let a child best you. Tell me what good you are to me?"

"Sorrrry, my veige. I vour servannnt," Vek groveled, slobbering and bowing his head into Stavros's feet.

Stavros snarled at the strighoul, rising to his full height. "Do you take me for someone who forgives? That is a weakness. You have failed me."

Magic punched through the room. Vek howled, his hands going to his head, his spine snapping back and forth like a kite tail, flaying over the floor with ear-piercing screams.

I hated Vek, death was too good for him, but I did not enjoy watching the brutal torture, hearing his screams.

Amara watched as though it were the climax of her favorite show, while the other strighoul froze in place, probably hoping they weren't next. Ryker was expressionless, but his Adam's apple bobbed and his shoulders tightened along the ridge of his neck.

I jerked back as blood spurted from Vek's eyeballs, blood vessels bursting, leaking down his face. A banshee wail spiked from his throat, and vomit rose to the back of mine. His nails dug into his scalp, trying to rid himself of the pain. Then he stopped screaming, a pop like a paintball splattering against the wall sounded through the silent space. He went still. Pools of blood poured from his ears and eyes, his mouth and open eyes resembling a horror mask.

"Finally, he shut up." Stavros brushed an escaped string of blood from his face. "Ugh. Such a mess. His blood better come out of the rug or I'm going to be awfully upset." Stavros rolled his eyes dramatically. "You." He pointed at the other strighoul. "Get him out of here. And make sure when you come back in here you have better news or you join him."

The strighoul bowed his head, fear twisting his already ugly face. "Yes, Majesty." He grabbed Vek's limp arms, dragging him away as quickly as possible, smearing gore across the wooden floor of Lars's office. If he were smart, he'd dump the body outside and run for his life.

"I guess that's what I get for taking in strays, right?" He held out his arms, his gaze darting between Ryker and me as though we would relate to the situation and laugh along with him. "Can't potty-train them, and they leave their guts all over the floor." He motioned to the red streak running to the door. The demon was no longer present, the crazy uncle was back in his place, like he had exorcised his demon by killing Vek.

Crap on ash bark. He was certifiably nuts.

He rubbed his neck, shaking out his arms, then refocused on Ryker and me.

"I'm still enormously upset with you two, but I will try to see the positive in this. We'll just have to roll with it. Those kids were my best threat, but I think a lot of people still care about you two. Certainly they don't want to see your brains leaking from eyes and ears. Right?" He chuckled, jogging in place, rolling his neck right and left, like he was warming up. "Mara, my love, can you go get my cloak? I want to make a grand entrance."

"Of course." A sensual grin curved her plump lips. "But you are *always* grand." She winked, walking through the door.

"That's why I keep her around." He watched her swaying ass leave the room. "Exceptional in bed and the only one who's truthful with me." If by "truthful" he meant telling him what he wanted to hear and manipulating him, then sure, Amara was the pillar of truth. "I'm shocked you let that girl leave your bed, Ryker. She's superb."

"I have far better," Ryker replied without a hint of emotion, as if he were simply stating a fact, but it was enough to insult Stavros that the King's taste was subpar.

"Get up," Stavros demanded, his lip hitching up. "It's time to go. We don't want to be late, especially when I'm bringing the appetizers." He nodded at us. "You will discover today what a true leader is. The people will be so grateful I have finally ended the Druid reign. Their horror will be over... and those who have been disloyal will finally see what happens when you defy a true King."

Insight zoomed up my spine as we walked, feeling the tingle of awareness.

Oh. Hell. No.

He wouldn't.

Who was I kidding? Yes, he would.

"You stubborn asshole." I shook my head, my boots clicking over the country road as our large group moved to the Seelie castle. Stavros led, using one of Nic's prized cars—a convertible Rolls-Royce Phantom, or so

I was told. He sat in the back like a king on parade while the rest of us marched behind the car. Ryker and I were tied with goblin-metal rope, and under watch by at least six strighoul with knives and spears directed at the back of our necks. The goblin rope was balanced to keep us on our feet and we were too drained to use our magic.

"What?" Ryker muttered, trying to move closer to me. I had a mad case of *déjà vu*. I swear, if Eli were here instead of the Viking, I would think I'd stepped back in time as another mad leader, with much better style, but otherwise no different, dragged me to the castle to use my powers against the ones I love. The mental health issues in my family were extremely alarming.

"I can't believe him." I turned my itchy forehead into my shoulder, scouring it against my sweater, my long hair falling across my cheek. I huffed out, blowing my grimy mane off my face.

The sizzle of Eli's blood in my veins called to me, longing to be reunited.

"You fae men know that we girls don't need to be saved, right?" I looked as though I were talking to Ryker, but I was really speaking to the fucker hiding in the forest along the road. "That sometimes all fae men do is create more work for us to save *their* asses?"

A deep laugh hummed through the dweller link.

Ryker's eyes narrowed on me. He probably wondered if I was going crazy. I flicked my eyes to the tree line, mouthing Eli.

Ryker nodded and looked forward.

Come on, woman, you're taking all the fun away from being your knight in shining armor. Eli's sexy voice purred through the link.

Knight in shining armor? I choked. *You're kidding, right? I recall a time you told me you were the furthest thing from one?*

How about a beast in the sheets?

Please. Stop. Cole's voice jumped in. *Or cut me out of this conversation. Between all of you, I am a step away from stabbing an ice pick through my temple, just to give me a moment of peace.*

Did Eli talk you into this? I linked straight to Cole. *Stavros is taking us to the castle now.*

Actually, it was Lily. Your mother is a force I can't even stop.

I sighed, bobbing my head in agreement. She really was. Even before the years she'd been locked away as Aneira's prisoner, she was a tornado of strength. After she returned, she became even more so. After being tortured by Aneira for so long, I didn't think there was anything she couldn't take on. And if you threatened Mark or me? Mama Bear got pissed.

We have a little surprise for you, Eli said. *You and Ryker be ready.*

What? What are you doing?

You'll see... just saying that Garrett guy is really handy with explosives.

Oh, crap.

"Be ready, Wanderer," I whispered.

"For wha—"

Booooom!

A flash of light and the Rolls-Royce, with Stavros in it, flew into the air, flipped onto its side, and rolled into the ditch. Strighoul, trolls, and other creatures near the car flew back, their exposed skin shredding on the asphalt.

The back half of the procession stopped in shock, staring at their fallen comrades and leader, not knowing what to do.

Our window of time to escape was already closing.

As if Ryker heard my thoughts, we moved at the same instant. His elbow slammed back into his captors, while I whirled around and used all my weight to ram into the wall of strighoul, knocking them to the ground like bowling pins. This would have been a lot easier if my hands were free and I didn't feel as though every move was similar to running through mud, exhausting my limbs.

Yells and roars slammed together, sandwiching the sounds of claws ripping through flesh. I didn't need to look to know Eli and Cole were the source of the anguished cries.

"Ryker!" I swung around darting out of the way of a group of trolls lurching for me. Ryker moved close to me, using his size and weight to knock into anything that came for us. We sprinted forward, my eyes latching on to two black beasts, their sharp claws swiping at a sea of creatures. Then I spotted my mother and her skulk family member, Olivia, both in human form, swinging swords like Xena the frickin' warrior princess.

"Mom!" I called out to her. Her petite build looked fiercely strong as she shoved her blade into the throat of a strighoul, blood raining down on the pavement. Olivia fought back to back with my mom, cutting through a troll as if he were butter.

Damn. All the women I knew were serious badasses.

"Ember!" Lily called out, joy flashing in her eyes when she saw me.

My boots pounded across the surface of the ground, every step bringing me closer to her. To Eli.

As though a noose had slipped over my neck, I was jerked by the throat and tossed into the air, my feet dangling above the road. I gasped, the hold around my neck cutting off all air. Panic thumped down my spine like a heartbeat, fluttering and jolting. My arms felt tied to my back, and I thrashed, gasping for air that would not come.

"Stop! Please! Stop!" I heard my mother cry, my vision going hazy as magic blasted into my head, squeezing.

"Brycin!"

Oh, holy shit. Pain. I had experienced a lot of it. In all variations and degrees. Lars even tried to get into my head before, applying pressure. But it was nothing—I mean *nothing*—compared to this. Agony so penetrating my mind flatlined because it could no longer register that level of pain.

The memory of Vek's ear-piercing howls echoed in my throat, but nothing could get past the hold Stavros wrapped around my neck. Every cell in my body felt his rage. His impulse to snap my neck and explode my brain over the street pumped through my stressed heart. Voices dulled, but I still caught Ryker's voice.

"Stop!" Ryker growled. "Let her go. You want to pick on someone? I'm fuckin' right here, demon."

The next thing I knew was the burn of my face as I creamed into the gravel on the ground. The pain did not register at first, only relief as the pressure disappeared inside my head, my lungs grappling for air.

"You move, dweller, and she gets another dose, and this time I won't be so kind." Stavros's voice swirled over me. I couldn't move, curled into a ball, trying to breathe. A buzz hummed in my head, but I had no energy to link to Eli, my head pounding.

Footsteps neared me. "You volunteering, Wanderer? You think your low demon half can take it better than her?" Stavros hissed. "She may be an abomination, but at least she has High Demon in her. You are nothing but a servant compared to her. Your father was a trader, scum of the demon world. I wouldn't even let his blood get on my boots."

"Scum? I won't disagree, but that's pretty rich coming from you," Ryker growled.

There was a moment of silence. Fear for Ryker, for my family, tugged my lids up, and I glanced out the corner of my eyes.

Stavros stood over me, his face dirty and blood drying around the healing cut and gashes he obtained from the explosion. The fur-lined King's cloak, which he must have found in a costume shop, was smudged with dirt and burn marks. Unfortunately, besides the superficial wounds, he appeared fine. Dammit.

251

A croaked gasp broke the silence. I twisted my head to see the Viking standing on the other side of me, his back bowing forward, the veins along his neck straining the skin, ready to pop. A trickle of blood dripped from his nose.

"Stop." Sitting up, my raspy voice wobbled. "Please. I will behave." I forced myself to my feet, propping my body in front of Ryker's, his head falling on my shoulder in torment. I captured Stavros's gaze. "Please, Uncle." Oh man, I can't believe I had to say this. "King." *I need a shower now.*

What are you doing, Brycin? Eli linked to me, but I ignored him, not breaking contact from Stavros.

"Love?" Amara came behind Stavros, running her hand over his back. "As you said, don't waste your energy on a lower demon. He's not worth it." She purred into his ear, but her gaze locked on Ryker. Did I detect fear in her eyes? "He might come in handy later. It's all about the long game, babe. We still need the stone, remember?"

Stavros inhaled, then dropped his hand. Ryker hacked and gasped for air. My fingers reached out to touch him behind my back, needing to be comforted as much as he might need it.

Stavros whipped around to face Amara. Her gaze dropped instantly from Ryker, a smile plastering to her face as he grabbed her head, kissing her fervently.

I took the moment to step closer to Ryker and look over at my family. Olivia, Mom, and Garrett stood in a group and farther behind were Eli and Cole. Naked as usual. I gave them a tiny nod.

I'm okay, I linked to Eli and Cole.

"My woman is always looking out for me. Always thinking ahead." Stavros grinned, flipping back to face the entire group. "While I'd love to crush all your brains into mush right now, she's right. You still have some use before I kill you. How's that sound?"

"Yayyyy…" I wiggled my hands in false cheer, the sarcasm dripping from me.

"Right?" Stavros waved his arms. "I am so generous, I can't even believe it. Who else would let you guys live after attacking me? The King!"

Shit, this one is several pancakes short of a stack, Eli rumbled.

No kidding.

"Well, the car is totaled thanks to you guys. And I didn't wear my walking shoes. We're close, right? I hate when my shoes pinch." Stavros huffed, straightening the cape over his shoulders, then stepping over a dead body. "Tie them up! And get those two clothes. I don't want to see their beasty parts swinging like pendulums the whole walk there." He motioned to a few of his men, then to the five attackers. "Hurry! I will be so angry if the battle starts without me. I don't want my entrance to be overshadowed." Stavros strode forward as though he did not notice the debris, blood, and dead bodies scattered over the road, a wake of devastation in his path.

TWENTY-FIVE
Zoey

The white stone castle rose over the tops of trees, declaring its splendor. Our progression silently came upon the Queen's citadel. Most of Stone's pets marched behind us, about fifty of them, all ages and types. And most were either a part of me or Sera. Our features and coloring still displayed a mark of who they originated from.

Even though they had my eyes and hair or my body type or smile, overall, I felt no attachment to them. The only exception was Zeke. Something about him seemed more human, more of me, which was extremely disturbing when I looked into a face of a man appearing to be my age.

Zeke and Zander, another of mine who had a barbed tail, flanked me, their weapons ready. I wasn't sure if they were ready to attack or protect me. Not that I would be doing anything Stone didn't want me to. He was in complete control, keeping me perched at his side. My silent partner, until his nails dug in deeper, controlling my voice along with my will.

If I'd thought years of abuse, of being violated, was the worst I would go through; I was wrong. At least when I was in a bad foster home, I was still myself. I could voluntarily retreat into my head. They had no claim over my will. Here Stone twisted my mind, making me bow to his wishes, dropping me into a new level of terror where you could lose yourself to the darkness forever. Would he mentally break me for good?

He still bequeathed me with sight and sound, clearly wanting me to watch and hear but not be able to do anything. I gasped inside my shell when we got closer to the gate where I spotted all the friends I had gotten to know since we came to the castle. The need to run to them, warn them, almost overwhelmed me. The stone used its power so they could not see the massive group of creatures walking through the gate into the kingdom along with us. No protective shield was powerful enough to stop a treasure of Tuatha Dé Danann.

I latched on to my sense of sight, searching everyone until I landed on a blonde dressed all in black standing near the blond dark dweller Cooper. Annabeth... my soul squeezed, then dropped when I saw what was bundled in her arms.

Wyatt! He was there. Safe. I shouted his name inside, a voice locked deep below the surface. Howling and wailing, my cries went unheeded. I was prisoner in my body, as though I were watching a film I was in but had no control over it. A viewer of this horror. My son was before me, safe in Annabeth's arms, and I could do nothing to get to him. To hold him, confirming he was unharmed.

"*Bhean?*" a voice called as a bird dipped down to Kennedy's shoulder. Sprig waved from the back, his mouth parting in a smile. The pure innocence and love crushed me. "*Bhean!*"

"Sprig, no." Annabeth shot over to him, grabbed him off the raven, and tucked him into her chest with one hand, her eyes narrowing on me with caution.

"What? *Bhean* is back! Maybe her tits are full of honey."

"It's not Zoey, Sprig." She tucked him next to Wyatt, and my son immediately stopped whimpering. He cooed and stretched his tiny hands out for the sprite, acknowledging his friend with a joyous gurgle. Sprig sat with him but watched me sadly, seeing the shell of the person he knew.

"*Bhean*," he choked out softly, as though he'd lost his best friend.

Another piece of me died. The trust and love he held felt fragile. If the stone made me hurt him, any of them, it would end me. Even if my body kept going, I would let Stone have my mind and soul. If he took my family from me, he could have me too. Just like he always wanted.

"Get the children inside!" Kennedy waved to a familiar man with a cane. I was pretty sure his name was Nic, the Spanish incubus who lived at Lars's and had been prisoner with Kate and the kids.

Speaking of—where was Kate? Or Ryker? Lexie? Croygen?

"No, you need me." The little girl, Piper, shook her head, trying to pull away from Nic, his grip tightening on her shoulder.

"Piper, please go with Nic," Fionna shouted back.

"But... I've seen..."

"Piper. Go. Now." Desperation sounded in Fionna's words. I could feel Stone perk up at her fear, licking his lips, understanding the power which came with that type of terror. Stone didn't stop Nic from taking Wyatt and Piper inside. To him, walls meant nothing. He could easily get to them when he wanted.

My friends understood the stone was formidable. They had seen a taste of it with Stavros, but they had no idea *how* powerful. It could take everything right now. End it all in a blink. Now I knew how long it had been planning this takeover. The only reason the stone didn't end it all was because Stone reveled in the chaos and game; otherwise it was bored and empty. It liked feeling alive. And this was the ultimate game—pitting humans and fae against each other. It didn't care who won. It drew strength simply from participating in the act, not the endgame.

Relief still swirled inside me when the door closed behind Nic, Wyatt and Piper behind the castle walls.

Sprig had jumped to Annabeth's shoulder, tucking himself next to her neck, his eyes still watching me. I also noticed the blond dweller next to her placing his hand on her lower back, bringing them both into him protectively. She let him, but she also stood strong, her chin lifted, one hand stroking Sprig's tail, her lids narrowed and defiantly telling me, "I will do what I have to do to protect them. Even from you."

"Good girl," I whispered inside. "And please do." I wanted her to take me down if Stone forced me to do anything to hurt those I love.

"I will win this war for you. There are just a few things I ask for in return," Stone's voice boomed over the courtyard.

"I doubt it will be beneficial to us," Kennedy said.

"Look around, Queen. Your people still live. Do you know what is waiting for you behind your barriers? Ships filled with monsters ready to tear you apart. Thousands of the King's warriors marching toward you right now. Soon the field will be nothing but blood and bodies. You will not win. I am giving you a chance. A way to save your people."

"And what do you want in return?" Kennedy's voice was cold and sharp, as if she were only humoring it.

The creepy uneven smile curled over Lars's mouth. "To rule all, of course."

Stone didn't want to rule. He wanted supremacy to have endless players for a never-ending war. That was where it found power.

"That makes you no different from Stavros," Kennedy responded, standing a few feet in front of everyone, declaring her sovereignty.

"Except if you give me what I want, everyone walks away right now, safe and sound. No bloodshed." *Lie.* The way Stone curved his top lip, I knew he was egging Kennedy on. He knew she would never agree. He was having fun watching the Queen squirm with the choice. I could only imagine the weight of her decision, all the lives on her conscience. "I kill

Stavros and his men, and we all go home. Well, except, this will be my new home. Yours will be either quietly at my side or down in the dungeons depending on how well you obey."

"No deal." Kennedy took a step forward, her fingers wiggling at her sides.

"Yes." Fionna stepped in slightly behind her sister.

"What?" Kennedy spun to Fionna, anger lining her forehead. Fionna stared at her sister like she was trying to tell her something, but Kennedy pinned her mouth together, turning back to Stone, dismissing Fionna. She took two steps closer. "I am still Queen. My answer is no. Making a deal with the devil to get rid of a monster is not a choice."

"You do realize I am being nice. Shields do not keep me out. No magic can stop me. I can end this all right now, with or without your approval, servant." Stone tried to smirk, as though he humored her.

"But you won't." Kennedy stopped only a few feet from him, her back rigid. "You wouldn't go through all this if you wanted that. You will kill Stavros anyway, because he is a nuisance to you. A fly in your soup. You are basically different sides of the same coin. You take pleasure in breaking me."

"You are going to be fun." Stone grinned, showing his teeth. The rush of desire he felt overflowed into me, his new sexual awareness taking over him. And physically showing.

A deep growl vibrated the ground. Lorcan's eyes flashed red, his teeth growing as he moved around Kennedy, ready to attack. She snatched his arm, the shake in her head so subtle I could almost have missed it.

This only amplified the lust coursing through Stone. He was equally turned on by either sex. Power and dominance didn't have a gender. Stone enjoyed being challenged by someone strong.

I was a survivor and learned early in childhood to wear different faces in different situations to survive. Each one protected me or let me fit into society. Fighting Stone would only give him what he wanted. I couldn't fight him with my will… it had to be something else.

"*It. Can. Offer. You. Nothing.*" I heard Lars's last words come to me. He had been determined for me to understand a deeper significance. But what did he mean? How was that supposed to help me?

A loud boom pulled my focus to the lake. The barrier over the sky at the gate to the open sea crackled, spreading out like veins across the surface, tearing at the protective shield.

The declaration of war.

"Time has run out, Queen." Stone motioned to the magic gnawing to be let in, a smugness twitching his mouth.

"Ken." Fionna reached for her sister, again her eyes trying to convey a message, but Kennedy never got to respond.

Another wave of blasts hit the barrier from multiple angles, showing the enemy had surrounded the castle in a crescent shape, attacking on as many sides as it could and shredding the shields like paper. Wails and ear-piercing screeches from monsters in the forest exploded into the air with their battle cry.

Boom! Boom! Boom!

Cannons and cries of attack from the water and land below stamped a chilling trail through my soul. The battle was here. This was the moment when everything would change. Stone was giddy with excitement, similar to a kid on Christmas morning.

I would be on the winning side, but I certainly would not be on the right side. My time was up; the stone had been easy on me. Today I would pay for what I did to it. It would revel in ripping my soul apart.

"It. Can. Offer. You. Nothing."

Lars's words hummed in my chest, but I had no time to think about them. A blast hit the gate, the force tearing everyone off their feet. I flew back, slamming into the ground, my bones crunching under the impact. Unfortunately, Stone might be in control, but I could still feel pain. Dust and debris fell like rain, clogging my throat, the lash of magic dissolving as the last bit of the protection spell fell away.

Strighoul rushed in, pointing weapons at us, Stavros strolling in, wearing a ceremonial fur cape like a king in a kid's play. As with the rest of him, it was covered in dirt and blood, looking as if he'd already been through battle. Stavros grinned, dirt also smeared over healed wounds. I couldn't help but notice the unsettling similarity between him and Lars.

"So... this is where all the cool kids hang out." He peered down at Kennedy, then his head jerked to Lars, lying on the ground. "Well, nephew, it's about time you showed your cowardly face." He shoved his foot into Lars's face, lifting his chin with the tip of his boot.

Oh hell. Did Stavros really think he was talking to Lars? All I could do was watch, as if it were a horror movie you couldn't look away from.

Adrenaline and hunger pumped through Stone, who loved the turn of events. He stayed on the ground, allowing Stavros to believe he was in control. I had a feeling he was already licking his lips with the thoughts of what he would do to him later. Right now he was enjoying this game.

"Before you get all puffy and righteous..." Stavros rolled his eyes. "It's so overdone anyway. You really need to change it up. Improvise. Be spontaneous." He pulled his boot off Lars's neck and turned to look behind him. "Know that whatever threat you toss at me, I will do tenfold to our lovely niece." He held out his arm, curling his fingers in a beaconing motion. Strighoul tugged something forward, pulling the figure from the thick of the throng, a girl, rope cuffing her wrists.

Ember. Like an urchin from a Dickens novel, she was covered in dirt and bruises, looking tired and unsteady on her feet.

Figures rose around me, the menacing growls from the dwellers, their bodies curving forward, revealing they wanted to shift into beasts. Stavros had one of their own, and each one would die to protect and defend her.

"Back off, kitties." Stavros stepped up to Ember, running his hand over her face. "Look at her. She looks so similar to you..." He smirked at Lars. "Are you sure she's not *your* daughter?"

Stone stood up, my body following his like a marionette. Stavros was expecting a response from Lars, but Stone just watched him, taking a thrill from the diversion.

"She does also look like Devlin, so I guess you will never know..." Stavros sighed dramatically, his fingers grazing Ember's cheek. She shuddered and glared at him with loathing. "Or will we? I might know something you don't." Stavros strutted around the same way as a peacock does, thinking he was in full control. Sounds of battle wafted from below. "I found journals in a back room. It looked as though you shoved his stuff there and never opened it. Did you know Devlin wrote in a diary like a ten-year-old girl?"

Taking Lars's silence for a no, he went on.

"Interesting what you find, and what people say when they think no one will ever know. Especially when he was losing his mind. Strangely, he seemed to get even more prolific."

"Get to the goddamn point," Ember gritted through her teeth.

"So impatient. Are you already forgetting my ferocity from earlier?" He patted her cheek, then sighed heavily. "My dance card is so full today— there's a battle to attend to, killing my nephew, bending the Queen to her knees, taking a bath, watching Netflix."

He tapped his lip, enjoying the theatrics. "But first, before I spoil the ending, I want to remind all of you it's not just her. You might have taken the kids, but I don't miss the slobbering, whiny, poopy things. We picked up a few along the way. Think some of these might belong to you?" He waved his hand back. More figures were shoved through the crowd.

259

Eli. Cole. Lily. Olivia. Garrett.

Amara, a sword in her hand, came forward, smugly smiling at me, tugging someone with her.

Ryker.

My body didn't flinch, but a wail shook my soul, my hands pounding against the watching glass, wanting to break out of my prison. "Ryker!" My heart cried out to him. His white eyes found mine, penetrating through the layers the stone controlled until I felt him inside. "Yes. I'm still here."

How did Stavros get him? I had missed so much. Was he the reason Wyatt was safe?

Fierce love poked at the enemy controlling my body. Slowly, Stone's head turned to me, forcing my neck to twist to see him, his eyebrow curving up. *Shit.* I tugged the emotion back, trying to numb myself. The more ammunition I gave him, the more he would destroy me piece by piece. And love was the biggest weapon he had to use against me.

"You honey-hating broomstick! Let him go!" Sprig bellowed from Annabeth's shoulder. "He's not yours, moldy toothpick. Get over it!"

A hint of a smile flashed over Ryker's face, but he quickly hid it behind his stoic mask.

"We should really call it a day; go get massages." Stavros rubbed a shoulder. "And by that, I mean you, Queen, will be giving me a massage while the rest of you slaves wait on me. Doesn't it sound like fun?" he said, glancing over at Lars. "After I kill you, of course. You understand? No hard feelings?"

"Of course," Stone replied, his tone so cool and controlled. If Stavros paid any attention, he would have felt the power pulsing under each syllable.

Boom. Boom

Cannon fire echoed from the sea, metal clanked, and screams of death rose from the field. Still, the true war was held right here where we stood.

"I'm surprised you don't want to know the secret before you die. You really are no fun today, nephew." Stavros went back over to Ember. "I thought you'd be *dying* to know." He chuckled at his own joke. "Get it?"

"Yes," Stone responded. It still enjoyed this, but I sensed a thread of boredom. He was ready for the foreplay to end. "Please enlighten me."

For a beat Stavros squinted at Lars, as if he grasped something was strange about Lars, but he shrugged it off, relishing his one-man play too much.

"Let me first say, the jealousy Devlin felt over you and Aisling…

wow. He kept it quiet, but sometimes he vehemently hated you... and he especially loathed you when Aisling told him she was pregnant. You see, over a year before, he had privately gone to the tree fairies. He wasn't ready for a child, sensing his sanity was faltering with the curse of our family's weakness." Stavros's eyebrows rose. Out of the corner of my eye, I saw Fionna grip her stomach, bending slightly over, beads of sweat trailing down her face. "So, you see, Ember couldn't be his. And he knew that. Knew while Aisling was with him, she still couldn't stay away from you. He kept quiet because he'd rather pretend and keep the only hold he felt like he had on Aisling. He'd have done anything to keep her from leaving him. Even claim the child was his, keeping her from you, the real father..."

Ember's mouth parted, her chest heaving, body swaying side to side.

"Aren't I nice telling you the truth? Your daddy isn't dead, Emmy dear. Or he's not yet. Enjoy these few seconds, because soon he'll be joining your actual uncle. And your slut of a mother. And you'll be a true orphan."

There was a beat when Ember's gaze strangely darted to Fionna then to Lars before she landed on Stavros, fury raging behind her eyes, turning them black. Wind sliced through the town's streets, a rumble of the storm brewing overhead, and whipped at her hair.

"Oh shit," I heard West mumble behind me, before an earsplitting howl flooded over her lips, ripping out from her gut, her arms yanked at the shackles, breaking them from her wrists, her skin paling even more than normal. A blast of magic billowed off her, slamming into each one of us, tossing us like dolls over the earth.

For only a beat, Stone let go of me, stunned when his form slammed into the dirt as well. I gasped for air, my bones feeling so light without the chains.

"Ryker!" I screamed, my need to touch him one last time moving me.

"Zoey," he cried back, his arms reaching for me. Chaos broke around us as the shock wore off and people regained themselves. All I saw was Ryker crawling toward me, his white eyes blazing with the need to reach me.

I cried out, my fingers stretching, touching the tips of his. He grunted, shuffling forward until he laced his fingers through mine.

"Ryker..." I choked, a tear spilling down my face.

"Fight, Zoey. Remember what you have. What we have together. Our family. Us. Fight for that."

I opened my mouth to respond, when I felt Stone slip back in, its mental manacles coiling around me, pulling me back down. I shouted my rage but no sound came out.

"I love you." Ryker grabbed my face, forcing me to look at him. "Fight, human."

All I could do was nod before Stone recaptured me, tossing me back into my cage.

Oh, Zoey. I've been so lenient on you. It's time you were shown how merciless I can be. The punishment for ticking me off... Stone spoke, his voice swirling around inside me.

My form rose over Ryker and all I could do was watch from the far corner of myself where the Stone had sent me. My soul was shoved so far into the dark, I could only look through a peephole into the world. Stone wanted me to watch, still be aware of what I did.

My hand shot out, gripping Ryker's neck. "You will be Zoey's first demonstration." My voice spoke, but the words were Stone's. "I will relish hearing her screams inside while I kill you."

Ryker smiled with a menacing twist of his lips. "Do what you want, but my girl got the better of you, and that will never change." Ryker winked, swallowing against the grip Stone had on his throat. "You can kill me, but the truth is already out there... you will always be a laughingstock."

Anger thumped down, twisting around me, loathing spilling into every pore, lacing it with the thirst for blood.

No... Ryker! I banged around. *Don't provoke him.*

Stone was going to have me kill him right here; I could feel it. And I could do nothing but watch my own hands squeeze the life from the man I loved.

"Remember what you have. What we have together. Our family. Us. Fight for that." Ryker's voice merged with Lars, whose voice was suddenly strong and loud, like he was there with me. *"It. Can. Offer. You. Nothing."*

No doubt Lars had been trying to tell me something, something my unconscious was latching to.

I needed to figure it out before it was too late. Before I destroyed everything... because Stone wouldn't stop at Ryker. He would use my hands to kill all those I loved, including my baby boy.

TWENTY-SIX
Kennedy

It was a pinch of time, a snap of a twig underfoot, a shatter from a dropped glass. Enough time to know it was happening, but no time to stop it. To grab the cup and save it from breaking.

Everything we had prepared for was no longer relevant. There had been no official declaration from me to prepare my troops. No warning the battle had commenced.

In a blink everything combusted. Chaos. Pandemonium. I never did well with being unprepared, but war didn't give you the luxury to think. You had to act.

Ember's magic slammed through the air, tossing everyone within her immediate radius to the ground. My spine kissed the cobblestone with a bruising force. Her irises were black, the spark of lightning that sliced overhead reflecting in her eyes. She leveled her head at Stavros, pinning him to the ground.

"It is you, Uncle, who only have a few moments left." She walked with even steps, calm power crackling off her, causing another strike of lightning to zigzag across the sky. I had seen my friend like this a couple of times, but nothing diminished my awe at her power. A zing of fear piped down my veins at the magnificence of her demon and High Fairy powers mixing together, creating the ultimate weapon. Even if she wouldn't personally hurt me, her powers had no understanding of friend or foe. If we were in their way, we could also be killed.

Stavros looked up at her from where he had landed, a smile curving his mouth. "You think even a dae can challenge the High Demon King?" He flipped his hand and Ember went rolling back, knocking into Eli. The dark dweller's eyes went blood red, his bones already shifting.

In a blink, turmoil broke out through the three groups blocking my view of Stavros and Ember. The Frankenstein creatures which belonged to the stone wailed a kind of battle cry and their half-human, half-fae bodies swarmed in, gnashing their teeth and waving their weapons. One creature with a spike-lined tail, whirled around, using one spike to impale an enemy strighoul's stomach, slicing it into threads. The strighoul screamed, its guts pouring onto the ground.

Crap times a billion.

Bodies swinging weapons, using claws, teeth, and magic all collided together in an aching crunch. Most of the dark dwellers jumped into the attack, slicing into skin as if it were paper.

Rain started to trickle down, Ember bringing in the angry sky.

"Ken!" Lorcan grabbed me, pulling me back to my feet, his green eyes twirling with panic. He pressed his hand to my stomach. We shared a look full of knowledge; I wasn't fighting for just my reign or my kingdom anymore.

I have even more reason to fight, I said into his eyes.

I know. He nodded understanding there would be no stopping me. Pregnant or not, I would fight beside my people. For our freedom. For our lives.

I love you, li'l bird.

I love you too.

The kiss was fast, brutal, and passionate, and then he was gone, a large mass of sleek blackness, joining his brothers in combat.

Cannon booms shrilled from the lake below, reminding me of the battle happening over the land and water. It all came on so fast. Had my people even been ready? I hadn't been able to declare war or give a speech to let them know I was fighting with and for them.

From the water, ships flamed with fire, a few already sinking as the enemy boarded. I could see Croygen, Lexie, and Jack on the closest vessel to me, already overtaken by the enemy. The echoes of "retreat" bounding from their lips as weapons clashed and people danced over the ship's deck in a tango of death. And Rez, the lone siren, even as she took a few adversaries to their watery death, was doing little to even the numbers.

Bodies and blood covered the field where the larger battle happened. The war had barely begun and already so many lives had been lost. Many of them, by the colors they wore, were my people.

Travil, Alki, Gabby, Torin, and Thara were in a group together, slicing and cutting down a group of strighoul as a large mass of trolls ran for them.

Sturt, Georgia, Rowlands, and Vander worked together to limit the numbers. But there were so many coming from the forest and from boat. Too many.

My heart clenched as I watched my friends and my loved ones being seized. Darkness swirled inside me.

A pack of strighoul leaped for Gabby, tackling her to the ground, their teeth sinking into her black fur. A pained roar blasted its way up the hill, shredding my nerves. *Gabby*. Her voice calling me *nerd* thumped in my heart, a review of all the moments we'd laughed and talked flashing through my mind. I would want to protect anyone I saw getting hurt. It was natural for a Druid; we were healers. But Gabby had become family. Not because I was a mate to a dweller, but because of the bond we had formed. I loved her.

More of her blood sprayed onto the ground as nails and teeth dug into her flesh. There were too many at once for her to fight all of them.

A cry from nearby jerked my attention to the samurai warrior who whirled in like a tornado, swinging his blade with precision. Heads of strighoul tumbled to the ground, falling away from the dweller. Alki's fierceness for Gabby seemed to pulsate through his sword as he cut them down with only a few fluid twists of his blade.

He tossed the dead bodies off Gabby, stroking her fur, taking his eyes off the battle, only for a second. That was all it took. A strighoul sprang from the trees, running for the preoccupied warrior.

"Alki!" The warning belted fruitlessly from me, my voice not carrying that far. He swung around, hearing the approaching foe, grabbing for his sword. But it was already too late. The strighoul was one step ahead, swinging his battle-axe. Horror froze in my throat as I watched the blade hit Alki's neck. Blood sprayed like a faucet as Alki's head flew away from his body, hitting the ground a few yards away, and his body crumpled to the ground.

"Nooooo!" A cry ripped through my throat as an anguished roar shook the ground under my feet. Gabby's pain sliced through wind and rain like claws through silk. More strighoul and trolls ran from the trees, heading for the group down there.

Rage coiled up my spine. Dark magic shot through my veins, lifting me slightly from the ground as my focus narrowed on the strighoul surrounding my friends, drilling into them with hate. My black magic skills were still limited, Fionna a lot more trained than me. I had no chance against Stavros, but the strighoul's minds were easier than water to step into. Control.

A cry broke from my lips as my mind claimed one figure after the other, turning them on each other and the approaching trolls. I watched with satisfaction as the strighoul buried their teeth into their flesh and ripped out their throats. Using them as my puppets, they became my slaves to wrath. A trickle of blood tickled my upper lip, but I ignored it, shoving my strength out farther. They killed Alki. If they touched Torin. Gabby... *I will destroy them all.* The darkness gripped me so tightly all I could think about was ripping apart each of my adversaries.

Boom!

Magic shredded my bubble, tossing me into the air. Bolts of lightning struck the street with their barbed tails. Two cars in the street flipped into the air, rolling and bursting into flames. The air crackled with Ember's rage, threatening to wreak havoc on the earth.

My bones cracked as I hit the ground, tumbling over the road, my focus broken from the field.

"Kennedy!" My sister crawled over to me, blood pooling below her nose. "Are you all right?"

I nodded. Fionna tried to help me to my feet but grabbed her stomach, crying out in pain, her face paling.

"Fi! What's wrong?" I clutched her arms, steadying us both.

"My magic... he's draining me. I can't—" She flinched, her jaw grinding. "I have to try now."

"Try what?"

"The cauldron. It's the only chance I have before it's too late... for all of us."

Another rod of lightning ripped through the lane where we were, scorching the row of houses and shops lining the quaint street. The shrill noises of battle clanked in my ears.

"Torin overheard you talking about a sacrifice..."

"I have to die, Kennedy." Fionna's face twisted in pain. "It's what the cauldron wants. What I was destined for. I was supposed to die in that cave. My life, my magic and blood, would have stopped the stone. This is all my fault."

"No." I shook my head. She had told me about what she and Lars did in the cave, altering fate and destroying the cauldron. But I didn't care. I would not lose my sister. "This is not your fault."

"Yes, it is. Stavros is powerful, but our real fight is with the stone. We all know it. The only way to win is with a weapon of equal power." Her hands rolled into fists as sweat dripped down her face. "I don't have a choice. I'm dying anyway. Better to use my life to save all of yours."

My mouth parted in a "what" but nothing came out.

"Lars… he's too much to carry. My human body can't hold him." Her palm moved to her stomach. "He's too powerful and substantial, even for me."

"Fionna…"

She grabbed my hand. "This is not a choice. It's happening. Please promise me you will take care of Piper."

My throat closed in, feeling the seriousness of what was happening. "No. We will find another way."

"There is none. The stone will destroy us all in a blink. The cauldron is the only thing which can challenge it. The cauldron was designed by our family to counter it. This is my job. My destiny."

Terror gripped my soul, and my heart pounded vociferously in my ears. My chest heaved with sobs. I had *just* found my sister. She was my only original blood family left. She was part of me.

"There has to be another way. I won't lose you," I gritted through my teeth. "Maybe it needs both of us again."

"I will not sacrifice you too."

I stepped into her face. "Was this your plan all along? You weren't even going to tell me?"

Fionna licked her lips, peering off to the side.

"Answer me!"

"I'm not good at goodbyes. I'm not used to people caring about me. It was easier this way." She licked the rain from her mouth. "You would've only tried to stop me. The only way to win against the stone is the cauldron. We need the stone to kill Stavros, then I will invoke the cauldron to quell the stone. Doing this, we can possible save Lars and Zoey. Please, Ken. I have to do this."

Screams of battle, of death, raged in my ears, thumping the ground. The fall of my kingdom was coming down bit by bit, crumbling the foundation. Literally and figuratively.

"I will do it."

"What?"

"I will try to get the stone to kill Stavros." I gulped. It actually was our best hope. Stavros was too powerful for us, but not for the stone. "Kill two birds with one stone."

"Horrible pun." Fionna shook her head.

"I know." I squeezed her hand, turning around.

What are you thinking? This is never going to work. My brain circled around and round, trying to come up with another list, an alternative plan to get us out of this mess, but nothing came. This was our only chance. Doing nothing was certain death.

My gaze drifted over the commotion happening. Parts of buildings had collapsed in large chunks, covering the street where cars burned. It looked similar to a war zone. Lars's form stood, his expression unruffled even though his clothes were torn, bloody, and wrinkled. Bodies lay in lumps around his feet as he watched the battle play out, a glimmer of amusement on his face, knowing at any moment he could step in and end it all.

A rush of *déjà vu* fluttered in my mind. I had seen this before. Like a dream, the vision flickered back with a rush of adrenaline that made my limbs tremble.

"Ken? Don't." Fionna's voice felt far away as I moved toward the man with an almost magnetic pull. I stepped through the clouds of dust and debris, his eyes locking with mine. Reality was slightly altered from my vision, as our choices always changed the visions. Sometimes they were more a warning of what was coming. Now I understood this one. It was not Lars in there. The black empty eyes staring at me were the Stone of Fáil. The most powerful object on earth… and I had to destroy it.

My jaw clenched as I walked to my opponent. Toward the object a Druid had crafted. My people had brought these into this world; it was up to me to take them out.

My feet stopped as the rest of my vision played out in front of my eyes. Drifting past the false Lars, Zoey stood there, her eyes empty of the emotion, energy pumping off her. A man's lifeless body lay at her feet.

Dead. *Ryker!* My heart screamed. *Oh gods, no.*

"Zoey is not here anymore. She's been a bad girl. Now it's *my* time." A robotic voice emerged from Zoey as she stepped over his body as though it were nothing more than a hunk of meat.

The stone grinned at her, then turned back to me, moving closer through the haze swirling in the air. Bile rose higher in my throat with every step he took toward me. I tried to move, but my feet wouldn't unpin from their spot.

"Watch and learn, Queen." Stone stopped only a few feet from me. "It is about to get fun."

It thrust out his arms, tipped his head back, and let out a deafening cry, chilling me to the core. Similar to an atomic blast, energy burst off him with a force I had never felt and could not have fathomed. I curled over with a scream. His magic was tangible; you could touch it in the air like jellyfish tentacles. It wrapped around me, dropping me to my knees, stinging and burning me inside and out. Buildings around us burst like balloons as huge chunks of cement and glass crashed down, squishing anyone in their path. Screams from victims shrilled in the air similar to crashing cymbals, adding to the symphony of war.

"I haven't even begun to dip into my powers. I can play with your mind. Make you believe anything I desire." He leaned over, running his fingers through my hair, his mouth brushing my ear. "Stop breathing."

My mind took his command as if it were the ultimate law; my lungs constricted, oxygen sticking in my throat. My hands flew to my throat, fear and panic clawed at my skin, digging at skin.

"This is the power of illusion. Your own mind is tricking you into thinking you can't breathe." My struggle was reflected in its black eyes, a hint of amusement on its lips. "I can make you believe and see anything I want."

Blackness spotted my eyes as I gasping for even a sip of air.

"You are going to be so much fun to play with." He tucked a strand of hair behind my ear. "Breathe, Queenie."

My throat gaped open, allowing air in. I fell backward as I sucked it in, my lungs clenching for every drop, my head pounding with lack of oxygen. This was different from Lars's or Stavros's power. Even in the grip of their powers, you could feel it was an outside force controlling you or choking you. This was completely me. My own body turning on me.

"With one word, I could kill everyone here. With one command, I could have you all as my slaves." The stone placed a finger under my chin, lifting my head to look at him. "Be grateful I am still enjoying myself. You are so amusing to me, but one day I will tire of you... of all life."

Oh. My. God.

There was no way we could fight it. None of us had a clue what we were truly up against. Stavros's tyranny was child's play. The stone would level us. Nothing would be left. He'd make it seem as though we had never existed in the first place.

The centuries this object soaked up power and magic from others prepared it for the chance to finally come on to the field.

TWENTY-SEVEN
Zoey

No! Stop. The cry went no farther than the cage of my body. A robot now. The scarred hand that had hit so many in the ring, had caressed and loved the man before me, was no longer mine to dictate. It wrapped around Ryker's throat with a strength no one could challenge, crushing his neck.

You will see what happens when you fight me, Zoey. You know you deserve this for your trickery. Stone spoke to me while his physical body moved forward, watching the battle dance around him, as if I were no longer a concern. *Now watch your lover die by your own hand.*

Ryker! I screamed inside. *Fight me! Kill me! Don't let me do this to you.* But the Viking only stepped into my grip, his jaw latching down, nostrils flaring in pain. Veins popped out from his forehead, but his eyes would not break from mine. *Don't do this,* I begged him. *Please, fight him. I can't live with myself if you let me do this.* Agony shredded me like a wood chipper, tossing bits of my soul away.

The loss of control, of my own will, stabbed at the wounded, angry girl residing in my broken soul. The men who abused me didn't win, but they had changed me, taken pieces of me I would never get back. With Ryker, my sister, my new growing family, I had begun to heal. The scars would always be there, but I could move on. Now I felt I was thrown back in time. Helpless and scared all over again. And I hated those feelings.

Dammit, Viking! Fight me!

My mouth parted, Stone's words moving my lips. "You had your chance, Wanderer. You carried me in your boot for too long, as though I were some trinket you found on the beach." A snarl came from me, and I pulled his face closer to mine. Ryker huffed, saliva dripping from the side of his mouth.

"Don't be mad I never gave in to you." Each word labored, Ryker's face turned a shade of purple. "You were not my type."

"I was surprised you were strong enough to resist my pull, but you were still weak enough to hold on to me. You never once tried to destroy me, did you? Never buried me in a cave or threw me into the sea. Secretly, I know you liked having the ultimate prize. It wasn't about protecting anyone from me or keeping me out of the wrong hands. You enjoyed stealing me. It was a game, and you got off on possessing the greatest treasure on earth. Having that leverage over everyone., even those you proclaimed you cared about. But you trusted no one. I think someone has daddy issues. Speaking of..." A menacing grin formed on my mouth. "Do you know daddy dearest is still alive? Zoey has been spending time with Vadik all week. Getting quite chummy, the two of them."

Ryker's expression didn't change. Knowing him, he probably thought it was a trick. But it wasn't. Vadik had somehow lived. "He's been my pet. Working for me for a while now, growing my army, sedating the breeding stock. Not much left to him, but I appreciate his determination to survive. There is nothing he won't do. That is always helpful, in my opinion."

"Hope you're happy together," Ryker snarled. "I couldn't give a fuck about him."

"Really? You could have killed him when you had the chance. But you didn't. You were *weak*. Even though he abused your mother and beat you, even after she gave up her life to save yours... how do you repay her? You let him live."

Ryker wiggled against my hand, trying to break free, but my grip only tightened until my knuckles went white. Ryker began to choke. "Remember this while you die: your father still lives, and the thing you kept in your smelly boot is going to squash you under his... well, actually, under your lover's boot. You dragged her into your world. She is here because of you, Wanderer. She will watch you die, watch her own hand kill you, then your son, and everyone else she loves. All because you were greedy and weak."

Rage flashed in Ryker's eyes, his shoulders expanding, the demon rising to the surface. "Touch. My. Son." He struggled to spit out the words.

"You'll what?" *Ready for your love to die, Zoey? Enjoy. You get the best seat in the house.* "I'm bored with you."

No! Please! I'll do anything!

Too late. I could kill him quickly, but I thought you'd enjoy these last moments with him... a more personal goodbye.

Like a cat thrown into water, I scratched and clawed against the walls locking me inside, not letting me turn away or stop my own body. Stone let me experience and feel everything, the familiar smoothness of Ryker's skin in my hand, the thump of his pulse in his neck, his struggle for air. My fingers dug into his airways, his eyes bulging. Terror iced every vein and bone in my body, bile flushing through my system as I wailed for the stone to stop.

"Zoe—I—lov—" Ryker gasped, the rest of his sentence dying in his throat as his eyes closed.

Noooooooooooooooooo! Ryker!

His body dropped. Crumpling at my feet, I felt the vibration of his fall resounding in my heels, through my bones, piercing my heart.

A wail shredded through every fiber of my soul. Pain impaled me like a javelin, crushing me under the grief, turning me into a wild animal inside. But my feet stood firmly, my outside empty of the anguish tearing me up on the inside. The stone let me look down upon him. See my heart on the ground.

Dead.

The agony was so unbearable I felt myself shutting down, retreating.

Come, Zoey. More to play with. My head lifted without a struggle responding to its master. In the distance, through the thick veil of haze, Kennedy stood facing Stone, her eyes on me, her mouth parted in horror, her gaze darting from Ryker to me.

"Zoey is not here anymore. She's been a bad girl. Now it's *my* time." My leg stepped over the body as though he were merely another object in my way, nothing of consequence, while I curled up in a ball inside, howling with grief.

Stone grinned at me, as if I was his prodigal daughter, then he turned back to Kennedy, his attention pinned on the Queen. Their outlines grew more obscure in the smoke, but I saw him lean his head back, throw his arms out, and release a deafening bellow.

A thunderous blast of energy exploded, bursting structures from the inside out. Glass and huge pieces of concrete sprayed out, crushing bodies and everything in its path like a whack-a-mole game.

I held my head high and not even a slice of glass touched my skin. Screams of victims rattled around me sounding like thunderous chimes. I stood there, the war exploding around me. Friends and foes fought for their lives as their deaths rattled in my ear.

Lightning struck near me, setting an abandoned cart on fire. The heat sparked off my face, but no pain registered. Nothing mattered.

The world was on fire. And I was the worst enemy of all. With the face of a friend, one you'd hesitate to kill, I sliced through you with a smile.

I *killed* Ryker. I would kill more…

Lexie. Annabeth. Croygen.

Wyatt.

The list would go on, until the last one fell at my feet. Stone would make sure of it.

Ryker would tell me to get angry. Fight Stone's control. To fight for our son, for our family. Us. But he was gone. He often had teased I would be his demise. And I was.

Empty inside and out, I stared at the burning frame of the cart. Hoping somehow, someone would come along and slice me in half. I would be grateful. Thankful.

"*Bhean?*" The familiar voice bounced into my ear. I had only enough control to tug my head over toward the sound of my best friend through the haze, smoke, and debris. *Sprig*. His face was streaked with soot, but it was the horror in his eyes that sawed another chunk off my heart. Noticing Ryker's body slumped behind me, his soft brown eyes locked on to mine with confusion and debilitating grief.

"*Bhean?* Why—why won't the Viking get up?"

Electric bolts of emotion darted through me. Seeing him was like stepping into a warm bath… that was full of acid. I wanted to snuggle into his fur and cry. To feel his warmth and heartbeat. Beg for forgiveness. But I couldn't.

When I was pregnant and not feeling great, many times he'd fallen asleep curled in the curve of my neck, or on my growing belly, talking to the future *Buachaillín*. He was my comfort. My happy place. Now I had betrayed him. Hurt someone he loved very much. His pure innocence and sweetness didn't understand the cruelty controlling me.

"*Bhean…?*" He leaped over concrete blocks and dead bodies, reaching me.

"Sprig…" I grunted through tightly clenched teeth, pushing back against Stone's power. I could no longer see him through the smoke, but he was near. His attention was focused on something else just enough to let up on me. "Go."

"No!" He jumped from a car to my shoulder. I froze inside, scared the stone would notice and make me hurt Sprig. "We're family, right? I mean, I shared my honey with you… if that's not love, then I don't know what is. It's more than I did for my own mother. That is a bond deeper than blood."

"Get. Away," I muttered, huffing through my nose. His hand came to my cheek, the warmth seeping into my skin.

"Do you need to borrow my cape?" He tugged on the pair of black undies he had around his neck. "What am I talking about? You have superpower tits. Those things can fight anything. They are blessed by the gods."

I swear I could hear my heart crack. With my love for him... for all my family.

Both tiny hands cupped my chin, forcing my face to look at him. He briefly peered down at Ryker, swallowing back the lump in his throat, his gaze coming to mine. "*Bhean*, I believe in you. Viking believes in you."

A sob welled inside, but I knew my face showed nothing.

"The honey gods are with you. Use them." He nipped on his lip, nodding toward my bra. "Ummm... they don't happen to be with you now? I mean, a little burst of sweet energy wouldn't hurt right now, that's all I'm saying."

"Go. Please," I whispered hoarsely.

"No." He shook his head. "You need me, *Bhean*. And... I love you. I never thought I would have a home. A family. A place where I belong. After what happened to me, I could never go home, never be accepted again. I thought I would be alone the rest of my life. A super freak. I'm lucky. You found me. Took me with you. You're my *Bhean*..." He tipped his head, stressing the last word. "No matter what, I will stand by you. To remind you of what we have." He dropped his hands away. "Plus, you have 'hallelujah, praise the gods' honey dispensers. Why would I ever leave that?"

"Remember what you have. What we have together. Our family. Us. Fight for that."

"It. Can. Offer. You. Nothing."

Something clicked inside me at last.

Holy hell.

The stone was only truly powerful when it had something to offer someone. Material things. Land. Money. A different life. To be famous. It offered your deepest wish to you, while it sucked you dry, getting its claws into you. At one time, I had wanted more. Family. Love. Friends. But none of it would have been real. Only the illusion of love and friendship. I had all that now. I wanted for nothing. I had my dream life come true. Beyond anything I could imagine. My business, my sisters, my son, my best friends, and the love of my life. And it was all real.

Ryker. I could wish...

No. He would not want that. Plus, it wouldn't be him, just an illusion of the actual man. A dream.

The stone had nothing to offer me! No power over me, except the agreement, and the mark on my hand. I had tried to cut it away before, but something was telling me to do it again. Except, the stone wouldn't let me hurt myself.

"Sprig." As I tried to get my idea across to Sprig, beads of sweat trickled down my body and my eyes watered from the smoke. "Cut my hand."

"What?" He gripped my shirt, eyeing me.

It took several tries, my head pounding with effort, but I finally lifted my hand, turning my palm to him. "Cut. It. Out."

"Is this some kinky stuff I really don't want to know about you?" His eyes widened. "Like honey-dipped-in-sugar-rolled-in-honey-and-fried-in-honey kind of twisted things?"

"Do. It," I croaked, perspiration gliding down my face. The clatter of war clanked around me as if I were in some strange bubble. Stone had probably done it so I wouldn't let myself get killed. He wanted me around. I tried before, but he wouldn't let me hurt myself... but even powerful treasures seemed to forget about lesser fae. "Knife. Boot."

"Fine. Only because I can never say no to your delicious honey melons." Sprig shook his head before crawling down my leg, grabbing the blade, and scouring back up. It might do nothing, but I hoped this would break a thread of his power on me.

"Okay, *Bhean*." He gripped the knife near the hilt so he could control it. "You owe me for this. You know I hate blood. Or bananas. Bananas are definitely worse, but blood comes in second. Well, maybe not. I don't particularly like cucumbers either. Gives me gas." He sucked in a breath then dug the tip into my palm. A jolt of pain dashed up my arm and zinged across nerves up and down my entire shoulder. "And if we're being totally honest, your green bean casserole is not my favorite. Salad night is just inhumane. But that triple honey cake you made for my birthday. Loved it! Death by honey is the only way to go."

He slid the blade deeper into my hand. I felt everything, but the cries of pain were on the inside, still making my brain flutter with dizziness. "If we get out of this, you are taking me to Izel's. I've been telling Cal about it. Oh man, the pancakes! She will be so happy to see us. She'll make me a dozen." He sliced deeper, blood pooling up and around the wound. "Ohhh... I'm gonna throw up... I'll need honey to recover. I'm not picky. If you happen to have one of those granola bars? Oh, how about those mango chips? Churros? I would never turn down one of those Inca Colas!"

"Keep. Going," I hissed. Each cut, I could sense it, like weeds being pulled in a garden, a connection to the stone being pruned. It was tiny, but optimism still curled inside with hope my leash could get a little longer.

"Zoey!" My name rang through the air, jerking my eyes to the side. Dressed in dark clothes, her hair in a signature Annabeth fishtail braid, my sister came running through the gate, cuts and blood covering her exposed skin. *Lexie.* My heart surged, but my body did not move an inch. "Oh my god... it's you, right?"

Lexie moved surprisingly quickly on her mechanical legs, Croygen yards behind her, jumping into the fight, slicing into anyone that hinted at leaping at her.

Oh, hell. If Stone saw my sister, he'd get another piece of his revenge.

"No," I growled, shaking my head. "Stay back." *I'm still not me. Please, run away from me.*

Her eyebrows furrowed, looking at Sprig, then at me. "But?"

A scream twisted my gaze away from my sister, landing on another. Amara stood a few yards away, her sword limp in hands, her eyes on the body behind me, agony etched across her features, her chest heaving.

Ryker. He was the only one Amara seemed to care about beside herself. The one person she wanted so badly after so long despite his continued rejection.

Fury rolled over her, twisting her mouth, hate finding me. Abhorrence flashed in her eyes, locking on me.

"You fucking bitch," she seethed, her lip curling up. "You did this, didn't you? I always knew you would be his end. I loved him, and you took him from me. And now I will thoroughly enjoy ending your life." She took large strides toward me, raising her sword, her tongue sliding over her lips, like she could already taste my blood.

"Please," I choked out a whisper, "*do it.*"

She halted, her forehead scrunching at my plea. She could hear I begged her to kill me, not to give me passage. Her sword was still poised to swing at me, but she tilted her head.

"Please, Amara." *Please kill me.*

Amara sucked in, skeptical of my motives. It was the first time I had ever seen her falter. And it was the first time I wished she wouldn't.

"*Bhean?*" I could hear Sprig call me. My energy was weak, but I dropped my arm, forcing Sprig to the ground, where droplets of blood pelted the concrete, the mark on my hand a marred bloody mess.

"Zoey?" Lexie took another tentative step to me. My eyes narrowed in warning, stopping her in place. She gulped. "Sprig." She motioned for the sprite to move to her.

"No." He still clung to the knife, staying near my leg. "*Bhean* needs me to keep reminding her to fight."

Well, well... I can't leave you alone for a moment. Stone's voice slithered through my head, wrapping around my throat. *I can feel you, Zoey. You think you can fight me. Think there is nothing I have that you want. You don't think I know your deepest wishes? I think there is one thing you will still want...*

Visons flashed in front of me, the battle disappearing in front of me, filling with the backyard of the house I used to see as my dream home. Again, I was draped in a long black silky off-the-shoulder wrap and sunglasses. The nondescript friends I used to fill my imagination with were now all the people fighting for freedom next to me. Ember, Eli, Kennedy, Lorcan, Fionna, and even Lars surrounded the table. Others played in the pool or lounged by the grill, laughing and joking. The table was full of food and drinks. Annabeth brought another tray of food from the house, the blond dark dweller at her side, his hands unable to stay off her.

There were no more imaginary parents, and this time Lexie was no longer a little girl playing in the pool. She and Croygen lay on the lounge chairs, whispering and smiling, like two on the verge of falling in love.

I looked over my shoulder at the man I loved. Ryker's white eyes danced playfully as he wrapped his arms around my middle, kissing my neck. "Just wait until I have you alone. Think the Chevelle needs to be taken for a ride."

This was everything I wished for, wanted. But it wasn't real. What I had was real. I no longer needed a huge house or nice things. Ryker and I had created an even better dream.

The splat of my blood hitting the stone echoed in my ears, pulling me back to reality, clearing my vision. The castle grounds drenched in blood filtered up my nose, centering my boots on the pavement. It had a strangely clarifying effect on me.

"No," I drove the response out of my throat.

"Excuse me?" Lars's image stepped through the fog of the battle. Not one blade or weapon touched him but moved around him like magnets repelling each other. Stone tilted his head, his black eyes clenched on me, then dropped to my hand. "You think cutting out my mark will stop me? You are so naïve."

"Not completely," I spit out. "Filing back the claws. You have nothing to offer me."

"Your lover is dead. Most of your friends will follow. You need me, Zoey. You always have. Even when you denied me, you still dreamed of me. Sometimes longed to have me back."

"The problem with being an object depending on people to live is that you need us, not the other way around." Every word came out stronger, my body still stiff, but I could feel prickling in my hand near the wound. And it felt like *my* hand. It hurt like a bitch, but the external pain was welcome, reminding me what was real. What was me. "Nothing you offer is real. Even if you showed me Ryker alive again. He's only a shadow of the man I had. An impression of the real family and love I have now."

This was what Lars was trying to tell me before he died. I had the power. Good or bad, it was real. I no longer dreamed of a better life, nor did I want power or money. I wasn't willing to live in a made-up world just to have family and friends surround me.

"Zoey…" Stone clicked his tongue, strolling over to me.

My mind drifted to Kennedy, wondering where she was and what he had done to her, but the sensation of his magic seeping in centered me in the here and now. I rolled my shoulders back, my head high. "You have no power over me."

Stone stopped, his eyes narrowing. Like a gust of wind, he shoved his magic at me. I stumbled back, the force burning my skin, his virtual claws digging back in.

I gritted my teeth, repeating my motto in my head at him, knowing he heard every word.

Stone took methodical steps toward me, his black pupils narrowing on me.

"Lars? What is going on?" Amara sputtered, looking between us, not understanding. She saw Lars. Lars attacking one of his own. Slowly he curved his head to her; a strange smirk tugged the side of his mouth too far up to be normal.

"Ah. Margo. Or is it Amara now? The woman who craved me so bad I could taste her desperation with every pulse. The years you longed for my power, not knowing how close I really was." Stone walked straight to Amara, taking her face in his hand. "Watching Ryker keeping you from me was my only entertainment. You were so desperate it was pathetic. And deep down all you really wanted me for was to help you keep him. You knew he never loved you."

"What are you talking about? I did not long for you. You were a means to an end. I was using you." She tried to jerk back out of his grip, but her body didn't move an inch. Fear opened her eyes bigger as she tried to move unsuccessfully again. Her mouth opened but immediately slammed shut in an audible crunch.

"You still think you're talking to Lars. How pitiable, Amara." Stone gripped the back of her neck, tugging her roughly to him. "You are such a small player; I should kill you for fun. There is no question why Ryker and I both chose Zoey."

She didn't speak, but it looked as though someone had slapped Amara across the face. Her cheek muscles tightened, her eyes widened, and hurt transformed her expression.

"Didn't you already have a chance to bed her, nephew?" A man's voice came through the fog, twisting all of us to the person who resembled Lars. "Seems an odd time and place, but desperation does strange things to men, huh?" Stavros, covered in dirt, his clothes torn and bloody, sauntered up, his arms open, as if he were the master of his domain. He acted like he didn't have a care in the world; he honestly thought he was the most powerful here.

Stone dropped his hand from Amara and stepped back, not looking at the Demon King. His mouth twitched as though he were amused. Amara's chest fluttered hastily. Her panic-filled eyes darted to Stavros, and she froze in place. Just as I did.

It was all an illusion. The power of our own minds working against us. The stone told our brains we couldn't move or speak, and our brains believed it. It was harder to fight yourself than an outside force.

Was there a way I could trick my mind out of it? Force it to push beyond?

"You will let everyone die for you, Lars?" Stavros waved at the rubble and bodies on the ground. Some of them were Rapava's creatures. My own children. Though I felt relieved there were fewer of them. "This could end now. But I doubt you could ever sacrifice yourself for others. It's not in our blood is it? In the end, demons will give up everyone they love to be the last standing." Stavros placed his hands on his hips. "Guess it makes it more exciting. I will probably be a little bored once you are dead. There will be no one to see me torture your lover or her child."

"Demon." Stone swiveled gradually to Stavros. "It's as if you are not even trying to make this challenging for me. I preferred the other High Demon King."

Stavros's brows furrowed as he dropped his arms and rolled his fists into balls. "I think the game is over. Time to die, boy."

Magic flowed from Stavros directly at Stone, the energy skating over my skin. I had been subjected to Lars's power before. It was crippling and painful. If Stavros had even more, I couldn't imagine the anguish he could cause... to a normal fae.

The potency of Stavros's power slammed into the bubble, but Stone bounced it right back into Stavros. Stavros stumbled, his forehead crinkling with deep lines as his own magic crackled against his skin. All humor and cockiness dropped away as fury rolled his lips into a snarl like a feral dog, thrusting more energy at the stone. Once again his energy slipped by or ricocheted back, Lars's body unharmed.

"What?" Stavros glanced around like he was being tricked. "What is going on? You have no power left."

Stone let his head drop back, an empty laugh chilling the already hostile air. Then the humor ended as his jaw clamped down. The shift to anger was just as abrupt and unsettling as the laugh.

Stone strode up to Stavros and wrapped his hand around his throat. Stavros's expression morphed into complete shock. "You are not speaking with your nephew. If you were any kind of demon, you would have known that. He is dead."

"Dead?" Stavros sputtered. "But I still feel him—"

"Stop. Talking." The rest of Stavros's words died away in his throat, though my brain latched on to his final words. He still felt him? Is that what he was going to say? It didn't make sense; I was there when Lars was expelled from his body. He couldn't live outside of it. That wasn't possible, right?

"You know the only weapon in the world which can kill a High Demon King is the spear?" Stone's voice was cruel and cold. It was the same one that haunted so many of my nightmares, vowing it would find me and make me pay. "Well, actually the magic of the spear. And guess who holds those powers as well." Stone lifted a lip in a grotesque sneer. "You are so far out of your element; this will be like stepping on a bug. Stupid, greedy, gluttonous, arrogant... with no reason to be. Do you know how many of you I've run into in my time? Thousands. Kings, CEOs, presidents. No different from the last. At first, I fed off your type, since you were never satisfied, always wanting more. I could suck you dry of life, and you'd come back again, your greed a drug. It outweighed any intelligence." He gripped his throat tighter. "I don't consume pig slop anymore."

Watch, dear Zoey. This one you might enjoy. The air shifted, and the prickle of death rolled over me, heading toward the Demon King. Stone's mouth parted, ready to order his death.

"Darz!" A little girl's voice cut through the middle of our little bubble, my heart dropping to my feet. I swung around just as Piper's tiny frame barreled through the battling men and objects on fire, running up to us.

Oh. God. No.

I wanted to scream, to jump to her, to cover her with my body. What was she doing out here?

Stone held Stavros's neck but stared at the little girl as if she were an alien, his nostrils flaring. I could hear Lexie and someone else screaming for her, but everything became white noise in the background, my attention tunneling on the girl.

She lifted her chin, looking so much like her mother, but with a certainty only a child could possess. She didn't flinch.

"Don't worry, okay?" Her Irish accent danced along with her toes, as though she had no doubt. "I will save you."

TWENTY-EIGHT
Fionna

My mouth parted as I called for my sister again, but she continued to walk toward the monster who wore my man as a costume. My fingers pressed into my gut, feeling Lars's presence expand. His demon was reacting, feeling the magic, the fear, and it wanted to attack. In the need to protect and fight for those he loved, he was draining me. My legs wobbled, and my body trembled, watching Kennedy disappear in the cloud of smoke. "Shite! Kennedy!" I took a few steps to follow her and crumpled over, my knees colliding with the ground. Gripping my waist, I sucked in deep breaths, trying to move despite the magic consuming my body.

As a child, I had growing pains and restless leg syndrome. This felt like my entire body was experiencing both, while diminishing my energy with every attack. "Will you ease up?" I said to my gut.

Pulse.

"Not sure if that was a yes or no."

Pulse. Pulse.

Fire shot down my nerves, his demon forgetting to be kind to the host. He wanted out. My teeth punctured my bottom lip, fighting back a groan.

"You are dying, Druid." Goran was suddenly beside me, watching me as if I were an insect pinned on a board, my muscles twitching in the final throes of death.

"Thank you," I snapped, the taste of blood on my tongue, my gaze searching for my sister. Through the haze, she was no longer visible. "You are very helpful."

What was she thinking? Why would she challenge the stone?

"She's giving you a chance. You need to do it now." He nodded at the rucksack I carried. "I gave you my word I would help save Lars before you let me go. If you die, my word will haunt me into the next life."

282

Suddenly the ground vibrated underneath my legs, pebbles jumping like popcorn as buildings exploded and rained down on the courtyard. I threw my arms over my head and curled my body over my legs. Goran grabbed me, shielding me from the large debris breaking over the pavement. I peeked up, barely able to see anything through the haze.

"Thank you." I tugged away from Goran's icy skin and awkward embrace. He dropped away from me, standing like an automaton.

Boom! My head snapped around following another explosion from below.

"Oh no." My hand went to my chest as several ships sank, their burning masts the last signs of their existence; the Queen's insignia flew off the mast. Flames flicked high in the sky, consuming it in a few gulps. Shouts and cries came from those jumping overboard.

"Shite." I gulped, realizing it was the exact ship where I'd last seen Croygen, Rez, Jack, and Lexie board. From my spot above, I could see the battle expand across land and sea.

We were losing on all fronts. Any strategy we had was long gone.

This is up to you, Fionna. It's time to set things right. At least you have to try to protect the future for your child. For those you love.

"Druid!" Goran growled with frustration, as though he had been calling me over and over. Blinking up at him, his empty features were uncomfortable to look at for too long. I had done that to him. He was supposed to die, and I forced him to live for selfish reasons. Just like Lars altered my destiny.

No. We create our own destiny. I've always had the idea that fate was changeable. Our choices and decisions were ours. To live or die, the choice was mine.

I reached around and grabbed the sack, and the cauldron tumbled onto the ground. My hands shook as I set it in front of me, suddenly bearing the weight of what I was about to try again.

A high-pitched cry tore my eyes away from the object to see a creature, half human, half lizard, sprinting for me. I had seen lizard shape-shifters before. This was nothing like that. It could never shift into one or the other. It was both... permanently.

A thick green tail swung behind him, full of thorny spikes running on either side of it all the way up its back. His human green eyes narrowed, a huge sword directed at my throat.

A spell came to my lips, but he was already on me, murder and hate sketched on his features as he swung.

Shite.

The blade hissed by my ear, and I closed my eyes, knowing I was about to die. Instead of feeling the blade pierce my skin and hack at my bone, the clang of metal on metal rang in my head, jarring my teeth. I opened my eyes to Goran's sword crossing in front of me, blocking the lizard man and shoving the thing back. With only a few moves, Goran's blade impaled the lizard in the stomach, as he pulled a knife from his boot and ruthlessly stabbed the creature in the throat.

The lizard choked, blood spurting from his lips, his eyes wide with the awareness of his own death. Dropping to the ground with red foam gurgling through the hole in his neck and his mouth, he looked at me one last time before his face smacked into the pavement.

Goran didn't hesitate to swipe the blade through the creature's neck, its head rolling into the gutter. The body still twitched and jerked before me, blood pooling in the crevices of the cobblestone.

Goran didn't even blink, turning back to me. "Begin."

All I could do was nod and focus on the cauldron, my entire body trembling as I ran my hands over the rim. A throb quivered in my fingertips.

Strange. My palms curved around the bowl, my brows drawing together.

"What?" Goran wiped off the blood on his sword, using the victim's clothes.

"Nothing. I could have sworn I felt energy come off it." So much magic and explosions swirled around, even my body shook like a shaved sheep in winter. Most likely, it was outside the object.

Wishful thinking, Fi.

I tugged the knife from my boot, energy and images of the blade's experiences flashing in my head. Excitement and magic danced off it, as though sensing another story was about to be added. My fear and resolve pumped straight into it. Gripping the handle, I dug the tip of the blade into my wrist. I would cut vertical, to follow along my vein, and bleed out into the vessel.

"Fuck. Fuck. Fuck," I whispered to myself, blinking back the tears. I never said my goodbyes to those I loved. We had no time now.

Pulsepulsepulsepulsepulse.

I tried to ignore the feeling of Lars, manic and violent, as he pounded inside.

I sliced a little incision at first, hoping Kennedy could somehow manipulate Stone into killing Stavros. It seemed impossible, but I couldn't wait long. I hoped Lars could survive inside me, use my body until he could get back in his own. The idea of taking him down with me was agonizing. I wanted so badly for the cauldron to weaken the stone enough that Lars could return back to full Demon King again… but this was all hope.

You fight, Lars. Stay alive, take my body somehow, some way. Raise Piper.

Pulsepulsepulsepulsepulse.

Yeah, he wasn't happy with me.

Words sang from my mouth, my world tightening to just the cauldron and me. Sounds and smells began to ebb away as the spell twirled over my tongue.

"Mummy!" A little voice jerked me out of my trance, my head snapping up, dread cascading over on me.

Oh gods, no.

My world tipped on its side, watching Piper run down the path, dressed in clean clothes, her washed damp hair sticking to her face as her boots trudged toward me.

"Piper! No!" A cry pierced the air, my voice shrieking, my legs rising.

She smiled. "Don't worry, Mummy. I will help. Darz needs us," she yelled, turning away, running straight into the battle.

A scream burned up my throat, my heart plummeted with terror. *No… this can't be happening.* My legs reacted as adrenaline shoved energy into the muscles.

"Piper!" I screamed, stumbling forward, the smoke curling in my lungs and blocking my vision. "Piper!"

Through the debris, my boots came to a squeaky stop, my stomach twisting into knots, my heart slamming against my ribs at the sight before me.

Amara and the faux-Zoey stood frozen, Lars's hijacked body before them, gripping Stavros's neck. They were both focused on the tiny five-year-old in the middle, her hands on her hips, looking as if she were schooling them.

Oh. Holy. Shite.

"Don't worry, okay? I will save you." She nodded at Lars's form, bouncing on her toes like she was excited.

"Piper." A guttural sound volleyed from my diaphragm, my bleeding arm shaking as I grabbed for her, taking careful steps. "Come here."

The stone's pitiless eyes flicked to me, then back to Piper, his head tipping in curiosity, still clutching Stavros's neck. What if it could feel her magic and notice how powerful she was? He could easily manipulate a child's mind and use her energy, especially when she saw Lars looking back at her.

Piper bounded back to me and my arms wrapped around her protectively, my guard up, ready with a spell.

Stone's stare did not break from her, his eyebrows slightly furrowing, as though he were trying to figure her out. And I knew whatever he was thinking was not good.

But if he tried taking her from me... The wrath of a mum would come for him.

The stone's mouth parted to say something, but instead Stavros tugged back, unsheathing his sword with a whoosh, the long blade finding Stone's midsection and sliding into his gut with a sickening sound of severed flesh. Stavros ran the blade in to the hilt with a gleeful smile.

"I win." Stavros twisted the blade. "I always win."

The stone took a step back, looking at the hilt sticking from its stomach, blood soaking in the clothing around the blade. For a second, I thought I saw shock flicker over his features, but it was gone before I could be sure. Slowly Stone lifted its head, zeroing in on Stavros. A cold, evil smile curved his mouth.

Oh shite. I knew it wasn't really Lars, but seeing the sword go into him made me cry out.

"Demon." Stone grabbed the handle, yanking the long blade from Lars's body with ease. "You aren't even on the sidelines. I am the Stone of Fáil, the Sword of Nuada, *and* the Spear of Lug. I am the very thing that can kill you." Before I could even blink, the stone flipped the blade around, slicing it across Stavros's throat, spraying blood everywhere.

I gasped, stumbling back with Piper, turning her away from the horror.

Stavros stood for several beats, his eyes wide before his head tipped to the side, dangling from his neck, a river of red liquid gushing in waves as a strangled gurgled cry came from his throat. A pained, devastated expression flushed over Stavros's face before his body fell to the ground, his head fully detaching at the impact, gushing like a squashed pumpkin. I cringed, turning my gaze to my daughter. She calmly held on to me, her face snuggled into my stomach.

For feck's sake. What kind of therapy is she going to need after this?

The moment the thought passed through my head, magic drove like a lorry straight into my gut, plunging me brutally into the ground with a silent cry. Pressure crammed in every corner, filling me like a balloon, ready to pop.

"Mummy!" Piper yelped, grabbing for me. Pure agony shredded my nerves as more magic funneled in, stealing my breath, sweat pricking at my hairline. *Holy. Gobshite.*

"Fionna." Goran grabbed for me, trying to get me back on my feet, but I bent over, moaning through the experience. My entire body shook violently, feeling Lars consume more of me.

Shite. He'd gotten his powers back with Stavros's death.

I was dying slowly before when he was just demon. Now that he was King again, my bones couldn't carry him. I wrapped my arms around my middle where it pulsed with agony.

I loved the bastard, but he couldn't make this easy, could he? My life was a fading tapestry, the strings unraveling quickly now. A low growl curled from my throat.

"Get up, Fionna. Fucking move," a voice whispered hoarsely in my ear. Goran's hand wrapped around my arm, tugging me up. "Stavros is dead. You have to act now."

"Aye. No shite," I grunted, letting him help me rise, my head swimming, bile burning my throat. I was retaining the High Demon King's soul along with my own. There wasn't enough room for both of us. Hopefully he could use me until the cauldron weakened the stone.

I stumbled and wobbled but rose to my feet. Lars's growing pulse echoed in my ears and chest. My purpose drove me forward. The precise thing I hoped for had happened. It was up to me now. While everyone's attention was still on the dead demon, I grabbed Piper, allowing Goran to walk us swiftly through the haze, back to the cauldron.

"Take her!" I hissed, pushing Piper to Goran. "Get her back to the castle."

"No, Mummy. I'm supposed to help." I'd grown so weak she easily wiggled from my grip.

"No!" I bellowed. "It's too dangerous. Go back to the castle. NOW!" I hated scaring her, or for this to be her last memory of me, but her life was on the line.

Boom! Boom!

My gut sank; that wasn't Ember, but cannons heading our way. Debris rained down upon us. My unstable legs zigzagged, shielding Piper, both of us leaping over objects and diving away from flames.

"Go! Now!" I screamed at Piper, wiping the sweat from my brow. "Get to Nic!"

"I won't!" Piper fisted her hands in anger, her forehead crinkling. Damn, she was so stubborn. One hundred percent my daughter. "You and

Auntie Ken need me. I make the third. I even memorized the spell." She stomped her foot.

The third?

It was as if a force shoved me backward, the realization snapping in my brain like a puzzle piece.

Of course. My daughter. My blood. Cathbad blood.

Kennedy and I weren't enough. It hadn't even crossed my mind to bring in Piper. She was too young to be part of this. But at five she was already more powerful than I had been for years to come.

Druid magic followed the laws of nature, coming in threes. For most spells, there was some form of three, like ingredients or the times you'd chanted a spell. It took three of the Cathbad bloodline to create the cauldron, my grandfather being the principal guide.

It would take three to bring it back, me being the guide.

"No." I shook my head. I understood this, but I still couldn't let my daughter me part of this...

"Fionna!" Kennedy's voice rang out, raw and frightened. Staggering through the cloud, she climbed over a huge chunk of a house in the middle of the street. Covered in wounds, her eyes were lined with broken vessels, as though she had been choked.

"Ken!" I screamed, rushing to her. "Are you okay?"

"I'm sorry, I tried. The stone is too powerful." She reached me, taking my hands, noticing them tremble in hers. "He told me to stop breathing." She shook her head, swallowing roughly, the memory of it still fresh. "I woke up and he was gone... and I was covered in rubble."

"It's okay."

"No." She gripped my arms hard. "It's not. It's so much more powerful than I thought. With one word, the stone can have us all on our knees or dead. Stavros isn't even a concern anymore..."

"Good thing. Stavros is dead."

"What?"

"Discuss this later." Goran walked up to us. "Look around. Your time is almost up."

Kennedy took a moment to notice the devastation, the piles of bodies on the field below, the ships on fire. Everything we loved and built was dying around us. He was right.

"Ken, I can't believe I'm going to do this. There is only one thing we can do to stop this." I nodded back at the cauldron. "It's going to take some badass Cathbad girls."

Piper bounced up to me, grinning, like she got her way. I could try to protect her, but if we didn't take down the stone, what would I be protecting her from? It was much worse leaving her in a world where she could be tortured, used, and possibly abused in ways which made my blood seethe.

Kennedy's eyes went to Piper in shock, her mouth opening to speak. I laid my hand on hers. "The power of three. Our blood created it. We can do it again." *I don't have much time.* I didn't say that, but I felt she understood, her expression dimming to grief.

Goran grumbled, irritated with our lack of action.

"Okay. Let's do this." Kennedy nodded, grabbing my hand, then Piper's. The three of us went over to the cauldron, dropping to our knees around it. Kennedy and Piper both placed their hands on it.

Goran stood guard, letting no one get near us.

"That tickles." Piper giggled, tapping on the pot.

"What tickles?" I asked.

"Can't you feel it?" Piper looked from me to Kennedy. "It's alive."

My mouth parted. "What? What do you mean?" I placed my hands on the vessel, not feeling anything.

"Piper, there's noth—"

"No, Mummy. Feel it." She pushed my hands firmer into the cauldron, then tapped her head. "And here. I can hear it."

Kennedy sucked in, closing her eyes. "Crap times a hundred. I think I feel something."

It took several deep breaths to steady my shaking hands, but after a while I thought I felt a magic tingle in my fingers. Was it alive? Did that mean I wouldn't have to die? How long had it been alive?

"It doesn't matter. The sacrament is still the same." I didn't want to get my hopes up, not when I would die anyway. If I didn't find a way for Lars to get home, I was doomed.

I almost lost focus at the sounds of people screaming in agony, gunfire, and metal crashing together. But I centered myself, starting the spell, and they followed my lead, Piper trying so hard to say the words she didn't understand.

Gripping the knife, I sliced a cut into Piper's finger. She wrinkled her nose in pain but didn't stop chanting.

With Kennedy, I made a deeper cut across her palm, then without hesitation, I sliced the blade down both my arms, my nostrils flaring as I forced the spell out, my blood dripping over my skin and into the pot.

The moment my finger clasped the edge again, I felt the thump of the cauldron's life. It lapped up our blood like it was milk, giving it more strength.

Yesss. The cauldron's voice hissed in my head, greedily taking our gifts. Its pulse grew stronger with every beat of our hearts, while mine diminished. *This is for the greater good. Look at the mess you caused for not following your destiny the first time.*

So you are going to kill me anyway?

It's the only way. The ultimate sacrifice.

As if it could feel my doubt, my fear at leaving my family, it latched on to me like a vampire, melding my hands to the surface. My spine went rigid, bolts of magic shooting through my nerves.

A scream ripped from me, my vision robbed.

"Fionna?"

"Mummy!"

I could hear a roar in the distance.

"Oh no." Kennedy sounded panicked. "I think the stone can feel it. He's coming for us."

Their voices grew distant. The cauldron tore through my mind, taking all function from me, my body responding as though it had been electrocuted.

Thank you, Cathbad. You will do fine. I've been wanting this for a very long time. Though it's a little more crowded in here than I planned.

Lars's demon flipped and scratched as the cauldron took possession. My lids popped open, my body rising, but I was no longer in control.

Shite. The cauldron was using me like Stone used Zoey and Lars. Bodies they could control while they locked us back, unable to do anything but watch.

"Fionna?" Kennedy said my name but reached for Piper, seeming to understand I was no longer in the driver's seat. The cauldron didn't even take notice of them, kicking over the empty vessel it used to reside in.

Shite. Shite. Fuck.

Yes, Fionna. You walked so easily into my trap. It's been you I've wanted all along. Isaac spoke of you so often and your blooming power he couldn't fathom in one so young. I knew it was you I would take. A Cathbad. It was easy to trick Isaac into thinking this was your destiny, to save the world. He set everything in place, leading the lamb to slaughter without even knowing it.

Thank you for telling me all I needed to destroy the stone. But dear girl, putting him back where he belongs is only part of the strategy. I will end the stone once and for all. With him comes the sword and the spear. I will become all the treasures.

Fuuuuucckkk.

Your demon saving you did put a hiccup in my plans, but it was simple to get back on track. Pretend to be empty, go silent. I left little ideas in your head. It was so hard to stay quiet after the blood sacrifice. You are enormously powerful, Fionna. I will enjoy your body so much.

This had all been a trick? The blood sacrifice gave it strength, while weakening mine, so it could take over my body.

You always had it in your head I was the good one. So easy to play with that notion. Truth is, Fionna, there is no good or bad. Just power. And I plan to take it all.

Cauldron and Stone were no different, each wanting to become more than objects. To become alive. Having all the supremacy and ability to act it out using our forms. And I had fallen for it.

Like a genie escaping its bottle, they were both free, ready to fight each other for the lead. And if either one contained all four of the treasures' magic? My mind reeled at the thought.

I was only able to watch as Cauldron took over everything else. My body moved awkwardly over the wreckage and bodies, set on the figure striding straight toward me.

Lars's beautiful face came through the haze, streaked with battle residue, the hole in his abdomen healing. His eyes black, his mouth set in a smirk. We stopped a few feet away from each other.

"I should have never doubted you would find a way to rise from the dead again," Stone said.

"Underestimating me will always be your downfall," Cauldron responded, speaking with my mouth.

"Don't get me wrong. You made this exciting. They were all starting to bore me."

"You get bored quickly, except hearing yourself talk, which I was most thankful for being buried deep in a cave for centuries. I didn't have to constantly listen to you."

"You know you can't beat me, Cauldron. You are a baby in that new body. I have the energy of both the sword and spear. I have armies…" He motioned behind him to his soldiers. "I am far more powerful than you."

"Are you?" The cauldron tilted my head, feeling magic stir inside. What was she planning to do? "I simply took my time. Listened. Learned. As weak as fae can be, if you go really still, they become comfortable, complacent. They will tell you all you need to know."

"And what could you have possibly learned from these things? After centuries of watching and controlling them, I realized how weak and prone they are to corruption and greed." He lifted his eyebrows in mocking. It was so strange to face-off with Lars. We had done it so many times, challenging and trying to break the other. It was ironic we were being used to do it again.

"Many things. I understood what these two would go through for each other. Felt their connection through the blood they spilt. How to put you in your place."

"Now it is you who is talking heedlessly."

"You may have purged Lars from his body, but do you think he would go so easily?"

Stone wrinkled its dark eyebrows, lids narrowing.

Cauldron motioned down my figure. "I got a two-for-one deal here. Took possession of a body carrying *two* souls. Love, it's the damnedest thing."

"You think I am that easy to fool?" Stone stared at her as if she were crazy, not unlike I had seen Lars do to me many times. Although, I could see a shiver of doubt twitching the muscles along his jaw.

Cauldron moved closer, becoming more confident in my body.

"Undoubtedly so. Killing the King only helped set my pieces in place. Made it easier to put you back where you belong, before I consume your power."

"What are you talking about? You can never beat me. I destroyed that pathetic excuse for a demon. He was no King. Now I will take his spot and rule."

"You are still a brash, stupid fool." Cauldron lifted my hand, touching the stone as she walked around him. Joy fizzed inside her, knocking against me like champagne bubbles. She leaned into his ear from behind. "You made it so easy. Technically, you could only become King if Stavros had no bloodline left, but guess what? He does." She flickered my gaze to the side, looking as though I were searching for someone.

"The dae. She's next in line." Stone whirled, his eyes searching for Ember. "Dae, come to me." Lars's daughter. His true bloodline.

Lars's soul rattled every bone in my body. His anger and power tripled with every minute that passed. I wondered if I was only alive because the cauldron possessed me. I couldn't have held out much longer with his energy bashing around inside. The cauldron pushed him back, her thoughts going through my head.

Be patient.

Thunder rolled above, lightning flashing through the clouds. Ember was pissed.

Like a goddess of death, Ember, sword in hand, walked through the haze, tall, proud, and striking. Streaked with blood, covered in new wounds and some healing, her jaw was set tightly, her eyes darting around in defense, taking everything in.

Flaming red eyes popped through the fog behind her. Eli's massive, sleek body growled in warning. A human form moved on the other side of her. West. For some reason seeing his familiar face felt calming. He had that way about him.

"Control your pets." Stone pointed to the dae. "Or they all become dinner for my men. And you will hand feed your lover's body to them."

One of the creatures next to him, an experiment which looked disturbingly human and similar to Zoey, snapped his teeth. He appeared human until he opened his mouth, and I realized he was a strighoul with an overdeveloped gland. His mouth was full of needled teeth, his jaw opening wide to tear apart his victims easier. The monster hissed in excitement, licking his lips at the prospect of a dweller cookout.

"This tall weed of a girl is keeping me from the throne?" Stone laughed flatly. "Can you at least challenge me?"

"My pleasure," Cauldron responded. Energy started to whirl inside, and I felt her grip Lars's soul. The air crackled, whipping through the group as she opened my arms, letting the power rush out of her. "And I wasn't talking about the dae, old friend." My voice vibrated, magic pushing people to the ground with shrieks and groans.

Holy fuck! The cauldron had heard everything, knew my ideas, the thoughts about how Lars could get back into his body. Fear and hope bashed around inside. I wasn't sure this plan was good anymore. I tried to reach for Lars, feeling his soul brush mine.

Let me go, Druid. This is our only chance.

What if it doesn't work? What if she kills you after?

I will be happy I got to love you.

No! Lars...

A blast exploded out of my body, and Cauldron thrusted it all at Stone; the power rammed the stone back. His expression shifted, realizing her power was greater than he had estimated.

Lars? The feel of him brushed by me, ripping away from my soul. *Lars!* I could make out the sound of his demon howling with pain.

Noooo!

Silence. Empty.

Lars's soul was gone.

TWENTY-NINE
Ember

Lightning sliced through the sky above my head, its power energizing my muscles. Tendrils of my energy struck a cart across the street, which exploded in flames. My demon side, which I tried to contain, would not obey. Wrath pounded at my temples, ready to strike down anyone in my path. Normal wariness of my demon, of being a dae, slithered off with every victim I took down.

This is who you truly are. Who you are meant to be. Feared. Awed, my demon spoke in the back of my mind.

A dragon creature leaped for me.

Shrieks pierced the air as my demon flew back and rammed the dragon into a sharp gate spike. Flesh and blood gushed as the monster slid down the ragged piece of metal, piercing its neck. Its tongue slid out and flapped like a squirming worm before his body went limp.

My black eyes narrowed. I felt nothing as I searched for my next prey, the dweller in me lusting for blood. Fear sang in the air, partnering with hate and death, but I only felt cold confidence. My demon vibrated through me, turning off frivolous emotions.

My boots crunched on the cobblestone, my sword humming, twirling in my hand preparing to strike. Some of the creatures darted away from me, having seen what I did to their kin, but there were always a few who thought themselves above a dae, that they'd be the one to take me down.

Bring it.

Though I was a good fighter, the stone's creatures were confident and tough to kill. Stronger, faster, and better trained, but I was a dae. There was a reason we were hunted and executed on sight. Daes couldn't control their powers and ended up destroying everything around them.

I licked my lips, sensing another enemy creep up behind me. I whirled around, my blade clanging with another's. Alki's training was still embedded in my muscles, his lessons part of me, his voice in my head.

"Dae," the creature hissed, his beady black eyes planning my execution. This one was a twisted version of human with dark hair and... Was it a gorilla? His arms and chest were corded with extra strength and extra hair. My demon took it in without faltering, but the humane part of me wanted to retreat from the frightening, tragic figure. Within I felt sympathy. I understood what it was like to be considered an "abomination," something that shouldn't exist and killed out of fear.

This didn't stop me from hacking at his leg when I had the opening. An enemy was an enemy.

Brycin, behind! Eli's voice linked in my head. Holding my sword at the gorilla-man, I pirouetted to the side, flinging the knife hooked into my belt at the troll bounding for me. The blade struck its breastbone, stopping it with a gasping squeal.

"Enough," I muttered, slamming my magic into both of my attackers, flinging them back like dolls. Bolts of lightning crashed to earth, striking objects around me. Explosions shook the already crumbling buildings, showering down more chunks of debris, and stirring up the smoke and haze resembling thick fog.

I was the cause of most of this destruction now. This was why I had to keep my demon under wraps. I was as much of a threat to my friends as the enemy. My magic had no filter between good and bad. It just destroyed.

In the distance, I spotted my mother sparring with a strighoul with grace and pure badassery. I idolized her so much. Even though she technically didn't give birth to me, she was my mother, through and through. And Mark was my dad, who stayed back in the castle along with Ryan, creating healing potions for the injured from plants he knew so much about. And now I had another dad, the reason I existed, creating me from pure love and heartbreak. If I lost him now... my wrath would reign down.

Nobody fucked with my family.

Stone and Stavros needed to die. Because Lars couldn't kill Stavros, I felt an obligation to be the one to kill him. We had to keep it in the family. Stavros's return started all this. And I would finish it, yearning to see his blood paint the ground.

"Dae. Come to me." A voice swirled around me, closing in like boa constrictor, its teeth sinking into my head, poisoning my thoughts, answering the command without a fight.

What. The. Hell?

Magic bent my legs and will, pointing my toes toward the voice.

Crap on ash bark. I had felt Lars take hold of my body in the past, but this was different. I felt this inside me, as though the magic had clicked an override button in my brain.

My demon faltered, bowing to the order as if I had told myself to move, twisting my brain like a pretzel. Thick tendrils of power swamped me, hauling me under its embrace. The magic was so dense and pure it laced along my limbs, marching me forward like a robot.

Brycin? What the fuck are you doing? Eli yelled in my head, but I continued to advance.

It's not me, I said back.

"Darlin'?" West grabbed my arm, but my feet didn't even hesitate as I jerked free and walked by. With every step my anger rose over the loss of self-control. Thunder rumbled around me, mirroring the storm brewing inside. I was not good at being told what to do. Being controlled was a million times worse.

Through the smoke, fire, and wreckage, I spotted Lars's outline standing there waiting for me to appear.

Stone.

My stomach sank, sensing the unimpressed appearance on his face was not in my favor.

My expression stayed cool, but panic fired through my heart, my grip tightening around my sword. I spotted Fionna standing slightly to Stone's side, a smirk on her face. What the hell was happening? What was Fionna doing? Why did she look so odd?

Eli's growl vibrated behind me. I could feel both him and West taking point at my back, protecting me.

The stone's eyes flicked back to my companions. "Control your pets." He motioned to Eli's beast. "Or they all become dinner for my men. And you will hand feed your lover's body to them."

I continued to take in my surroundings. The creature that took so much after Zoey stood close to Stone, his mouth open, baring his hundreds of daggered teeth at us. Zoey stood off to the side, Sprig wrapped around her ankle. A figure lying on the ground behind them.

Holy shit. No.

Ryker.

Pain pierced my heart. I blinked back the shock and horror at seeing him. Was he dead? It seemed impossible someone like him could fall.

Ryker and I had created a bond through our time in captivity, and I could feel devastation lurking in my chest. I gritted my teeth. *Not the time, Ember. You can mourn later.* I tried not to think of how many I would mourn if I survived.

Amara stood near Zoey, with Lexie a few feet away from them, her attention on something to my far side.

Following her pallid gaze, I twisted enough to see. My limbs slightly jolted in repulsion. Bile and shock coated my throat.

Stavros's lifeless eyes stared at me from his severed head feet away from his carcass. Blood and bits of brain matter were sprinkled between the two, like the debris of a shipwreck.

Stavros was dead. Really dead. My first feeling was anger that I didn't get to do it.

Shit, I heard West exclaim through the link. *The King is dead. What does that mean?*

I don't know. What did it mean? The one who kills the current King becomes King. Did that mean Stone was King? Did it matter? He would take over anyway.

"This tall weed of a girl is keeping me from the throne?" The stone's mocking laugh drew my attention back to him, his pitless eyes grazing me with derision.

Crapping hell.

"Can you at least challenge me?" He curved toward Fionna, making a slow smile curve her face.

Looking closer I could see Fionna's eyes were black. Similar to Lars.

Something tells me Fionna isn't home, I linked to the boys.

No. I know her. That's not Fionna, West replied.

Who is she then? Eli asked.

I don't know, but I can tell you whatever has taken her… it's not good.

Seriously? Can we get a break? Is it Monday or something? I mentally sighed as I lifted my sword, ready to act.

"My pleasure." The faux-Fionna tilted her head, dropping her hands to the side, opening her palms. The atmosphere popped and sizzled; magic flooded from her, flogging us as it lashed out. "And I wasn't talking about the dae, old friend."

A strange howl echoed through the courtyard, flooding the space with magic. As though a tsunami crashed down on me, I smacked against the cobble street under the weight, curling into a ball, a scream tearing from my throat.

I was no stranger to tangling with powerful fae. Aneira had torn my magic from me, tortured me, and almost cut my head off when her magic pinned me to the floor. But nothing the High Fairy Queen had thrown at me was equivalent to this. Withering under the gravity, my bones cracked, every nerve burning. The magic radiating from Fionna filled every cell and felt as if it were compressing my brain.

At the sound of a howl from behind, I twisted to the side. I pried my lids open, knowing it was from one of my boys.

West was hunched over his legs, his dark dweller shredding his clothes, deadly spikes sprouting out of his spine, his face shaping into the beast as he roared.

Holy crap.

He had not been able to change since Aneira had tortured him. Having lived on the Light side too long when the worlds were still split, he could no longer shift into a dweller. But this magic was different and was powerful enough to crack through the cage, the beast flying out. His red gaze locked on mine for a brief minute, joy and elation danced in his eyes.

Free! I could hear his beast cry.

Another agonized cry rose over the other screams of pain. I dropped my gaze back to where Stone had stood. Fionna now stood over Lars's body, most of the magic funneling into him, a glowing golden trail running from her core to his. The pained cry died away, his mouth froze in a large circle, and his body jerked as though with a seizure.

Then the tail of the link left Fionna, the glowing essence sinking inside the stone's chest. The magic snapped back into her, dissipating from the atmosphere in a whoosh. Stone crumpled to the ground, lifeless.

Oxygen zoomed back into my lungs, my bones groaning with relief, free of the oppressing weight. I had a strong idea of what was controlling Fionna.

"Ember?" Hearing Eli's voice, I raised my head. Naked and back in human form, he crawled to me. "You okay?"

"Yeah, you?" My eyes raked down his body, taking in that he was okay, then darted to West. Also nude, he lay on his side, staring into the void, grief etched in his expression.

"West!" I scrambled over to him. "Are you all right?"

He didn't respond, his gaze finding mine, the sorrow so deep he didn't have to say a word. I could feel it. Leaning over, I wrapped my arms around him. West and I had a close bond, and seeing him in pain made me feel as though it were my own.

The sound of a gasping cough bolted all three of us to our feet, where we huddled together in protection.

Lars's form burst up, sucking in air, his hand on his chest, green eyes blazing back.

"Lars?" I straightened to my full height, hope pounding in my chest.

His head turned, blinking. "Ember," he croaked out.

What Stavros had said earlier—about Lars being my real father—was he playing with us? Was it true? Every ounce of blood in my body hummed with truth, finally having proof of what I always felt. Somewhere in my gut I had sensed a deep connection to Lars. He was more than my uncle. He was my father. And it sat in my soul like fact. I knew this with every fiber of my being.

"Oh my god. Lars…" I ran to him, feeling Eli reach for me, but I crashed down at Lars's side, my arms wrapping around him. "You're alive." Emotion tangled my words and dampened my eyes as I held tightly to his neck. I was overwhelmed by the urge to cry in my father's arms like a little girl, something I had never gotten to do with him. I took a deep breath, fighting back the tears.

His arms circled me, crushing me into him. For a moment we didn't move, until his hand grasped my hair, yanking it back painfully.

"Sorry, Daddy had to step out for a moment." Black eyes dug into my soul, a snarl dancing on Lars's mouth. "I did not miss sharing space with him. I will make sure this time he is permanently taken care of."

My nose flared with rage and dread. The stone yanked me to my feet by my hair, nails digging into my scalp, his gaze landing on Fionna's form.

"You thought you could get rid of me so easily? I am vastly more powerful than any little trick you can brew up." The stone snarled like a feral dog, tugging me around with him, his feet moving as if he stopped he might fall over. "All of you put together couldn't even begin to challenge me," he barked out at the crowd circled around.

His men and our people still bristled, ready to fight, but many of Stavros's hired strighoul and trolls slunk off. Their benefactor was dead. They had no reason to put their life on the line anymore.

"It's humorous you are trying to be grand while you can't even stand. No outside help will be needed to end you." Fionna circled him resembling a tiger coming on its prey, motioning to the throng hooked on her every move. "Just *inside* help. He will help put you back in your cage."

Magic swirled around my feet, pulsing off Stone, his grip clenching down, like he used me as a crutch. Energy balled up, shooting forward, pummeling at Fionna. A fae version of dodgeball. The skies echoed with pops and flashing colors as their forces collided.

Cauldron tipped her head back, a laugh pealing from her. "That was adorable. Close to being hit with bath bubbles."

A grunt emanated from Stone as he shoved me away, his full attention on his true enemy. The rest of us peons were nothing compared to the treasures.

Eli grabbed me, pulling me back between him and West.

"It's about time you and I had it out. You have been a thorn in my side for centuries," the stone snapped, saliva flying out of his mouth. He flinched as if in pain and grasped his stomach. For a flicker of time, yellow-green eyes pushed through the black pits, then disappeared.

Lars. He was fighting.

My heart twisted in my chest, wanting to help him. Could we do anything or were we doomed to lose him all over again? *No.* Screw that. I would not lose my father. My *father.* What a strange and natural thing to say. My dad. Not my uncle, but my birth father.

My dweller part was exceptionally protective of my family. I leaned forward, needing to act. A growl hummed on my lips

"Don't you fuckin' dare, Brycin," Eli muttered in my ear, gripping my arm tighter.

Sometimes I really hated the bond between us. I couldn't get away with shit. My impulsive nature occasionally needed to be reined in, but I still hated it. I wanted to jump in, protect what was mine.

"How wrong they were about you. Always cast you as the good one to balance me. You are no different from me." Stone ground through his teeth, motioning at the cauldron. "You longed to be freed from your cage as well. You twisted and played with these creatures like it was a game. Because it is. They are nothing to you either."

"You're right. I don't feel anything for them. I wanted to experience life through my own body. To taste food, to have sex, to do all the things I had to watch, but never experience." Cauldron stepped closer. "But I was still created to counter you. There is room for only one treasure at the top."

"Yes. There. Is." His boots touched hers. A gust of magic swept in, like the tip of a hurricane just hit land.

"Oh crap," I mumbled, realizing two formidable treasures were about to fight each other, and we were right in the crossfire. "Run!"

Magic exploded into the courtyard, rocketing through the space. Cars, debris, and bodies tumbled away from the sources, as though an atomic bomb detonated. A train of energy slammed into me, flipping me up in the air.

I smacked onto the ground, rolling until a wall stopped me, my head cracking against the cement; my vision blurred. Magic banged and popped in the air with overpowering density and smoke, causing my lungs to spasm.

Brycin!

My head jerked up. *Eli!* I called back, my eyes trying to break through the haze. My head throbbed, but I stumbled to my feet.

Eli's outline strode for me, tugging me into his body the moment his fingers could reach me.

"We need you to get everyone out of here. The war is now between them, and we will have to deal with the last one standing, but until then, it's best to stay out of their way."

He nodded.

Another flash of magic caused us to stumble to the side, and it brushed over my skin like fire. His body bent forward, his beast forced to the surface.

"Come on." I dove in a little deeper, grabbing any of our people I could and sending them out the gate.

"Kennedy? Have you seen Ken?" Panic scraped at my throat. I hadn't seen her in a while.

"She's at least alive." Eli hunkered close to me, dodging the loose items flying around in the air. Magic echoed around like a tornado and two treasures were at the heart of the storm. "Believe me, you'd feel Lorcan through the link if anything truly bad happened to her."

"You know, Dragen, that's not very helpful," I snapped dryly.

"My lady! My lady?" Simmons zipped past me, not able to slow down, his body tossed through the air like a dust particle.

"Crumbling crackers in dung sauce!" Cal rolled through the air after him. Eli reached up and plucked him from the sky. "Turtle dumplings, my head feels as if it's been put on spin cycle!" Cal rubbed at his head, looking dazed.

"My lady!" Simmons zipped by my ear, his mechanical wings twirling wildly, flipping and circling along with the loose debris.

"Dammit, Simmons, stop spinning. You're making me dizzy." Cal leaned his head into Eli's grip. "I'm gonna vomit."

"If you throw up on me, pixie, you'll be wearing your tongue as underwear."

301

"You think I want to throw up? Lose all that wondrous juniper juice in my belly?" he exclaimed, then tilted his head. "Wait... if I tossed my cookies... I *would* get to experience it a second time around..."

"No. Just no." I grabbed for Simmons as he zoomed by me again.

"Don't be so snotty, girlie. If we were in a dire situation... and had no juniper juice around... I don't think you'd be so firm on that stance."

"Yeah, I would." I continued to search the area, tucking Simmons into my neck. He gripped my hair, holding on against the wind pummeling us. In the distance, I spotted two forms lying on the ground.

Oh gods. Piper. Kennedy.

"Kennedy!" I screamed, running to my friend, her arms wrapped tightly around Piper, guarding her from flying debris.

Blood gushed from Kennedy's head, but she blinked at the sound of my voice.

"Em?"

"Are you okay?" I dove down next to her, touching both her and Piper, needing to feel they were real and breathing. Piper stared up at me but didn't talk, appearing a little dazed.

"Yeah. We're okay."

Kennedy sat up, pulling Piper into her lap, peering at me with agony. "The cauldron. It tricked us. It has my sister..." She trailed off, sobs choking her throat.

"I know."

"Kennedy!" Lorcan rushed to her, practically pushing me out of the way, panic carved into his features. He ran his hands over her wounds from her head to her belly.

"I'm fine." She cupped his face, making him fully look at her. "Really."

His shoulders did not budge an inch, still riding tight with tension, but he nodded, bringing his head against hers briefly. Their love was so strong it brought tears to my eyes.

Kennedy pulled back, glancing over to where her sister's body battled with Lars's body, looking utterly defeated. "I felt it take her, heard the cauldron's plans. It wants to destroy the stone, which is what Fionna first wanted, but now I understand. If it succeeds? If either of them does? We are doomed. One will possess *all* the treasures' powers. It will be too much. We not only lose Lars, Fionna, and Zoey. But *everyone*."

My attention shot to the two figures battling. The magic swirling around the stone and the cauldron was tangible, a ray of colored magic spitting off them. Kennedy had me watch Star Wars enough times to recollect the big fight between Vader and Luke. But this time there was no good side. Only the emperor's side.

"Fionna wanted to use Cauldron to put the stone back." She pointed at the rock lying inside the cauldron. "The cauldron wants to take Stone's power back, but that's not its only plan." Kennedy's eyes grew wild and full of fear. "I can't let it happen. But... I don't know how... if I can." Sorrow crumpled Kennedy's features. "No matter what I do. They die." She curled forward, clutching her face.

In that moment I felt hopeless. Bleak. Useless. Terrified. We'd come all this way, and it was still going to end the same.

"Guys, look!" West's voice tore my gaze to the side. He stood a few yards away, pointing down at the field. My neck twisted around, following his finger.

For a moment I had no idea what he meant, until I noticed dozens of figures coming through the port. Not on a ship, but *swimming*.

"Sirens." I gaped, watching the cluster move in, surrounding the enemy ships. Forms started jumping off the deck, giving themselves over in abundance to the siren call. "They came..."

"Oh my gods." Kennedy rose, her gaze not on the water, but latched on to a hill by the field. "I can't believe it."

A handful of figures charged toward us, weapons high, magic chanting from their mouths in unison. None of them I recognized, but I knew what they were. Druids.

"DLR." She shook her head in wonder. "They're here. To fight with us."

I had heard of them from Kennedy. The Druid Liberty Republic was a group Fionna had founded to fight against the fae after centuries of their massacring Druids. And here they were, to stand alongside fae, to come to the aid of the Queen.

The sight of the sirens and the DLR coming to assist us sent a surge of optimism in my stomach like excited butterflies.

"Hope." Kennedy plucked the exact feeling from my chest, clutching my hand.

I turned to her, straightening up. "Do you think you can try to pull the stone and cauldron back into their original forms?"

"I don't know." She fluttered her lashes, pushing through her doubt. "But I will give it all I have."

"Me too, Auntie Ken. I help too." Piper tugged on her aunt's shirt.

Kennedy stared at her, and I could see the horror of letting her niece participate. But this was war. We had no other choice. Piper was an extremely strong Druid already.

"We're gonna get Fionna back. And I'm getting my father. This is not over. We fight until the end," I said.

"Until the end." Kennedy nodded in agreement.

"Whatever I can do for you, my lady, and Majesty, I am at your will." Simmons bowed his head.

"Thank you, Simmons. I am grateful for your help." Kennedy smiled at him.

"Such a kiss arse!" Cal voice shot over to us.

"I want Mummy and Darz back." Piper curled into Kennedy's side, wrapping her arms around her waist.

"I know, sweetie." Kennedy nodded. "We will get them back." She kneeled to face Piper. "Do you understand what we have to do? I know you are scared and tired, but I need you to be extra strong. Together we can try and save your mummy."

"I know, Auntie." Piper cupped Kennedy's face. "I am strong. I will fight for both Mummy and Darz."

Wow, this little girl. I blinked back tears.

Kennedy grabbed the vacant cauldron lying a few feet from them, setting it upright, then yanking out the gray rock next to her. I could see her mind working through the problems.

"Piper and I will be here with the cauldron and stone. Ember, I need you to use all your strength to break through their field. If they kill each other, all is lost. We need to stop that. They're both going to have to fight like hell, but I hope Piper and I can draw the treasures out of the bodies enough to at least give Fi and Lars a chance."

"What do you need us to do?" Eli set Cal on my other shoulder, ready to shift if he needed to.

"Kill every one of those things." Kennedy nodded at the Frankenstein creatures, her queenly persona back in place. "And keep anyone from getting near us. Piper and I can't break out of our spell once it's started."

"On it. Be safe, li'l bird," Lorcan whispered, kissing her, before shifting back into a dweller along with Eli. Then Lorcan, Eli, and West dove back into the throng, spreading out in an arch around Kennedy and Piper, protecting them from attack.

"Cal, Simmons, stay here and be another layer guarding Piper and the Queen." I nodded to my two boys.

"Aye, my lady." Simmons saluted me, while Cal hmphed in my ear, but flew off my shoulder, landing near Piper. He hated when I left him behind.

"Come back to us. Me and Ryan need our spice." Kennedy squeezed my hand.

Swallowing the lump in my throat, I nodded, not able to find my voice. I turned, parting ways with my friend, knowing this might be the last time I see her.

The stone and cauldron's battle filled the air like being on a tarmac next to a jet, roaring energy into my eardrums. Pushing forward, wind slashing my skin, as though I were walking into a tornado, I forced myself closer to the fight, using the electricity to fill me up, my dae clawing at the surface.

My demon smiled, a bolt of lightning zigzagging across the sky, the clouds rumbling angrily. "Oh, this is going to be fun." I opened my arms and turned my face to the sky, magic building and ripping across the grey afternoon. I always held my dae on a leash, scared to let her out. But now I needed her free.

Completely.

I closed my eyes, pulling away from the driver's seat, releasing both my demon and high fairy out of their binds. Electricity zapped around me buzzing me with adrenaline and power. Imagining the child amplifier, Asim, touched me and enhanced my powers, I summoned every molecule of fire and electricity down on one target.

Heat thrashed in the sky, building as I shoved my demon forward, switching off all emotions.

Boom!

A hungry current zapped to earth, scorching it, peeling away all magic like a cheese grater.

Turning everything to embers.

THIRTY
Zoey

Pain volleyed up my backbone and into my head, the hard stone gouging my scalp. I blinked furiously, every nerve in my body responding to being crushed into the cold ground, the cauldron's force leveling everything that had a pulse to the ground.

The pain didn't bother me because only one thing dominated every thought and feeling… when the cauldron's magic lifted off me…

Freedom.

The sensation of liberty and release was so great I felt as though I might rise off the ground and float into the stormy sky. I wanted to flex my hands and stretch my legs. I could almost taste it—the freedom. I desired to cry with relief, but I didn't dare move. Not even a twitch of my mouth; the stone would realize he had fully vacated me and raid my body again.

Cauldron had broken Stone's tie to me, declawing the parasite sucking on my soul. It wasn't the same as before when I had moments of freedom, where he still lingered somewhere on the perimeters. He was completely gone, but in leaving, he seemed to have wiped me of my strength. My magic barely hummed in my body, dormant for so long.

With a gasping cry, the stone rose from the pavement. His hand pressed to his chest as he sucked in gulps of air. His back was to me, but I didn't need to see his eyes to know they were green. In an instant, a strange buzz vibrated in my chest and heart because we went through the same thing together, created a link no one else could understand.

Lars was alive.

I fought back tears of joy. I had no idea how he survived outside his body, but I didn't care. Knowing he was back gave me hope. Strength. Maybe we could actually fight this and win.

"*Bhean?*" Sprig's fur brushed my hand and I turned to my best friend. His soft brown eyes stared up at me. "It's you."

Opening my mouth to speak, no words came out, only a hiccupped sob. I scooped him up, cradling him against me. He snuggled in, releasing a heavy sigh of.

"I am so sorry," I whispered, rocking and stroking his back. This tiny thing took up so much of my heart. The love I felt for him was immeasurable. But then I remembered, as if a dagger were twisting in my heart at the thought of the man lying a few feet away from me, I shut my lids in agony.

No. Zoey, don't let yourself think of it now. If I let myself even breathe in Ryker's direction, I would curl next to him and never move again. Wyatt, Lexie, Annabeth, Sprig, Croygen—they were all reasons to get up, keep fighting. But I relived the horror at what I had done. No matter if the stone had control of me, I had felt his throat under my fingers. In the end I wasn't strong enough. I didn't fight hard enough.

"Zoey?" Lexie's voice cried out. I turned to see her inching toward me, her eyes wide with hope.

"Lexie…" I croaked, another wave of emotion obstructing any other declarations.

"Oh my god, Zoey!" She ran, her mechanical legs pinging against the ground as she fell down next to me and wrapped her arms around me.

A sob caught in my throat, hugging her, her loose curls tickling my nose. Squashing Sprig between us, she clasped me tighter.

"I've missed you so much," she blubbered into my ear, her sobs drenching my chest. I held her, stroking her hair as she wept. "I was so scared… that we lost you."

"Me too," I whispered, struggling to find the right words.

"I love you, Zoey." She gulped, pulling back to wipe her eyes. "I don't say it enough. You have always been so amazing to me. Even when I was being bratty and hateful, you stayed. You could have left Jo's, but you stayed for me."

"Lexie." I cupped her face. "You are my sister. There isn't anything I wouldn't do for you. I love you so much." I brought her to me again, kissing her temple.

"Unless you both become honey bread, I'm not lovin' this sandwich right now." Sprig wiggled against my hand, but I heard no seriousness in his voice.

"You love it, furball." Lexie rubbed his head, sitting back.

"Only if her bra was producing those honey packets." He pointed at my chest. "But they are dry. Why would they do that to me? Do the honey gods want me to suffer?"

I grinned as he sighed dramatically.

My family. My world.

"*Mother*." Hate hissed over my shoulder, making me stiffen. With one word my whole world came to a stop. A jolt of fear raced down my spine. I scrambled to my feet, Sprig clasped to my chest. I shoved Lexie behind me. Zeke stood a few feet away, his sharp javelin poised in his hand aimed for me. Green eyes glared back into mine, full of hate and revulsion. "Finally." His lip hitched in a snarl. "We're alone."

I shoved Sprig into Lexie's arms, my eyes locked on the strighoul hybrid, my hand grabbing for the small blade on the ground.

Zeke took a step toward me, ignoring the commotion his master and the cauldron made a short distance away. Magic pounded down on us like a hammer, the wind whirling furiously, threatening to absorb us all in a final bite. But in that moment all I saw was the threat standing before me. The fighter stepping into the ring with me.

"I have been dreaming about this for years." A tongue slid over his jagged teeth, hate stamped across his face. "I longed for your death since the moment you left us all to die, your own flesh and blood, abused and forgotten." Zeke's fingers rubbed at his spear handle. "What kind of mother deserts her children without even a thought? You only saw us as mistakes. Abominations." The javelin twirled in his hand as he inched closer. I had seen him train; I knew how good he was.

I tried to summon my magic but it was like finding an empty well. Come on magic. Where are you when I needed you? "Zeke." I held up my knife, backing my sister and me away from him. "You don—"

"Don't want to do this?" He snapped his teeth. "This is the *only* thing I want to do. I have been patient, pretending you were our queen. But I knew if I stayed quiet, endured every wretched moment I had to bow to you, I would get my chance. Sometimes he would leave you unguarded," he snarled back at the stone.

My heart pattered wildly against my ribs. I didn't know if Zeke was alone in his hatred or if they all felt this way. Either way, this was not good for me.

I could fight the best of them, but Zeke was designed to be better, faster, and stronger than both human and fae. That was why Rapava had created them—to challenge fae and destroy them.

My mind raced with different scenarios, slowly slinking us backward with every move he made forward. Out of the corner of my eye, I realized I was near Ryker's body and my chest compressed with grief.

"You're going to die, Mother. And so is the girl you consider your family more than your own blood. You think we don't feel? That we didn't understand your rejection? We were kids… I cried out for you, watched my own mother desert me, because you *wanted* me to die."

I had. I still did, but now I felt a shred of remorse. What kind of person was I not to feel anything for them? It wasn't their fault they were born the way they were, but I had been violated too. Rapava had stolen my eggs from me when I was unconscious. They were a result of his horrible deeds, and they weren't supposed to exist.

But neither was Sprig. Neither was I.

"Zeke, I am sorry."

"Don't," he snarled. "It's too late. I feel nothing but revulsion for you. I want *you* to die." Zeke lunged for me, his lance whirling in his hand, pointing for my heart. It moved so fast I had no time to react, but my brain registered I was going to die.

"No!" Lexie's scream tore through the air, her hands shoving me to the side, my body tumbling to the ground beside Ryker.

All I could do was watch the javelin continue its journey, Zeke ramming all his strength into it.

Straight into Lexie.

A guttural scream tore from my mouth as the slurping sound of skin and bone being shredded against metal banged in my ears. With a pop, the pointed dagger burst out her back, her body stiffening, a silent scream froze on her mouth.

"Guess you're first, little sister," Zeke growled with elation, twisting the javelin in deeper. Then he jerked it out, her body collapsing to the ground.

I knew I was still screaming, but nothing made sense anymore. I scrambled over to her, a wail rising from my lips.

"Lexie?" I gripped her face. Her eyes darted in fear, her hand covered mine. Then she went still, her hand falling from mine to the ground. "Lexie! No! Lexie, don't leave me. Please!" I gripped her harder, shaking her. "No… Please. No!" I screamed, desperation screeching in my voice.

But it was too late.

Her eyes stared lifelessly at the sky, her body twisted in the position she fell in, blood pooling around her. A cry hiccupped in my throat as I bent over, my forehead taking in the warmth evaporating from her body.

She was dead. Because she tried to save me.

"Now you know how I felt when I saw many of my brothers and sisters die because of you," Zeke jeered over his shoulder.

Anguish rotted in my chest, in my soul. Ryker. Lexie. The loss was too much. Violence shook my limbs, grief mixing with unfathomable wrath. And I felt the switch.

Zoey was no longer. The Avenging Angel rose in her stead.

My eyes locked on the creature. No human words crossed my lips. A feral wail belted from me as I leaped for the monster with only a small blade in my hand.

He jumped back, turning to face me, tossing down his stick. "I want to kill you with my bare hands and tear into your flesh with the teeth. The ones that make you cringe every time you look upon me."

Magic whirled thickly in the air, shouts and lightning dancing in the sky, but nothing else mattered except killing Zeke.

Neither one of us danced or bounced around each other. We went straight in for the kill.

My blade nicked a long trail along his arm as he spun, a snarl hitching up his mouth. He curved around me, his teeth snapping at my neck. I dropped, swinging my knife for his gut. He jumped out of the way, smirking at my failed attempt. This only drove the anger deeper into me, enraged me more, tunneling my vision and thoughts.

Primal. Feral.

My bones cracked as I rolled over the pavement and jumped back on my feet. With a shriek of hate, he sprang for me, long nails protruding from his buff human arms scraped my skin. My nose flared with the smell of blood and pain, but I only fought fiercer. Twisting around, I kicked my boot into the side of his knee, going for a tendon. A scream belted from his mouth as his leg dropped to the ground. I rammed a fist into his temple, barely feeling the pain that speared down my arm. Zeke pitched toward me, his mouth clamping on my arm.

It felt like a thousand needles embedded into the bone of my arm. I cried out. Blood gushed around his teeth. I managed to ram my foot right into his crotch; he opened his mouth in a scream, letting me tear away from his hold.

"I enjoyed killing her. I wish I'd done it slower. I'll make sure I take my time with you." He dove forward, his nails scraping my stomach. "And I'm going to love eating all of you for lunch. I'll use that monkey as a toothpick to dig your guts out of my teeth."

He already destroyed my world, if he even touched another…

An animal sound broke from my throat. Ignoring the ache pounding in my arm and gut, I jumped on him, the force of my fury driving us both to the ground with a crunch. My fists pounded into his face, cracking his teeth and cutting up his face. And my hands. Blood poured from both of us, streaking down his face.

His green eyes bore into me with fury. Roaring, he shoved me off him, my body flying back, landing roughly on a car. I heard the sounds of bones snapping, as a piece of glass stabbed through my spine. I tried to rise, but my body failed to respond. Coughing up blood, I felt every broken rib, my lungs rattling.

I would fight until my body gave out, for my son, my family, but I couldn't deny the part of me that wanted to let go now. To follow my sister and Ryker to another place. To feel peace. No more heartache and pain.

Zeke rose up, grabbing his spear. "I think it's time to say goodbye, Mother." He slurred through broken teeth. Limping over to me, he lifted his spear, aiming it at chest. "And yes, I will take great pleasure in your death. Sweet justice." His arm went back.

Move, Zoey! But my muscles didn't respond. Hell. This was it. And maybe I deserved it.

A glint of a blade whizzed through the air behind Zeke and embedded itself into the hybrid's neck. Zeke made a strange gurgling shriek, the spear falling from his hands, as his head detached from his body, flying several feet before splattering onto the ground. His body took a few seconds to respond, then it crumpled to the ground.

I blinked through the blood and sweat at my savior standing over me.

"Human." White eyes glinted at me. My sword was propped on his shoulder, dripping with fresh blood. On his other shoulder sat Sprig, a happy smile curving his mouth.

"Ryker?" I gasped, afraid if I blinked I'd find this a hallucination. Or maybe I had died. I didn't care. He was here. "Oh my gods…" I found the strength to rise, ignoring the dizzying pain tears flooding my eyes.

Ryker dropped his weapon, which clanged loudly to the ground as he grabbed for me, his large arms wrapping around me. At his touch, a whimper rose from me, my body falling into his.

"How are you alive?" I sobbed, touching him over and over. "I-I am so sorry…"

"Shhh," he muttered against my ear. "It's not your fault. And as you see, I am a lot harder to kill than even the stone thought. And it never decided to check to make sure. Had a good nap though. Woke up to a monkey farting on my face."

I gave the ghost of a laugh as an agonizing cough rattled my lungs. "If I'm going to die, I want to be in your arms."

"You are going nowhere, human. You belong here with me." He folded himself over me. "You know I will hunt you down for eternity."

I blinked, willing my body to heal. But I thought of Lexie's last moments, that awful sickening sound of the spear slicing through her. As though sensing my heartbreak, Ryker's lips brushed my head, my cheek, and found my lips softly. The feeling of his mouth against mine made tears flood my cheeks. I had thought I would never feel them again. That I'd lost him forever.

"She'd want you to fight. Don't let her sacrifice be in vain." He broke away, the love in his eyes burning into mine. He was right; she would want me to fight. She'd be furious if I gave up.

Wiggling from his grip, I crawled to her, my body shaking with effort. Kneeling next to her corpse, fresh tears cascaded down my face. With trembling fingers, I gently shut her lids. "I hope you find endless adventures, Lex." I gulped, my throat closing in. "I love you, little sis. Forever." My soul shredded into pieces hearing myself say goodbye. It made it real. True.

Ryker moved in next to me, pulling me into him. I watched Sprig climb down his arm, moving to Lexie's face; he leaned into the side of her face, his hands running through her curly locks, his shoulders shaking the grief.

"*Leanbh*," he whispered softly, palming her cheek. "I will miss you."

She was so fearless and full of life. She had so much more to live and experience. I shook my head repeatedly, not ready to accept it after everything she had been through it had all been taken from her. She had lived through so much. It wasn't fair. She deserved a beautiful life. And selfishly, I wanted her with me. I knew my time with Lexie and Annabeth would be shorter due to my extended fae life, but this was far too soon.

"Lexie?" Croygen's voice crashed into me, hearing his desperation. "LEXIE!" His scream tore the last bits of my soul, bending me farther into Ryker. I had never heard him scream that way. Croygen fell to the ground on the other side of her, wailing like an animal in pain.

"No! Lexie... Nooooo!" He pulled her into his lap, wrapping his arms around her, smearing himself with her blood. "No, you promised me. You promised me, li'l shark. You and I." He cried as he dropped his head onto hers, rocking and holding on to her life as if she were his entire world. "Don't go… please… stay here with me."

Ryker held me tighter. Croygen's wails shook and wiggled Lexie's lifeless body. I knew they liked each other, but until this moment, I didn't realize how much. He was in love with her. Something he'd tried to deny, saying she was like a kid sister. She had always loved him, and along the way Croygen had fallen in love with her. Deeply. How could you not? She had been so full of life and love. Curious and smart. Ready for adventure and to take life by the horns.

Now that light had been put out.

And a part of me went out with her.

THIRTY-ONE
Kennedy

Lightning cracked and thunder bellowed overhead, answering to its mistress. Piper's little hands trembled over the empty cauldron, her eyes squeezing tight with every bolt that rumbled near us. She bit back a whimper when the thunder vibrated the ground. She was being so brave.

Ember's magic scared the hell out of me too. It was raw and brutal with no awareness of good or bad. It just lashed out as nature did. She had gotten better at controlling it, but it was still wild, exactly like her.

"Piper." I reached out, touching my niece's face, her blue eyes flashing up to me. I couldn't believe what I was asking of her. She was so young. She should be back in the castle, wrapped in a blanket, safe and comfortable, letting us adults take care of this, but unfortunately, she was a Cathbad. A powerful one. We needed her. "You and I have to do the chant all the way through. No matter what is happening around us. You understand? I know it's scary, but we need to do this for your mummy. Okay?"

She nodded, running her tongue of her lips nervously. "And Darz. I'll help him too."

"Yes, of course." My thumb rubbed her dirty cheek. "Are you ready?" *Crapping nerf-herder.* Was I ready?

"Yes, Auntie Kennedy."

"Okay, wait on my word. And as I said, we can't stop chanting until the end of the third time. Don't stop." I peered over at Ember. She stood, arms open, head back, her eyes shut. Magic crackled around her as she internally summoned her power.

Crap a million times. This was a bad plan; not that I had a good one. Rules and plans had flown out the window the moment this battle started.

314

Fear clasped my lungs, but the need to protect my unborn children and my kingdom roared inside me like a bear. If we were going to perish, I wanted us to go out fighting for a better world.

Lightning bolts zigzagged through the sky and shook the ground. *Booooom!* White light blinded me as the power of Ember's magic shot to the ground, slicing through the barrier the treasures wrapped around themselves.

Bam! Energy and flames burst against their magic, ripping through it, blasting everything in a hundred-foot radius back like paper dolls. My bones popped as I rolled, heat burning my skin. The cauldron went flying, clanging as it hit the stone several feet away. The stone flew out, tumbling into the gutter.

Crap!

"Piper!" I screamed, scrambled to my knees.

Coughing, Piper lifted her head, blood trickling down her temple and nose.

"Shit." I ignored the throbbing aches in my bones. "Are you okay?"

She nodded, her head jerked to where the lightning struck. "Mummy!"

Fionna's body lay a few yards away, her black eyes glancing around in confusion, landing on Ember. A dae's powers were always talked about with terror and awe, but Ember had never exhibited her full strength. The fact she could tear through the magic of the most powerful objects on earth—I was starting to understand why they were so feared.

"Mummy?" Piper got to her knees, staring over at Fionna.

"Piper, no!" My voice was raw yelling over the commotion. "She needs us to chant okay?" Setting us back up, I grabbed the cauldron and stuffed the rock inside. Then I wrapped my hands over Piper's and placed them on the vessel, my lips parting to start the chant.

Piper didn't hesitate. Closing her eyes, she spoke each word with me. Energy drained from me faster than I could make up for it, but the strength of my niece, her warm little hands under mine, pushed me on.

Magic swirled around us, and my hair snapped at my cheeks. Voices shouted and wailed, but I blocked everything out, lifting one hand to pick up the knife Fionna had left behind. Drawing both the cauldron and the stone back to their cages would call for a sacrifice. I just hoped it wouldn't be a life.

Slicing my wrist, I let my blood drip into the cauldron, painting the lifeless rock inside. Our words danced around it, circling us.

A hiss parted my lashes. Fionna whirled around to us, her face contorted, rage hunching her over like an animal ready to attack. "No, Druid. You will not send me back. I will rip both of you apart before you can utter your next line." Her voice sounded nothing like my sister, or human. It rattled with power and wrath.

A small whimper escaped Piper as she continued to recite with me. I gripped her hands harder, trying to reassure her.

Fionna strode closer, magic bubbling out of her. She raised her arms and shoved magic toward us.

I could protect Piper from a lot, but even my magic couldn't defend against Cauldron's power. Summoning my black magic, I volleyed it at the ball heading for us. The energies cracked against each other, but my effort shredded into vapor, only denting the power coming at us.

My mouth parted, a squeak of a cry coming out as I folded myself over Piper. It would do nothing, but if we were going to die, I wanted to hold her. I shut my eyes, cradling her to my chest, the last of the chant uttered.

Lorcan, I love you.

I waited for death, for the darkness to take me. My heartbeat thumped, hearing a sizzle crackle near my head. *Still alive. Still alive.* My lashes flickered up.

"Nerf-herder," I whispered, seeing what had prevented our death. A shield of magic cocooned Piper and me. The cauldron's magic sparked against the defense and faded away.

Piper did this. She protected us. *Holy crap.*

I looked at her in awe. She stayed curled in my arms, her limbs trembling. My gaze shot to the black eyes who held my sister captive. Cauldron stood in shock, her eyebrows furrowed in disbelief. For a moment I saw brown eyes look back at me before they returned to black. Fionna was fighting. We had to as well.

Ember didn't let up, her discharges of fae lightning raining around us, knocking the two figures off center. Rage roared from the two treasures, blasting magic back at Ember. Each time, bloody and broken, Em rose to her feet, doing it again. How many times could she do this before she didn't get up again?

"Piper we have to do it again. Can you do that?" I pulled away, looking directly into her eyes. Her lids fluttered, exhaustion weighing down her tiny frame. A desperate cry rose from my throat. I hated I was demanding this child to push herself to this dangerous edge of her own power, but I could see no other way. Cathbad blood was the only way to do this.

Shit. Shit. Shit.

I realized what would have to be done.

"It's okay, Auntie." Piper seemed to already know what I had just comprehended.

"No." I shook my head.

"I-I have to." Piper picked up the knife from the ground, reaching for the black cauldron. How could I let a five-year-old slash her wrists? How could I let her bleed into a stupid pot?

Because it's the only hope. Otherwise we all die anyway.

Blasts and screams rang in my ears, death stinking up the air. Ember cried out in agony as the face of her father tossed her body across the yard.

"I can't... I can't keep the bubble up." A tear slid down Piper's face, as though she were letting me down.

"It's okay, sweetheart. You are being so brave and strong."

The shield dropped, slapping my skin with magic so thick it clogged my throat. If Cauldron noticed, we were dead.

Piper choked back a sob, clutching my hand, leading it back to the vessel already drenched in her mother's and my blood. Darkness crept in at the outskirts of my vision, my essence slipping freely along my arms. This was it. Our last chance.

Our hands melded together, the spell spilled over my tongue, my body slouching to the side and I slumped to my knees. I forced the world to disappear, giving everything I had to each syllable. Piper gripped the knife, her face crumpling as she inhaled sharply. Then she carved the knife down her arm, red liquid pouring out after the blade. Tears streamed down her face, but she never stopped chanting, getting to the end of our third chant.

"Now," I yelled.

Piper fell over the cauldron, her blood spilling out, a huge droplet falling on the stone inside.

The sky pierced with high-pitched wails so loud they were painful, each one shredding my nerves. I could feel them echoing around in my skull.

The more pure a sacrifice, the stronger it was. Nothing was purer than a child's, one who was willing to die to save the world. Piper was no ordinary martyr.

1. Child
2. Druid
3. Cathbad

All done from the innocence of her heart. The love for her mom.

The magic Piper put out into the atmosphere was like a missile, directed right at the stone and cauldron.

317

"Nooooooo!" Cauldron shrieked, falling to her knees. Stone gripped his stomach, crashing upon the ground. Their cries filled my chest, cleaving my skin.

Fionna's face twisted with hate, black eyes daggering into me. Then I watched as they switched to brown.

"Fionna!" I scrambled to her, sinking beside her. My sister sobbed in pain, her hand pressed to her chest as she curled over onto herself. Black pits flipped to brown, then back to black, over and over. The battle inside was for the death. "Fight. Please... I won't lose you. Fight for us!" I wept, watching her body twitch and flip as though she were possessed.

"You. Will. Die. For. This. Druid," she hissed, black eyes drowning out the brown. "Ahhhh!" she cried, bending over farther, clutching her stomach.

"Mummy." Piper stumbled over, barely able to walk, blood trickling from her wrists and nose. "You can do it, Mummy. I know you can." She brushed at the loose strands of hair covering Fionna's face. "Don't give up."

"Lars!" I looked over my shoulder at Ember's cry. My friend ran to the King, kneeling next to him. "Don't give up!" Blood and wounds covered her, her frame looking as if it were about to topple over.

I could feel people move in around us. Eli and Lorcan were close, but all I could think of were the two people I loved in the fight for their life. It was out of our hands now. Were they strong enough to fight the magic of the treasures?

A strangled cry came from Fionna's throat, black eyes staring up at the sky, her muscles locking stiffly. Then her body went limp, slumping into the ground.

"Fionna!" I grabbed her arm, shaking her, her body flopping around. Lifeless. "No! No... please."

"Mummy?" Piper's whispered in fear, her chest puffing in and out shallowly. "Mummy?" Her head shook as she pressed her ear to Fionna's chest. "No, Mummy. Don't die. Please don't die." Sobs choked her throat, tears dripping down her face.

"Fuck! No... not you too. Lars!" Ember's desperate plea froze my heart. We were losing both of them.

My shaking hands went to Fionna's throat, searching for a pulse. Nothing. Dread set the word *no* in my head on repeat. Jared had died in front of me, along with so many others, and I had done nothing to stop it. I couldn't let my sister. I had the power to bring people back to life. Fionna had done that to Goran. And he hated her for it. He was a shell. A zombie stuck in a body.

But desperation did not let me think past my own suffering. I had lost my parents. Friends. Companions.

"Li'l bird." Lorcan's voice was in my ear, his hands pulling me into him, like he had sensed what I was going to do.

"No! Let me go." I fought him. "I have to save her. I can't... I can't let her die."

"You have to." His arms circled around me tighter. "Let her have peace. If you brought her back, she would not be Fionna. She would hate and resent you."

"I don't care!" I wailed, but I knew he was right. She would hate me, longing to die anyway. To bring her back and have Piper witness her mother as a zombie. She wouldn't be the person we knew.

Piper's sobs were silent as she laid her head on her mother's body, holding tight to the corpse. I tried to draw Piper into me, but she shoved me away, her head jerking over her shoulder.

I followed her gaze to see Ember leaning over Lars's frame.

"Nooooo!" Ember clutched his face. "Lars, no!"

"Darz?" Piper stood up.

"Please..." Ember's choked, tapping her forehead to his in a desperate plea. "Dad."

"Daddy!" Piper cried out. In unison the two girls screamed, their grief merged.

As if Ember had caused lightning to strike down, magic flamed from Lars, shoving me back into Lorcan. Colored energy burst from his torso, rocking his body with a gasp. Threads of tangible energy shot out, glowing bright gold, and sent its magic over Fionna. Silver and gold sparks clashed as energy flowed into her body. She convulsed violently, flopping and arching. A chilled inhuman scream wrenched from her, piercing the afternoon sky, coating my skin in goosebumps.

The energies sparked and crashed into each other, billowing into the air with fireworks of magic and pressure. Bones cracked under the weight, and I was shoved harder into Lorcan's arms. The density of the air spiked in a flurry, wrenching a pained cry from my lips, as the magic lashed at my skin. Darkness curled around my vision, the compression of magic carving apart my consciousness.

A thunderous crack vibrated my lungs. With a whoosh, the energy shot past Fionna and dropped into the actual cauldron. Power burst out of the pot, heaving us back like a sonic boom, the object flying into the air. Lorcan dove over Piper and me, guarding us from the force.

At last, stillness descended around us, the only sound was from the crackling fire from burning objects nearby. I opened my eyes, looking at Piper curled in my arms. My attention shot to where the treasures lay near each other on the street.

"Mummy?" Piper wiggled away from Lorcan and me, crawling over to her mother.

Fionna lay only a few feet away. My heart in my throat, I clambered after Piper.

Brown eyes blinked at the sky. "Fionna!" I cried out. She turned to her daughter and me. Dazed, wounded, and exhausted, her lips parted in a soft smile, her hand reaching to touch Piper's cheek.

"I knew you could do it, Mummy." Piper wrapped her arms around Fionna.

Fionna ran her hand over Piper's hair, holding on to her tight. "You did?"

"Of course. You're like a superhero."

"No, Piper. You are my superhero." Fionna's face crumpled and tears wracked her chest as she hugged Piper closer, her other arm grasping for me.

"So are you. You did it," she whispered to me in awe.

"We all did it." I wrapped my arms around them both, squeezing harder as though the hug could hold my heart together.

"Can I get in on this family hug?" A deep voice cut through the silence. Lars climbed shakily to his feet, badly injured, clothes shredded, and wobbling on his legs, but his chartreuse eyes stared down at Fionna and Piper with love.

Fionna slowly stood up, her gaze never leaving Lars. They stood staring at each other for several beats. With a sob, Fionna leaped into his arms, tears wracking her body. Lars nestled his face in her neck, picking her off her feet, a guttural sigh croaked out of his throat as his muscles relaxed into hers. They clung to each other, their expressions a mix of agony, joy, and relief.

He kissed her neck, breathing her in, before he set her back on her feet. The moment he did, Piper ran up, barreling into them, wrapping her arms around them. Lars scooped her up, quickly wiping the moisture from his eyes.

"Darz." Piper curled around his neck, squeezing him tight. "I love you."

An emotion I had never seen from him, flickered over Lars's face, crumbling with such softness and deep, unconditional love.

"I love you too." He kissed her temple. Oh my god. I was melting. "You saved me, Piper. Thank you."

She leaned back, a proud smile on her lips.

"Actually, both my daughters did." Lars glanced back at Ember, awe and love glowing deeper in his irises. Ember wiped her eyes, leaning into Eli. "I'm an incredibly lucky man."

"You're going to be." Fionna mumbled barely loud enough for me to hear as she cozied in closer to her little family. Lars cupped her face, staring at Fionna as if she was his world before he drew her mouth to his, kissing her.

A hand wrapped around my stomach, and I turned to Lorcan. He pulled me to him, love burning in his eyes. "They okay?"

"Yeah." I nodded, rubbing my flat belly, already sensing them. "They're strong."

"No shit." He snorted, his fingers sliding up my jaw. "They're ours."

THIRTY-TWO
Fionna

Lars's mouth covered mine hungrily, hinting at what it would do to me later. The need for him, to have him inside, to claim, taste, and feel every inch of him, almost overwhelmed me. The only thing that stopped me was my daughter. I didn't want to be parted from her for a moment.

This five-year-old was my champion. I could not believe what she'd done, how scared she must have been. But she never gave up. As a mother who barely got the chance to be one—I had only brought pain, danger, and loss. What damage had I already done to her? She was strong, determined, and stubborn, but she was still a little girl. A child who had chosen to be locked up in a dark dungeon with a baby, because she never doubted she could save him. Who ran into war because she understood she had to save us too.

Except I had not been saved.

I had died.

The cauldron had won.

I had felt death take me into darkness and nothing.

In the end, the stone had shoved my soul back in my body when it ripped the cauldron from me.

"I died," I whispered, pulling back from Lars, my head already turning to the side in pursuit. "I was dead…"

"What's wrong?" Lars's brows pulled down, sensing the agitation in my body, my head jerking from side to side. He set Piper down as I moved away from them. "Fionna?"

Inside, I searched for the connection. The link I created to him, tethering his life to the earth. I felt nothing. If I died, then my magic keeping him tied to life would break.

"Goran," I said just loud enough for Lars to hear me. Rubble, smoke, and dead bodies enveloped every inch of the village lane and courtyard, my mucky and bloody boots hiked over the obstacles.

Only a few yards away, I spotted blond hair sprouting through debris. I already knew the truth, but my stomach still plummeted to my feet.

"Goran." I went to the dead man's side. Lars came around the other side of him, his jaw twitching. "I am so sorry for what I did. I hope you find peace now."

"He has," Lars replied softly, a slight croak in his throat.

Staring at Goran, I knew it was true. Goran's lifeless eyes stared up into the sky like it was calling him, a slight smile set on his mouth. Serene. Content.

"I vow I will never do it to anyone else." I lowered Goran's lids. At one time, we hated each other; now I peered down on a face who had become an ally, if not a friend.

"FRIEND OR FOE!" Kennedy's voice rang out. I swiveled around. My sister stood on top of the roof of a smoldering car, her hands raised as her words traveled over the field, circling around the courtyard. Dressed in black, her hair wild and blowing in the wind, blood and dirt streaked her face. Their Queen had fought right by their side. She didn't hide behind her soldiers or inside the walls.

"Fuck," I muttered. She looked like a goddess of war. A true Queen. Ruthless but also kind.

"The war is over. Stavros is dead." Cheers arose from below and from our group. "Surrender now. If you continue to fight, you will sacrifice your life for nothing."

It was the first time I truly looked around. Only allies of the Queen stood around. Almost all of Stavros's men were in pieces scattered across the courtyard. Quite a few of the stone's experiments were dead, and any who survived had slunk off in the commotion.

"The stone's tie to them broke." Lars came up to my side. "They were his prisoners as much as I was. Their loyalty died the moment the stone's power could no longer hold them."

"That means they are out there now."

"Yes. More of them than you realize." Lars's hand came to my back, looking down at me. "But that's for another time."

"Stavros, the false King, is dead!" Kennedy shouted, her arms waving in the air. "Long live the Unseelie King! King Lars."

Cheers and yells poured in all around. Kennedy turned to Lars, a smile on her lips, joyous and heartbroken. Lars might have been back on the throne, but we had lost so many in the pursuit. Probably many more than I even realized.

In my periphery, I saw Zoey and her group crouched as though in mourning over someone. I saw Cooper and West helping Cole, who was bleeding badly from a wound in his torso. Healers from the castle ran out to attend the injured.

"Lars?" Kennedy waved him over to her. He leaned over and kissed my temple before jumping on the car with her. The screams of excitement rose with his presence.

Piper came up to me, and I lifted her up on my hip. "Look at Lars up there." I pointed.

"He's my daddy." She placed her head on my shoulder.

"Yes." Emotion caught in my throat. "He is."

"My friends," Lars called out, his voice booming. "I cannot thank you enough for staying and fighting. The sacrifice you made will not go unnoticed or unrewarded." Lars slipped back into his role so easily, but I noticed a reluctance in his shoulders, a sadness in his eyes he could no longer hide. "A lot will change going forward. Humans and fae need to be represented equally in government. But right now, I want to acknowledge your Queen. Without her, I would not be standing here. She has fought by your side, shed blood, sacrificed loved ones—all for a better world. For the kingdom. For *you*. She has proven herself over and over as a true leader and Queen. One who will no longer be looked down upon or questioned because of her age or the fact she is a Druid. She is *my* Queen. And *I* bow to her." Lars bent his head deeply before her.

Kennedy stood in shock, her eyes filling with emotion. In the history of the fae kingdom, not one King or Queen ever bowed to the other. They never wanted to give up power or seem like the weaker one. It was unprecedented. Lars went against tradition and custom, not to mention his nature, by honoring Kennedy with his respect and loyalty.

"You are amazing, Kennedy. Don't ever doubt it."

"Y-you called me Kennedy…" She blinked, her mouth parting.

"I suppose I did." Lars winked at her, turning back to face me, love scorching his features.

It seemed the moment we felt any happiness, it was ripped away.

It was an instant.

A flash of magic.

Pressure gripped my lungs, slamming my knees to the ground,

toppling Piper to the side. Lars tumbled off the car, smacking hard into the pavement. A woman cried from behind me, and I knew in my gut it was Zoey. Her cries echoed my own pain, our voices coming together in a communal union.

"Oh my god... Lars? Fionna?" Kennedy scrambled off the car, running to us. My vision blurred, not noticing the group crowding around us.

You think you can get rid of me so easily? A voice hissed in my head. Shite. The cauldron was back. *I've marked you. You are mine, Fionna. I have your blood. And when I've used up your body, I have other Cathbad blood I will claim.*

"Lars!" Ember hovered over her father, her face twisted as he jerked and twitched under her hold. The stone had hold of him. Probably had Zoey as well. Their claws had gotten into us. We were easy to take hold of again.

Sweat spread over my body as I turned my head toward the black vessel. It pulsed with magic, both the stone and cauldron together. We had stupidly thought we had won. We might have sent them back to their original form, but they were too powerful to simply disappear, especially together. They had regrouped and were coming back for us.

"Fionna. Talk to me." Kennedy's hands moved over me with panic, not understanding what was wrong.

"Treasures." I spit through my teeth. The call to go to them, to touch them throbbed in my body like a heartbeat, my muscles aching to move.

I caught sight of Lars digging his fingernails into the road toward the objects, his nostrils flaring. Zoey made another strangled cry.

"I have to... Let me go," Zoey screamed.

"No." Ryker rolled her body back into his, wrapping his arms around her. "I won't ever let the stone control you again. You are mine. You promised me, human. For life."

"It will go after Wyatt... Let me go."

It wasn't just the cauldron threatening my family. The stone and the cauldron must have decided to work together until they got what they wanted once again.

"They're calling you, aren't they?" West strolled over to the treasures, staring down at them, his tongue sliding over his bottom lip, his toe inching toward it.

"West." Eli drew up from his squat next to Ember, his voice full of warning. "What are you doing, man?"

"I hear them." West nodded at the objects. "They know."

325

The hold the cauldron had on me lessened as it shifted its attention to the dark dweller, realizing it had a new target it could manipulate.

"West…" I pushed up from the ground, fear lodging in my throat.

"What do they know?" Eli spoke evenly, prowling closer to West.

The southern dark dweller gaped down at the items, his back curving as if they were pulling him to them.

"What I truly want. My weakness. My desire. They say they can help me. Make me whole again."

"They are lying to you, brother. Don't listen to them." Eli took another few steps. Lorcan had moved to West's other side, creeping up.

West's forehead wrinkled, and with a heavy breath, he shut his eyes. His hand tapped impatiently at his side.

"West?" Eli repeated his name.

West rolled his hands into fists, fury flashing across his face. "What would you do, Eli?" He jerked his head toward him, spitting out each word. "How would you feel if you lost your beast? What would you do to get it back? *It's who we are*. My entire identity is missing. My heart. My soul." West's feet shuffled, his bare skin twitching, like he was coming down from a high. The treasures had their claws in him, sensing he might fall.

"Don't, West. I know it's hard, but you have to resist them." I held my chest, practically pleading. I barely got a taste or a choice when the cauldron took me, but I still understood the power of their call. If they wanted you… they would have you.

West swung around, sensing Lorcan's movements.

"Of course. The Dragen brothers." West snarled at them, his voice tightening, eyes flashing deep crimson. His beast might not have come out, but he was just as feral. Possibly more. "Once again you think you know what's best for me? The last time you forced something on me, you got an innocent girl killed." West crouched, ready to attack.

"Shite. They're taking over." If I had to blast West across the square to get him away from the objects, I would do it. But West must have sensed me, for he swung to me, baring his teeth.

"Don't even think about it, Druid." His voice was no longer his own. Stiff. Cold. Robotic. "This time I'll be certain you're dead when I drop you off a cliff."

West was no longer himself. This was not the charming man I had gotten to know in Ireland. Even when we were on opposite sides, I liked him. Actually, I kinda fancied him, but at the end of the day he was still a fae. And he was clearly in love with someone else.

Lorcan edged closer, compelling West to inch even closer to the items, his hand hovering over them. Eli and Lorcan stopped dead in their tracks. If he touched them. Game over.

Kennedy caught my eye, and I gave her a nod. West's bare, sexy arse was about to get spelled. Magic sat on my tongue, ready to spew out.

"West. No!" Ember cried out as West's fingers reached for the cauldron, not even flinching at her voice.

"Stop!" A woman's voice sprinkled over us like a song, halting everyone in place. Her voice shoved the spell back inside my throat. "You are stronger and better than that, West Moseley."

My attention jerked toward the gates.

Rez stood there, her hair wet and hanging down her back, dressed in damp shirt and pants, but looking like the most beautiful woman I had ever seen or heard.

"You are far more than that."

"Rez…" he whispered her name, his hands squeezing tighter.

"You're enough man and beast for me." She strolled up only a breath away from him but didn't touch him. "You will always be enough."

Torment contorted West's features, his fingers still inching closer to the cauldron. "I can't. I need them…"

"No." Rez grabbed for his arms, turning him to her. "Please, West. I know you think you are not complete, but you are."

"So easy to say now that you have yours back, huh? But I know the truth." He growled through his teeth, trying to move her out of the way. "You tried to pretend you were fine, but you weren't. You felt incomplete; don't deny it." He tapped at his gut, his jaw clicking with tension. "I'm *hollow* without the beast."

"You are anything but hollow. You are the most complex, wonderful, aggravating man I have ever known. And if you do this, you will lose everything that actually makes you, you." Rez shuffled in his way again, trying to get him to look at her. "Your family, your friends. Me."

Muscles flexed along his jaw and a strangled cry softly curled from his chest.

"I can't be without you, West. It took me long enough to find you. What we went through to be together. I will not let them take you from me."

"I'm not strong enough to fight them," he whispered, his body leaning forward. Their claws dug into him, compelling him to touch them. He moved her away, his fingers hovering over the cauldron.

Shite.

327

"You fought Aneira and climbed out of the darkness. You can fight this. Don't leave me. Please, West," she whispered hoarsely, still sounding like the sultriest singer you ever heard. "*I love you.*"

His head bowed forward, a howl vibrating up his throat.

"You are my future. The man I want to be with. Have a family with."

He sucked in, his fingers wiggling, only a centimeter away from the cauldron. A heart-wrenching roar cried up to the sky, goosebumps rising up and down my arms. He huffed and grunted, slowly turning away from the vessel.

"West…" Rez grabbed him, pulling him to her, wrapping her arms around him. West shut his eyes again, leaning his forehead into hers. He grimaced as though in pain, his chest heaving.

Kennedy's voice hummed, her magic shoving the treasures far from West's reach.

He still clung to Rez, as if she were his anchor.

"I love you." She kissed him softly.

"I know that, darlin'. I'm a fuckin' monster in bed." He tried to smile, but it wobbled on his mouth.

"That you are." She winked at him.

He wrapped his arms around her, kissing her before he peered back at the treasures. "They need to be destroyed."

"You will lose any hope of getting your beast back." Lars rose from the ground, his tone serious. "I want you to understand that, Mr. Moseley."

"I understand." He nodded, pain flickering over his face. "They're too dangerous to have around. I will cave to it… I know." He gripped Rez's face. "And really, all I need is you and loud, primal sex."

"I am certainly willing to do that for you." A grin engulfed Rez's face.

"They can't be destroyed," I said, getting to my feet. The link to the cauldron was still there, but I shoved back at it, not letting it get in my head. "They are too powerful to fully destroy."

The cauldron's power inside let me know I had been a fool to ever think they could fully be destroyed.

"Then what do we do with them?" Kennedy stared at Lars, West, Zoey, and me, not saying what I knew everyone was thinking. We weren't strong enough to fight them. They had literally gotten under our skin and in our heads. Marked us. We would always be susceptible to them.

"The only thing we can do." I faced Kennedy. "What our ancestors did. Hide them."

"Hide them?" She shook her head. "No. That's not good enough."

"Ken, we have no other choice. They have to be hidden by Druids, and I only trust you. It must be us, but I want you to spell me after. Force me to forget so I will never search for them again."

No! You will not discard me. I have been waiting for centuries. I will not go back. The cauldron screamed in my head, pounding in my temples. I bent over gripping my head with a cry of pain. Lars reached for me, tugging my hand in his, his own face flinching with discomfort.

"They will not have us again, Druid," he growled in my ear.

"Leave my mummy and daddy alone." Piper stomped over to the objects. She pulled her foot back and spouted a spell, then kicked the cauldron.

"Piper, no!" I yelped. Pushing through the pain, I took a step toward her.

Pop! The cauldron's magic rippled out like a lasso around my ankles, knocking us off our feet. I hit the ground and as though a knife cut a chord, my connection to the cauldron went dead.

"Piper!" I belted, sitting up, searching for my daughter, ready to destroy Earth if the treasures did anything to her.

Everyone was scattered around on the ground. Except Piper. She stood over the objects, grinning back at me.

"Holy shite." My mouth dropped open, staring between my little girl and the treasures. The treasures floated in an encased protective shield.

What the feck? Her magic could hold them?

"Piper… how are you doing that?" I went up on my knees, fear lacing my voice.

"They were hurting you." She shrugged, as though it were no big deal.

Fuck. Her powers went beyond even mine. Like my grandfather gifted her *all* his magic, passing down his irrefutable line of power.

"We're gonna have to watch this one." Lars sat up next to me, staring at Piper in amazement. "Especially in her teenage years."

I searched my head and gut. I felt no link to the cauldron. All their magic was contained inside the barrier, their tentacles reaching for us, but they were locked behind the sphere.

I couldn't believe she could project at her age. To have magic strong enough to hold the most powerful treasures in the world in a magic-proof bubble was astonishing. Should I be proud… or scared? Probably both.

"Freck." I breathed out. "We're so screwed when she hits puberty."

"Yeah, we are." Lars clutched my chin, twisting my face to his, his mouth brushing mine. "And I'm going to love every minute of it."

THIRTY-THREE
Zoey

Cool wind from the water blew my hair back, soothing my skin as I stared out at the port. The sun was peeping through the clouds like it was still nervous to show itself fully. The only warmth I felt was from the two tiny bodies curled against my chest. Sprig coiled next to my son, both holding Pam for security.

My hand absently rubbed Wyatt's back as he slept soundly in the Baby Björn, unaware of the devastation and loss which took place three days ago. The moment he lost his aunt, my heart, my world.

He would never know her. Never remember her voice or know how truly amazing she was. He would not have the memory of her smile when she held him.

My chest clutched, a hiccupped sob catching in my throat. Sprig mumbled in his sleep, calling for Lexie. His sorrow had kept him silent for the last couple of days, which only further broke my heart. The first night, he had fallen asleep repeating her pet name over and over.

I still could not come to terms with her death. I probably never would. Presently, I couldn't even imagine how I was going to get through the rest of the day, not alone the week or month. Life without Lexie in it was too much to bear. But then I'd look at my son and I had no choice.

And now I was watching another piece of my heart sail away.

"He'll come back," a deep voice rumbled next to me, Ryker's hand pressed to my back, his body coming to my side. His axe glinted in the hazy sun. It had taken several dives for him to remove it from the bottom of the lake, but its pull had been too strong, calling to him, wanting to be reunited.

I nodded, not trusting myself to speak. My gaze drifted slightly to the side, catching blonde hair flying in the breeze. Annabeth sat alone on a rock, watching the same ship sail away. The loss of Lexie had muted her as well.

At night, through the wall, I could hear her wrenching sobs; during the day she would walk around like a zombie.

We didn't speak much, neither of us having the words to console the other. It was hard to comfort someone when you felt the same utter emptiness. But we would silently hug each other or squeeze hands, both trying to come to terms with Lexie's death. They had only been family for a handful of years, but the two couldn't have been closer. They were sisters through and through.

My eyes caught another tuft of blond hair atop a figure striding up to where she sat. Annabeth didn't react to Cooper's presence or his touch, her attention still out at sea. He sat on the rock next to her and put his arm around her. She let him pull her into him and rested her head on his shoulder. Even from here, I could see her body quaking with grief. His love would help her through. That was my only consolation. I had no doubt she had found her partner in life. They were perfect for each other.

Wiping the tears slipping freely down my face, my attention went back to the water. The ship's black banner lashed in the wind as it made its way for the gateway out to sea.

Ryker pulled me firmer into his side, his arm curling around me, no longer able to hold back my sobs. "I can't... I can't lose him too."

Ryker wrapped both arms around me, kissing my hair.

"He just needs time." Ryker engulfed me in a hug, his chin on my head. "He'll come back. He needs to deal with this the best way for him."

My shoulders shook as I cried. I understood that, but it still felt like another death. Another hole in my heart.

If I thought Annabeth's response to Lexie was heartbreaking, Croygen's was paralyzing. The easygoing pirate had become violent and detached. Turning to drink, he had spent the last three days drunk and fighting anything in his path before he would finally pass out. He fought Ryker when he tried to approach him. He brushed off Rez and avoided seeing Morweena before her clan left; although I heard Morweena didn't want to see him either. Think it dredged up too much pain, things they could never change, heartbreak and misunderstanding that could never be rectified.

The only time Croygen even got near Annabeth or me was to tell me he was leaving.

"What?" My stomach pitted, my red-streaked eyes blinking up at him.

"Yeah. It's fucking time." He growled, running a hand through his hair. "It's pathetic I've been living with you guys so long. I'm a fucking pirate. It's about time I got back to it."

331

"Croygen…" My voice caught in my throat. "No. You can't leave. What about me? Annabeth? Ryker or even Rez?"

"No!" He snarled. "Are you fuckin' kidding me, Zoey? You think you're my mother? Sorry, you can't tell me what to do. My daughter is a grown woman who has lived this long without me. She's better off with me gone. Actually, you all are."

My hand shot to my chest, feeling as though my heart was going to fall out on the floor.

"Croygen, please. We need you. You are my family. Your home is with us. She wouldn't want you to go. Lexie—"

"Don't." Croygen stepped closer, his head bowing, getting right in my face. "Don't you fucking dare bring her into this. Don't use her as a guilt trip to tie me down."

"Tie you down?"

"*My home* is on the sea; *my family* is my crew. For one moment I let myself be domesticated." He snapped, clenching his fists. "But now I see clearly again. Her death reminded me I was not meant to be tied to people or things. I don't need anybody. And I certainly don't belong to anyone. My *only* love is the sea." He spun around, trudging down the hall.

"When?"

"This afternoon," he barked back, not even turning around, and walked through the door.

The instant the door slammed, my knees buckled, my back sliding down the wall, and my chest constricted. My mind understood he was in pain, his heartbreak dictating his cold words, but my heart didn't care. All it gathered was it was losing another piece of my family. Another person I loved.

I had my suspicions Croygen was in love with Lexie, no matter his denials, but until I saw him rocking over her body, I didn't realize how deep it went. It was as if he broke, shutting off his humanity, so he wouldn't feel the grief so much.

Her death was a domino effect; one by one, we were falling apart.

Now, staring at him and Jack drifting away with what was left of their crew, I didn't hear Croygen's hurtful words. All I felt was his loss. The echo of his laughter and smile blowing in the breeze.

"Did you find the underground base?" I leaned back, needing something to pull me out of the quicksand of grief.

Ryker stepped back, nodding. "Yeah."

"The women?"

"We got them to the Honey House as you wanted. Some ran, but for those who wanted help, we got them food, clean clothes, and a bed. They are going to need a lot of counseling."

"I know." I swallowed. The only moments that ebbed the grief of Lexie were those when I focused on my plan to help the women who had been so terribly abused by the stone. I could relate to them, and I wanted to provide them a safe place, counseling, and a way to get back on their feet. For some, it might never happen, being far too damaged by what occurred to them. But if I could help even a few, it would be enough.

Lars and Kennedy both said they'd pay for a new facility and all the expenses for the women, eventually opening it to all. But for now, we'd begin with the girls from the cave. Until it was built, they would stay in the Honey House. It wasn't until the idea formed that I realized this was something I really wanted to do. Because Annabeth and I were both survivors of sexual abuse, we wanted to help others who had gone through it, expanding our business beyond foster children.

Kate said she wanted to help with their recovery as soon as she was done with her own. She still had a long road of healing from the stab wound, but I knew she would get better. She was feisty and strong. Dunn, the fae father of her daughter, hadn't left her side once.

"And Vadik?" I asked.

"Escaped." Ryker flicked his white eyes to the side. "Rez is still searching the tunnels even though I told her it was pointless." Ryker wasn't the only one who had a past with Vadik. I discovered Rez was one of the fae Vadik drugged and prostituted in one of his sex clubs. When she'd found out he was still alive, she'd bared her teeth and demanded to be part of the group that went after him, showing both anger and heartbreak. She wanted to face her demons. Literally.

"Vadik waited until I saw him, winked at Rez, saying he had missed his favorite concubine, then vanished down one of the passages. I ran after him, but he is like a ghost. No, he's a fuckin' cockroach and will always somehow survive."

"He and Amara both." I shook my head. The moment we looked up from the battle, Amara was gone. I wasn't really surprised. Amara was the ultimate survivalist. In a strange way, I was glad. I think if she ever sacrificed herself or did the right thing, the world would truly be ending.

I had no doubt Vadik and Amara would be all right. They would find their next prey, their next swindle, and someday their paths would probably join with ours again. But they meant so little to me in comparison to what had happened, I didn't have the energy to worry they were still out there.

"I'm sorry for Rez. I feel disgusted I'm related to that monster." Ryker shook his head, tendons tightening in his neck. "After what that fucker did to her, to others like her, death is way too good. But if I see him again?" His fists tightened at his side. He would shred Vadik into tiny pieces. And I would happily watch.

I leaned into him, rubbing his taut back. We both stayed quiet for a moment. Dread over my next question coiled in my stomach, my tongue slipping over my lips. "And all the creatures?" I wouldn't let myself call them children, that dozens born and trained in that cave to be monsters. I couldn't. If I let myself think about Zeke's words, his hurt over my betrayal, I might want to make another choice and I knew I couldn't. They could not exist.

Ryker tucked a strand of hair behind my ear, his mouth compressed into a firm line. "All you need to know is they have been taken care of." I had seen the explosives Garrett had designed. I knew what that meant.

Ryker, the dark dwellers, Rez, West, and Lars had gone back to deal with the experiments and get the women to safety. Lars had asked if I wanted to go back to the cave, if it was something I needed to do.

I didn't. There would not be closure for me. I never wanted to step in that place again. For Lars, I think going back was his way of dealing with his trauma. Perhaps it restored his sense of control and power. He never outright showed it, but in private moments I could tell the King had been shaken to his core.

Humbled.

Humiliated.

The all-powerful King had been brought to his knees by his own greed and fear.

When taking his throne again, he made it clear he would do everything in his power to secure the kingdom. Most countries were behind him, except the Eastern bloc in Europe. They wanted to cut all ties to the King and Queen. Their people had already begun protests in their streets to extricate from the kingdom.

Lars and Kennedy had a lot of work to do, to get everything back on solid ground, but because of this battle, Kennedy's popularity had risen high in the polls. Most thought she was a strong and capable Queen and did not appear to care that she was Druid, young or mated with a dark dweller. She had proven herself.

"Kennedy and Fionna took off right after us. They should be back in a few days." Ryker rubbed my bare arms, the cool wind chilling me. The two Druids were the only ones who would bury the treasures far apart from each other. Then they would each perform a forgetting spell on each other. I hope the treasures would be forever lost. "Lars is hoping we'd stay around for a bit, until they come back."

"Actually, I was thinking…"

"Staying here permanently," he finished my sentence.

An empty smile wobbled my mouth. He knew me so well. Our main house was in South America, but I couldn't imagine staying in the house Lexie and Croygen had shared with us. They would haunt me, the echoes of their laughs, the ghosts of their figures wandering the halls.

"Casa de Miel is running fully without me and Annabeth anyway. I can still pop in… And I know Annabeth is going to want to stay here now… and…"

"I know." He leaned in, brushing his mouth across my forehead. "I can live anywhere, human. If you guys are there, I'm happy." He rubbed Wyatt's head, causing the baby and Sprig to stir.

"Thank you," I whispered, gripping him and shutting my eyes. I tried to hold back another wave of emotion. Even in the despair, I knew how lucky I was to have him and the family we created. Lexie might not be here physically, but she would always be part of this family. Wyatt would know of his aunt.

"Stop, honey bears! No, that tickles!" Sprig giggled then sputtered, pulling me back away from Ryker. Sprig's head popped from the Björn, looking around in a daze. "Huh? What?" He smacked his lips together. "Is it breakfast time?"

"No," Ryker responded.

"Oh good, lunch then," he squeaked, wiggling out of the Björn. "Only time I want to be smooched like that is alone with Pam and some honey."

"I really didn't need to know that." Despite my torn heart, I smiled, needing Sprig's presence more than he knew. He slid out from beside Wyatt and leaped to Ryker's shoulder. The last three days he hadn't left either of our sides. Going from one to the other.

Sprig looked past me, rising onto his legs. "Why is the smelly butt-pirate waving at me? Where is he going?"

I turned my head, staring back to the ship sailing between the gates. With my fae sight, I spotted a figure standing on the first rung of the mainmast, facing back our way.

I gave a small gasp and pulled away from Ryker, stepping closer to the edge of the lake.

Croygen.

"He's leaving for a bit," Ryker answered Sprig.

"Whhaaatt? Nooooo!" Sprig cried out, his eyes going wide. Then he sat back folding his arms, his lids blinking rapidly. "Good. Good riddance to that swashbucket. Never liked him anyway."

"Sure, furball." Ryker snorted.

"I mean, I'm fine he didn't even say goodbye. Whatever. I don't care." Faster than I almost could grasp, Sprig wiped his eyes with his tail. "See if I ever share my honey with him, or that juniper honey he liked so much. If he ever dares to show his face again…"

Annabeth came up beside me, her face forward as her fingers laced with mine. Cooper stood on her other side, already a member of our family.

All of us stared out at the diminishing figure, the ship slipping into the setting sun.

"Please," I whispered into the wind, staring at Croygen's outline. "Come home to us someday."

As if he heard my plea, he lifted his fist into the sky, then brought it to his heart, tapping it six times. One for Ryker, Annabeth, Sprig, Wyatt, me and… Lexie.

A hiccupped cry broke from my lungs, feeling my heart crash against my chest.

In unison, the four of us tapped our hearts, motioning back to him. I couldn't see it, but I felt it in my gut… He smiled.

There was hope.

One day he would come home.

EPILOGUE
Ember
(Eight months later)

Lights twinkled off the tree, enveloping the room in a cozy warmth, and snow softly pelted down outside the windows. Fire crackled in the hearth and the scent of cinnamon and baking bread danced around the room, making my mouth water. Wrapping paper, tissue, and boxes were spread all over the floor, covering it like wall-to-wall carpet.

Sighing contently, I looked around the room, taking a moment to process the idyllic scene before me. I dreamed of having Christmas in this house, all of us together under one roof. It had come true, but at a very high cost. The absences of those we lost in the battles echoed loud, but the promise of new life gave us hope.

In the upstairs living room at Lars's, the growing group of those I cared about and thought of as family, spread over the room.

"Sprig, stop. You had enough," Zoey yelled at the sprite holding another one of Marguerite's breakfast honey muffins.

Sprig moved to put it back, until Zoey looked away, then he shoved the entire muffin in his mouth.

"I saw that." She scoffed, reaching for Wyatt. Ryker sat on the sofa, Zoey between his legs on the floor, watching their son play with the bubble wrap, not interested in the toys he was given. Their dog Matty was curled up beside Zoey.

She put on a brave face, but I could see the pain of her first Christmas without Lexie, the silence where Croygen should be.

Beside Ryker, Annabeth and Cooper sat on the couch, whispering and touching each other like teenagers.

Love. You could see it blooming vibrantly between them. I had never seen Cooper so happy, a content grin on his face, his gaze raking over Annabeth as though she were his world. Eli felt it as soon as he saw them after they were together the first time. It still took me a little longer to feel it. When I noticed the link to Annabeth, I realized what it meant. She had become part of our family. A pack member. And with the link I shared with the group, I knew Cooper wanted Eli to help him find a way to extend her life. Fae food no longer existed since the worlds had meshed as it had when it changed Mark and Ryan. He needed to find another way.

Burying the treasures not only terminated West's chance to become full dweller again, but it possibly ended the chance for Annabeth to have a long life, as well. But if I knew Cooper, he wouldn't give up. He would find a way. When it comes to your mate, there is nothing you won't do.

Rez was proof of that. West chose to let the treasures go, but she still wanted to find a way to restore his beast. None of us would stop searching for a way to return him to full dark dweller again. He sacrificed a lot for the greater good and not one of us would forget it.

Rez was hurt about Croygen's departure, feeling abandoned once again, but she was trying to understand. He lost someone he loved and was dealing with his broken heart in his way although I think it hurt she wasn't enough for him to stay. She talked about going to find him, but Ryker thought it was better to let him come back on his own terms.

"Look at her," Rez cooed, rubbing her Christmas gift. She and West sat on the floor, their brand-new husky puppy sound asleep in the wrapping paper next to Wyatt. Dwellers weren't normally pet friendly, but he knew she had wanted a dog. Raising it from a pup, it would be used to the dominant males and become part of the pack. It was amusing to see all these alphas cooing over the fuzzball. And the way Rez looked at the puppy, with unconditional love exploding across her face, I had a feeling children wouldn't be far behind.

"Nerf-herder," Kennedy groaned, grimacing in annoyance. She and Lorcan took over the entire other sofa, her legs in his lap as he rubbed them. "I have to pee again."

"Seriously? It's been, like, five minutes." He rubbed the large bump of her belly.

"You tell them that." She motioned to her stomach. "Whoever is pressing down on my bladder, get off please." Kennedy swung her feet onto the ground. Lorcan got up, helping the extremely pregnant Kennedy to her feet. The healer told her she was having a boy and a girl. Their parents so powerful that both their traits were adapted. They would also be a new breed of fae. As far as anyone knew, there were no half-dweller, half-Druid children, so this was a first for all of us.

They were going to be a handful. But those babies would be so loved. I couldn't wait to be called Auntie Ember. Piper talked to Kennedy's belly all the time, telling them of the mischief they would get into.

Lorcan kissed her forehead. "I'm gonna get you a catheter or bedpan."

"Don't think I haven't thought of that." She went up on her toes kissing him. She was huge for her tiny frame, but she looked beautiful. Happy.

"Look, Auntie Kennedy. Look what Darz gave me." Piper jumped around her, holding up a book. "They're Irish tales. He says we'll read one together every night."

"Wow, your book looks amazing." Kennedy leaned over and kissed Piper on the head. "I'm jealous."

"Of the book or Lars tucking you in and reading to you at night?" Lorcan muttered playfully to her, making her laugh.

Piper grinned before she bounded off to show Wyatt, promising she'd read them to him. Wyatt only spoke in single syllables, but Piper could understand him without a word uttered. They had a connection none of us understood.

"My Darz is the best." Piper hugged the book to her chest.

My gaze drifted to Lars across the room. My father. His arms were wrapped around Fionna on the sofa. Dressed in jeans and a T-shirt, he looked almost human. Relaxed, like for the first time in his life he was letting himself be loved. Happy. He was still the King. Strong and ruthless, but his priorities had clearly shifted. Fionna, Piper, and his family came first, then his work. Looking at him as Piper jumped on his lap, snuggling between him and Fionna with her new book, I felt as though my heart was going to burst. He deserved happiness.

We were spending more time together, but deep inside I think we had always been father and daughter, so not much had changed. He really did like to use that "because I'm your father and I said so" line. Not that it ever worked on me.

There had been a lot of alterations and redecorating of the compound since Lars's return. Besides getting rid of anything reminding us of Stavros or places his bare ass might have touched, they had constructed entirely new secret exit tunnels since the others had been exposed. Piper had a new playroom, but the toys managed to escape and drop all over the house. The compound felt much more like a home, even though we all still missed those we'd lost.

Travil was now Lars's right-hand man. Cadoc was being trained to take Travil's old spot, but mostly everything ran much as it had before. Rimmon's spot had been filled with kin of the ogre's, but it wasn't the same. I knew Lars missed Goran and Rimmon, but he was good at compartmentalizing. You didn't live as long as he did and not get used to death.

Fionna helped Lars as a secretary but was rallying for him to hire a new one. ASAP. She had her plate full with her own organization: a group fighting for equal rights among all fae and humans. And sleeping with the King didn't always mean she was able to get laws passed easily or that things changed overnight. Too much racial, species, and class prejudice still existed in the world. Fear and hate would always be a battle.

Mom and Ryan helped Fionna organize groups around the world. Mark's interest was still in plant life, and he kept in constant contact with Kate. They were seeking new medicines for fae and human. Kate still used a cane from the injury Stavros inflicted on her, but that woman was tough. During recovery her daughter visited a lot, but it was the sexy fae named Dunn who wouldn't leave her side—no matter how much she told him to. I really liked her. She and her family were supposed to stop by later. Even on Christmas she was at the labs.

Lily's laugh took my attention to the fireplace. She, Mark, Ryan, and Castien sat in front of the fire, drinking and laughing. Their little unit only grew stronger. Mom and Dad had taken them on as their kids, and I suspected they would never live too far from each other. Someday Ryan and Castien might want to adopt and have their own house, but right now they were all so happy and content where they were.

My gaze drifted to Cole and Olivia, looking to be in a heated discussion. His eyes glinted with life as he shook his head, replying to her comment.

I grinned to myself.

"Don't." Arms slid around my waist. "Leave them be."

"What?" I peered at Eli over my shoulder, his eyebrow hitched up.

"You know what. Don't play matchmaker." He drew me in closer, pressing his body into mine.

"Look at them. I don't think I will have to." My hands rubbed his powerful arms. Eli and I would be back to work tomorrow after a group of rabid imps in Australia. This was our life, and I loved it. Right now we were happy. I didn't know if kids or staying home would ever be for me. But that was the good thing about living so long; we didn't have to decide for a long time, if ever. I loved being free, traveling around the world, and kicking ass with my man and two pixies.

He pressed firmer into me, so I could feel every hard inch of him. "We have a moment before dinner?" He nuzzled the back of my neck, thrusting heat through my veins. His hands tracing the exposed skin along the top of my jeans.

"Crap on ash bark, I hope so." I gripped his thighs, squeezing.

"Mr. Cal! No! Get off the table!" Marguerite's voice shrilled from the dining room, carrying a tray.

"But my weeeeeeeee bitzzzz feel so good."

"Dammit," Eli grumbled. "Ten seconds and we could have been halfway upstairs."

I peered into the connecting room where Gabby and Nic sat, getting drunk. Cal lay on his back close to Gabby's cup. Alki's loss had brought her and Nic close, bonding in their heartache. Lately, I noticed they were *always* next to each other. It was far too soon, Gabby's heart was shattered from Alki's death, but for some reason, seeing Nic and her, I felt a glint of something. A hope for more. At least a friendship.

"Gabs, stop getting Cal drunk," Eli yelled at his dweller sister. "We are going to eat there."

"Too late." She winked with a snort, watching the naked pixie do snow angels. "Naked pixie ass imprints are all over this table." She motioned her hand over the surface with a smirk.

"Frickin' sisters." Eli set his forehead on my shoulder. "Think we can still disappear for a few minutes?"

"Dinner!" Marguerite called out, making Eli moan softly.

"Doesn't look like it." I laughed.

"Too bad." His fingers trailed over my skin, his voice husky. "The things I had planned for you, Brycin..."

My teeth clenched, my body flaming with desire as he walked away, winking over his shoulder. He was so going to pay for that later.

We all moved to the table, helping Marguerite set the dishes, holiday music softly playing in the background.

The years had brought death, devastation, betrayal, and headache. But they also brought love, friendship, laughter, and family. And those were everything to me.

Torin was the one friend not here. He stayed back on duty at the castle. This time Thara was back at his side again, reinstated to a lower position.

They were inseparable. The amount of times we had found them kissing in a corner or making eyes at each other was insane, especially for a man as straight-laced as Torin. I guess when you find that person for you, all propriety goes out the window. Thank the gods he finally woke up and saw what was in front of him. It was a long, tortuous road, but I doubted he would ever take her for granted again.

With all of us around the large table, our glasses filled, I lifted my cup. "A toast to my growing family." I looked around the table, my heart filled with so much love it almost temporarily lessened the loss and pain. "I am so thankful for each and every one of you. You have taken me on a journey which has changed my life. And I couldn't be more grateful. I will never forget those we've lost, they will never be far from us. But tonight, I want to celebrate. To what is to come. To new beginnings."

"To new beginnings!" Everyone raised their cups.

"Cheers to the saint of the delivery of sweet nectar." Sprig rose on his hind legs between Ryker and Zoey, his hands in the air. "Saint Honey Tits. May her bra never be empty."

"Now that's something I can toast to." Cal sat up lifting his cup full of juice.

"Me too." Eli held up his glass, winking at me.

Simmons stood next to Cal, his face pinched, before he grabbed the other tiny cup set out. "Ah, screw it!" Making everyone laugh.

I had a feeling this was going to be a new tradition.

We all reached for each other, clinking glasses.

"To Saint Honey Tits!"

The kingdom would always have enemies. Just because we won this battle didn't mean more weren't in our future. Life was a never-ending ride. And even when it burned to the ground, we would get up—rise from the embers—and start again.

That's what we did.

Especially when we had Saint Honey Tits to fight for.

ACKNOWLEDGMENTS

I can't believe it's over. Three series that have been my whole world for the last five plus years. These characters are so a part of me, I can't imagine them not being there when I start a new book. They are my friends, my babies, and the reason I am where I am. They've had a brilliant ride, and it's all because of you readers. Truly you guys have been my inspiration. The love and support you've given me. I have no words. This is bittersweet for me, but I hope my next series will bring as much love as these have. Though, I don't think I can ever top Sprig, so maybe I should just stop now!

I'm trying not to cry while I write this and stay strong to end them the best way I can. I want these books to be a place you can come back to over and over, not roll your eyes that it should have ended five books ago, but a world you constantly want to jump back into and find something new.

Again, I'm totally choked up right now. I feel so lucky that you have loved all these characters and their journey as much as I have (don't cry, Stacey… don't cry).

My thanks are many. But first it's to you all. There are so many I can't name, but those on my Squad page, you guys are my backbone and I thank you for being there!

Colleen Oppenheim - I couldn't function without you. Thank you for dealing with me, my waves of crazy, and always being so supportive and having my back. I love you lady.

Kiki at Next Step P.R. - Kicking and screaming you push me to do better. Thank you for all your hard work! **https://thenextsteppr.org/**

Jordan - You have been with me since the end of Darkness Series. You have helped develop these characters and made their journey better. Thank you! And now I have your voice constantly in my head as I write. Thank you. **http://jordanrosenfeld.net/**

Hollie "the editor"- Don't ever, ever leave me. I will wander the streets in my slippers, mumbling your name. **http://www.hollietheeditor.com/**

343

Dane at Ebook Launch! Thank you for doing your thing and designing such beautiful covers! **https://ebooklaunch.com/ebook-cover-design/**
To Judi at **http://www.formatting4u.com/**: Awesome as always! You always have my back.

Because I can't thank you enough, to all the readers who have supported me, shared posts, written reviews, and forced books in your friend's hands because you knew they'd love it too: My gratitude is for all you do and how much you help indie authors out of the pure love of reading.

To all the indie/hybrid authors out there who inspire, challenge, support, and push me to be better: I love you!

And to anyone who has picked up an indie book and given an unknown author a chance. THANK YOU!

ABOUT THE AUTHOR

USA Today Bestselling Author Stacey Marie Brown is a lover of hot fictional bad boys and sarcastic heroines who kick butt. She also enjoys books, travel, TV shows, hiking, writing, design, and archery. Stacey swears she is part gypsy, being lucky enough to live and travel all over the world.

She grew up in Northern California, where she ran around on her family's farm, raising animals, riding horses, playing flashlight tag, and turning hay bales into cool forts.

When she's not writing she's out hiking, spending time with friends, and traveling. She also volunteers helping animals and is eco-friendly. She feels all animals, people, and the environment should be treated kindly.

To learn more about Stacey or her books, visit her at:

Author website & Newsletter: www.staceymariebrown.com

Facebook Author page: www.facebook.com/SMBauthorpage

Pinterest: www.pinterest.com/s.mariebrown

Instagram: www.instagram.com/staceymariebrown/

TikTok: www.tiktok.com/@staceymariebrown

Amazon page: www.amazon.com/Stacey-Marie-Brown/e/B00BFWHB9U

Goodreads:
www.goodreads.com/author/show/6938728.Stacey_Marie_Brown

Her Facebook group: www.facebook.com/groups/1648368945376239/

Bookbub: www.bookbub.com/authors/stacey-marie-brown